REVIEWS OF CHA

CW01506641

'Unmissable. Proud is a brilliant, economical and poetic
writer who brings a character and period of British history
previously shrouded in mystery to vivid life.'

Maggie Gee OBE, FRSL

The dangers threatening Togidubnus, both in Rome and
in Britain, are serious enough to keep readers hooked, but
Chariot of the Soul is essentially a novel of character and ideas,
both philosophical and spiritual. Its style recalls some of the
finest novels about ancient Britain, from Rosemary Sutcliff's
Sword at Sunset to Mary Stewart's *Merlin* trilogy – but with the
benefit of further decades of archaeological findings to draw
on. Readers hungry for more novels of that high quality will
find *Chariot of the Soul* a worthy successor.

Margaret Tomlinson, Substack

These people lived in a vibrant and artistic society, open to
new philosophical ideas from as far as Greece, and at last we
have an author who does them justice. This book does for
early Roman Britain what John Cowper Powys did for the
end of Roman Britain in *Porius*, and like that great novel is a
masterpiece.

Revd Prof. Martin Henig FSA

With her lucid, captivating prose, Linda Proud conjures
an immersive world so real you can touch it, peopled with
powerful characters, and driven by an irresistibly compelling

story. This is historical fiction at its most convincing: entertaining, enlightening and unforgettable.

Robin Mukherjee, Senior Lecturer and Programme Leader of MA Scriptwriting at Bath Spa University

Engrossing from start to finish, this book is an historical tour de force. The research and writing are excellent, with insightful period detail that is authentic at a deep level. The intertwined destinies of Delfos, and his people, with the might of Rome make this a wonderful novel, which has its own spiritual depths and surprises. The book charts that perilous edge where loyalty, enforced rule, and betrayal create heart-breaking human choices which will determine everything for time to come, in a land whose people must speedily adapt or die.

Caitlín Matthews, author of The Art of Celtic Seership

Another splendid adventure of the visionary imagination which, as well as re-awakening us to a crucial time in this island's history, speaks in so many ways to vital issues and the crying needs of our own spiritually beleaguered times.

Lindsay Clarke, winner of the Whitbread Prize for The Chymical Wedding

The characters feel completely real and, just as I like it, never come down firmly on the side of either black or white: Togidubnos himself doubts his mission, his motives and his loyalties many times, as he assimilates back into his boyhood world. Proud also incorporates some of the more mystical elements of ancient British life, to an even greater extent than Manda Scott did in *Boudica*: we don't only have druids, but also the ethereal Shee and the time-bending powers contained within sanctuaries and stone circles. Sometimes this kind of thing bothers me within novels, but it works here because it feels like a plausible extension of the landscape, its lines, ridges, barrows and ageless chalk figures cut in the hillsides.

It conjures up the strangeness that's buried only a little way under the surface of the British landscape and its mythology, and succeeds in feeling mystical rather than fantastical.

Although this is a new departure for Proud, it rings with confidence and authenticity and, excitingly, seems to be only the first part of a longer story. Dreamlike and pragmatic by turn, it's one of the best books I've read by her. While there is obviously much research here, it's worn lightly. It forms a satisfying complement to the *Boudica* novels and, if anyone's just finished Manda Scott and is wondering where to get their next ancient-history fix, I'd nudge them this way. Highly recommended for those who want a thought-provoking story about Britain's history that prizes negotiation above violence, peace above war and philosophy above blood.

All in all, a compelling tale of Britain, Rome and one man's quest to know himself.

theidlewoman.net

THE ALBIOS WAY

THE ALBIOS WAY

SECOND IN THE AWEN SERIES

LINDA PROUD

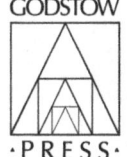

GODSTOW

·PRESS·

First published 2025 by
Godstow Press
60 Godstow Road, Oxford OX2 8NY
www.godstowpress.co.uk

Typeset by Amanda Roberts

Printed and bound in Great Britain by Hobbs the Printers,
Totton, Hants.

The paper used in this publication is procured from
forests independently certified to the level of
Forest Stewardship Council (FSC)
principles and criteria.

Dedicated to my constant companion, David, and his remarkable patience in having this read to him again and again and again.

They make a desert and they call it peace. Tacitus

CONTENTS

GLOSSARY

Atrebatic Lands Hampshire, West Sussex, Berkshire
(as was – see below), included the lands of the Belgae
around Winchester

Breghed   (became known as Reghed) Lake District,
Cumbria, home to the Carvetii people

Brigantia   Most of northern England, including Yorkshire,
Lancashire and Northumberland
    Lopocares – sub-tribe, Corbridge
    Gabrantovices – sub-tribe, Bridlington
    Setantii – sub-tribe, mid-Lancashire

Cantia   Kent

Catuvellaunia   Bedfordshire, Buckinghamshire,
Hertfordshire; also parts of Berkshire, Cambridgeshire,
Essex, Greater London and Oxfordshire

Corieltauvia   Leicestershire

Cornovia   Shropshire

Deceanglia   Cheshire

Dobunnia   (northern) Gloucestershire, west Oxfordshire,
Monmouthshire, south Herefordshire, Warwickshire,
Worcestershire, Breconshire

Dobunnia   (southern) Somerset, Wiltshire

Dumnonia   Devon

Durotrigia   Dorset

Icenia   East Anglia

Ordovicia   north Wales

Trinovantia   Essex

Siluria   south Wales

PLACES – BRITAIN

BERKSHIRE
Calleva   Silchester, near Reading
Hill of the Albios Horse   White Horse Hill, Uffington
(With changes of county borders in 1974, much of
Berkshire became Oxfordshire, now known to locals as
'occupied north Berkshire'. The rage at losing the White
Horse, which was and remains the county emblem,
has not lessened. For those interested in this 'cultural
vandalism' see https://www.bbc.co.uk/news/uk-
england-oxfordshire-68515410)

ESSEX
Camulodunum   Colchester
Stony River   Colne

GLOUCESTERSHIRE
Corinium (Kyronion)   first settlement was at Bagendon,
Cirencester
Creig   Crickley Hill, Vale of Gloucester
Ferylloog   Forest of Dean
Gleva   Gloucester
Hills of Cuda   Cotswolds
Llyn Llyw   Sacred Lake of the Salmon of Wisdom, silted up
by the Middle Ages, possible locations include Longford
and Horsbere Brook, Gloucester (Yeates, S. J., A Dreaming
for the Witches, Oxbow Books 2009)
Rim of the Cauldron   Cotswold escarpment, Birdlip
Severn River, 'Torc'   the Noose, Newnham
Temple of Cuda   Littledean, Forest of Dean
Temple of Nodens   Lydney, Forest of Dean
Twelve Elms   Ditches, Bagendon

HAMPSHIRE
Ford of the Alders (Venta Belgarum)   Winchester
Sacred Isle   Hayling Island
Vectis   Isle of Wight

HERTFORDSHIRE
Verulamium (Verlamion)   St Albans

LANCASHIRE (GREATER MANCHESTER)
Rigodunum   Cartimandua's southern capital, whereabouts
    unknown but here located at Castleshaw, Oldham, near
    Manchester

LEICESTERSHIRE
Venonis   High Cross

OXFORDSHIRE
Cuma's Hill   Cumnor, near Oxford
Sanctuary of the Wheel   stone circle under Keble College,
    Oxford
Ford at Two Rivers Folly Bridge, Oxford
Yellowhammer Hill   fort at Ambrosden, near Bicester

SHROPSHIRE
Blackstone Hill   Titterstone Clee
Brei Dun   Breidden Hill
Caer Ogyrfan   Oswestry
Hill with druid altar   Bury Ditches, Lydbury
Viroconium   Wroxeter
Wrikon   Wrekin

SOMERSET (THE SUMMERLANDS)
Hot Springs of Sulis (Aquae Sulis)   Bath

WEST SUSSEX
Noviomagus   Chichester

WILTSHIRE
Hill of Sovereignty, Kennet   Silbury Hill, Avebury
Sanctuary at Kennet   Avebury stone circle
Swale   Swallowhead, near Avebury

WORCESTERSHIRE
Bare Hills   Malverns

WALES
Copper Hill   Llanmynech Hill, Powys
Llanmelin   hillfort near Chepstow, Powys
Mona   Isle of Anglesey

PLACES – GAUL

Burdigala   Bordeaux
Celtica   one of the three main regions of Gaul and home to
    a people who called themselves Celts
Land of the Veniti, Armorica   Brittany
Narbo   Narbonne
Sea of the Basques Bay of Biscay
Via Aquitania   Roman road running between Bordeaux
    and Narbonne, an overland route connecting Atlantic with
    Mediterranean

ROADS

Akeman Street   followed an ancient track linking
    Verulamium to Corinium via Calleva and Yellowhammer
    Fort. Metalled by Romans
Albios Way   Fosse Way
'Lindinis to Lindum'   Ilchester, Somerset, to Lincoln
'where the Albios Way runs into the sea'   Axmouth, Devon
Via Claudia linked Dubris (Dover) to Viroconium, later known
as Watling Street, now A5

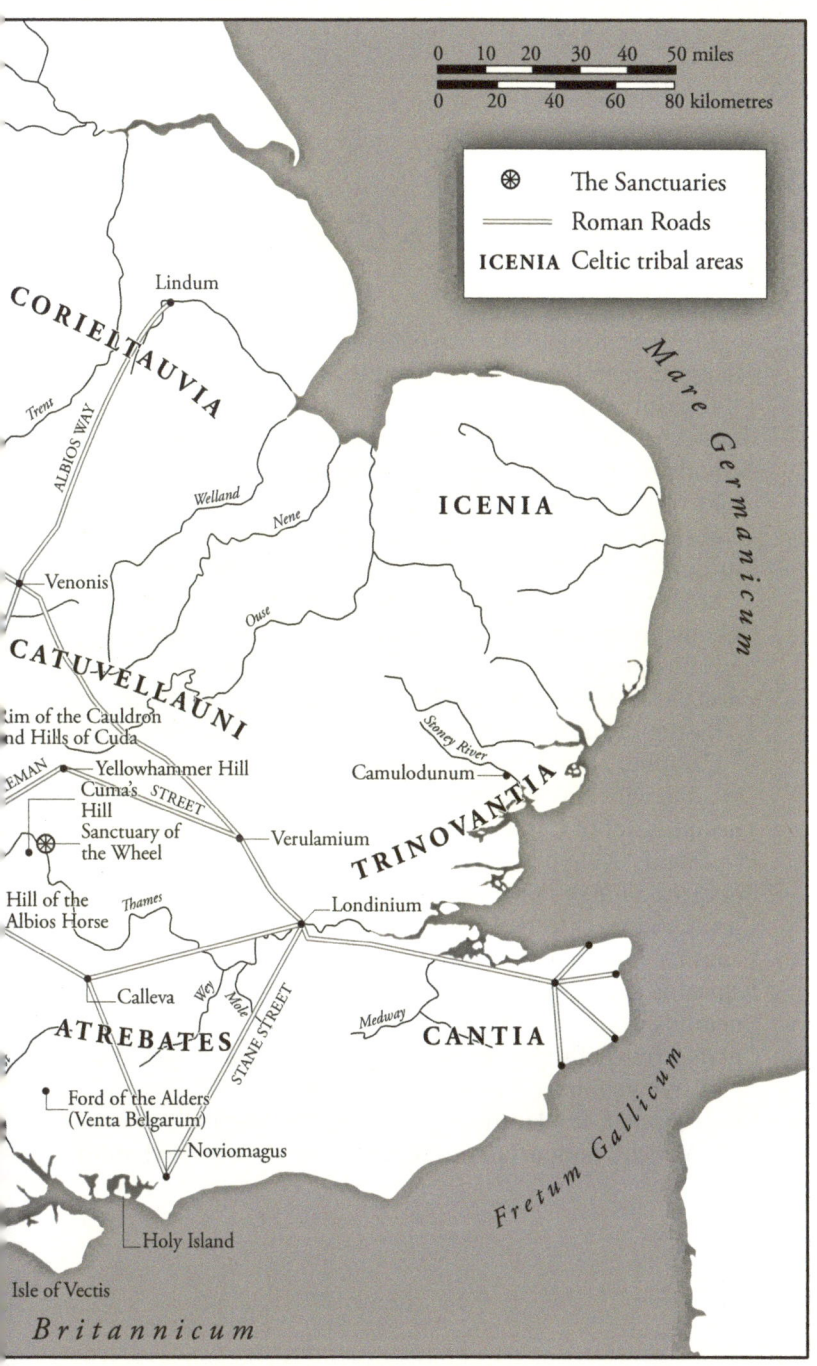

CAST OF CHARACTERS

Britons

Togidubnus, King of the Atrebates

Mandred, member of the Durotriges tribe, now freedman of Togidubnus

Branwen, Queen of the Dobunni, enslaved in Rome

Apnodens, previously head of the bardic order, now in hiding Ricoba, last of the people who held the Royal Seat of Kings at the Creig (Crickley Hill, Vale of Gloucester)

Katuaros/Catuarus, foster brother of Togidubnus and joint holder of the role of king of the Atrebates

Debonia, wife of Katuaros, a midwife of a branch of the Cuma people

Caratacus, King of the Catuvellauni, resistance leader in hiding in Siluria (British name: Caratacos; Silurian name: Caradoc)

Dryadia, wife of Caratacus

Theana, sister of Caratacus

Prasutagus, King of the Iceni

Boudicca, wife of Prasutagus

Cartimandua, Queen of the Brigantes

Venutius, husband of Cartimandua

Velocatus, shield-bearer and lover of Cartimandua

Enemnos, warlord with claims on Dobunnia

Celatus, head of the workshop of bronzesmiths at the Grove of Twelve Elms

Cow Crippler, Ten Horns and Mouse Ears, originally warriors in Verica's fianna, later captains in the Cohors Atrebatum

Characters who died before or during the conquest
Togodumnus, brother of Caratacus
Verica, King of the Atrebates, father of Togidubnus
Kommios/Commius, grandfather of Togidubnus
Innogen, wife of Verica and mother of Togidubnus
Esius, King of the Dobunni, father of Branwen
Draumur, harpist to Togidubnus
Regalis, archdruid and father of Apnodens
Cunobelinus, king of the Catuvellauni, father of Caratacus
    (known in early histories of Britain as Cymbeline)
Biccos, king of the Belgae and father of Katuaros

Romans
Claudius, Emperor of Rome
Aulus Plautius, first governor of Britain
Publius Ostorius Scapula, second governor of Britain
Vespasian, legate of the Second Legion
Messalina, third wife of Claudius
Agrippina, fourth wife and niece of Claudius
Domitius, became Nero, son of Agrippina
Britannicus, son of Claudius
Gaius Sallustus Passienus Crispus, consul in AD 27 and 44.
    Husband of Agrippina, step-father of Nero
Lucius Seneca, philosopher, writer, tutor of Nero and, later,
imperial advisor
Sextus Afranius Burrus, prefect of the Praetorians, tutor of
    Nero and, later, imperial advisor
Manlius Valens, legate of the Twentieth Legion

FOREWORD

This is a remarkable tale for our own unsettled times. It is told from the perspective of Togidubnus, scion of Britain's Atrebatic dynasty, a man born of British parents but sent for education in boyhood to Rome, from which he has emerged with a Stoic philosophy of life (as we learnt in *Chariot of the Soul*).

Now he has come home as an obliging client king in dangerous times, with Roman citizenship and some very interesting personal relationships. He is a sympathetic, sometimes exasperating, character with high principles but conflicting loyalties, resented by many at home for his role in promoting the Roman occupation, but striving to keep some sort of peace amongst people who themselves were far from united, and whose traditional ways of life and understandings were being trampled upon and overthrown. Thus it ever was under a colonial régime. The conquered must accept what they cannot change, including interference in their festivals and customs: as one character puts it, 'We are not Romans, that much is certain, and yet we are not what we once were. We have to find out what – or who – we are.' In this splendid novel, we watch them all begin to do just that.

As one who knows this period's history, and its archaeology, very well, I found myself swept happily along by a sensitive novelist into a world whose landscape settings, at least, I did actually know, and found vividly evoked, but that was otherwise of course imaginary, even dream-like in places, and all of whose characters, historical or purely imagined, were credible as people of their own time – and ours. Did I really think I 'knew' Seneca, Claudius, Ostorius Scapula, or Caratacus from previous reading? I was made to think again! All the characters we meet, Roman and Briton alike – some known to history, many simply imagined – are richly three-dimensional, caught up as they are in epoch-making clashes of world views and values both in Rome and in Britain. There are many touching scenes of inner conflict, love, goodness, disappointment, and personal loss. You may think you are getting to know some of these people – but do you really know them? Veil after veil drops from your eyes as the narrative unfolds, with some startling surprises en route.

There are also some hilarious interludes, brilliantly sketched, as when Togidubnus tries, half-heartedly, to explain the maddening Roman calendar to Britons on whom it will be imposed,but who already have their own perfectly satisfactory and entirely rational system. I had to laugh aloud, remembering my own incredulity aged 14 when we were introduced to Roman dates in Latin class at school, and given a jingle to help fix it in our innumerate heads: 'In March, July, October, May....' Linda Proud knows how to make you laugh as well as cry.

This is a wonderful novel, rich in human sympathy, and beautifully written. It bridges different worlds. I am reminded of something Ursula le Guin – an equally fine wordsmith – put on the lips of a character in Tehanu (1990) to describe the role of a bard in a traditional (and in her case, purely imaginary) society, but which also describes Linda Proud's The Albios Way: these are not only the great stories everybody learns, the heroes and the kings and the things that happened long ago and far away, but stories that only she knew.

Dr Daphne Nash Briggs, author of Coinage in the Celtic World

AD 43

1

RETURN TO CALLEVA

I was born of rape. My father, king of the Atrebates, violated a druid priestess in the circle of stones at the Sanctuary of the Wheel. After that, everything began to go wrong for him, with the attacks by the neighbouring Catuvellauni becoming ever more ferocious. He tried to mollify the gods by marrying her but it didn't help. He always had to take what was not given and suffer the consequences. My mother often disappeared into the woods that surrounded Calleva. Once I found her crying in a glade, head down, hugging her drawn-up knees, her slender toes wriggling in the cow parsley. I snuggled up to her, sat there for a while, not knowing what to do or say, and then asked, 'Has he hurt you?'

'No, not the cuts and bruises kind,' she said. 'I cry for my goddess. I was not made to be a mother, dear one.' She squeezed me against her, bronze armlets clinking. My breath shortened. What was she saying? Did she hate me? I stared up at her pale face, glistening with tears. She was gazing at the trees around us, trees she had been introducing me to since I could walk, teaching me their lore, their properties. I knew the names of them all, could recognise their winter skeletons and their summer fullness. I knew them by the sound they made when the wind blew through their leaves and by the smell of their resins. She taught me that treecreepers run up trunks and nuthatches run down, the different kinds of woodpecker, those that drum and those that laugh like maniacs. Any fear I might have experienced in the woods, she removed, only to put it back at night when she told me terrible stories about snakes, ogres and magical boar. 'It is not wise', she told me when I

3

was older, 'to be completely fearless. That's the delusion of warriors and look where it gets them.'

But on this day when I found her crying, she told me about my conception although I was still at an age when the word 'rape' had no meaning.

'I had dedicated my life to the goddess Cuda, but your father snatched me away from her. You, my little Delfos, you were given to me by the goddess to help me in my sorrow.' At my birth ceremony she named me Delphidius of the temple of Belenus which, shortened to Delfos, was my cradle name, and she never used another. 'Togidubnus' was my father's name for me; meaning 'deep strike', it was usually shouted. 'Delfos' I took to mean dolphins, leaping happily in the sea. It was only when I came to study Greek that I discovered it meant 'womb',

'I hate him,' I said.

'No need for that. Every time he forces himself on me, he loses something – more lands, the health of his livestock, the loyalty of his warriors. It's about time he understood the connection but he's too arrogant to think anyone has control of his life other than him.' She gazed down on me with her periwinkle eyes. 'What do you want to be when you grow up?'

'A good father.'

'And a good husband?'

'Yes.'

'Never take what has not been given to you.' She bent down to kiss me on the scalp, her beads of stone warm against my cheek. Nut blossom came down on us like soft rain.

'What are you thinking about?' my companion, Mandred, asked as we approached Calleva through the woods. The familiar scent of the trees was making my heart beat faster. I remembered Calleva as a busy place, the hub of four major routes; as a happy place to grow up in; as a place of danger, occupied by the Catuvellauni. I expected to find all of this and more as we rode the track through the woods to the oppidum.

As an infant, I had lived with my mother in Noviomagus on the south coast while my father, King Verica, was away fighting to regain Calleva. On his victory, we moved back and I found my companions in the animals, birds, trees and spirits of Calleva's woods.

'Mother's boy!' King Verica boomed on my fifth birthday. 'You need to start building some muscle!' He arranged to foster the son of Biccos, king of our friendly neighbours, the Belgae. I left my mother to her herbs and medicinals to crash through the trees after my new brother, always after him, since he was fitter, fleeter – and fearless. His bare legs from the back were as shapely as amphorae. Katuaros taught me to ride without reins, how to use the sling, how to stalk the boar, and not make a sound when being branded with the symbols of my tribe. When I had a simple eight-spoked wheel inked into my forearm, he had a ram-horned serpent running from shoulder to wrist. Each morning we outdid the woodpeckers with the knocking of our wooden swords.

'I was ten', I told Mandred, 'the last time I saw Calleva. Things were quiet with the Catuvellauni under the rule of King Cunobelinus; however, Verica arranged to send me to Rome. He said it was for my education. Of course it was a tactical pledge of loyalty to the emperor. But my mother understood it as a punishment for loving me as she never loved my father.' When had I turned for my last view of her, it had been Katuaros I saw, white-faced with the effort of appearing unmoved.

I might have stayed in Rome forever except for events at home. Then two years ago, when I had been away for eight, Verica had suddenly appeared at the imperial palace, asking for help from the Romans. With the death of King Cunobelinus, the Catuvellauni were now split between his three sons.

'The middle one, called Caratacus,' Verica told the emperor, Claudius, 'has taken Calleva and driven my people south. We've lost Calleva before, I know, but not so definitively, and I've always won it back. Caratacus, however, is savage and brutal.'

There had been a battle. I had been living in Rome at the time yet, having heard the story so often, I almost believed I had seen for myself the war-painted second son of Cunobelinus bursting through our gates, firing thatches, spearing anything he found:

horses, dogs, babies; the Atrebatic warriors rushing to fight but losing the battle. My two elder brothers, whom I barely knew, had been slain. It had been Katuaros who was the hero, taking on Caratacus one-to-one. The fight ended with a mighty slash of the enemy's sword that nearly destroyed his ram-horned serpent and his shield arm with it. Calleva was lost.

To my surprise, Claudius agreed to help. It soon became evident why. He sent me home with a mission: I was to persuade the kings of Britain to submit without a fight and enjoy the benefits of the Roman way of life. 'Tell them that peace is preferable to bloodshed.' It was to be conquest, then, not liberation. Verica didn't care either way, so long as he got back what was his.

Only when the woods ended in cleared land did Calleva come into view. What did I expect to find? My mother? My dog? My people going about their daily tasks? Corn-grinding on the quern, crushing it fine in a mortar while the women sang the pounding song; bringing in the fruit harvest on carts attended by wasps; plugging holes in houses against winter's draughts. What I found was a wreck.

We entered by the east gate, its great doors hanging off their hinges, open on to streets befouled by wandering pigs, goats and geese. No one was sweeping up or transporting the muck to the fields. There was no harvest: the fruit rotted on the bushes. Buzzards circled overhead. The only activity was the slaves dragging decaying corpses out of the oppidum. The late autumn sun shone down on ruin.

A month after the 'conquest' of Britain by Claudius, I was on my way back from the formal submission of kings at Camulodunum, where we had celebrated the emperor's personal victory in subjugating the wild barbarians. In truth the conquest had been made in the summer by the legions, based in the friendly kingdom of the Atrebates. I had thought I was coming home to Calleva but, faced with this scene of wreckage, I suddenly felt rootless.

Four ways, north, south, east and west: Calleva was the hub of central Britain. We walked slowly through the grid of streets that had once thrived with merchants and tradesmen jostling at shops where you could buy just about anything, from a loaf of bread to a necklace of Roman glass beads. It had been a long journey and I was wincing with the pain of bruised ribs, my expectation of a trip to the baths dashed. There were no baths. Never had been. My mind was playing tricks. At the crossing of the four ways was the King's Hall, now occupied by military officers. I could smell barley beer on the wind and hear the drunken laughter of warriors. Surrounding buildings had been demolished and surveyors were pegging out the land for new building. 'What's the plan?' I asked them.

'This will be the forum. Over there a basilica. Over there, the House of the Commander.'

I turned away, aware that my fury would be showing on my face.

'You hadn't been consulted?' Mandred asked as we walked on.

'My father would have turned purple,' I said.

'And you?' Mandred asked. 'You're not far off purple yourself.'

'It will pass – just anger and I can control that.' Mandred had a way of looking at me when I came out with philosophical precepts I'd learned from books: eyebrow cocked, smile playing on his lips.

'To be honest,' I said, 'I shall be glad to see Calleva demolished and if they wish to civilise my birthplace with their fine buildings, let it be. Perhaps they overstep the bounds but to have Calleva back, the Catuvellauni quashed, Caratacus beaten and on the run, the whole territory of the Atrebates restored: the Romans have liberated Calleva as they promised. I can forgive them anything.'

There was a sudden crash ahead. An old man had stumbled and banged into a legionary. The soldier shouted at him, demanding his name; the old man shouted back. Neither could understand the other. Mandred ran to intervene but a centurion on horseback got there before him.

'Do as you were asked!' he thundered at the cowering wretch. 'Give us your name!'

Twisted and toothless, the old man shouted in a dialect which I doubted anyone could understand. I ran forwards but was four paces short when the centurion whacked him across the face with his vine staff. The grinding crack of splintered bone. Disgusted by the man's howls, the legionary grasped him by the neck of his tunic and hurled him under the wheels of a passing cart.

'One less for the census,' said the centurion, breaking the pall of silence. He turned to me. 'What are you staring at, scum?' He clearly did not recognise me as king of the place, but then why should he? I quickly apologised, knowing that, with the damage to my ribs, I could not survive a beating.

'Anything?' Mandred asked, with his skewed smile and raised eyebrow.

'Eh?'

'You can forgive them anything? Even a pretence of liberation?'

He was right. The incident buried its tip in my soul, there to fester until its appointed time.

2

THE FORT AT YELLOWHAMMER HILL

Summoned by the legate of the Second Legion, we left Calleva for the newly completed fort where the legion would be garrisoned in the winter. By the time we arrived night had fallen and we had to pick our way carefully over many dykes and ditches. The fort loomed black against the star-silvered sky, lamps glowing in the watchtowers at the gates, outlines of men patrolling the upper walkways.

The legate, Titus Vespasian, refused to leave his bed to welcome me and I was told he would see me in the morning. On our way to our allotted quarters, we passed slave pens crammed not only with beaten warriors but also their wives and children, who bawled all night long. By the many lamps set here to prevent escapes I could see their bruised and filthy faces staring back at me.

I tried not to think of Branwen, my betrothed, being kept in such a pen. She was only a child and any feelings I had for her were those of an older brother. She was a free spirit, daughter of the woods, devotee of the goddess Swale, youngest and best in the bardic college of Apnodens. Caged, transported, she would wilt and die like a plant torn from its roots.

'Are you all right?' Mandred asked.

'Let's get away from here. The smell is making my head spin.'

'It is cheesy, isn't it? Makes wet comfrey smell like perfume. Can a body decay before death?'

'You are not helping,' I said, gulping the bile down. I was relieved to find incense burning in the quarters allotted to us.

9

Vespasian invited me to join him for breakfast. 'I hear you woke the fort up last night. What were you doing arriving at that hour? Clattering through the gates?'

'I thought there was a clear road here from Calleva but it became a track across bog. We pressed on, but then we met the defences. All those dykes and ditches!'

'Yours, not ours. We're flattening them where we can.'

The fort had been sited where three territories meet: that of the Atrebates, the Catuvellauni and the Dobunni. Of the three warring tribes, the Atrebates and Dobunni had formed a shaky alliance to meet the challenge of the rapacious Catuvellauni, who ate up other people's possessions as rootling pigs, leaving churned mud behind them. For generations they had snuffled and grunted the entire length of the Thames, on the northern side of the great river. Unlike his predecessors, King Cunobelinus had played fair, but his sons, now that the great king was dead? Of the three, the eldest had fallen in the first battle against the Romans; the youngest was occupying the lands of the Canti on the eastern coast of Britain; and the middle one, ah, the middle one . . .

'Any news of Caratacus?' Vespasian asked, slurping his way through a bowl of bread soaked in hot milk. He usually ate in the barracks with the men but, in my honour, was taking breakfast in his quarters. The menu, however, remained the same: barrack food. Slops from camp cauldrons.

'No, none.'

'When did you last see him?'

A lump of stale bread stuck in my throat. I had to cough it up and chew it. The last I had seen of Caratacus? He was throwing at me the blood-matted head of Esius, king of the Dobunni. My host. My ally. The father of my betrothed. My harpist was dead at my feet, a spear buried in his ribs. My foster brother, Katuaros, lay unconscious in the rocky basin below the track. My fianna, the small band of warriors I had inherited from my father, had scattered, preferring to hide in the woods than maintain their reputation as warriors. Although weary after weeks of battle with the Romans, Caratacus still snarled with the self-confidence of an immortal, jeering at me, waving his sword. He would have killed me there and then except that he tripped on a bramble which seemed to twist itself round his leg. As he cut himself free, I went at him but he caught my blade with his. I would have fallen had not Apnodens come up the rock steps from the sacred springs with raised arms and a sound so high-pitched it was like a whine in heaven. A *vocos* – a spell created by sound that only druids can cast. Caratacus was exhausted. He had done nothing but fight since the Romans had landed and was now on the run. He stood there limply, head hung low, shoulders pulled down by the weight of his sword and shield. 'Go!' commanded Apnodens, chief of the bards.

'Last I saw of him,' I said to Vespasian, swallowing again, 'he was on his way to safety in Siluria.'

'Safety? He won't enjoy that for long, not when we extend the empire to the western sea.'

'Is that your intention?'

'Not at the moment. Before advancing, the governor wants us to consolidate what we have, which, thanks to you, is the whole of central southern Britain.'

He took me on a tour of the fort, the barracks, the baths, the market stalls, the headquarters, the stables, the watchtowers and upper walkways. 'So, what do you think?' he asked.

'Impressive.' Squirrels leapt ahead of us along the palisades, looking for somewhere to bury nuts in this changed land.

'We have half the legion garrisoned here. The other half remain fighting the Durotriges in the south. At the Armilustrium we shall celebrate our victories and, by all that is right, retire for the winter. But will that happen? You barbarians take no notice of the rules of war and attack whenever it suits you. There will be skirmishes and ambushes all along the frontier. In the winter! You have as much understanding of civilised engagement as a swarm of enraged hornets.'

It irked me, this use of the second person when it came to barbarians. We were passing the transport pens. 'What a stink!' I said, holding my kerchief over my nose.

'Yes, nearly a thousand captives. We scoop them up like mackerel. We need to start exporting them – and soon.'

I noticed for the first time that there was a pen within a pen, filled with young women. And then a prickling sensation, like sweat running down my back: the unnerving feeling of someone staring at me.

'All Catuvellauni, I presume,' I said, trying to keep my voice level.

Vespasian followed my gaze. 'I see your attention is on our whores.'

'I doubt they consider themselves whores.'

He shrugged. 'It's what they've become. There are a few strays from other tribes, but the majority are Catuvellauni, captured at Calleva. As we promised your father, we have regained your native place for the Atrebates.'

I nodded. 'I know. I was there two days ago.'

'How does it feel to have your birthplace your own again?' he asked.

It felt good, except that Caratacus was still free. He was to blame for it all: the loss of Calleva; my father fleeing to Rome for help; Claudius granting it; the invasion, the conquest, the new boundaries, the constant skirmishes – all the fault of that arrogant, jumped-up second son of Cunobelinus. Three sons the old king had, and a daughter, Theana. Now I stood locked in her gaze. Those eyes . . . They made the hair on my arms stand up. Was it really her? Chained and caged like a captive animal?

Those green eyes . . .

An optio approached with a message for the legate. Vespasian took his leave of me, saying to help myself to anything I needed. 'But avoid the whores. They are riddled with crabs. We'll discuss the Dobunni later,' he said, 'when the governor is here.'

'The governor?'

'He's coming with the Fourteenth for the Armilustrium. Yes, help yourself to what you need or want but make sure that includes a bath and a shave, you filthy, unkempt savage.'

'King to you,' I said.

'Since when? The death of your father? Is that all it takes to make a king? Surely there is more to it?' He strode off, laughing.

I remained, staring at the pen within the pen where the young women were. Theana, swathed in a mantle, stood in the midst of them, staring as if she would turn us to stone.

'Is that who I think it is?' Mandred asked.

I nodded wordlessly.

Theana, the sister of Caratacus. Did the Romans know who she was? Vespasian had made no mention of it.

At the horse field they were practising acrobatics for the Armilustrium, when the legions come together to mark the end of the summer campaigns. The Second and Fourteenth were to muster here, the Ninth and Twentieth at Camulodunum in the east.

We stood at the fence, disparaging the riders and their laughable antics, not that we dared laugh in this company. Two horses, a black and a grey, trained to run together, were led out. The cavalry commander invited anyone to chance his luck with the Roman Ride, the trick that could either kill a man or catapult him to the rank of hero. We watched men struggle to mount, starting off on one beast and then moving a leg over to the back of the other. Within moments they were tumbling. One even did the splits which made all the onlookers groan in sympathy.

Mandred was scathing about the Thracians, Germans, Gauls – all idiots. As for the Romans, they did not even volunteer.

Despite their training, the horses were growing fractious, especially the black one. 'They remind me of the allegory of the Charioteer in Plato's *Phaedrus,*' I said, 'where the black horse and the white horse represent—'

Mandred looked at me sideways. 'And that's your idea of wisdom, is it? To stand apart spouting Plato?' With that he vaulted the fence.

'Mandred! No! Come back at once!' I thundered.

The man who until recently had been my slave exercised his independence by striding to the mounting place. Recognising a Briton, the onlookers started jeering. *Britunculi!* Little Britons. Something of a misnomer considering how tall we are, but the way the word was spat out was the jeer of the conqueror at the conquered. It was only a month since I had seen Mandred running the pole at a chariot race yet I could never shake off the image of the lame cripple I had bought cheap at the slave market in Rome. His suppurating neck, his lurching gait caused by months in ankle chains – my tutor, Seneca, had told me off for buying rubbish. But I had seen his spirit and potential.

He removed his breeches and sandals to a storm of wolf whistles and, tightening up the girdle round his tunic, approached the horses slowly and from the front. The commander asked him which auxiliary unit he was from. 'None,' he said. 'I am the secretary of the king of the Atrebates. I wish only to show your loons how to mount two horses at once, the easy way.'

He took his time about it. First he introduced himself to the pair and knelt before them until, with a nudge, they bade him rise. He ran his hand over their flanks, guiding them down to sit. Moving between them, he put one bare foot on the back of the black horse, and the other on the back of the grey. I was not the only one feeling breathless. All jeering dwindled into silence.

'Up, please,' said Mandred, and together the horses rose. He wobbled a little but his feet maintained their grip. 'So,' he said to the commander, 'that's how it is done here in Britain.'

'Will you take them on a few circuits?' the commander asked.

Mandred agreed but only if the bridles were removed. The gathered crowd gasped. My head sank into my arms. I knew he had trained in this art when a child, and then again when he used to hang around at the racecourse in Rome. When I had given him his liberty, and he left me, he all but lived in the stables there. But I had never seen him perform the Roman Ride unbridled before. Even the centurion looked nervous as this living triangle set off on the circuit. Mandred had found his feet – his supple legs, so recently cured of lameness, took the ups and down as a boat bobs on water. The horses ran together as one, guided by what to them was an invisible third, known only by a slight pressure on the back and some tongue-clicking.

When Mandred finally brought them to a halt, jumped down and returned to me, he was mobbed by admiring horsemen and soldiers.

14

'Now tell me,' said Vespasian when we met again later, 'what's south of here? I sent scouts but when they returned they were witless, claiming they had been away two days when it was more like a month.'

I'd had that experience myself: the scouts had my sympathy.

'It's a confluence of two rivers, Thames and Charwelle, overlooked by one of our ancient temples, now just a stone circle in ruins and abandoned long ago.'

'What could have happened to them?'

Truth makes the best bricks when building a lie. 'There are legends.'

'About what?'

'There are many spirits in this land, and not all of them are open to propitiation. Some will lure you into bogs; some will set rats on your grain stores; some will cut off your horse's tail during the night. They do not like human presence. They certainly will not be liking the Roman presence. That broken ruin is an ancient sanctuary where such evil beings gather. They are taller than men, can change form at will and make a nonsense of time. Boggarts, marsh sprites, spriggans, call them what you will.' Shee . . .

He was staring at me as a child stares at his grandfather spinning a yarn but then blinked and snapped out of it. 'Storyteller!'

I could hardly have hoped for a better outcome. I tell him the truth and he accuses me of making it up. I relaxed. But the smile faded from Vespasian's eyes. 'For a man of truth, it's quite remarkable how many lies pour out of you. Togidubnus, King of the Atrebates, a man who traps flies with his sweet words, but you won't trap me.'

'Put it this way, whatever is there is not human. There are wild ponies, geese, swans, a few cattle but no settlement – on that long gravel spur, no one lives. So avoid it. Waste no more scouts. It's of no use to you.'

'Well,' he said. 'I thank you for the entertainment, but I need to get on.' Vespasian was eager to get back to his desk and the multitude of arrangements for the winter, assigning different units to different tasks, building the fort, filling in ditches, flattening dykes.

'Don't worry,' he said. 'I'll steer clear of the fairies, eh? By the way, I'm deputing you to go into the Far West and find out where Caratacus is.'

I bristled. I, the king, did not take orders from generals. 'Do you have that power?' I asked stiffly. 'Deputing me?'

'Asking, then. Delfos, believe me, all we have to do to end hostilities is capture Caratacus. It's in everyone's interest. While he lives, there will always be rebellion.'

I rejoined Mandred, still at the horse field. 'Hail!' cried a passing knot of soldiers. My secretary acknowledged them with a dip of his head.

'Vespasian considers me a liar,' I told him.

He feigned surprise. 'You?'

'I like to think I value truth above all things.'

'You certainly demand it of others, especially me.'

'He said I am honey-tongued, that the lies just pour out of me. He's sniffing about in the south. I told him about the Sanctuary of the Wheel – had to – but in such a way that he didn't believe me.'

Mandred smiled. 'To steer a man away from that which he shouldn't know about is not lying, just obfuscation. It's what the Shee do, after all. Why has he called you here?'

'The governor is due to arrive and wants to discuss affairs, specifically the whereabouts of Caratacus. They want me to look for him.'

'Well, you can't. Tell him from me, it has exhausted you coming this far with injured ribs. We're going to spend the winter at Corinium where you can rest.'

Units of the Fourteenth led by the governor, Aulus Plautius, arrived in the afternoon. As troop after troop marched in, the fort became crowded and I made my way with difficulty to the House of the Commander to meet him. 'The Durotriges are proving tenacious,' Vespasian reported to him. 'Each time I win one of their hilltop camps, I swear they create a new one. This could be a long campaign. The tribes west of the Severn, the Silures and Ordovices chief among them, are equally obdurate. The Dobunni—'

'Dobunnia is ours,' I said. 'Esius had turned. As you know, I am betrothed to his daughter, but the Fates have reduced her to slavery in Rome. All we have to do to win the loyalty of the Dobunni is to bring her home.'

'As I told you last time we met,' said Plautius, 'we are trying to locate her.'

'She is in Rome?'

'Yes, but not at the imperial palace. We don't know what happened.'

'You must find out. She is a queen!'

'How old is she? Ten? Eleven? A child, a female child. Not my idea of a strong ruler,' he said. 'Establish yourself as king in her absence, double your territory and quadruple your wealth.'

'Property and possessions are burdens I can do without,' I said, sounding pompous even to my own ears.

'Didn't Esius have a fine herd of horses? One of the finest?' Vespasian nudged me. 'Was that the ripple of an expression that just crossed your impassive features? For all your Stoicism, you are very young – what man in his twenties can resist horses and chariots?'

'To want to own horses', Plautius assured me, 'is natural, especially for you, Togidubnus, a Briton. A fine herd, eh? How many?'

'Only fifty or so,' I said. 'Caratacus took the bulk of them.' But he had failed to find the mares and foals kept in hidden paddocks. A small herd, perhaps, but so carefully bred as to be the very finest in all the land. Chariots, too. Only the Iceni had finer chariots.

'Why do you keep them hidden?'

I gave a short laugh. 'You don't know the Britons too well if you must ask that.'

Vespasian's gaze flicked my way. 'But you'll tell us where they are?'

'No, and for the same reason.' I grinned to relax the tension.

Aulus Plautius had been on campaign all summer. His normally marble complexion was now like fine doe hide, lightly tanned and uniform, unlike that of most Britons who reach the autumn with dead skin peeling off blotchy redness and freckles.

17

'What's the situation at the frontier?' he asked Vespasian.

'We've established our line on the Albios Way, as you know. But within Dobunni territory we have a double boundary, ours and nature's. Severn river lies a day's march beyond the frontier. We're clearing the people off the land and opening up areas for battle, but the rebels do not like honest fighting. They prefer subterfuge and surprise.'

'And one-to-one combat,' I put in.

'They won't be getting any of that,' said Plautius. 'So, they are camped on the west bank of the river?'

'That's so forested we can't tell where their camps are,' said Vespasian.

'Which tribal territory is that?' Plautius asked.

'Still Dobunnia,' I said, 'though often in contention.'

'So, it is your land,' said Plautius, feeling his chin for bristle.

'It will be if the people accept me as king.'

'Your next task is obvious. The Dobunni are caught between rebels and Romans.'

'Dobunnia is physically split down the middle by your frontier.'

'Sort it out. Use your eloquent charm to persuade them to stay loyal to us. Anything you need by way of troops, supplies or defences, let us know. We owe you everything.'

Mandred, standing apart, glared at me, willing me to refuse.

'I wish to establish relations with Corinium,' I said. 'The rest can wait until the spring.'

'Excellent. Yes. It's a strategic place and we intend to build a fort there in due course. Establish yourself as king of the Dobunni, double your territory and quadruple your wealth.'

'I told you, I'm not interested.'

'Apart from the horses.' Vespasian's furrowed face creased up in a rubbery smile.

'Not even women?' Plautius wondered.

I carelessly stretched my arms and cracked my knuckles. 'It is true that right now I have a more pressing need than even horses.'

'I told you,' Vespasian said to me, 'those girls are infected.'

'All of them?'

'Well, we keep one or two apart, including a green-eyed beauty, a priestess apparently. Governor, what do you think? Can we add to this young man's burden of gifts?'

Plautius smiled and nodded. 'Enjoy yourself. But we'll have her back in the morning, thank you.'

'I am not going to rut on foul straw like an animal,' I said. 'Have her brought to my rooms.'

I strode back to my quarters, Mandred hurrying beside me. 'What's your plan? What's your intention? You're going to free her, aren't you? How are you going to do it?'

'I have no idea,' I said.

Theana, the proud, the haughty, the cruel. Theana, the needy. Needing me. The thought of it inflamed my brain. 'They did say I was to take anything I wanted.'

'They meant barley or some bacon. Plautius told you to bring her back in the morning.'

'I'll say I misheard.'

'We need to think this through!'

'Talking of barley,' I said, 'have a wagon loaded with grain to go with us to Corinium. The harvest rots in the fields for want of labour. The governor would approve of it, without doubt, and it will buy my way into the affections of the Dobunni.'

Corinium. Once the lofty citadel on the edge of the Hills of Cuda, the northern seat of the Dobunnic kings, it was now a new settlement down in the valley. Beyond the now-abandoned royal house, however, a mile or two through high woods, stood the hidden paddocks and the Grove of Twelve Elms, the place where I had been betrothed to the daughter of King Esius. There, I hoped to retire into seclusion for the winter, alone with the woman who had the power to render me senseless.

3
THEANA

My foster brother, Katuaros, was followed everywhere by girls beguiled by his smiling eyes and strong limbs. It irritated him and he was always off in the woods, hunting with spear and sling. When it came to girls, I was the one doing the following and there was one I stalked whenever the Fates brought us together, usually at the great festivals. It was Lughnasa, being celebrated at the confluence of Thames with Charwelle. I saw her walking off alone and followed her to a pond, where she stood naked up to her waist in murky water. She was expecting me. Her eyes, emerald, looked on me with such soft invitation that I felt like a dog hearing its master's whistle. I waded and then swam to her, glimpsing her navel as I stood up. I was nine. I hardly knew what was happening to my body. She was older, taller. We gazed at each other. She reached out and gently cupped my head as if she would draw me into a kiss. And then the bottom of the pond fell away. Or so it seemed. I was falling. I was being pushed. I was under the water with a heavy weight on my head. All my struggles were in vain until, at what must have been the last moment, the weight lifted and I was pulled up to the surface, gagging and coughing and crying like a baby. Such utter humiliation. I thought I hated her as much as her brother but, whenever she was present, my eyes overpowered my thoughts.

The door opened. She was ushered in. 'Delfos?' she breathed. It was just a moment, one brief moment of vulnerability when

20

a woman recognises a man as her security and protection. And then she was raging.

'You conniving Briton with a Roman tongue!'

I said nothing while she railed.

'How dare you send for me? You who have betrayed the Britons! Betrayed! Did I save you from Caratacos last Beltane for this? Did I?'

'I am in your debt.'

'You have compromised! You have made treaties with the enemy! That empire which would suck us dry, you bow down before it. They call you king. They are laughing at you! You just make things easy for them, and for that they reward you, over and over again. By Sulis herself, you are disgusting, self-serving, deluded. You lack all honour. You have the warrior spirit of a stillborn lamb!'

'When you are done, Theana, I need to talk to you.' I could see a curse forming behind her eyes. 'Save your energy', I said, 'for the superstitious. You have no power over me.'

Then she launched herself, all claws like a cat. I held her by the wrists while she twisted and writhed, moaning, crying, trying to get the words out. *Voces mysticae* – the language of the curse – a language unknown to anyone, even those temple-appointed curse-scribes who scratch into small lead tablets and toss them into sacred waters. She was making it all up as she went. Gibberish. I disdained her antics, designed for weak and impressionable minds. I was above and beyond it all, a man of reason as impregnable as this fort. But she began to screech and, within the screech, I heard words and made the mistake of listening. And then, and then, it was as if the room, the fort, the world itself, everything burst into roaring flame, an explosion of fire giving off unendurable heat in the face of which we could only burn and melt. When everything went dark again – leaving a smell of cooked flesh and singed hair – we found ourselves clutching each other. I pulled her tight to me as if to absorb her. I felt her voice through my sore ribs.

'It is done now,' she said. 'The curse is laid and cannot be unlaid.'

'Against me?'

'If you stand with them, yes.'

'Theana, if you tell us where Caratacus is, they will let you go.'

She moved back so that she could stare at me. 'Tell me the truth.'

'You will be spared an interrogation.'

She looked at me through narrowed eyes. 'You mean they will kill me once they have what they want.'

'Yes. Believe me, it is better.'

She thumped me hard on the collar bone. 'All right for you to say.' Then she subsided and peered at me creased up in pain. 'Did I hurt you that much?'

'My ribs . . .' I muttered. 'I was unhorsed by one of your brother's warriors.'

It had been during one of the staged battles that Claudius 'fought' on his way to claim Camulodunum. I'd been in indulging in a moment of pride, giving myself credit for the peacefulness of the invasion. Suddenly there was a flash of light, sun off a helmet, and I was once again in the Temple of Apollo at Delphi, standing before the gate on the lintel of which was inscribed 'GNOTHI SEAUTON'. *Know thyself.* When I came back to this time, I was flat on my back and painfully winded. A British spear, not cast by anyone play-acting, had failed to penetrate my cuirass but had hurled me off my horse like a stone from a sling.

'Do you want me to have a look?' Theana asked.

'No!' I wrapped my arms around myself protectively.

Mandred, who helped me dress and undress, had given vivid descriptions daily of bruises which had begun 'the colour of Roman vomit after wine' and were now yellowing into 'the colour of British vomit after mead'. I was doing my very best to ignore it all. As Seneca once told me, 'pain tests brave men', and I meant to pass the test. But one thump on the shoulder from a beautiful woman and I was close to tears. 'I don't need any help,' I told her. 'It's you who needs my help. I'm going to get you out of here.'

'How?' she asked.

I shrugged. 'Not sure.'

'And how do you intend to explain my absence?'

I shrugged again.

'What we need', she said, 'is a great distraction.'

I did not sleep with her that night, too frightened since she did not offer herself. And what Vespasian had said about crabs dampened my ardour. My eye ran over her body as she lay on her side, glowing and peachy in the flickering light of the lamps. It had the rising and falling profile of chalk hills but my attention snagged on the film of grime on her skin and that smell of the slaves. Chalk hills, muddy and malodorous. I would take her to the baths, yes, in the morning, somehow, to the baths. Jump together into the caldarium and maybe, just maybe, push her head under the water and keep it there until she submitted to me utterly.

'Did you have a good night?' Vespasian asked when we met in the barracks for breakfast.

'Please have her removed as soon as you can.'

Vespasian beckoned to his optio and gave him the instruction. 'Beauty isn't everything, eh?' he said to me.

'She's absolutely crawling, and the stink she's left behind!'

'We're expecting another delivery of livestock in a few days – perhaps we'll find someone cleaner for you there.'

'More slaves? You haven't got the space.'

'No, we haven't. This lot needs to move on.'

'When?'

'Day after the Armilustrium. Crawling, eh? I did wonder at your choice.'

'What do you all do? You can't go years without a woman.'

'We use the locals.'

'If you'll take my advice,' I said, rising from the bench, 'you'll look after your slaves better. Get them cleaned up for sale.'

He shrugged. 'They have no value. Too many of them.'

'Then clean them up for the sake of camp hygiene.'

The rest of the day passed with the clatter of military rehearsals and the howling of slaves being marched to the river beyond the fort, unshackled and thrown in. When they all came back, one was missing and no one noticed, not immediately.

'Your woman has escaped,' said Vespasian at the practice grounds.

I watched the equestrian acrobats without expression. 'She's not mine. And in my opinion not worth the bother of searching for,' I said.

'I'm of the same mind. I have a whole unit scouring the woods and fields when we need them here. Clever, aren't they?' He nodded towards men handstanding bareback.

'We train our boys to do those stunts at the age of five,' I said.

'I heard about your limping secretary's feat with two horses. Impressive. If the Britons want us to respect them, more of that and less of the spears, eh?'

The Armilustrium, when it dawned, would be a long day of sacrifices to Mars, cavalry parades, dancing priests and the ceremonial putting-away of the weapons. It was late in the afternoon when the entire fort gathered to see Mandred repeat his triumph. I slipped away, back to the stables where my own horses were being kept, and the wagon loaded and waiting to go to Corinium. I looked about. No one around. In the distance everyone was cheering the barbarian who could ride two horses, unyoked and without reins.

I knocked on the side of the wagon. 'Are you all right in there?'

'What do you think?'

'Not long now. One more night and we'll leave at dawn.'

'You want me to sleep in here? Let us leave now!'

'That would arouse too many suspicions. Theana, be good, be quiet. Not long to wait and you will be free.'

4
LIFE AT TWELVE ELMS

The new road flanking the Hills of Cuda halved the journey and we reached Corinium in a day. The new settlement, which had come down from the hill to the valley, had now crept south to the crossing of four major routes and the proposed site of a Roman fort. We turned off before we reached it and ascended the hill to the ancient capital of the Dobunni, high on its flinty plateau overlooking the rolling lands to the southeast. The hill, as well as all the dips of its natural folds, was skirted by broken-down defences and earthworks. At the top, the rubble of the royal house and a few deep-thatches of those who preferred to live in the past rather than the future. A few miles along the ridge was the deserted grove called Twelve Elms where we arrived at twilight. I had my mind on the wagon and its contents but flitting bats made me stop and stare up at the trees, their still-leafy tops black against the darkening sky. The wind soughed in their waving branches. The wind, the bats – I felt unwelcome. The spirits of the place disapproved of me. Perhaps I should have taken Theana somewhere else. She emerged from between the sacks of grain, shivered and rubbed her arms. 'Someone here needs placating,' she said, looking up into the canopy. Mandred offered her a thick mantle to wrap herself in.

Esius's retreat house sulked in the shadows. Since the death of the man who had built it, it had been neglected. We got the fire going while Theana cleared mouse nests out of a pile of hides, not with a broom but with a song that charmed the little creatures out and away. The *vocos*, the song used to change things, is not the same as the crying of the Mother

25

that I sometimes hear. That is profound, chthonic grief; this was enchantment. My friend, the druid Apnodens, could send a message through miles of woodland in a voice I could barely hear, though animals in the vicinity came running to find this Orpheus. Only one other man had the same power to make himself heard for miles and that was Caratacus. With the coming of the Romans, however, he had broken the law of the druids and used his voice to stir up men to battle. Where deer and wild ponies came to Apnodens, long-haired warriors bristling with spears came to Caratacus.

When everything was the best it could be, we all three lay by the hearth. I stared into the cone of the thatched roof with the coil of smoke rising as if joining us to the sky by an umbilical cord. She was there, next to me, that woman who could strike men dumb with desire, who rode naked on a white mare at Beltane, who could by pleasure take a man to the threshold of death.

Take nothing that has not been offered. Especially her!

I was long practised in Stoicism. I had slept on stone floors without a pillow on a two-day fast to 'embrace poverty' as Seneca called it. That was nothing to this. I wondered if even Seneca could resist this. I thought I'd never sleep but just burn up in a shivering fever of lust and abstinence but I awoke in the dark, a soft hand stroking my cheek.

'Are you going to resist me all night?'

'If I can.' I raised my head to see where Mandred was.

'I put a gentle sleeping spell on him,' she said, her breath warm against my ear as her body pressed into mine.

Self-control went out of the roof with the smoke.

'Do you remember the first time we met?' she asked, fully awake while I was drifting in and out of this world on a warm cloud.

'How could I forget? You pushed me under the water. I thought I was going to drown.'

'I was just about to kiss you when you turned the colour of pond scum, fainted, got entangled in water weed. Do you remember that? No, I thought not. I didn't drown you: I saved you from drowning. I saved you from drowning and I saved your pride.'

Could that be true? 'I didn't realise!'

'Why did I save you, do you suppose? Because you are everything Caratacos is not. Now here you are, grown into a solemn man bearing the burden of the world, one who neatly folds his clothes before he goes to bed.'

There were slaves for such work, of course, but I liked to brush away the dust and make everything fresh for the new day to come.

'My brother will be carousing somewhere, or just plain drunk. He doesn't care about anyone but himself and his own. But you – you do care. I love you for it. Yes, you heard me right.'

At this point a stupid man would be thinking about settling down with this treasure but Theana rubbed her cheek against mine and said, 'Give no harbour to thoughts of forever. I may love someone else tomorrow.' She kissed me on the nose. 'As the years pass, we shall meet like fork-tailed kites in the sky, kiss and part, kiss and part, until the day when we shall meet no more.'

I awoke properly when dawn seeped through the gaps in the house. Had any of that been real? Just as she had put a sleeping spell on Mandred, she could have put a dreaming one on me. I left Theana asleep and went outside. A threatening silence enshrouded the Grove of Twelve Elms. The occasional squawk of a rook up in the trees only made the silence more pronounced. Once a bustling fortification high on the ridge overlooking the road to Siluria, the site was now an ancient circle of elm trees growing through piles of fallen stones. One large boulder had been split in two by the force of an elm sapling and was now in the grip of the mature roots of a grown tree. This boulder and tree, made into a shrine, had been abandoned with the death of Esius.

Ivy and nettles encroached on all the buildings in the grove – workshops, outhouses, stables. Decay does not take long in Britain. When I returned to the house, rats darted at my approach and scurried under the overhanging thatched roof that almost touched the ground. I was making a mental list of things to be done when Theana came out wrapped in a blanket, grey against the grey of the morning mist.

'The thatch needs to be smoked, if not entirely replaced,' I said. 'The ground gutter needs clearing – your *vocos* for the mice, does it work on rats? Then these piles of wet leaves must be removed or they will threaten the integrity of the daub.'

Her eyes widened angrily. 'Would you domesticate me, Delfos? Is that what you want? A woman who is concerned with blocked gutters?'

'I'm not asking you to do the work!'

'But you want me to organise it, to have it in mind, to keep myself busy with house maintenance while you go about your kingly duties.'

'Not at all!' I was wrong-footed. I'd presumed she'd be off on the road to Siluria at first light but she seemed to be suggesting she stay. On her own terms.

'So, where are you going today?' she asked.

'I've arranged to meet the elders of Corinium.'

'Without me?'

'It has to be. I'll only be away two nights.'

'I might not be here when you get back.'

Was there ever a woman to keep a man's soul in such a state of imbalance?

The track to Corinium led back along the ridge to the burnt-out ruin of the royal house and a huge pile of blackened skulls. From here, King Esius had governed all Dobunnia, a territory stretching from the source of Severn river in the western hills down to where the great river flowed into the sea. The house had reeked of Esius: the smoky gloom, the boar tusks over the lintel, the hides used as hangings, the wolf skulls placed in a ring around the purlins, their empty eye sockets catching the warm light of the hearth. Now it was just so many charred pillars poking out of the ash.

A group of uncles who had come up from the new Corinium to meet me uttered meek apologies for the state of the place.

'We should have pulled it down,' the chief elder said, looking with disgust at the ruin.

'Or repaired it,' I replied.

'Or repaired it, of course. But it is no longer in use.' They invited me to sit in council but I turned back towards the ruins, imagining the house ablaze.

'Who fired it?' I asked.

'Caratacus,' said the chief. 'He came here after his defeat, calling for the death of our people and our king, shouting accusations of betrayal. He himself threw the first torch into the thatch. While the king was still inside. Esius ran out unarmed to remove the flaming torch and stop the fire but Caratacus caught him by the hair, twisted him so that he fell to his knees with his throat bared and . . .'

'Yes,' I said quickly. 'I've seen the head.'

'You have? What happened to it? Caratacus took it away, when by all that is right it should have been left to take its place among the ancestors.'

'He ambushed me at Seven Springs, killed my harpist. Then he threw the bloody head at me, saying he didn't know what to do with it.' The elders gasped at the sacrilege. I raised my hand to calm them. 'My foster brother, Katuaros, who had dislocated his shoulder in a fall, went south for healing to the Temple of Sulis. He took the head with him, there to be stripped of its flesh and added to the skulls of the great Dobunnic kings.'

That the head of Esius had safely reached the Temple of Sulis caused them to soften towards me. Some continued to regard me as the cause of all their woes, since the plan for the Dobunni to desert Caratacus and join the Romans had been mine, but others were more forgiving. To these men, I was the betrothed of the king's daughter.

'Did you see what happened to her?' I asked.

'They carried her off squealing like a piglet.' The elders looked distraught. I told them that I'd heard from the governor himself that she had been sent to Rome as a slave, a gift for the wife of the emperor. I said nothing about her being missing. They glanced one to another, not knowing whether or not this was welcome news.

'It is good to know what happened, at least,' said the chief elder. 'She is safe. Is she safe?'

I said that we could presume so, and that the emperor, Claudius, had promised to find and return her. 'Are these ancestors?' I asked of the pile of blackened skulls at the threshold of the burnt house.

'No, they are our enemies. We've taken the ancestors to a new temple down by the river where we will put them on the bone fire at Samhain. They are badly damaged, halfway to the Otherworld. It is time to be done with the past.'

They took me to the new settlement, a two-hour ride along the river valley to where a host of new deep-thatches clustered around the area being cleared for the fort. There was a temple on higher ground which we approached in formal procession, a deep-thatch with intricate woodwork decorating the niches where the heads of Corinian ancestors rested. Once we were seated in a circle around the hearth fire, I formally addressed the council of elders.

'As you know, at the midsummer gathering I was elected to be the successor of my father as king of the Atrebates. The Druid Council also proposed that, as the betrothed of Branwen, I should succeed Esius as king of the Dobunni and unite our two nations.'

'That is not right. Branwen is the successor.'

'But she is enslaved.'

A collective groan came from the company.

'I am willing to stand in her place until she returns, at which time we shall rule jointly.'

Much muttering, mostly positive.

'It is your decision,' I said.

'If Branwen were here, and you were married to her, we would have no trouble in accepting you into our tribe,' said one of the elders.

'But he is the son of Innogen,' said another. 'He's half-Dobunni.'

'Perhaps, but born of rape by the king of the Atrebates. Togidubnus was born of rape and is the son of a rapist. We have no precedent for this, and no druids to guide us.'

'No druids?' I asked.

'A few bards remain but no priests. They have joined the exodus west.'

'Are you saying they have decided to support Caratacus?'

'No. They just feel the need to go beyond the empire. They say Rome intends their destruction.'

'That is nonsense. Rome intends no such thing.'

'Whether it does or not, we are left without anyone to consult on such matters as this one.'

'I shall send for Apnodens, the son of the archdruid. Would that be acceptable?'

There was much discussion, the elders muttering, even bickering, between themselves, before giving their conclusion. Those who had been at the great gathering knew that the archdruid had announced to the assembly that I was a just man who would 'give birth to something new'.

'On that basis,' they said, 'and given that you are the son of our great druid priestess Innogen, and that on solemn oath you undertake to bring Branwen home, we of Corinium are content that you be our king-in-waiting, but only on return of Branwen will your role receive divine sanction. Bring Branwen home!' they said.

'Your wish is my wish,' I told them.

That sealed it. Corinium, capital of the northern Dobunni, was mine.

When I returned to Twelve Elms I found to my relief that Theana was still there and had taken charge of the renovation of the grove and its dwellings. As I arrived she was overseeing hurried attempts with local women to rethatch and limewash the plaster before winter took hold. The air was noticeably sweeter, robins were singing, leaves beginning to gently fall. 'I work for the goddess!' she said when I made some wry comment. 'Cuda wishes this grove to be restored.' She had been a whole day at the boulder shrine, singing incantations, putting herself in a trance, communing with the goddess.

'Cuda?' More than a local spirit, she governed the rolling hills of north Dobunnia.

'This is a more significant place than it might seem. Esius chose his retreat well. Now that harmony is restored, you can rest properly, heal those ribs.'

Her eyes searched mine. I ran my hand over her long waves of black hair. 'You are wondering . . .' she prompted me.

'Yes?'

'How did I make myself welcome here? I tell you as I told Cuda: by the time Branwen returns, I shall be gone. She was satisfied with that. Are you?'

On free days Theana and I joined in the work of restoration. To be rid of the pervasive smells of woodsmoke and stale urine, we had all the dross of the past, old hides, old hangings, unidentified bones, thrown on to the bone fire being built for Samhain, all under the watchful gaze of some aunts whom I had deputed to keep us in check. They allowed most things to pass but every now and then protested that I couldn't possibly send this wooden cup of finger bones to the fire, or that weird scrap of leather which turned out to be the face of a great-great-great-uncle renowned for his horse-raiding. It was strange, handling the relics of those who lived on in the songs of the tribe.

What to put in their place? There was so much of Rome I missed. I wanted the sun inside the house, a fountain, green things growing, a hypocaust under tiled floors and a garden with a nymphaeum. None of these was feasible, not in a round house. Besides, it would alienate me from the people. I limited my desires to a bed in the Roman style, commissioning a local carpenter to do the work. He came to see me but declined the commission, saying it was beyond his skills, that I needed a Roman carpenter to make a Roman bed.

On the day of painting its interior, Theana wanted the house free of men so that she and the aunts could perform their sacred duty 'in peace'. I went with Mandred along the ridge, down through woods and apparently impenetrable undergrowth to the hidden paddocks. Caratacus had stolen the herd to replace his own horses lost in battle, but the mares in foal had been kept separately and he hadn't found them. Depleted though it was, it was still the basis of a fine herd, requiring only a stallion or two come spring.

'Do the Romans know this location?' I asked.

'Not yet,' said the head of a family of grooms who had looked after the royal horses for generations.

'Until we have established my legitimate ownership, we must remain very discreet, or the Romans will take them for meat,' I said. The grooms gasped. Perhaps I was exaggerating, but it did the job of having them accept me. I might not want the kingship but I certainly wanted the horses that came with it. Esius had begun a breeding programme, crossing Roman beauty with British strength, which I intended to continue to create the finest herd in Britain. My horse Scipio would make a perfect stud.

In the paddocks but penned separately were some Catuvellauni horses that Caratacus had left behind. We went amongst them, running hands over withers and legs to get a sense of health and form. 'Inferior stock,' I said, and the head groom agreed.

'Sell them off?' he asked.

I nodded. 'Keep those you deem fit for haulage and sell the rest. No, wait . . .' I reflected awhile and changed the instruction. 'Send them back home.'

Everyone looked astonished.

'There is much to atone for, on both sides. Send them to the Catuvellauni as a gift from the Atrebates with our hope that we might work together in peace to build a new Britain.'

We walked back to the grooms' cluster of houses. The head man was not one to hold back but said things others only thought. He was old, he was ready to die, he couldn't see the benefit of being circumspect. 'What you've just done – the gift to the Catuvellauni – it was shocking. Good, but shocking.'

I smiled and dipped my head in deference to his great age.

'Who's the woman?' he asked.

'What woman?'

'At the grove.'

'Just a slave.'

'A bed slave? Is that why you want a Roman bed? To make her comfortable?'

Corinium – the seat of stories and gossip. Nothing could be private here, but I was getting the sense that if I shared my secrets, they would keep them.

'She's the sister of Caratacus.'

'Well, yes, we know that. The carpenter recognised her. What's her name is what I'm asking.'

By the following day, everyone in Corinium knew that a daughter of Cunobelinus called Theana was living with the king at Twelve Elms. This knowledge stopped at the gates. No one outside Corinium knew it. Theana began to live more openly but, from her own choice, kept to the grove.

Back at the house, its daub walls still drying out, I was shown the designs scratched in the compacted chalk floor. Seen in trance-induced visions, the patterns were ordinary, extraordinary and downright confounding. What was clear was that Theana had mastered geometry. Circles, semi-circles, crescents, all intersecting, overlapping, sharing points on a circumference but not a centre: our druid geometry looked so odd to the Romans yet was something Euclid would have recognised. Theana asked me to choose which pattern to use to decorate the walls. 'For it is by our patterns that the gods recognise us,' she said.

5
SAMHAIN EVE

Samhain, the night of the ancestors, approached and the people of Corinium were busy building the great fire on the royal plateau, carving turnip lanterns and ceremoniously digging up the horse's head they had buried the previous year, now stripped of all flesh by the worms. I had sent a message to Katuaros in Noviomagus, inviting him to join me for the feast but making it sound like business to deter his wife from coming. I did not want Debonia meeting Theana. Oil and fire.

As young boys ran through Corinium delivering invitations, acceptances, apologies, a military messenger from Yellowhammer Fort arrived with a letter from Vespasian.

> There has been a diplomatic rift between Claudius and Passienus Crispus, consul-elect. A barbarian princess, destined for the imperial palace, was intercepted at the docks and taken to his house. I know the man and see no cause for concern. She will be well cared for.

Although I had never met Crispus, I knew the name for he was rich, influential and had a network of informants that permeated Rome. Even the emperor would not cross him. While relieved that my betrothed had not become the slave of my ex-lover, the emperor's wife Messalina, I was still annoyed, for Claudius had promised to return Branwen as soon as he found her. With this conflict of desire, I felt the first tug of the Maenads as they laid hands on their victim to tear him apart.

On the eve of Samhain, the crisp, autumnal weather became wintry. Rain lashed down, spoiling celebrations and turning tracks to mud. People scrabbled to protect the enormous heap of wood and bedding that would be the bone-fire with ramshackle awnings. The summer was over; days were shortening. Although not late, it was after dark when Katuaros came sodden into the royal house high on the plateau and squelched to the fire. I embraced him despite the sliminess of cold, wet leather, and called for fresh clothes to be brought. As his personal escort came out from under their capes, I recognised members of our old fianna. The last time I'd seen them, I was cursing them for hiding when Caratacus had attacked us at Seven Springs, but in truth I was pleased to see the dished face of Cow Crippler, who had broken his nose in a steer-wrestling contest, Mouse Ears with the bush of hairs behind the lobes that had given him his name, and Ten Horns, a quiet giant who had gained his name by killing a stag with ten tines on its antlers. They regarded me with the hopeful eyes of beaten dogs, wondering if they were still loved. With the briefest of nods, I let them know that they were.

'So,' said Katuaros, wrapping his hands round a cup of warm wine. 'King of the Dobunni, eh?'

'Only so far as the Corinians are concerned,' I said. 'I have yet to approach Gleva, and then there is the south of the territory.'

'You won't find it so easy down there. A local warlord called Enemnos is charging travellers heavy tolls to visit the Hot Springs.'

'That's a crime against the gods!'

'He's like a snake wrapped round gold. He even charges those who go to the Temple of Sulis for healing. He has claimed southern Dobunnia as his own, saying the only usurper in Dobunnia is you. First task for the new king: deal with him.'

'I will, if Sulis doesn't see to him herself.'

Slaves went about serving stew from the ever-bubbling cauldron; soon the house was filled with the steam of wet things drying out and the chatter of men recovering from a journey with the help of beer. Katuaros looked around, his disapproval clear. 'Not the house of a king,' he said.

'Ten days ago it was a pile of ash,' I said, 'burned down by Caratacus.'

He growled and muttered a curse against the man who had killed his father in the battle for Calleva.

'We've been working hard to get it this far,' I said, hesitating to tell him about Twelve Elms, where we had made even better progress on rebuilding. If I took him there, I would lose Theana to him. No woman could resist Katuaros and his twinkling eyes, his way of muttering in your ear as if you were the only person in the world who mattered. Lost in thought, he rubbed at his shoulder. The light of the hearth fire glinted in the waves of his hair.

'How is your shoulder?' I asked.

'The priest at the Hot Springs put the bones back in place and had me sleep in the temple for three nights. After that, I did not know what to do. On horseback I could not go far and I thought I would come back here.' He looked pale at the memory of pain. 'I was resting where the road forked, north to Corinium, east to Kennet, when a small party from Cuma approached, bringing a stunted baby to the Hot Springs. Debonia was with them and arranged for a wagon to take me to her people's stead at the Sanctuary of the Wheel. And there I stayed until we were married. She looks after me well.'

Debonia, the widowed midwife of Cuma, red of cheek, red of hair. Debonia the fearless. Debonia the terrible. Debonia his wife.

'She sends her good wishes, Great King, and says if I'm not home by full moon she will skin me.'

'Good reason not to go home, then.'

He rolled his eyes. 'Come on, out with it. What is it you have against Debonia?'

'Why did you marry her?' I asked. 'You could have had anyone. Someone younger, someone noble. Not a midwife from a community at one with their pigs when it comes to intelligence.'

He jumped to his feet as if he were sitting on ants. 'By Taranis, Delfos! I never took you for a snob.'

Nor had I and was just as surprised. In truth, I was annoyed that, having promised to find Branwen, he had gone to Cuma to recuperate. He had explained it all to me, how hopeless the quest had been; how, in the flood of slaves being exported, it had been like 'looking for a twig in a river, and you don't know which river'. He had been in agony I had asked too much of him.

37

'I don't understand the attraction, that's all. What is it about her?'

'She's pregnant,' he said, sitting down again.

'Yours?'

He nodded. 'While I was recovering from the first dislocation.' We had been crossing Thames river from the Sanctuary of the Wheel and he had fallen from the ferry boat or, in his version, been pushed by the Shee.

'I still don't understand. It's no reason to marry her. Please, tell me, what is the real attraction?'

'I want sons. You know that. I need to restore the dynasty of my father, Biccos. If you hadn't noticed, Debonia has a wonderful pair of hips on her. And she is a midwife!'

'That doesn't make childbirth any easier.'

'But she's strong. I married her strength and certainty.'

This took me aback, that he of all people could choose according to quality rather than prestige or beauty.

'And you?' he asked. 'Do you have a woman?'

'You know I do.'

'I mean a real woman, not a child!'

I remembered how fond Branwen had been of Katuaros. Why do girls like glib men? Glib men with laughing eyes, soft voice and the muscles of a warrior.

'I am betrothed to Branwen.'

'But, Delfos, a child! Even if she were here, safe and sound, you'd still need a proper woman, for five years at least. Have you looked around here at Corinium? We could find someone for you. This is, after all, the night when the Sky beds the Earth. All the lads will be out. We'll find you someone.'

Everything in me longed to rush home and bed Theana but if Katuaros found out about her I'd never hear the last of it and I could do without his mockery. Katuaros knew how to keep his affairs light: I did not. Always quick to identify hypocrisy in others, he'd have made a meal of it. Twelve Elms was sacred ground and I was defiling it. I, not Theana, I, with my addiction to her body.

Although he was a broken spear, I was still jealous of him, my foster brother, he who always took charge as if his superiority were a law of nature recognised by the gods;

he who, when we were boys, had planned our days and devised our adventures; who had humiliated me with his protectiveness; whose stride I still believed I could not match.

'You think I'm being harsh about Branwen?' he asked. 'I miss her, too. Her brightness. A flame of curiosity flickering about us. I sometimes lie awake at night wondering where she is. Poor child! Can you imagine what she's going through? Half-starved, forced to work dawn to dusk for some patron who barely notices her, her hands raw with scrubbing, her bones aching from fetching water, or—'

'Hush now,' I said. 'She is in Rome, in the house of the consul-elect. She will be well treated.'

He sat back with a long sigh of relief. 'How long have you known this?'

'I've had a letter from Vespasian.'

'So, it was all wasted effort on my part, but that is of no consequence. She's alive . . .' he said. 'We'll get her home, and then . . .'

'And then what?'

'Once she is of age, you will be married and rightfully king of the Dobunni.'

'Am I, are we, even kings of the Atrebates and Belgae? We have had no investiture.'

'I have.'

'When?'

'After you went to Rome. I returned to Ford of the Alders to take charge there. I was only twelve but I had uncles to help run things.'

An investiture! Was I destined to spend my life envying my foster brother?

'I should have one, too,' I said.

Katuaros pulled a face. 'I can't see the Romans allowing that. They just about suffer us calling ourselves kings. Best that we don't strut about in traditional robes and regalia.'

He was right. Yet still I yearned . . .

As we sat talking by the hearth fire, planning the new house Katuaros wanted to build at our harbour close to Noviomagus, the rain stopped. Noises outside grew ever more boisterous with children running about screaming, their high-pitched sound bright against the low tones of the busy adults. Music started up. I noticed Katuaros tapping his foot.

'The Atrebates are at peace,' he said. 'The Roman army has moved on, leaving the mustering ground which, well, it's a huge, deserted space with a few granaries, nothing more. But consider the site: right at the harbour, the sea lapping a short walk away. All those cargo ships coming in, subject to our tolls.'

'Why would you need so much space?'

'For a king's house, something in the Roman style that could host any dignitaries who come our way. A governor, say, or an emperor. Anyone landing at our harbour, anyone important needing a formal welcome.' Again he looked about him at my deep-thatch lined with darkness. 'Somewhere with underfloor heating,' he said.

'I can't see the need. What's the need? Just to impress our overlords?'

'I don't understand you. The more titles and territories you acquire, the more you retreat into hovels. The Romans have no respect for kings but if we were to have a palace . . . I can build us one, if you will put up half the cost.'

'What is the cost?'

'I haven't considered the details yet.'

'Well, when you have, I'll put up the money if I deem it viable. Or I could give you the money now to build a royal house without ostentation, in the British style.'

'No marble? No fountains? No gardens?'

'Such things are luxuries.'

'No bathhouse?'

I groaned. He knew my weak spots.

'Delfos, Delfos, Delfos . . . Stoicism – it's like spitting in the eye of Fortune.' He rose up again. 'Shall we go outside?'

'Stoicism teaches equanimity.'

'Is that why you look stony at the mention of Branwen? Is that the face of equanimity? No! It's the face of concrete! The only rightful response to grief is to howl.'

'If you would be an animal,' I said. Mandred, who was sitting with us, glanced at me, one eyebrow raised. He had heard me howling in the hills when I thought I was alone. 'Like a wolf in a trap,' he had said.

40

'I,' Katuaros continued, 'I embrace good fortune and spit at the bad. I am alive. The whole object of life is to increase the good and avoid the bad.'

Epicurean, I thought. 'You have no control over these things,' I told him, following him outside as I had always followed him.

We sat by the communal fire, watching children running around dressed as headless giants, toads, bats and ghosts. It was the night of the dead, a night to remember the ancestors. Around midnight, Katuaros and I withdrew into the royal house and fell asleep at the hearth like two boys, curled up together, each of us believing he protected the other. I had intended to sneak away while he slept and have my Samhain night with Theana, but I fell asleep before him and only awoke to the sound of children banging metal on metal and shouting, 'Feed the horse! Feed the horse!'

I stumbled blearily to the doorway, where Katuaros was praising the reddened skull that snapped its jaws above a swaying body of horsehide drapes. 'Fine horse!'

'Beware the Shee!' cried the children. 'Protect your house from the Shee!' Having given the horse gifts of food, bones and scrap metal, it called down a blessing upon us and swayed on to the next dwelling, circling the plateau sunwise. We made our oblations to our gods and the ancestors, lit brands from the hearth fire and planted them around the wall of the house; then, gathering in the centre, we ceremoniously doused the hearth fire. It hissed wildly and died.

Roman units were active on all roads running west across the frontier, so it was natural that Corinium, which overlooked a major route, should be visited. When they came, however, it was a ceremonial unit of cavalry headed not by a decurion but a tribune, come to attend my proclamation. It was a nice touch on Vespasian's part, to recognise and honour a local king, but I could see the unit had a double purpose and sent Mandred off to Twelve Elms to take Theana somewhere even safer.

'We're looking for an escaped slave,' the tribune said. 'The legate said that, while I was here, I should search Corinium since you had a fondness for her. Would you have any objections?'

'Do you honestly think a woman dragging chains would go unnoticed?'

'She wasn't shackled.'

'Are you talking about Theana?' I asked.

'Theana?' Katuaros gasped. 'Here? I think we'd know about it.' Ah, gods, how you favoured me! My foster brother's unfeigned surprise mixed with offence persuaded the tribune that he would not find her at Corinium. But he still had orders to follow and sent his men off through the oppidum, commanding them to respect the inhabitants on this auspicious day. Everyone in Corinium professed ignorance – never heard of her, let alone seen her, she must surely be on the road west.

Returning from Twelve Elms, Mandred took me aside and told me that Theana was gone, 'and has taken one of your horses'.

'Was she startled by the Romans?'

'No, she had already left, having spent Samhain Night alone,' he said, pointedly.

My face crumpled.

'What is it?' he asked, concerned.

'She took a horse? The bitch . . .'

Not for a moment did he believe I'd been so violently felled by the loss of a horse when I had so many.

'Where do you think she went?' I asked.

'West,' he said. He took me firmly by the arm. The pressure of his grasp spoke to me, reached me through the sickening grief. 'You knew she wouldn't stay.'

Kiss and part. Kiss and part.

I sat down heavily. 'The Corinians told the Romans she must have gone west. And she has gone west!'

'It's half a day to the river from here. She'll be across it and into Ferylloog by sunset. They won't catch her.'

Ferylloog – Iron Woods. Yes, she could hide there easily, betwixt Severn and Wye. Katuaros, who had attended the sudden departure of the Romans, returned to the royal house to find me sitting morosely on a bench at the hearth.

'What's the matter with him?' he asked Mandred.

'He's had a horse stolen. It was a favourite.'

'Oh,' said my foster brother. He came to me and laid his hand on my head. 'I'm sorry to hear that. But, Delfos, you have a herd fifty strong.'

'It was a favourite,' I muttered, wondering why now? Why today? I wanted to go after her, to persuade her to stay with me, but this was the day of my proclamation as king. And on my return to the grove there was to be a more private ceremony, one I had imagined her playing a part in. She would be over Wye river and into Siluria by then.

Agitated beyond endurance, I wanted to go and kick things. Where the Stoic now? Perhaps he was present in the man who, despite the turmoil of his emotions, did nothing, but it wasn't detachment I felt, it was failure. Failure as king and lover.

A proper investiture would have been held at some sacred place such as the Hill of Sovereignty at Kennet. Instead I was to be proclaimed king at the royal house high on the plateau in a perfunctory ceremony and had to submit to the fussing of aunts before the ceremonies began. They painted my face with the same skill – and patterns – with which they had decorated my house. Patterns reaching to the sky for new life. They plaited my hair. They dressed me in an embroidered tunic of doeskin hung with golden chains and drapes of beads. There was talk of my wearing the boar-toothed helmet of Esius but I refused it. Instead they put on me the helmet of the grandfather of Esius, a Dobunnic warrior of renown. The helmet itself was close-fitting, and the crest, a sun disc made of exquisite filigree bronze and plumed with red feathers, increased my height by a head. It was hard to keep it upright; as I was led out into the compound, I realised I should have rehearsed this moment. In the gathering dusk the elders stood in concentric circles on the plateau in their feather mantles, antlered headdresses and torcs for the Samhain Rites of the Dead. Up hill, down dale, two worlds, past and future. 'Boduocus fought in that,' one of them said, staring at my precarious headgear. 'You can't even stand upright in it.' There was an undercurrent of objection. Most were content for me to assume the kingship, but not all. I heard

43

someone mutter, 'Atrebates!' and spit, but I let it go. They had no reason to love me. Given the mood I was in, I felt I deserved such insults. I concentrated on the rites. Having bidden farewell to the Summer King, and welcome to the Winter King, we called upon the ancestors – our teachers – to guide us, and the ancestors – our families – to come to us, to meet us at this thin time when this world meets the Other. It's a rite, a ritual with long chains of verses invoking memories of all one has known and lost. Into my mind came images of my father, Verica, then of Esius, father of my betrothed, and of Draumur, my harpist. As I began inwardly to recite my own genealogy going back to Kommios and beyond, there came another spirit who overwhelmed the rest: Innogen, my Dobunnic mother. She had been a priestess in a druid line that stretched back forever; a royal line; a supernatural line begotten by gods. Heady stuff.

Somewhere in these lyrical dreams, in the palpable presence of my mother and her kin, I was formally pronounced king-in-waiting of the Dobunni.

On the rising of the moon, we gathered at the Samhain fire which had been built in the royal enclosure. It was a great pile of rubbish, as high as a tree: broken furniture, old bedding, fouled rushes, all thrown on to burn away the year. After a prolonged ceremony around the altar, I turned to the fire and lit it with three brands. To the relief of all, it took and, as the night progressed, people came up from new Corinium to offer to the flames the bones of their dead. We stood in silence, remembering those who had passed, and that which was passing: the very life these people had lived for generations.

Devotees of Cuda performed the swan dance three times round the fire – something I had once seen Branwen do. Where was she now, on this night? In Rome they would be celebrating the Victory Games of Sulla. Branwen would not be interested, her face puckered up with disdain at this display of muscle. She'd want to fly away, my swan maiden. Her arms moving up and down, up and down, if only in her imagination. She'd be wanting to fly home. But how to get her back?

'Delfos!' said Katuaros. 'Where are you?'

'Annwn, the Otherworld. It is the night for it.'

44

At daybreak, a procession of Corinians laboured up the hill bearing brands to collect new fire for their hearths and to hear me address them. I told them in as booming a voice as I could muster of the new laws we were to live under, and how things would change. I did my very best to make it seem it was all for the better, but some of the announcements were met with fuming silence, some with angry outbursts. The chief of the elders called for peace, 'For this is a sacred time and a sacred space. Set your troubles aside, at least for a while.'

The priestly augurs presented themselves to tell of the year to come. For once they seemed uncertain and said that the omens were 'murky'. It could be good, it could be bad, it depended. What they could discern without difficulty was the weather. By the order in which the trees shed their leaves, how the leaves fell, and the shape of the piles that gathered, they could tell us we had a week before the next rain came, and that it would be presaged by a terrible storm that would flood the valleys. Katuaros decided to leave as soon as the ceremonies were over.

As the great bone fire began to die down, each family lit a fresh brand from it to take back home and relight their hearths. The snaking column of light went down the hill to the new oppidum. Autumn had become winter; Kyronion had become Corinium; Esius had become Togidubnus. The song of the tribe had a new verse. I know now what I did not know then: it was to be one of the last.

As Katuaros took his leave, apparently keen to return to his stocky matron, I noticed a sense of distance between us that had not been there before. I had become something he had not: king of two territories. I did my best to heal the rupture but the truth was that our status had irrevocably changed. He was now the junior who had to match my stride, and he did not like it, as if something unnatural had come upon his life. After that, he tended to make his own mind up on matters which should have been joint decisions and I, still trying to heal things, allowed it.

6
APNODENS

Ahead on the track leading to Twelve Elms was a solitary figure with crinkly grey hair hanging down almost to his waist. He had a leather bag slung across his back, bulging like a tinker's and clattering as he walked. Sometimes he went faster, sometimes slower, sometimes he stopped or skipped, as if he and his bag were joined in some percussive song. A druid swathed in a sodden mantle, his feet bare, he knew I was behind him and turned with a smile. The last time I'd seen Apnodens, back in midsummer, his hair had been foxy red.

'Where are you going, pilgrim?' I asked.

'To greet the king of the Dobunni. I hear he dwells in a grove hereabouts, with living trees as the pillars of his palace, the floor a mosaic of woodland litter and the blue sky its glorious ceiling.'

'It's not always blue,' I said, dismounting but holding back from embracing him. 'You wet old dog. What happened to your hair?'

'The colour bled out.' He looked momentarily absent, remembering the murder of his father. Then he shook himself free of sorrow and we walked on together. It was not just the colour of his hair that had changed. The dutiful, solemn head of the bardic college, who had held me captive in his grove at the Sanctuary of Kennet, who had found in me a friend for his lonely soul, had become scruffy, rebellious, indifferent to anyone's rules and regulations.

As we approached Twelve Elms, we passed chickens scratting in the undergrowth for worms and slugs. 'Hail sacred harbingers of the dawn!' said Apnodens and they ran out to him, heads up, regarding him full-face with both eyes, as if they knew he carried seed, which indeed he did. 'Blessings on this place,' he said, casting a handful to the birds. Twelve Elms didn't seem blessed to me on that day. It seemed even colder and more neglected than when I had first arrived. I had been at Corinium for only four days yet the grove dwelling felt robbed of warmth.

I took him to the king's house, a burst of colour amid the browns and greens of the trees. Theana's patterns glowed and Apnodens 'read' them with approval before we went inside to the hearth.

'How did you know where to find me?' I asked.

'I put myself in your place and wondered where I would go.'

'Are you still in hiding at the Hot Springs?'

'I left the safety of my cave to find you, to warn you about what is happening in the south. A warlord called Enemnos is ruling the territory. While you ride hither and thither doing the bidding of the Romans, you are losing what is now your own ground.'

The fire – which had been relit with the Samhain flame – was blazing and the cauldron bubbling but, still mourning the loss of Theana, I felt shivery.

As an attendant approached with fresh, dry clothes, Apnodens stripped off. His muscles were tight as ropes under his brown skin. He passed over his own clothes reluctantly, as if they were his children being taken hostage, removing from his mantle ('woven by the Shee', he told me once) a silver brooch formed of two swans with their necks entwined. Apart from the brooch, and the knife thrust in his belt, everything he wore and owned he had made himself, often from the skins of animals he had sacrificed. He was not dressed in clothes, but in spirits. He took the tunic and breeches offered, and a fine woollen mantle woven by an aunt. Wriggling and complaining that it was coarse and itchy compared to his own, he fastened it at the shoulder with the swan brooch. Given a bowl, he helped himself to the stew. 'A truly royal feast!' he said approvingly. 'I hear you were proclaimed at Corinium.'

'King-in-waiting.'

'Waiting for what?'

'Branwen.'

At the name of the child who had been his best student of voice, his cheerfulness disappeared like the sun behind a cloud. 'Branwen,' he sighed, as if she represented the whole of his previous life that could never be reclaimed. 'Have you any news?'

'She is in Rome and the property of Passienus Crispus, a man of rare honour, designated to be consul for a second time.'

'Slavery is an offence against nature! Can we get her home? Can you not appeal to Claudius?'

'I already have, of course, but Crispus is one of the richest men in the empire so we can't just buy her. In Rome everyone is linked together in a web of patronage which you disturb at your peril. Being so rich, it is Crispus who has the upper hand, not the emperor.'

'Then we must pray to the gods, make sacrifices and oblations, to bring this about.' He told me about the past months spent hiding in the hills around the Hot Springs. 'In my refuge I am free, but down in the valleys the Romans are everywhere.'

'Have you not discovered yet,' I asked, 'that there is no need to hide?'

'Not yet, no. I disbanded the college of bards and many have accepted your invitation to live freely in your territories but others are moving west into Ferylloog.'

'Which is now my land,' I said. 'It's on the far side of the river but still Dobunnic.'

'Are you sure? With their carving up of territories, the Romans have cast the Feryllooges into the lap of Siluria. What are you doing, taking on a territory split east from west by the Romans, and south from north by that upstart Enemnos? A wise man would have walked away. And I wouldn't be too confident about Ferylloog wishing to remain Dobunnic. Since the invasion its loyalties have swung to the Silures. I believe Caratacus himself is often there, using it as a base to harry the frontier.'

I winced at the thought of him hiding in my land. Ferylloog was a place of terror in my childhood imagination, thanks to the stories of my grandmother, but I did not wish it violated by grim reality. 'Is it as bad as that? A split in the union and Ferylloog lost?'

'According to the stars, yes. The premature deaths of Esius and my father caused a fissure in our story. You have to mend things, somehow.'

'Have you met Enemnos?'

'I have not. As you know, I prefer the company of rocks, springs and ferns to that of men. Most men. But I have heard stories. Few have met him. He weaves his webs, sits in the centre and sends others out to do the work. He has a savage reputation.'

What had he done? Been merciless to prisoners? Treacherous with friends?

'They say he killed his grandmother. She told him off when he was a boy, in front of others. He never forgave her and one drunken night he pushed her into the fire.'

Whether this was true or not, I had heard that Enemnos killed his own wife for bearing a daughter. I didn't want to see him ruling anybody.

I sat back and closed my eyes on the world for a while. Silures overrunning Ferylloog, a north–south split of Dobunnia, a missing queen – how long before I would become caught up in conflict? 'Tell me what you know to be true about him.'

'Oh, he's just a common man with common greed and a common lust for power. There is nothing honourable about him. He is merely using the turbulence of the times to advance his own selfish cause. They say he dribbles when he uses the word "gold" but I have it on better authority that he's after your horses.'

I stiffened. King of a divided territory, under the rule of an empire that despised kings, I felt as if I'd been given the fragments of a beautiful vase broken in transit. How to heal? How to put it back together again? How to save my herd from some scabby raider from the south? I glanced at Apnodens. His large eyes were full of compassion.

I had not seen him since we had fled together from the great gathering at Venonis where all the tribes met in the centre of the country at midsummer. I wondered whether to broach the subject or let it drop into the lake of the past like a stone. His father, Archdruid Regalis, had stood at the Speaking Stone on the Hill of Assembly calling for a peaceful transition into a new way of life. A faction of young druids, who equated peace with submission, bayed like wolves. Master of the *vocos*, the archdruid spoke over them without apparently raising his voice. In place of loudness there was penetration: you couldn't hear anything but his voice. Urged on by Caratacus, who did raise his voice, the tribes shook their spears, stamped and hollered. The archdruid was compelled to finish his address by shouting that this would be the last Gathering of the Tribes. But at once up went a chant among the thousands: '*Next year in Venonis*' – the customary farewell once a gathering had finished, and a pledge to return. The archdruid raised his arms and called upon the gods. It was a priest of the Parisi who came up behind him with the sacrificial knife and drew it across his throat. There was a flash of metal and a gush of blood.

Apnodens and I had stood frozen, witness to the murder of his father by a new breed of druid, young, militant, led by a self-appointed druid king, Caratacus. Suddenly fearful of being recognised, we had squirmed out of the angry throng and run down into the badlands. Caratacus, his rebel army and the militant druids moved west into Siluria and from there mercilessly harried the patrols on the frontier while I spent the rest of the summer in careful negotiations, continuing the work of the archdruid in trying to achieve peace in the south without conflict.

I poked at the fire and threw on a log. Perhaps Apnodens was caught in the same memories, for he said, 'The way of peace is not easy.'

'Is it a way we must walk unarmed?'

'It is not.'

'Explain that to me.'

'When you kill, as you will have to, do it as a sacrifice and not from any rage or thirst for revenge.'

'A sacrifice? At an altar?'

'No. In the moment. It's all in the intention. Make all your acts, acts for the good.' He rummaged in his leather sack. His possessions were few: a small harp, a long war trumpet in

50

several pieces, rattles. 'I own what I can carry, and only carry what no man owns.'

'A carnyx?' I said, looking at the trumpet. 'The trump of war?' Designed to be held aloft and upright – a feat in itself – it had a boar's head and a clapper tongue and would make a dreadful noise to frighten the enemy. 'Where did you pick this up from? A battlefield?'

'It's not ideal but, with my breath blowing through it, it can summon spirits.'

'And the god Camulos, I shouldn't wonder.'

'Perhaps that's who we need,' he muttered.

I felt a cold hand on my spine. Surely he did not mean that? I blinked to clear any image of the god of war.

'Before you ride off into battle,' I said, 'I'd like this grove to be cleared of any evil spirits and reconsecrated. Would you perform the rite for us?'

'Anything else?'

'An investiture?'

'Not yet, not until you are king of yourself.'

7

KING OF THE SACRED GROVE

The druids arrived in procession from who knows where. They came through the woods from the west, from the temples of Ferylloog which are the most sacred of all in Dobunnia. We heard their cymbals and clinking adornments first: a sound which always made you hold your breath. 'They're coming! They're coming!' cried the children of Corinium, running ahead of them. They were led by the chief priest of the Temple of Nodens, taking the place of the archdruid while the seat remained empty.

The priests performed rituals of cleansing before we made a sacrifice to Cuda on a new altar. Each of the elms was swagged with garlands of evergreens, and the ancient shrine where a tree seemed to grow out of a boulder was resanctified. As I knelt before it, many hands dressed me with a flowing mantle, a golden torc around my neck and a golden circlet for my brow. The torc was the crescent moon, the circlet the sun and the blue mantle was embroidered with silver stars. The function of a king, after all, is to bridge worlds.

'Welcome, King Togidubnus,' said the chief priest, bidding me to stand. 'Nemetona and the spirit of the sacred grove welcome you. The animals of the undergrowth, the shy deer and the crafty fox, welcome you. The birds of the sky, soaring on outstretched wings, welcome you. The owls and the squirrels and all who live in the trees welcome you. The worms in the soil and the beetles under logs welcome you. We welcome you, Togidubnus, King of the Dobunni, elected by the authority of the last archdruid.'

As I stood in the centre of the grove, it seemed my feet put down roots. The druids bowed to the four directions; they bowed to the four spokes of time and invested me with true kingship, not the kingship of three vast territories – that kind of king belongs to the middle world and has to fight for his life against a multitude of enemies. This was an inner kingship, when a man begins the work of mastering his own nature. The chief priest saw that I understood. 'King of the Sacred Grove,' he said.

There was a ceremonial feast afterwards but I changed my robes for breeches and tunic and slipped away to the paddocks, telling myself it was to check on the mares when in truth it was to be alone with them. As I arrived, the darkening sky went black. There was a searing gold fissure and a blue flash, followed by a bolt of Taranis which shook the ground and made the trees gasp. Grazing horses jumped sideways then went back to eating grass, but there were sounds of distress in the stables. The brood mares were whinnying and rearing up, outdoing the thunder with their clattering in the stalls. A few of the stable men – so adept in the skill of riding that we called them the centaurs – were trying to calm them but just making things worse, the horses catching and reacting to their anxiety. Another bolt crashed in the sky and the paddocks lit up blue. Had my election angered the god? It was to calm myself that I began to run my hand over the trembling flanks of frightened horses, their eyes and ears swivelling. 'There, there, hush now,' I said softly to each one, as if to a baby.

There was a lead mare, mother of the herd, who was quieter than the rest but still troubled. I stroked her repeatedly from withers to rump then took a comb to her tail, loosening knots to take my own mind off the storm. The next bolt was not overhead: the wrath was passing. 'There, there, hush now.' I combed and combed until the mare was at peace. As she calmed, so did the others. I ran my fingers through her tail. Two fingers separating it into three strands. Where did the memory come from? Where the knowledge? My Dobunnic grandmother had taught me braiding songs and how to plait. I used to practise on Katuaros, taking his thick, lustrous hair into my hands, dividing it into three strands, and then entering the rhythm of the braid. It's one of those activities where your mind cannot be involved or you end up staring at your hands full of hair, not knowing what to do next.

53

'Stop thinking!' my grandmother used to counsel me. 'Listen to the song.'

It was a song of threes. I don't remember the verses, but everything comes in three.

Truth – Beauty – Goodness.

Man – Woman – Child.

Night – Day – Twilight.

Wisdom – Reason – Imagination.

'The wind in the tree,' she sang as she plaited my own hair. 'The air in the babbling brook. The cry of a newborn baby. These are the three great melodies of creation.'

Right over, twist. Left over, twist.

If I'd forgotten most of the words, I remembered the tunes and hummed as I braided. The mare let out a sigh of contentment. With the rain crashing down outside I hummed as if it were a sunny spring day in the pasture, alive with bees dancing over the flowers and grasses.

The centaurs lounged on hay bales watching my skilful fingers deftly transform rough horsehair into the three tails of the horse emblem of the Dobunni. From the tail, I moved to the mane. It had been one of the tricks I used to play on the old, the young and the stupid, braiding manes and tails during the night to make them think the Shee were about.

By the time the trees had stopped creaking and groaning and the rain had reduced to a patter, six of the best mares were done up in a ritual finery of knots and braids. (I heard later that the young lads who came in to feed the horses in the morning fled out in terror.)

The storm passed, leaving a clear sky and enough starlight to see my way back to Twelve Elms. The druids had settled for the night but Apnodens remained awake, staring into the fire. 'Where have you been?' he asked.

'The other side of a storm.'

'Better now?'

'Yes.' I squatted down beside him. Apnodens went back to gazing intently into the flames dancing over the log.

'Why do you hide?' I asked. 'You know, don't you, that there is no need to hide? Indeed, I suspect I could persuade the governor to support your claim to being archdruid.'

'Oh!' he said, noticing some woodlice hurrying out of cracks on the log to find themselves facing an inferno. He reached into the fire with his bare hands and pulled the log out. 'Go, friends,' he told the woodlice, taking the log to the door and throwing it into the night. 'Archdruid? That can never happen. I broke the law of obedience and I do not regret it. Obedience and discipline. I was a good student, you know that. Assiduous in both my studies and my duties. I wanted to train for the priesthood but my father would not allow it. He said I was being selfish, that I was one of the finest bards and needed to teach. The thirst for knowledge, he said, is a kind of greed. He told me never to leave Kennet.' And Apnodens would have obeyed but that the Romans came. Needing his father's advice, he had had to leave his college and travel to Venonis to get it. Regalis gave him his advice and then banned him from the order.

'That was a blot on his reputation,' I said.

'Not at all. He was himself obedient to the law. It pained him to do his duty. But then, unwittingly, he gave me what I most needed and wanted: freedom, to bend with the wind, to be carried by the wave, to walk the earth. Freedom to study what I want, to act from instinct, to pursue my own choices.' The direction of his study was not as arbitrary as he made it sound. When a boy, and in attendance to the archdruid, he had met philosophers of many nations who came to study in Britain. Our druid colleges attracted the wisest of men: Brahmins from India, magi from Persia, philosophers from Greece, Jews with great learning of the deepest mysteries of the ancients. 'I study the stars, as I have always wanted to do, and I am also learning about number, geometry and true music. Free! If only I were free to live where I wanted, you'd not find any man more content. But I must hide.'

'You could live with me openly, under my protection. No Roman has any intention of harming you.'

'Caratacus would not agree.'

I bristled. 'I promise you,' I said, 'they intend no harm, so long as you don't resist them.'

'How can I not resist them? Just being who I am is an act of resistance. I don't want – I utterly reject – what they have to offer.'

'What, peace and prosperity?'

'To surrender the ancient ways for some small personal gain in wellbeing. Peace? Can peace be imposed? The Romans are luring the Britons with luxuries, luring you all into slavery. Not me. They need to offer me a bit more.'

'Such as?'

'Freedom to be who I am.'

Awkward, Apnodens, always awkward. Always quick to kill off your opinions with a sharp stab of truth.

'I've missed you so much,' I said. 'At least stay with me here at the Grove of Twelve Elms. Officially, should anyone ask, you are my personal bard. I could do with someone who sings of the gods rather than Dobunnic ancestors – who all seem to have the same name – someone who sings the stories that pulse in the veins of Britons.'

'Am I not a master of bards? Demoted perhaps, but I can sing those stories. And add in a vocos or two.'

'No,' I said, 'at least, not long distance. No beacons and no calling. I've agreed that with the governor.'

Apnodens looked like a wolf who had just had its teeth pulled. To cry into the wind and be heard on every hill in view – that was what he had trained so arduously to master. I knew then that he would not stay. Perhaps for a while, but not forever.

Winter was coming fast upon us. The farmers were spreading the fields with pig dung and the ash from the bone fires. The hunting season had started and our fighting men were out beating the woods for game. I wanted to show Apnodens the paddocks, but he went so slowly it would be dark before we got there. He had no interest in stock-breeding. His interest lay between the roots of trees and on dead logs: mushrooms and toadstools of a thousand kinds. And he had to stop and examine each one of them. When the sun began to set, we turned back for the grove. Apnodens was restless. He didn't want to go indoors, not yet. He wanted to say goodbye to the day outside, on the high point facing west. Down in the valley below and stretching into the distance was the ancient track leading to Severn river and Siluria. Despite a chill wind, he sat there bare-armed and barefoot, chanting a prayer to the setting sun, while I huddled in a heavy cape. We talked about the past, the present and the future, our interpretation of events, our hopes and fears. Then he took up a flute and began to play to the local spirit, who he said is called Lemana, to Nemetona, and to Cuda herself, the mother of these wooded hills.

The sun went down, striated by clouds glowing in its dying light: sunset on the old life. Copper, amber, gold, the colour of dried blood: the leaves were falling in the woods of Britain and night threw its blanket over the land.

Again I felt the heavy weight of foreboding but then Apnodens pointed to the ancient limes. Hanging in their branches, becoming visible now that the trees were finally yielding their leaves, were great evergreen balls that seemed to glow in the twilight. 'Look! The mistletoe. The spawn of new life. Death, birth, always recurring.'

8

THE SILENCE OF THE POUR

As winter's grip began to tighten, I received a deputation from a family of bronzesmiths asking to establish a workshop at Twelve Elms. In Corinium we had two blacksmiths and an armourer; each of them had approached me, claiming to have secrets they needed to protect, secrets so secret they could not even tell me what they were. In truth they were scared of having their metals requisitioned by the Romans. The mint that had struck generations of Dobunnic coins had closed down and the skilled goldsmiths had left Corinium to seek work elsewhere. These bronzesmiths, however, were seeking to protect their art, not their metals. They were, they said, the seventh generation of masters in bronze. They were not only casters but knew how to spin sheet bronze to make anything from small bowls to trumpets and horns 'of great length and supernatural thinness'. No one knew how they did it, and they liked it that way. They didn't want any Roman stealing their art or, worse, torturing them to reveal it. They needed a sanctuary, somewhere secluded.

'How noisy is your process?' I asked.

'The hissing of the fire and the sighing of bellows. Some tapping.'

'How much tapping?'

'Not as much as with iron.'

'But how much?'

'Some consider it musical. Iron dongs, tin tinks, bronze chimes.'

I made enquiries and was advised that, if I were going to give them harbour, then it should be as far away as possible

58

from the houses. 'It's not just the constant tapping, it's their curses,' I was told. 'They roar when a spark lands on them or they cut themselves on a sharp edge.'

I met the bronzesmiths again. 'Will you undertake to make no weapons of war?'

'Not even spears for the hunt,' they agreed. 'That's all in iron these days. No, our work has its source in Annwn, the secret of the alloy is life, not death. Marry zinc or tin to copper for bronze, but how much? How much? Only we know that, that and how hot the fire is, working in the dark so that we can see the colours of the heat of birth.'

'My mother was buried with a bronze bowl over her face.'

'For life, not for death. We made those bowls. She is with you still.'

And for a moment, she was. Together we are emptying my father's box of gold coins that led back to the chief of our tribe, Kommios. Innogen teaching me how to look at a coin: first right way up; then upside down; now the side with the symbol of the king who is named; next the symbol of the tribe on the reverse. My father's symbols included a vine leaf and the running boar of the Atrebates, but the most common emblem on the reverse of coins, and not only in Atrebatic lands, was the triple-tailed horse. My mother's voice making me drowsy with her story of the Sacred Mare, which is the land, and how she brings fecundity and abundance to all who honour her. Right way up, upside down. See the eight-spoked wheel of the year. See the face. Do you not see the face? Here, turn the coin to an angle, look across the surface of it. Now you see. Now you are looking with the inward eye.

I used to dream of a coin stamped 'TOG.REX', with the Sacred Mare on one side, a pattern of blobs on the other that made no sense until you turned the coin obliquely, but it was not to be and never will be. The mints in my territories have been closed down. Now we have coins of Claudius and his forebears which do nothing except look upside down or back to front as you turn them.

'Well?' asked the chief of the bronzesmiths. I gave them the most distant quarter of the grove to build a workshop and a house, asking in return that they make the best bronze horn their skill could fashion. 'Like a carnyx, but dedicated to peace.' They said they knew how to do this.

I was intending to build for myself a rectangular house close to the deep-thatch. Not a house in the Roman style – that would be too provocative – but a British house built with right angles. Best of both worlds, and not without precedent. Apnodens thought this idea was risible. 'Think of the trouble and expense you would save if only you had round furniture,' he said, 'or no furniture at all, but as you will, as you will,' and he made himself at home in the deep-thatch. He was rarely in it, however, preferring the sky as a blanket on all but frosty nights.

He drew me from my bed one dawn to go with him to find mushrooms. It was a bleary day and we walked through a heavy dew, Apnodens patting trees as we went, whispering as if stepping carefully through a garden that was asleep. It was the end of the season and pickings were few, but he was looking for something particular. 'Where are your paddocks?' he asked. 'Take me to them.'

Thinking he might have suddenly developed an interest in my herd, I led him there gladly, but while I was being nudged and greeted by a couple of mares at the gate, he went in to explore the ground, poking at grass clumps with his staff, muttering to himself. Then, with a low whistle of relief, he stooped to collect what he had sought: a pale mushroom with acorn-shaped caps, made distinct by their smallness and plainness as he added them to his colourful basket. The Mushroom of the Opening Eye. I cleared my throat like a grandmother expressing her disapproval of the activities of men. Crouched over his prize, lifting the whole clump from the ground, he glanced up. 'Not for you, I think.'

'Certainly not!' I'd heard of men losing their wits to this mushroom and never regaining them. I'd heard of men going into trance and never coming out. I'd heard of men visiting the Otherworld and not returning.

Back at the grove, Apnodens cooked up onions and blewits for breakfast. After we had eaten, he took the slimy little pale ones from the basket and began to prepare them with the care of a sacrifice, cleaning them, cutting them, skewering the pieces on a slender stick to dry high over the fire. Everything Apnodens did was done with care. While the rest of us impatiently pushed on to the next thing, he remained with the task in hand, making sure nothing or no one was offended by his actions. Just being with him, watching him, was a time of healing and restoration.

'Hmmm,' he said, quietly turning his sacred mushrooms, whether to himself or my unspoken thoughts I could not tell. 'Midwinter is a good time for the Dreaming Cup. They'll be ready by then.'

On the two occasions I had drunk from the Dreaming Cup, no mushroom had been included. It was a powerful enough experience without it. Apnodens glanced up questioningly.

I shook my head.

'You bald-faced Romey,' he said.

'Hairy wizard,' I replied.

It was cold that winter, cold enough for Apnodens to retreat indoors after dark. I frequently visited the bronzesmiths with their incandescent pot in which they melted down broken bits and pieces. At first I had been annoyed, thinking they had deceived me with their sing-song recipes of minerals, but one my own age called Celatus explained that the cost of ore was beyond them, and so they recycled.

'Iron,' he said, holding up a hammer. 'The only thing it is good for is shaping bronze.'

To pay for my warmth, I was put to work breaking up copper and tin artefacts the smiths had collected on a tour of Corinium, when they called on the people to donate to Gobannus, the god of metals. I could stand there half a morning, fascinated by the melting of scrap, the removal of dross, the recovery of true metal. To become a sheet, bronze must be hammered and hammered, with frequent annealing, until the metal is as fine as silk. And soft. So soft. A sheet taken up by his brother was turned on a lathe and shaped into a bowl which, when polished, took on the glow of gold.

61

Sheet bronze was beautiful, but the magic of the art was casting in a mould. Celatus was the master of the fire, and it was a process done in the dark. He fuelled the fire with charcoal and poked it into flame while his young sister operated the bellows, bending over them, one in each hand, singing the rhythm. The puffing bellows, the hissing of the fire, the palpable patience of the workshop as we waited for the fire to come to its most tremendous heat, a moment known only to the master who could read the colours of fire. The clay mould placed on the reddened charcoal and cooked until Celatus raised his hand for the pour; the emptying of the fiery crucible of molten bronze into the mould; everyone who had gathered to watch liquid fire cool and darken holding their breath; the silence of the pour. Then the darkening of metal as it cooled and the sucking sound as it shrank inside the clay. The mould broken, a god appeared, or a diviner's spoon. Bronze does indeed chime when struck, a lustrous sound that carries and lingers and seems to cleanse the soul. The older smiths claimed they could hear it day and night, even when everything was quiet.

Dedication to the craft kept the men intent on their work in full and careful concentration but, when they stopped to rest, then came the jokes, mostly about local widows, Silures and sheep, or Roman legionaries in latrines. They laughed hard, these men of clay and charcoal, with ash-black fingers and long, matted hair. Breaking the mould – when the shiny treasure born of fire is revealed – was a stage they had yet to reach within themselves.

At the celebrations of the winter solstice, I gathered them together in a circle of log seats in the deep-thatch where I gave them a feast of roast meats and jugs of spiced wine. Before we ate, they presented to me the long bronze horn, as tall as a man, as slender as a willow wand. 'Ah,' I said, 'it is not for me. Give it to the druid.' With a look of wonder, Apnodens received what he called 'this most sacred of gifts'. He tried playing on it and an ethereal sound came from his breath moving inside the bronze. It startled some, for it was otherworldly. Apnodens himself looked bemused, for what was coming out of the instrument was so much more than what he was putting in.

62

'I need to practise,' he said, laying it aside and staring at it.

The hardened smiths dressed in old leather, their skin so tattooed or scarred, so weathered by the elements that they were all the colour of yew bark; these knotty men sat round like children, munched, swigged, made their merry curses against Rome and disdained everything I tried to teach them. I had everyone in Corinium taking lessons in the new ways they were to live under. Under Mandred's guidance, schools were established for young and old. Only warriors were exempt. Warriors and bronzesmiths who said they were too busy to traipse down to Corinium to be taught how to be ignorant. So whenever I was at home at Twelve Elms, I gave them lessons myself. Or tried to.

'What day is it today?' I asked them.

'Why, it is midwinter!'

'By what other name is it known?'

They looked baffled until one said, 'The night of sun-stillness in the Month of the Darkest Depths?'

And another: 'Shortest day?'

'The Romans live by another calendar, one reformed by Julius Caesar . . .' There was a sudden hiss as a glob of phlegm hit the fire. 'No spitting in my presence!' I said.

The culprit looked abashed and wiped his mouth.

'You need to learn it. Do you remember the last lesson?'

'Yes,' said Celatus. 'There are twelve months in a year – that we know – and the year ends with the tenth month.'

Sounds of scoffing and snorting.

I told them I agreed, it was very confusing to have months called after gods, emperors and numbers. 'But if you recite them using your fingers, you'll see there are twelve. Repeat after me, Januarius, Februarius, Martius, Aprilis . . .'

And so our chanting began – they were getting the hang of months – but we all doubted they would ever understand days.

'You say there are only seven days?' said Celatus. 'We people of the moon know full well there are fourteen.'

'Seven,' I said.

'What are their names?' Celatus asked.

'Drink!' Apnodens said, passing round the beer. That helped, but only a little.

'They don't have names,' I said.

They looked at each other askance. No names?

'Kalends is the first day of the month,' I said. 'Nones is the eighth day – or ninth, depending on how you're counting – and is nine days – or eight – before ides, which means "middle". We have to count backwards for nones, forwards for kalends.' I should have read the crowd at this point but, proud of my knowledge, I continued. The gathering began to seethe.

'Perhaps you should leave it to Mandred,' Apnodens said.

That only goaded me into persisting, explaining again, only louder, about nones and ides, and the more I tried to drum it into them, the less sense it made even to me. The Roman organisation of time: here in Britain, it seemed jarring.

'The moon is our clock,' said Apnodens. 'We know when to meet by the moon. Anyone would understand "full moon in Anagantios" whereas "the fourth day before nones" relates to nothing anyone knows. Our calendar places us in the cosmos, gives us our place in the cycle of growth. The moon is the goddess who has always guided the Britons. Must we give her up? Must we adopt the practical calendar of Roman bureaucrats? All numbers, no poetry?'

The smiths drummed their feet on the ground in agreement with the druid.

'Think of the great eight-spoked wheel of the year,' Apnodens continued, 'the turning seasons, the moon, the tides, our round houses that tell us exactly where we are in space and time, our shadow-poles, our knowledge of the rising and setting of stars: is all this to be surrendered for an arbitrary calendar of unequal months, some named after gods, some after emperors, some after numbers? Weeks of seven days? Each hour of the day of equal length? Days and hours grow and shrink according to the season, we all know that. Here in Britain, between Samhain and winter solstice, night comes earlier and earlier, and the morning rises up to meet it. But the numerating Romans, wishing to control the cosmos as well as the world, contort this breathing of time into a system that suits administrators.'

Then they erupted, these smiths who had grown up counting time by the moon, and I thought I had a rebellion on my hands. They went off, loud in their dismissal of crass Roman ignorance. The following morning they came limping past in mockery of a unit of infantry, led by their 'centurion'. Apnodens and I stood at the door to see what was going on. Once deep in the trees, the 'centurion' called them to order. 'Men, line up!' There was shuffling and the sound of twigs breaking underfoot. 'All together now, one, two, three – piss!'

And howls of laughter came out of the wood.

The smiths, having proved that they could urinate to order as well as any marching soldier, came back in a rolling British swagger. 'What day is it?' one asked.

'It is the forty-fifth day of the Emperor Jug Ears.'

'That makes sense, given that yesterday was the forty-sixth.'

'So tomorrow will be the forty-fourth?'

'Of course not! Weren't you listening to the king? Tomorrow is the first. Which is to say, the fourteenth before the fifteenth.'

Some kings keep comic bards to remind them that, for all their pride, they are the same as anyone else. I had bronzesmiths. Often, when I came back from a visit to Corinium, I found them loitering at my door on some pretext or other, when all they wanted was news. Not news of Roman advances or various skirmishes along the border. No. News of other forges. What were those idiots at Churn forge doing? Or Perrot forge? Was it true I'd closed the mint down? Or that the ironsmiths at Overhill had a big commission? What for? Who from? Didn't anyone realise that iron turns to rust within the year? Whereas bronze . . .

But when asked what they were working on, they clammed up and said only the gods had the right to know that. And they'd go back to the foundry to hammer, emboss, polish with grinding stones, and in their skill and their meticulous attention to their work, touch divinity.

9

THE DREAMING CUP

Since being stripped of his place as the head of a college and dismissed from the order, Apnodens had changed, become less formal and tight-lipped, less the serious and ambitious student. Everything stopped being theoretical. He no longer spent his days learning what he was taught; now he used them finding out for himself. While living with me at Twelve Elms he collected things found in the woods and made music with a bunch of dead beech leaves that clung tenaciously to the twig, a blown eagle's egg filled with dried peas, a flute made from a hollowed stem, a drum of taut hide, a flat piece of bark pierced and threaded on a string that buzzed as he twirled it above his head. He spent that winter playing to Nature her own song. With his instruments, his 'bag of music', he developed ways of mewling, howling and crying like the beasts of the wood; he snuffled like the badger; he made the sound of the sea withdrawing over a shingle beach or the wind in a pile of leaves. Unwary visitors were often disturbed by the sounds of birds not known in woodland groves: curlews, gulls, bitterns.

All these things endeared the creatures to him, but it was the spirits who came to the sound of the bronze horn. Thus he played it with care and never for mere entertainment. He longed to try it in a cave, where the echoes would add another dimension, but had to make do with sitting in a large deep-thatch. One evening I joined him at the hearth and, as usual, involuntarily grunted as I sat down.

'Are you in pain?'

'I was unhorsed by a British spear. No blood, just bruising.'

'How long ago?'

'Three months.'

He made me stand and, from behind, grasped me like a wrestler and squeezed my ribs. I felt nothing, but when he suddenly let go, I yowled.

'Ah, some of your ribs were cracked. Nothing I can do about that – time will be the healer here – but perhaps I can help with that wounded heart, which I suspect is the real cause of your pain.' Turning me to face him, he placed his forehead against mine. 'Name it. Name your pain.'

'Branwen is lost,' I whispered.

'Nothing else?'

'That Branwen is lost – my fault. I failed to protect her.' I wasn't sure if he could hear me; I could barely hear myself.

'Nothing else?'

Why did he keep asking?

'Nothing,' I said, and I believed it to be true.

He stood back. I opened my eyes and saw as if in a mirror that we both suffered the same pain. He was not angry: he felt as guilty as I did. 'Branwen . . .' I whispered. The name of the one we never mentioned. His favourite pupil and best of all singers. Our Little Sister.

'Yes,' he said, also barely audible. 'Branwen and Britain. You have abandoned them both.'

'I thought it was the right action! I do nothing without cautious consideration; everything I do, I do for the good. By the gods of the waters and the woods, did I get it wrong?' Looking over the past months since returning to Britain, all I could see were my actions causing the death or loss of others.

He took me by the shoulders and stared into my eyes.

'And how would it have been if you hadn't acted as you did?'

'What do you mean?'

'Think of all those who have lived because of your actions. I am not won over by your idea of collaborating with the Romans, but I do see the Atrebates thriving, an oasis of peace in a troubled land. And yet, by those same actions, you have lost your betrothed and you are abandoning Britain. You have left the moon for the sun. This calendar you would foist on our people: it is an offence to our gods.'

'Help me,' I groaned.

'We need the Dreaming Cup.'

'You know I don't . . .'

'I know you have, once or twice.'

True enough, once or twice I had, and on each occasion I had been scared witless. The Dreaming Cup calls for nothing less than total self-surrender. You give yourself up to the god. It is riding at a gallop bareback in unknown territory. Exhilarating. Terrifying.

'I will not!'

'You need the help of the gods. They speak to you all the time but you can't hear them. You will not listen. Dreaming will help. It will be my brew. I promise you illumination and peace.'

'Very well,' I whispered.

'But not here. I need a cave.'

Caves are not so common in the Hills of Cuda.

'A tomb will do. Come,' he said, standing up and collecting some things together. 'At dawn we'll go to your mother.'

The long night grew quieter and quieter, the muffled silence that comes with snow. When I woke up, Apnodens was already out, making tracks in his bare feet. His toes were pink with cold but he claimed not to feel it. 'Try it!' he said. I demurred.

The West Way was the shortest route to the escarpment which we called the Rim of the Cauldron, but Apnodens said it would be dangerous to take it. 'We could meet a patrol.'

'So?'

'We should keep to high ground and follow the sheep.' And go on foot, of course. There were indeed sheep tracks to follow but it was the best part of a day before we came to the precipitous edge of the Hills of Cuda. We stood looking out over the Vale of Gleva and its several hills, the closest being a promontory of the escarpment and a place so ancient that it is just called Creig, 'the Hill'. Once upon a time, the birthplace of kings. Those same kings are buried along the Rim of the Cauldron, for that is what the Vale of Gleva is: the cooking pot, the source, the womb of the Dobunni. And among those ancient burials was a comparatively recent one, that of my mother, Innogen, herself born at Creig. I felt a cold shiver, for I remembered the Hill from my childhood, the reverence in the voice of my mother's mother when she had told me about the seat of her family, ancient beyond ancient, and royal. Creig had fallen to the southern Dobunni. Esius had won it back but by then it had been abandoned.

Apnodens named all that we could see in the wide, extensive view over the vale. Another promontory of the scarp was where the Glevenses chased burning chariot wheels in an annual festival; the hill ahead was Chosen Hill; in the mid-distance the woods of Ferylloog; to the right and northwards, the distant hill of Wrikon.

'Caratacus is there somewhere,' he said, pointing to the blue line on the western horizon. 'Beyond the two rivers, hiding in Siluria.'

The snow of the night remained on the shadowy scarp. All the other hills and promontories within view were wreathed in smoke from the many houses and farms on the higher ground. Occupation in the vale was minimal: a few huts on stilts. A fortified dun, below where we stood, was the chief gathering place of this scattered folk. It all seemed remote and not a little threatening, in the way of the unknown. Although these were my mother's relatives, I had yet to meet them as their king. From this lofty viewpoint the dwellings looked primitive indeed and I was glad to postpone that pleasure. We walked along the ridge to the cluster of deserted deep-thatches that had housed the tomb-keepers who tended the many royal graves and barrows. They had left their homes and their duty, crossing the two rivers into a new life in Siluria. A life beyond the empire.

'There,' I said, pointing out the cairn that marked the place of Innogen's simple tomb. We knelt down beside it and touched the cold ground with our foreheads. Outwardly, I greeted my mother and asked for her blessing. Inwardly, *Delfos* . . . her voice rose up in me like incense, a whisper of the soul. I had seen her body the last time we were here, knew what she looked like in death, but that is not what I saw now. I saw her in Annwn in the prime of her beauty, wearing her torc, her circlet, her jewellery. She held out her arms to me and I, her lost child, ran to her embrace. Her warmth. The hardness of her stone beads against my cheek. The smell of herbs in her clothes.

We communed. I will not say what passed between us. A man has some pride, and it does not do to portray a king as a sobbing wretch telling his mother he has lost his betrothed, that he is a failure as a man and unfit to be a king. I was just grateful that her spirit did not need to hear it in words. My breaking heart was enough. When I was limp and spent and only able to do what I was told, Apnodens led me onwards to the most noble of all the tombs of the kings of the ancient star-gazers. Tombs of our own age, such as Innogen's, are crude in comparison. She lies crouched in a stone chest with a great slab as a lid whereas the ancients have several chambers within man-made domes of soil and turf. The entrance to this one lay between two turf flanges Apnodens referred to as legs. 'Here', he said, 'is a good cave in which to spend a night.'

Oh no . . . He had done this to me before, made me endure hours of darkness in a long barrow near the Sanctuary of Kennet, terrifying my men with the sound of bees. What was he intending now? Stooping under the stone lintel, he passed into the passage that led 'down inside the Mother, into her womb'. There were four chambers, two on each side, and a fifth chamber at the back.

While I shivered as if to shake my bones from their joints, he made a fire in the fifth chamber. As usual, just watching Apnodens perform a task was to feel the power of healing. The way he rubbed the stick, caught a spark and blew on the bundle: it was all ritual done with rapt attention. When the kindling caught light, he sat back to gaze on the fire with what appeared to be love. My juddering subsided into normal shivering. He took from a pouch some pale powder which he emptied into a copper dish on the fire, adding a little water. Steam soon began to coil from the dish.

The preparation was long and careful, Apnodens evoking the god with soft chanting, drawing him out of the steam. I grew increasingly agitated until suddenly I reached the point of acceptance. At that moment, the rituals came to an end. Swilling the liquid around in the dish to cool it, Apnodens poured it into a cup of chased bronze. I recognised the design: a pattern of deer ran round its lip, and its handles were cranes. My smiths, I thought, are masters of their craft.

'Drink,' said Apnodens, proffering me the Cup of Dreams.

Usually there is a circle of men sharing the cup, served by a medicine woman. This time it was just the two of us. Apnodens did not partake of it himself, saying he must stay behind to guide me home.

I drink. The liquid runs down my throat. It tastes warm and earthy. Mushroomy. I wait for something to happen but nothing does and, as I fall into the space of nothingness, Apnodens begins to play the song of air on a bone flute. He plays so that echoes sound in all five chambers and, listening to him with my eyes closed, it seems there are at least five Apnodenses. Sounds come and go like visiting elements: water, fire, air and earth, ghosting about in the fifth, which is aether. Then, when I am in deep sleep but still awake, comes the sound of Annwn. I open my eyes. He is blowing on the long bronze horn. Voices come up the tube, stopped and started by the breath of the player. I begin to float in a warm bath of wonder at the beauty he coaxes out of the instrument. Putting down the horn, he rattles the eagle's egg, blows on teasels and pounds on the drum, all at once. I don't know how long this lasts, but it feels like hours, or no time at all, and I begin to drift. To leave behind that which I think I am yet I am not. Pipes again. Mournful pipes. A clatter of stones. And then that piece of bark on a string he can make roar like a nest of disturbed hornets. The mournful pipes, a flute of bone, the bronze horn crying like a lamenting woman, a woman in the agony of sorrow. She cries and cries again. Is it the bunch of dried rushes that whisper *Branwen*? My spirit moves this way and that, a reed underwater, and then leans to the quickening drum which starts with a trot, breaks into a run and then a gallop. I am riding the downs on a horse whose step never falters. I am. Or am I? Perhaps I am not riding the horse. Perhaps I am the horse. I gallop over the soft chalky sward of the downs on a sunny day of eternal spring. I am the horse. I am the horse on the hill. The sudden crack of a pair of clappers acts like a smack on the rump and I go, launching into the sky, heading south. *Branwen, Branwen,* sing the birds in the mouth of the druid. And then there is silence.

AD 44

10
THE TRIUMPH

She is standing with the boy and his mother at an upper window, looking across the river to the Field of Mars and the city hills. They can see the great parade assembling, the low winter sun glinting on chariots and armour. It will be a torturous procession to the Capitoline Hill which, although only a short walk away, will take two days to reach. Leaving the Field of Mars at the end of December the Triumph will arrive at the Temple of Jupiter on the kalends of January. The boy's excitement mounts until it threatens to burst him at the seams. Since dawn he has charged about the house, being an elephant, being an emperor, being a dying Gaul, furious that he will not be allowed to cross the river and follow the procession step by every ponderous step. Trumpets blare. A wretched group of captives joins the head of the tremendous line. Domitius howls with frustration, so hard that his mother clamps her hands over her ears, her face contorted.

Branwen cannot ask, Shall I take him to see the Triumph? She does not have the language. She asks the question with her eyes and the mother, who has a headache starting, understands, nods in acquiescence and orders a Nubian slave and two of the Praetorians assigned to her husband, the consul, to take them across the river.

Now Branwen and the boy are in the Field of Mars, watching the procession set off. The view is not as good as they had hoped. The delirious crowd is ten deep. The Nubian picks up the boy and puts him on his strong shoulders. Branwen stretches as high as she can on tiptoe and then, not thinking, forgetting she's also a slave, she squirms to the front. There are hundreds of captives passing, thousands perhaps, mostly Catuvellauni, but she studies them anyway, looking for someone familiar, seeing instead a thousand stories of wretchedness and pain. They shuffle along in their chains, heads down. The dreary column is interrupted frequently by carts trundling past piled high with glittering spoils; the crowd hoots and whistles at the displays of golden treasure, bronze cauldrons, beautifully wrought swords and shields. Every hour on the hour the procession will stop to give a performance, to re-enact a battle in some public space, or to parade the machinery of war, the siege engines, the catapults and ballistae.

The first enactment takes place while they are still on the Field of Mars. Branwen, pressed by Romans on this bright winter's day, watches a fight to the death between one soldier, dressed up as General Vespasian, and a captive who is naked but for the torc around his neck, a barbarian noble who fights for his life in this re-enactment. Naturally he cannot win: for the sake of authenticity and the pleasure of the crowd, he is slaughtered by the sword. She is so close, blood spatters her face. She doesn't have the language. What she hears, what she makes out is that this 'play' shows the death of Togidubnus. 'Togidubnus?' she asks the man next to her.

He says something unintelligible. Seeing her confusion, he nods and confirms, 'Togidubnus.' More strange words fall from his lips but Branwen is not listening. She is watching the murder of a man playing Togodumnus, King of the Catuvellauni, but thinks it is my death they are re-enacting. Does she cry? No. She is bereft of hope now. I look deep within her, but all is darkness there, shrouded by hurt and rage. Stepping backwards, she is squeezed out from the crowd like a splinter. She reaches up for the boy who has become the burden she must carry in her new life and the Nubian sets him on the ground, this flame-haired child of freckly face and blue eyes. She clamps her hands on his shoulders or he will be away. There is something about him. If he were a grub you found under the sod, you would have to squash him. He's too pale. Nothing good will come of him.

The procession has restarted and now the senators and magistrates are being borne along on this river of triumph, at their head the new consul, Gaius Sallustius Passienus Crispus.

'Father!' the boy screams, kicking Branwen in his struggle to be free. The Nubian takes him back and holds him tight. Domitius is not really the son of the consul, only when it suits him. After the death of his own father and during the exile of his mother, he had lived in the household of Passienus Crispus. When Agrippina was eventually recalled to Rome, she was more or less a stranger to him, and he hid from her in the folds of the toga of Crispus. It was soon arranged: on the orders of the emperor, Crispus divorced his wife to marry Agrippina and was rewarded with the highest office. The boy likes Crispus. He's old, he's kind and he's fair. 'Father!' he shouts to him.

You'd think he was three, not six, the way he gets over-excited, but when he is handed back to his British slave, and reaches out to squeeze her small, budding breasts, then he has the expression of a lascivious old man. She cannot slap him down or pinch his ear or do whatever it would take to make him stop. So she whispers curses as if they were lullabies and smiles sweetly while she damns his soul. Her speech is as incomprehensible to him as his is to her. They communicate entirely by expression, and when no one else is looking, she pulls faces at him. Not the jokey kind. The various faces of hatred. To his credit, he finds her funny and laughs.

She doesn't know how she came to be where she is. There was an altercation at the port on the Tiber, some fierce bargaining with the trader, protests, Passienus Crispus sternly intervening, money changing hands. Then she was brought in a cart to a beautiful house on the Palatine with its marble floors and painted walls. She'd always presumed Rome was like Corinium, only much larger. Instead she finds herself in a city of marble and brick where houses echo, the property of a man so wealthy that his string of country houses begins here and ends at Pompei.

When Branwen arrived, a fellow slave, a British woman of the Cantii, was deputed to explain things to her and teach her some Latin. She showed Branwen a bust of the previous emperor, and pointing to the mistress in the distance said, very loudly, 'SOROR.' Later she pointed to a pair of slaves who were twins, saying 'soror et soror'. So Branwen's first Roman word was the one for sister. Agrippina, her mistress, is – was – the sister of Caligula.

Gradually the story is revealed to her, that there were two sisters, Agrippina and Julia Livilla. Accused of attempting to assassinate their brother, they had been exiled to small, barren islands. The new emperor, Claudius, in his kindness, in his respect for the ancestors, had recalled them. Julia Livilla had only been back a matter of months before she was returned to exile on one of the Pontine Islands, there to starve to death. Her crime? She was accused of adultery with Lucius Seneca, but her real crime – according to the gossip of slaves – had been to say that the hairstyle of Messalina, wife of the emperor, looked like a sponge. *Soror – soror – frater* . . . Agrippina was the great-granddaughter of the divine Augustus. On the death of her husband, she was given by Claudius to Crispus, the richest man in Rome. Wisely Claudius wanted to keep her young son with his Augustan credentials within view.

The Nubian finds them a good place to watch the lictors in their red war robes march along, followed by four white horses pulling a golden chariot. The emperor, dressed as Jupiter in a purple and red toga, the laurel crown making his ears stick out, stands there waving to his people, now to the left, now to the right, accepting the roar of the crowd as a god accepts a libation. The chariot rattles and clinks with all the charms it carries, the largest of them the winged penis suspended underneath to ward off envy and the malice of the onlookers. To Branwen it seems the emperor considers himself something of a stallion.

A small boy, the son of Claudius, is peering over the rim of the triumphal chariot. On this day his name will formally be changed to 'Britannicus'. Domitius frowns at his sort-of cousin, second cousin, step-cousin, or whatever he is, his great-uncle's son, somehow a usurper, because it is not right that he, Domitius, great-great-grandson of the divine Augustus, is a spectator and not himself in the tremendous parade. Something is definitely not right. He sets up a squall that only Branwen can cure. She drops to her knees and begins to sing quietly in his ear. He likes the feel of her breath. He likes her song and her narcotic voice. He hums with pleasure and presses his cheek against hers.

The procession continues, chimes of bells and bones, clouds of incense rising up, dried flowers strewn under the feet of those marching to the slow, slow beat. Until, at last, with the passing of the two white oxen with gilded horns destined for sacrifice, you'd think it all over. Except . . .

'Elephants!' shouts Domitius. 'Here come the *elephants!*' and they are condemned to watch and wait another hour until the armoured war elephants have plodded past. Domitius is disappointed that they do not trumpet and wants to run at them with a goad but is more than placated when one of the beasts raises its tail and deposits a pile of steaming dung. He hollers with orgasmic joy.

As they return across the river to the garden house, Branwen continues to calm Domitius with song which makes Agrippina, who is waiting for them, look wistful. She smiles weakly and thanks Branwen. 'You have a beautiful voice,' she says, not for the first time trying to be friendly. Branwen avoids her eye, retreats into her usual sullenness. Domitius opens the window, looking for a route to escape the house and rejoin the parade.

'It's too cold . . .' moans Agrippina. 'Close that window.'

Domitius snarls – his exotic cat impression – and his mother smiles and ruffles his hair.

To her surprise, Branwen is growing rather fond of her charge. Despite the severe difference in their status, she is beginning to look on him as a younger brother. He does not look upon her as an older sister: to Domitius, Branwen is a slave-princess who must do his bidding. It is his self-imposed task to make her smile. He doesn't like moody girls.

Branwen doesn't know that it was her sullenness which saved her from being sold to Claudius's wife, Messalina. During the aggressive bartering at the docks, Passienus Crispus in his toga of purple stripe, had loomed over Messalina's agent and told him that it was common knowledge that the barbarian princess had the ability to sour milk with a glance. 'Look at her face and see if that is not true. Tell Messalina', Crispus had continued, 'that the girl's knowledge of herbs is dangerous. The last thing Messalina wants is the company of a hostile witch.' And once the man had scuttled off, Crispus bought Branwen at a knock-down price and took her home as a gift for his stepson, who loved exotica. 'Be grateful, girl,' he said. 'I have saved you from Messalina.' She looked at him blankly, not having the

Latin. 'Why saved, you ask?' he continued, in the face of her silence. 'Well, I happen to know that her previous lover was Togidubnus.'

Branwen twitched, recognising the name, and squinted up at the consul.

'Yes, her ex-lover and your betrothed are one and the same man, and should Messalina ever get wind of that, she'd give you a slow death for sure.'

The distant sound of a bronze horn draws me through curtains of tattered reality. I return to the cold world of the tomb and see a large hound sitting on its haunches, staring at me. For a moment I believe that Apnodens has shapeshifted but then by the feeble light of lamps I see my friend sitting close by, smiling, the bronze horn resting across his knees. The greyness of the dog's shaggy coat and the darkness of its eye persuade me that it belongs to this world. It stares at me, tongue lolling. Apnodens reaches out and strokes it, but the hound will not be distracted.

I struggled up on my elbows. 'Where did it come from?' Even as I asked, I noticed a tall woman standing in the shadows. It was hard to tell her age, for she was lithe and had a faded beauty. A woman of age but not bent of back. Straight as a spear. I squinted at her. She was both familiar and strange. 'This is Ricoba, the wise woman of Creig, mother of all, mother of none,' Apnodens said, 'and this her hound, Maglos.'

As I tried to rise, the hound stood up, came to me and pushed its head into my chest to make me lie down again.

'He's telling you that you need to rest longer,' said Ricoba.

I gazed at the hound, now wondering if it and its owner were Shee. I said to Apnodens, 'You told me that the Creig had been abandoned and no one lives there.'

Ricoba squatted on her heels beside me. 'I have lived there alone for a generation, caring for the shrines, but the spirits have gone now, following the Shee westward. I was sitting there, waiting for death, when I saw lights among the tombs and heard your screams.'

Screams?

Apnodens nodded. 'At one point you screamed. I thought you were being murdered.'

'Which point?' I asked.

'How should I know?'

Ricoba was unsmiling of mouth but her eyes were kind. She took up my hand and stroked it. 'What did you see?'

'Branwen,' I said.

'How is she?'

'Unhappy, angry, but not ill-treated. She is in the house of the *consularis*, Passienus Crispus, looking after his stepson. There was a parade, the Triumph awarded to Claudius for his conquest of Britain. A re-enactment of the death of Togodumnus, whom Branwen mistook for me. She thinks I'm dead . . .' My words petered out. 'It wasn't me screaming,' I said. 'It was her. Sometimes I seemed to be looking out of Branwen's eyes, and knew whom to like, whom to be wary of and whom to hate. I felt only her emotions, never mine. Although my Latin is good, I understood so very little of what people were saying, and yet I knew what they were saying. I felt her misery, and worse. Rage burns within her like a furnace. It is not possible for her to be happy.'

'You say she is in the house of the consul-elect?' Apnodens asked. 'Not that of the emperor?'

'Passienus Crispus knows of my . . .' I glanced at Ricoba. '. . . past indiscretions with the wife of Claudius.' Ricoba remained expressionless. 'He realised that should Messalina discover that Branwen was my betrothed, she would be cruel to her. I have to go to Rome.' I tried to rise, only to be floored once again by the hound. 'Of course, it could all have been a dream,' I said.

'Of course.' Ricoba gave a short laugh.

Throwing his long hair over his shoulders, Apnodens bent his head over the bronze cup to end the ceremony with thanks to Cuda and an offering of the dregs as a libation to the fire. While he performed the rite of Closing the Portal, Ricoba continued to stroke my hand. 'Delphidius of Creig. Home at last.'

'I am Togidubnus, King of the Atrebates,' I said.

'Only to your father's people,' she replied.

'To the Corinians, I am king of the Dobunni. Or king-in-waiting. Will the Glevenses accept me as their king?'

'Of course! Their true king. Whether or not Branwen returns. For you are the son of Innogen. They had no time for Esius the warlord. It is not might which makes a king.'

'So Branwen, his daughter . . .?'

'She is a true royal, like your mother. Branwen's own mother, Gwynedd, was also born of Creig, and was a bard.'

'Are we related?' I asked, suddenly worried about taboos.

Ricoba shook her head and told us that royal families from all over Britain once sent their pregnant women to Creig to give birth. She laughed. 'Creig is far from being a nest of Glevan inbreds. Outbreds, all of us. Any woman who gave birth here was known as "of Creig" – Innogen and Gwynedd among them.'

'What happened to Gwynedd?'

'Despite all our ministrations, she died giving birth to Branwen. The girl has never forgiven herself.'

'Through Innogen,' said Apnodens, 'you are related to all local kings. Any thought you have of the Glevenses as strangers is false. All your mothers were of the Dobunni since the beginnings of time.' He chanted my maternal line, going back ten generations, all of them Dobunni, but each from somewhere different: Kyronion (now Corinium), Hot Springs of Sulis, Gleva, Ferylloog.

'Do not delay in visiting the Glevenses,' said Ricoba. 'While they are west of the Roman frontier, they are in peril, caught between the Silures and the river. Dobunnia is split, east–west, and now we hear that the union of north and south is threatened. There is a warlord I scryed in my mirror prowling the south bank of Gorge river.'

'No longer,' said Apnodens. 'Enemnos has crossed the gorge and has established a camp overlooking the Hot Springs.'

'By Sulis!' exclaimed Ricoba.

'Whatever you thought of Esius,' I said, 'you must allow that he kept Dobunnia peaceful during his rule.'

'True enough,' said Ricoba grudgingly.

I seemed to be engaged in a staring match with the enormous dog.

'Everything beautiful in Branwen came from her mother,' Ricoba said. 'You are to marry Branwen – the gods will it – and you are to treat her well. Make her happy.'

As my stomach lurched suddenly, I pushed the dog off and went outside alone into the dark for the necessary purgation. Apnodens packed up his bag of music and, once I'd stopped retching, came out to join me. 'So,' he said, 'back to Twelve Elms.'

'In the dark?' I asked.

Ricoba invited us stay overnight at the Creig where she lived alone in a hovel with only Maglos for company. Hovel perhaps, but it was warm and preferable to walking through the freezing night. She fed us from her cauldron and made us comfortable under blankets of many subtle colours she had woven from wool she gathered herself.

When we awoke, the place was cold. Dawn revealed an empty hearth. I thought she had been part of the vision, but then we heard her whistling outside, calling to a raven she liked to feed. When she returned inside, Ricoba announced – no, not announced, let it quietly be known – that she was coming with us.

'Leaving the Creig?' Apnodens was shocked.

'As I am destined to, one way or another.'

She was my height, which was disconcerting. 'You are my destiny,' she said, eye to eye.

'Are you sure you want to come? Mine is a troubled, peripatetic life . . .'

'You think I am too old at seventy?'

My argument blocked by her tone of derision, I said no more. She could have passed for forty except for the whiteness of her hair and the state of her teeth.

She walked with us, easily keeping pace, talking with Apnodens, who would learn from her what he could of the healing arts.

'Dogs,' she said. 'They are the best healers.'

'They are, so they are,' he said, nodding. 'Is it true that you will help anyone in need, irrespective of tribe? There is a story that you once revived a band of Silures left for dead by the Dobunni.'

'True enough,' she said. 'All life is sacred.' She turned to me with a quiet smile. 'Except for Romans . . . That's stretching it.'

'Mother,' I said, 'even you have things to learn.'

She laughed and ran her hand fondly over the back of Maglos as he loped along beside her.

A letter was delivered to me at Corinium from an imperial secretary which told me in brief that my betrothed had been bought by Gaius Sallustius Passienus Crispus as a present for his new wife, Julia Augusta Agrippina, and that it was not considered diplomatically advisable to secure her release and return. 'Had she entered the household of the lady Messalina, as had been intended, the outcome would of course have been different.' Claudius trusted I would understand.

11
PROVINCIAL COUNCIL

We made a house for Ricoba at Twelve Elms, following her own instructions. Bending and binding a circle of saplings into a cone, we formed the framework of a deep-thatch, wondering how long it would last when the trees grew. 'Longer than me,' she said. We made walls of wattle and daub and plastered them with mud. The floor, pounded with chalk, glowed white during the day and red by firelight. It became the glowing heart of our grove.

Here she ate, slept and practised the art of dyeing, with as much secrecy as any smith. Forbidden to enter, I stood at the threshold and looked into a chaotic scene of colour. Ricoba was adding plants to the cauldron that hung bubbling over the fire while singing a song of weld, woad, madder and tansy. Linen threads and hanks of spun wool already dunked in the cauldron hung on lines she'd had set up across the house and there they dripped. Runnels of blue, yellow and pink dribbled over the pristine floor.

'Mother?'

'Go away. I'm busy.'

This was her repeated response, until the Wheel of the Year was moving towards Imbolc and the first flowers. 'Mother?' I said from the doorway.

She was whispering over a bowl full of lichens. 'Go away.'

'I am going away. That's what I've come to tell you. I've been summoned to a Provincial Council at Calleva.'

Ricoba, who had appointed herself my right-hand woman and travelling companion, dried her hands on a cloth.

'I do not require your attendance,' I said.

Crossing to me at the door she met a chicken wandering in, chancing its luck. 'Get out of here!' she stormed. The chicken ran out clucking, beating its impotent wings.

'Mother, remember whom you speak to.'

'I don't care if they are divine! I don't want their dirty droppings on my floor!' She was in a poor mood. 'I'd better get myself a horse.'

'You are not coming with me.'

'A quiet mare. Which one would you suggest?'

Since she would never be able to keep company with Romans without speaking her mind, Mandred and I left for the council without her, sneaking out of Twelve Elms the following dawn to meet my men waiting for me at Corinium.

The land of the Atrebates is thick with trees. No other territory has so many. Elm, ash, beech, but mostly oak, gnarled and twisted, rough-barked, king of the trees. All were still naked of leaves and apparently dead, except for the hazels and their pendulous blossoms we call cat's kittens. Under the trees, the woodland floor was becoming a carpet of new green sprinkled with celandine but the tracks had been churned into mud. The squelching sound of our passage, the whinny and snicker of our horses, were comforting. It was safe in these woods which, miles deep, encircled Calleva. Yes, there were boar about, but no wolves or wildcats. I thought of us as a model of the civilised barbarian but the other tribes considered us soft. There were no rebels in our territory. I couldn't imagine there ever would be. The people were too engaged in enjoying themselves hunting with their dogs or rowing about in their boats. Peace for the Atrebates was being allowed to live lives of pleasure without interference and thus I'd had no trouble in getting them to agree to Roman terms and to sign treaties.

The last time I'd been to Calleva, the place had been a wreck. Now, less than a year later, our ride through the woods was brought up short by the vision of steep, earthen ramparts and wooden watchtowers. It was rare to get a glimpse of Calleva, known as 'the place in the woods', from a distance, except on the eastern side. Now it stood bare, like a slave stripped naked. The track was no longer bordered by trees but by fresh stumps.

'What have they done?' I complained.

'Rebuilt the defences,' said Mandred.

'But they are felling my woods! They have no right!'

'They are just trees to them.'

My earliest years, lonely in the opinion of others, had been spent being king of these woods, my palace a den made of branches and leaves, from which base I explored further and further afield. I was never alone. Everything had a name, each brook, track, tree, flower, a secret name that only I knew. I and the Shee. These Shee were not the shapeshifting kind who can take on human form, but the kind that guard the sanctuaries. These wood sprites lived in leaf litter and tree boles and liked to play tricks, making you lose your way and get confused. We blamed them for every mishap. Had they died with the trees? And where was the cacophony of birds, where the shy animals known mostly by their spoor, where the healing herbs that my mother had taught me to recognise?

I had had no sense of being alone but then, when I was five, Katuaros ap Biccos of Ford of the Alders arrived in my life like a storm in spring. I had presumed my foster brother would be my trusty companion and right-hand man, but he soon put me straight on that.

Surrendering to him my kingship of the woods, I had accompanied him on rampages through the trees, looking for Catuvellauni to hack down. Sometimes he demanded that I play the part of King Cunobelinus so that he could fight me to the death – my death. How often as King Cunobelinus did I fall writhing to the floor, only to bounce up again. 'Dead!' Katuaros would shout. 'You're supposed to stay dead!' And I had to fall again, this time to lie still while he danced round me like a wild man, hollering his triumph.

When not fighting, he was teaching me to ride, or to stalk deer. Each day servants of Verica came out of Calleva to search for us: we became the prey and would scramble up a favourite oak or beech to hide from those who were searching for us, usually because it was time for supper.

As we grew, play became training and Katuaros retained his status as the greater warrior. I learned more about how to defend myself in those blunt fights than ever I have in my time with the Roman army.

I looked for those sanctuary trees now in vain, for the Shee, the birds, animals and herbs. The road to the oppidum ran through a field of stumps, dead bramble and blackened nettles. Surely this was once Willow Woods? And that sluggish ditch – East End Brook? Loss stabbed me like a knife in the heart.

Within the fortified gates of Calleva, we were assaulted by the sweet smell of new wood; where once we had been deafened by woodpeckers and chiffchaffs, now it was the rasping of saws and tapping of chisels. We were escorted through busy streets where soldiers off duty lounged at taverns swapping tales with postal carriers. Hunting dogs awaiting transport to the harbours of Noviomagus growled in their cages and furiously scratched holes in the ground. Pens filled with Catuvellauni slaves were opened for prospective buyers to check the livestock and make a deal. Passing Atrebates spat on the Catuvellauni for luck.

The building of the forum had not yet begun and the governor had taken up residence in the long timber hall that had been the king's house, built by the Catuvellauni when they had first taken Calleva from us not long after I was born. My earliest memory is of being scooped up, swaddled and laid in a basket on the back of a chariot, the jogging sky as we bounced over the ruts, the women keening, the men shouting, and the face of my mother peering in at me to tell me all was well, cooing and stroking my cheek, when clearly nothing was as it should be. I do not remember anything of our journeying, or stays in southern capitals, but I do remember coming home a year or so later, after Verica had ousted the usurpers. Home. That was what Calleva meant to me.

The hall had been cleaned up but I could still smell stale woodsmoke which hung in the rafters, spilt mead and rancid fat. You could almost hear kings and their warriors carousing. Whatever I thought of my father, he had not been one of them.

Not for Verica drunken nights spent feasting and bragging. He'd rather sit morosely by the fire in a deep-thatch with only his closest friends for company, playing a game of Black Raven as his harpist sang songs of heroes.

Vespasian was waiting for me at the door and escorted me along the length of the hall to where the council was meeting in a circle of benches at the end. I stared about me.

'It's yours again,' said Vespasian.

I shuddered. 'No thanks. No one who has seen Rome could be interested in this barn.'

He grinned but advised me to accept it graciously when Plautius offered it to me.

Is there such a thing as the ghost of a smell, an odour that lingers long after its cause has passed? I shuddered, for a moment thinking Caratacus was here, reeking of that sweet oil he rubbed into his skin, the garlicky sweat, the greed, the pride. The scent of him lingered in the very fabric of the hall. I lifted my nose, as Katuaros used to do in the woods when we hunted boar, claiming he could smell one that had passed this way a week before. Said to impress me, of course, but always followed by a kill.

Verica's triumph over the Catuvellauni was short-lived. Seven or eight years later, the great king Cunobelinus died and his vast territories were divided between his three sons. Caratacus, the middle one, occupied the north of the Thames and, like a drooling wolf, hankered after the south: the land of the Atrebates. I was enjoying my education in Rome when he attacked. While my kin were dying in the second battle for Calleva, reports from beyond the empire arrived sporadically and there was nothing I could do.

Did my father prepare his defences? It would seem so. Did he strengthen his militia? He must have done, but the onslaught of Caratacus on Calleva was so devastating that Verica took flight once again, this time not stopping at the southern shore. He fled to Rome to plead for help. In his weakness, he threw open the gates of Britain to the empire. Hatred of Caratacus ran through my veins like a poison that robs the body of heat. The smell of him made me stop, sway, wait for it to pass, for Reason to regain her sovereignty.

'Togidubnus?' Vespasian asked gently. 'Is all well?'

'All is well,' I assured him and went forward to join the council.

Several kings and chieftains who had arrived before us were in conversation with the governor and the procurator. Most were from tribes friendly to Rome. Others were more neutral but ready to negotiate. The Brigantes, a large, sprawling federation led by Cartimandua, were friendly to Rome but beyond the frontier. It was at meetings such as this that the governor, Aulus Plautius, aimed to unite all friendly tribes, the way raindrops on metal join up if you run your finger through them. I dipped my head formally before him, he of the sculpted face.

'Ah,' Plautius said, 'the king of the Atrebates.'

'There has been no investiture as yet.'

'All in good time. I leave that to you and your druids. What do you think of your oppidum now, cleared as it is of the Catuvellauni?'

And trees, I thought. 'It is reborn,' I said. 'We are free.'

'The Atrebates have been returning here in increasing numbers since the liberation last year.'

I nodded. 'I have been encouraging them.'

'So these people are your people.'

'They are.'

'And this is your house and your oppidum, which the emperor has asked me to present to you with our gratitude for your help in the conquest.'

'The gratitude is all mine, speaking on behalf of the line of Commius and all my ancestors. This, my native oppidum, has been a seat of contention my life long, and good men have died trying to defend it.'

'Its future safety is now guaranteed.'

His words were like a warm bath for aching muscles but I had learned that when Rome gives you a gift – especially when it was yours in the first place – the wise thing to do is to give it back.

'Legate, you have chosen Camulodunum as the capital of the province of Britannia, but it seems to me that Calleva, more centrally placed and hub of four routes, is better situated to be your administrative headquarters.'

'Then we are of the same mind,' said Plautius. 'The only thing that makes this rotting heap tolerable to live in is its strategic position.'

'I thank the emperor for his limitless generosity and would be honoured if he would accept Calleva as a gift from me.'

Plautius exchanged a smile with the procurator. 'No, no, Togidubnus,' he said. 'You go too far. It is yours.'

Mine, but for their use. The full implication of this took a while to reveal itself, but then I am a believer in the essential goodness of human nature, which makes me gullible.

'We must build a house for the governor,' I said, 'something more fitting.'

'Indeed we should.' He uncovered a model of the new oppidum. 'Calleva Atrebatum,' he called it. In the centre of the model was the forum with a basilica, the Governor's House, law courts and temples. Plautius pointed out the relationship his official residence would have to the forum and the baths. All carefully sited at a distance from each other to allow for ostentatious processions between them. I could see him walking behind six lictors, swathed in his toga of purple stripe, followed by every man of the oppidum who sought favour.

When the Romans were distracted by the arrival of a messenger, Prasutagus, the priestly king of the Iceni, came close, his forked beard soft against my ear. 'You are too young for your role,' he said. 'How old are you? Twenty?'

'Coming on twenty-two.'

'What are you doing giving them all your property?'

'Hardly all of it.' Did vanity creep into my voice then? I confess I enjoyed reminding the king of the Iceni that I was in possession of most of central southern Britain, whatever my age, while he just had the windswept flatness of the eastern coast.

'Think of the future, of your unborn children,' he said sharply. 'Do not make paupers of them with careless generosity.'

'You heard the governor – he rejected my gift.'

'I never took you for a dimwit. Who do you think is to pay for all this?' He pointed to the model of the new Calleva.

The blood rushed to my face.

'You see! Look at you. Now do you understand?' Pity for my youthful ignorance softened him towards me. 'Be sure to recoup anything you spend. It's the people who must pay. Look to your tax collectors. Make sure they are good men, and by good I mean good for your coffers. Don't let that procurator get his sticky fingers on it.'

Prasutagus offered to be as a father to me. Should I ever need his advice, I was not to hesitate. It was meant kindly. It was certainly true that I had no one else, but what twenty-three-year-old ever believes he needs help from anyone? Especially one of the Iceni, whom everyone considers a little blasted in the brains by too much sky, marsh gas and the effervescent spirits of the fens. He turned sharply and made his way back to his flame-haired wife, Boudicca, who glanced at me with a sympathetic half-smile.

All three legates of the legions had arrived at Calleva with days to spare, but the chiefs drifted in like dandelion seed, including the king of the Corieltauvi, a neutral nation north of the frontier. Katuaros was two days late because of confusion about dates. 'Why didn't you say Imbolc?' he demanded, cutting across Plautius's remonstrance about his punctuality. 'Then I would have known.'

Volisios, the king of the Corieltauvi, agreed. 'Fourth day before nones? What is that supposed to mean? When is nones? – and don't tell me four days hence. We need an interpreter. We have no intention of foisting your calendar on our people. In our land we live by the moon and that's that.'

I agreed. 'My farmers and metalworkers are refusing to learn the new system.'

'But it's so simple!' Plautius protested, and when we countered that it was not, he called his chief augur to explain.

'You can't have a calendar based on the moon,' the augur said. 'Time slips and next thing you know, you're celebrating harvest in the winter.'

We all looked at him with such disdain that he flinched and seemed momentarily not so sure of himself. I glanced around the Britons, looking for a druid of Time. Finding none, I explained to the augur, as if to an idiot child, about intercalary months.

'Of course we know about intercalary days,' he said, 'but a month? Break your devotion to the moon, divide the year by twelve and all becomes simple. In the system devised by our divine Julius we have one extra day every four years, and it falls in this month of Februarius. Now that is simple. Just one day every four years. And you? A whole month every two years.'

'Is that true?' Plautius asked.

'Every two and a half years, alternately spring and autumn,' I said, 'the Month of the Eagle and the Month of the Bear.'

'The augur is right,' he said. 'That must be confusing.'

'Far from it. Both are holy months for us, months of fasting and sacred rituals.'

'When's the next?'

'Spring next year.'

Plautius reflected in silence for a moment.

'Our calendar is of the gods and is divine,' Cartimandua of the Brigantes explained sweetly to him, considering herself to be a bridge between cultures. 'Forgive us, but our peoples consider yours to be man-made, a contrivance.'

'As it is, except that man was Julius Caesar, whom we call the divine Julius.'

Cartimandua did not even blink. She smiled on the governor as she smiled on all men, her cheeks round and rosy, dimples at the corners of her mouth. 'Of course,' she said. 'But, Legate, some people are quick to learn and others not so quick. Would it not aid punctuality if all dates were given according to both customs?'

Her husband, Venutius, standing beside and slightly behind her, looked down on his wife with affectionate pride.

Plautius inhaled and nodded, irritated that a solution offered by a woman made sense.

I glanced at Prasutagus of the Iceni; by his expression he was clearly reappraising Cartimandua, whom he had only ever known as exasperating.

After consultation with his augurs and chief priests, Aulus Plautius announced at the end of the council that there would be no change to our calendar. 'For a while, perhaps as much as a generation, the Britons will have to live under two systems. For now, keep your extra month. The next one is . . .?

'The Month of the Eagle,' I told him.

'Fitting,' he said. 'Do the people go on pilgrimage?'

'No. If they are scattered, they return to their homes. It is a time for families to come together.'

'Excellent,' said Plautius.

The procurator agreed. 'A good time for the census,' he said to the governor.

'Please hold to your word,' said Volisios of the Corieltauvi, 'for if you change it, my quiet people will be quiet no longer. It took me much effort to calm them after you stopped the festival of Samhain.'

As a favour to me, the Atrebates had received a special dispensation to keep the fire festivals. For the other tribes, all public fires had been forbidden. I began to sense their unease, as when your foot comes down on the edge of a bog and the ground gives way beneath you. A rapid sinking sensation that gets you in the stomach.

The noble Plautius, grandson of republicans, rose to confront Volisios, his usually expressionless face now stern. 'Romans always keep their word.'

As they left the council, Cartimandua and Venutius passed by me. Cartimandua looked up with a bright face and a smile in her eyes, as if we had arranged this outcome together and had succeeded. I smiled back. Of all the chiefs in the council, she was the one I trusted most, for it seemed we shared the same aim: the best for our people.

Mandred stepped forward to accompany me out. He'd only been able to hear half the conversations. 'It was like gazing on placid waters and glimpsing a violent current beneath.'

I nodded. 'The Romans seem to believe that Britain is beaten but the real sense here today is of suppressed fury. Perilous times lie ahead, my friend, perilous times.'

12
THE PEOPLE MUST PAY

It was the Festival of the Dogs, a custom peculiar to Calleva when children fed strays and tried to put garlands of ivy round their necks. Walking the lanes, we came across a knot of boys huddled by the pens where hunting hounds for sale were kennelled. I boomed at them, hand on the hilt of my sword.

A scruffy lad of about nine approached boldly to tell me that the dogs should be released.

'They are of great value in Rome,' I said.

'It's the Festival of Nodens. It will bring bad luck if they are not freed.'

'Touch that cage and I'll have your hide for breeches,' I told him. The boy, half my height, puffed out his chest and glowered at me. Mandred stepped in to tell him that the man he was facing up to was the new king. The boy deflated and ran for it.

All Calleva was a confusion of baying, barking and shouting. Gradually, amongst the scramble, I became aware of being stared at by one hound which, seated on its haunches, was quite still. There was a quietness to his eyes which was disturbing. As shaggy as the best of hounds, and as long-snouted, he was every inch a fine hunting dog except for those eyes, which seemed human. The hounds in the pens howled as if they knew what day it was. Our dog was not one of them: he sat quietly, staring at me.

'Nodens himself, perhaps,' said Mandred in a low voice.

The hound got to his feet, stretched and came to join us. We offered him an oblation of water but he ignored it.

'What is it you want?' I asked him. He pawed the ground and whined softly.

'He could be a scout,' said Mandred, 'from the Temple of Nodens in Ferylloog. They have magical dogs there.'

'What's it doing here?'

'Scouting.'

'Or looking for me?' I wondered.

'Perhaps it is our guide and we should follow it.'

As if understanding, the dog took a few steps and then turned to gaze at us with its human eyes. Content that we were indeed following, it loped off towards the west gate. We made our way in obedience to the hound, wondering where he was taking us and why. When we reached the west gate, he carried on through to the ditch that encircled the oppidum where he barked three times. Mandred and I gazed at each other, wondering what to make of it. There were piles of corpse bones in the ditch, being picked over by ragged scavengers. We huddled in our cloaks against the stench and the cold wind blowing across from the east.

The hound whined. Had its owner died here? I reached out to lay my hand on its head but it stepped backwards with a growl.

'What are you trying to tell me, boy?' I asked it.

'This is the spot where Caratacus fell,' said Mandred.

'Oh? Fell, perhaps, but he did not die,' I said bitterly. 'The coward who had called on men to fight to the death fled west.'

Which is when I met him at Seven Springs, carrying the head of King Esius in a blood-soaked bag.

Mandred had his head turned away, staring into the ditch of bones being lethargically picked over by those searching for anything of value. But I could hear him well enough. 'Had it not been for your deception, Caratacus might have won. Had the Dobunni troops reinforced the Catuvellauni, the Romans would been driven back. Britain would be free. All Caratacus needed was the help of the Dobunni, but you put paid to that.'

'You go too far!' I snapped. Although as my companion and secretary Mandred had licence to be brutally honest, he was overstepping the mark, but he turned to face me, surprised by my tone. 'What is it?' he asked.

'What you were saying . . .'

'I wasn't saying anything!'

We both looked to the dog, but it had vanished. 'Shee,' we said together. A shapeshifting member of that tribe of the Otherworld who challenge our sense of reality.

'So,' I said, somewhat unevenly, 'the Shee think I am on the wrong side.'

'Are you?'

'You know very well my intention is to be on neither side. To find harmony between these opposing forces I must stay neutral.'

That wind, that chilling easterly, carried the voices of ghosts. 'These bones,' I began.

Mandred was examining them. 'Died in battle,' he said. 'It would have been here, at this gate, that the Dobunni arrived as if in answer to Caratacus's call for reinforcements. When their general formally surrendered to Aulus Plautius it must have stunned everybody. That was such a clever idea of yours.'

Yes, it had been my idea, and it had worked. Within the day Caratacus was on the run and Calleva had been restored to the Atrebates, as Claudius had promised.

'Your deceit gave the Romans the advantage,' Mandred said.

'So?'

'So the consequences were your fault.'

I felt giddy, as if the ground beneath me had suddenly turned molten. I could hear the whirring in the air of stone balls fired from ballistae, the whoosh of a passing bolt from a scorpion, men and buildings falling. The ground heaved beneath my feet, as if all the dead would rise up and claim my soul. He was right. Caratacus had taken his revenge against the Dobunni by murdering King Esius and abducting his daughter. Branwen. My betrothed. Sold into slavery. All my fault? Now the world was tipping and I wasn't sure if I was going to be sick or to faint.

I gazed down on the bone ditch, its flutter of rooks and the human scavengers. The world righted itself. 'Has anyone organised clearing this up?' I asked them.

'Clearing up? What do you think we are doing?' said one bent-back old woman.

'Make a note', I said to Mandred, 'to raise this with the governor. We need burial pits here and some respect for the dead.'

'Even if they were Catuvellauni?'

'Even so.'

Somewhere in the far distance a dog howled at the sky.

We made our way to the court that had been established in a temple dedicated to Sucellos where, as king of the Atrebates, I sat in judgement over numerous breaches of the law. Most of them, it would seem, made by the Romans. The people all but battered me to get redress for their losses and I staggered away at sunset to cleanse myself of the day and settle down with friends and some good wine but I was too troubled by what I had heard to relax and enjoy myself.

In the next session of the council, Prasutagus of the Iceni grumbled about 'trouble at home' and said that, though Caratacus had been defeated, there was still a threat of uprisings. Virico of the Wrikon wanted to know exactly where the frontier was – Severn river or the Albios Way? Volisios of the Corieltauvi asked if a successor had been found for Esius and looked peevish under his low brow to hear that it was me. 'So you set off a chain of events that ends in his death, and you take over? How convenient.'

'I hardly knew that was how it would end,' I protested.

Plautius banged his gavel to stop us bickering. 'You all have problems, I am aware of that,' he said, 'but the purpose of this Council is to gather intelligence about rebels, Caratacus in particular – where in Siluria he might be hiding, where we might expect insurgencies.'

'I believe he's in the uplands between Siluria and Ordovicia,' said Virico.

'We have no evidence for that,' I said, 'but it's a favourite haunt of his, full of valleys in which to hide.'

'A good place for springing traps and laying ambushes,' said the husband of Cartimandua.

'Why can't he play straight?' Plautius growled. 'These devious tactics are dishonourable. Barbaric.'

I refrained from asking what honour lay in the use of siege engines.

'The rebel army is swelling with new recruits,' said Vespasian. 'Not only the Silures. There is an increasing number of Britons moving beyond the frontier and into Siluria. They are crossing the rivers in nutshell boats they call coracles and we can't stop them. The Second is too stretched to patrol the whole length of the frontier from the sea to Gleva.'

'Why are people fleeing the empire?' Plautius asked. 'For what reason?'

'They are the landless, the disaffected, the frightened, those who cannot accept our ways,' said Vespasian. 'But my scouts tell me that by far the greatest proportion is druid.'

'Druids? Going to Siluria?'

'And further north, into the mountains of the Ordovices,' said Vespasian.

'Well,' said Plautius reflectively, 'at least they are not fighters. If they want to leave, let them go. It will be for the best.'

'How so?' I asked.

'If they continue being cantankerous and obstructive, they will have to be dealt with. Best that they emigrate.'

'There are some druids of the order of priests', said Prasutagus of the Iceni, 'who are determined to remain with the temples.'

'That's already been decided. They stay and become priests of our gods.'

Prasutagus grunted. 'What about our gods?'

'They will be assimilated with due respect,' said Plautius. 'It is our way.'

Prasutagus, high priest of Andraste, could not imagine his fierce goddess having much in common with Rome's Victoria. Neither could his wife, who swung round to stare at him wordlessly.

Cartimandua sided with the governor. 'We must move forward,' she told her peers, 'and not look back. Leave the past to gather dust. If our old gods had any power, we would not be in this situation.'

Boudicca, the wife of Prasutagus, drew herself up to her full height, which was head and shoulders above the Brigantian queen, and steamed like a dragon. Cartimandua ignored her.

'In Brigantia,' she continued, 'we have already begun the work of assimilation.'

We all knew this was an exaggeration, for Brigantia is huge. The largest tribal territory in Britain, it stretches from coast to coast, separating the south from the Far North, and neither Cartimandua nor anyone else had control of all of it at any one time, but she stood there, brimming with good cheer, and none of us dared to argue with her. Venutius, the chief of the Carvetii, gazed appreciatively at his wife. His marriage to Cartimandua had been brokered by the Romans yet they seemed genuinely in love. He stood there, a British chieftain with magnificent bronze hair, skin like tanned leather, the ideal of a warrior. Not for him the toga. He was a man who had surrendered to the empire on his own terms, which were the queen of the Brigantes for a wife and power in the largest territory in Britain.

Our discussions were interrupted by a ruckus outside. An optio ran in to tell the governor that the hunting dogs had been released by children who were now running about trying to catch them again. The meeting came to an early end and we went out to witness the spectacle of the children trying to get the ivy garlands around the necks of the dogs. But these dogs had been penned up and were not in the mood for play. Katuaros, Mandred and I rescued at least nine squirming infants from being torn apart by the 'nice doggies'.

By sundown the dogs had been netted by Roman soldiers and returned to the pens. That was the last Festival of the Dogs and a poor reflection of its glory days, when it had honoured the god Nodens in his dog form, and every dog – for who knew which one was the god? – was fed from a silver platter.

'I think we have the god with us,' muttered Mandred. Our shaggy companion certainly seemed uncanny enough, reappearing when we least expected it. Vespasian had advised me to find a site for a house 'away from the centre'. When I asked the hound for help, he set off down the slope to the southern boundary, close to the earthen ramparts. The site was below the spring line and, despite the ramparts and their shadows, caught the sun when the sun chose to shine.

Mandred expressed bewilderment at the choice until I pointed out that this was an excellent place for a bathhouse. We shared a love for plunge pools and, although Roman bathing required a certain decorum, if it were my own bathhouse, we could do what we liked after hours, and what we liked was flipping about in water like merry dolphins, splashing each other, diving down to catch the other's legs and pull him under, our laughter bouncing off the vaulted ceiling.

Vespasian came to see my 'wretched camp' and wanted to know why a king should wish to live in a tent in scrubland under the ramparts but, having walked the small site, he understood my choice, praised me for finding it, and said, 'Get possession of this ground as fast as you can.'

'It's all mine, surely?'

'Did you not give Calleva back to the emperor?'

'The governor rejected the gift.'

'Did he? It might have sounded like it.'

I inhaled sharply and, within the day, was buying the site from the Romans plus other plots of land including the tombs of my ancestors. It was galling, to have to buy what by rights was mine, but I gritted my teeth and thought of the future. Once the bathhouse was built, I would put a high fee on its use by the army and its officers.

On the final day of the Provincial Council, Plautius announced that a census would be held during the intercalary month due to occur in just over a year. All land holdings were to be declared and recorded to establish the worth of each community.

The room grew stormy.

'You want to tax us?' Prasutagus asked.

'Of course, but based on proper records. What system do any of you employ at the moment? As kings, your only interest is with your treasury. You have no idea of how the money is being collected or by whom, just so long as it arrives in your coffers. Corruption is everywhere.'

That was rich, coming from a Roman! But true, according to what I was hearing in the courts. My fellow kings yowled in protest as if their sole means of sustenance was about to be cut off.

Aulus Plautius raised his hands to still us. 'Our emperor insists that we be fair in our dealings. So if, say, we establish that the tax payable on your community is one million sesterces, and you collect one and a half million sesterces, you keep the surplus.'

Everyone subsided, except me. 'How is that fair?' I demanded. 'It might suit the leaders, but it will not suit the communities.'

'That would be true if your leaders keep the money for their own enjoyment, but we would hope and expect that you spend it on improving the communities, on roads and defences, new buildings, new temples. Otherwise we are talking about tax-farming and we all know that was done away with by Augustus. As Tiberius once said, shear the people, do not flay them. Fair dealings and good profits are not mutually exclusive.'

I looked about and could see by the keen light in the eye of the king of the Iceni, who relished the thought of surplus tax, and the terror in the eye of the king of the Trinovantes, who was in a sweat about the costs of building at Camulodunum, that Plautius was being more than a little idealistic. I turned to the gathering and addressed them. 'Our systems of tithes and customs have built up randomly over the years like limpets on a boat's hull. At every stage, someone is making money. With a census we can start again.'

Volisios, king of the Corieltauvi, was livid and did not wish to be lectured by 'the jumped-up son of old Verica'. He addressed his peers. 'Do you see what this means? The Romans demolish our settlements and oppida to make way for buildings that we have to pay for. All the buildings and roads: our expense.' A sound like whimpering came from Agrios of the Trinovantes. 'So what are you saying?' Volisios demanded of the governor. 'That the kings must pay? Well, count me out. It is my people who will pay, through their taxes.'

'We must treat the people fairly,' I said, holding firm, 'or else take the consequences.'

The king snorted but Plautius agreed. 'Togidubnus is right. That is the purpose of the census – to make levies and tithes uniform and fair.'

'Not to mention profitable.'

The argument continued back and forth until, in the end, after one or two had stormed out, the room was won over. If we cleared our tax-gathering from corruption, then we would be ten times richer than we were, and easily able to afford the new projects, although it stuck in everyone's craw that those projects would be dictated to us. Even I was irked by that. As for Agrios, he had to sit down. For a generation the Trinovantes had lived under the rule of the Catuvellauni. With the Catuvellauni now subjugated, when Plautius had invited him to the council Agrios had presumed it was to redress past wrongs and give his people their lands back. It was not to be, and here he was, getting the first taste of reality. The requisitioning that had robbed the Trinovantes of Camulodunum, now the capital of Roman Britain, had only just begun.

When the meeting was over, Plautius asked me to stay behind. I had sent him a list of things that had come to court involving the army. Crimes, I called them, but Plautius referred to them as misdemeanours. 'I've looked into the particulars of your complaints,' he said, 'and find many of them justified. Any misappropriated land or reckless damage will be compensated.'

I thanked him for it.

'Regarding the rapes . . . It would be better if you protected your women with your own troops. Do you have your own militia? No, thought not. Listen, you are young. You're a Stoic and, like me, an initiate of Eleusis. A philosopher, in a word. But not a wise one. You cannot continue expecting the best of people by going barefoot amongst them.'

'I don't . . .'

'You know what I mean. You need to wake up to human nature. You are being robbed blind behind your back. Who collects your taxes and tithes? Your customs? With your amount of boundaries and borders, not to mention your harbours, you should be dripping with wealth. What happens to the money?'

'Well, I . . .'

'Exactly. You don't know and you don't want to know. So long as you have enough for your basic needs and a superfluity of horses – yes, we do know about the herd. If you want to stop my men raping your women, get some muscle and flex it. That's my advice to you. And if you heed it, I shall advise my troops to leave you and yours well alone. After all, you are going to need money,' he said, 'for the rebuilding of Calleva.'

'So, you are to pay for a forum and basilica?' Vespasian chortled as we rode together at the head of a column of troops to Corinium.

I growled.

'Don't worry. It won't come to that, not so long as you're loyal. We absolutely depend on your loyalty.'

'I've offered to build a public bathhouse.'

'Fair enough. Whatever you do, don't get into borrowing,' he said. 'It's a road to destruction with no means of turning back. Once you're on it, you're on it.'

'Why should I need to borrow? I'll use the tax.'

Vespasian sighed. 'You will find there are gaps between expenditures and receipts. When they occur, stall the project. Do not borrow. For now, your expenses will be mounting faster than your income, so stall,' he said. 'Promise nothing.'

At Corinium we parted, he to rejoin the Second further down the Albios Way.

At the spring equinox I called for a council of elders, inviting every chieftain, every magnate, anyone involved in the collection of dues. This alone helped me to discern what was going on: I only had to note the names of those who did not turn up. The more I investigated, the more I uncovered, as I'd been warned, layer upon layer of extortion. With the help of Katuaros and Mandred, I appointed good men as magistrates in each of our capitals to act as local procurators. As to the militia I needed: that came to meet me.

AD 45

13

THE MONTH OF THE EAGLE

As Plautius had promised, we kept our intercalary month but the Romans pushed their seal into the wax of it, using the sacred gathering of families to hold the census. I spent the month at Noviomagus with what family I had – that of Katuaros – taking only Mandred and Ricoba with me.

A new road linking Calleva to Noviomagus streaked like a spear over the undulating downs. For the sake of efficiency, it passed the great hill overlooking the coastal plain where once all visitors used to pause and pay their respects to the local gods. We left the road and climbed up to the windy summit. O ancient hill, landscaped with ditches by the ancestors of who knows whom. We looked down not on Noviomagus but straight ahead to the blade of silver on the horizon. I felt the pull to run down the hill, over the plain, on to a boat and away, to sail gently in light-filled water to warmer, safer climes that had a cultured life I could not find here.

After the conquest a large part of Noviomagus had been 'cleared' to make space for a temporary fort as a garrison for the Second. Now, assured of peace in my territory, the Romans were dismantling it for use elsewhere. As we descended the hill we saw trains of carts westward bound, transporting planks, poles and stakes to be reassembled at a new site on the frontier, leaving nothing behind but foundations and their pattern of right angles on the place.

Katuaros was waiting for us by the north gate. I had expected to be accommodated in Noviomagus but he escorted us to the harbour and the house he was having built – the one I was paying for – of timber, wattle and daub. It was still under construction and was very far from the grandiose schemes of his imagination. Only the southern end of the house was complete and his wife, Debonia, was waiting on the threshold to receive us, straddling her hip a yearling boy who only had eyes for his father. Katuaros chucked him under the chin and kissed him on the forehead.

Debonia was learning Latin from slaves and vowed to speak nothing else. 'Our home it is to be hoped too small for you is not,' she said to me, glancing at Ricoba as if she were something the cat had brought in.

I introduced them, plainly stating that Ricoba was of Dobunnic royal blood. Debonia, considering herself a queen, and an Atrebatic one at that, was not impressed. 'Bless you Juno bless,' she said.

'I still live in a deep-thatch myself,' I told her, 'out of preference.'

Debonia stared at me. 'I know but you a king is that fitting?'

'I have grander accommodation when I'm a guest at places such as Calleva.'

'Oh, ourselves we have soon.' She smiled acidly at Ricoba. 'Understood me are you not? We must find interpretation.'

'Indeed we should,' said Ricoba, whose own Latin, though it lacked grace, was at least correct.

While I tried not to laugh, Katuaros, standing behind his wife, smiled lovingly upon her.

'Gutter bitch,' Ricoba said to me later. 'What was Katuaros thinking of, choosing her?'

'Her hips,' I replied.

'Well, yes, that's the best you can say of that woman with wool for brains. She can't even speak her own dialect well. Good hips. But that's not the foundation of a lawful marriage.'

'He was more concerned about her ability to produce sons than her bloodline, and she seems to have fulfilled his wish.'

Ricoba agreed. 'Sweet little thing, that boy,' she said. 'And so handsome. Takes after his father.'

The following day, I was at the harbour seeing for myself how busy it was with many small boats ferrying cargo from ships in the anchorage. I stood on the saltings as I had as a boy, watching the sea breathe in, breathe out, bewitched by the dancing light on the water, waiting for that point where it had withdrawn into a deep river – Fish Creek – before filling out to become sea again. Not only cargo came in, but other, more lively imports – smiths, potters, stonemasons – Gauls who had learned their skills from the Romans and were ready to pass them on.

Back at the building site of the new house, I was met by the remnants of my old fianna led by Mouse Ears, Cow Crippler and Ten Horns. When Caratacus had come upon us at Seven Springs, my protective warriors had vanished into the woods, after which, in bitterness, I had disbanded them. They were sorry, they said, they were cowards, it was unforgivable, and yet I was the kind of man who could forgive. Would I forgive them?

Once all that was over, they turned to business. The Romans were going to use the census not only to organise tax collection but also as a means of enlisting men into the army. Or else, why were they asking the age of every man? And his fighting skills?

It was true and I knew it.

'We don't want to be part of the army. What, us? Line up and march in time wearing skirts and sandals? Can you imagine it?'

I laughed and said I could not. 'But listen,' I said. 'I've been asked to form a militia for the protection of the Atrebates.'

'Under whose command?'

'Mine.'

'But you're half-druid, son of a priestess. You're not supposed to fight.'

'I will not take up arms, but I can still lead.'

I charged them with the task of enlisting others.

'How many?'

I had no idea. Fifty? A hundred? They thought two hundred and fifty. I flinched at the cost of it.

The next occasion when I met Plautius, I told him that I had a militia forming. He sat back and gazed at me, long enough for me to begin to feel uncomfortable. 'I know what I said but, on reflection, I don't like the idea of a private militia. Expand your men to six hundred and they will be officially designated as an auxiliary cohort.'

'Don't auxiliary units always get based abroad?'

'Yes, but this is a specific and delicate case. We need you here, making the south safe for us, and you need protection. At the same time, we don't want a private militia to act on your behest and not ours. So, we shall form a cohort – Cohors Atrebatum – to be deployed in their own country.'

'At whose expense?' I asked.

'The army's, of course.'

The farmers, the fighters, the merchants: that was the make-up of our communities. But now we had a new stratum. 'Nova-togas' we called them, those British high-borns who, to achieve citizenship, shaved their faces, cut their hair short and made deals advantageous to the Romans. Awarded the toga, they wore it with overweening pride, gathering in the new forum amidst the soiling dust of demolition, impervious to the derision of the people. Why should they care? They were rich and getting richer.

Katuaros could not understand my reluctance to wear the toga. On being granted citizenship by Claudius himself, he had been presented with a gold signet ring that was blank. His Latin was much better than his wife's but, when he had carved his new Roman name backwards on his signum ring – Tiberius Claudius Catuarus – it was in letters that looked almost childish. He took his duties seriously. As chief magistrate of Noviomagus, he was out each day with the official *censuales,* making lists of land holdings. I asked him what he did when he uncovered injustice. He shrugged as if to say, What can I do? Stories were coming in from other territories, not least those of the Durotriges and Cornovii, of armed clashes and many dead, protecting their property, the reports said, from 'imperial theft'. 'Refer such cases to me,' I said. We might be sharing the kingship, but I alone had the ear of the governor.

On its way out to sea, Fish Creek passed the Sacred Isle of the Atrebates, Verica's last refuge when the Catuvellauni had driven him south. To celebrate holy month, I joined a pilgrimage passing through the mudflats. The mournful calls of curlews accompanied our sad reflections as we looked back rather than forward, remembered our dead, honoured those ancestors we had never known. Barefoot through the sucking mud we went to a jetty to wait for the next ferry across Fish Creek. Dressed in a simple robe, I was part of the crowd and stood listening to the slap of the waves, as Apnodens would, and was rewarded by a kind of deepening where only those sounds existed. Slap – slap – slap. As regular and rhythmic as breathing in deep sleep. A deepening, away from the day and into the soul and its memories.

'Togidubnus!' The familiar, dread voice of my father. 'Come on, boy! Stop your dreaming!' My mother is wading with her skirts tucked up and knotted round her waist. 'God's knuckles, woman,' Verica growls. 'Are you sure he's mine?'

Innogen turns to him. 'It was you on top of me at the Sanctuary?' she asks.

'There could have been others.'

'Not before, as you well know, and not after, as you also know.' She glares at him momentarily, like fire catching resin in the wood. 'He's yours all right.'

Verica grumbles into his moustache. 'Born of the Shee, then, a changeling child. Good for nothing but staring into space.' He whacks me across the shoulders. 'Go on, get out there with your brothers. Get your head wet. Fill your bucket with oysters.' My brothers, years older than me and of a different mother, have gone into the creek and are upending like dabbler ducks, their muscular legs waving in the air. Every now and again the legs disappear and heads bob up spraying out water. They knock and punch each other, brother stealing the catch from brother. I want to listen to the waves, the shingle and the curlews. Verica cuffs my ears hard – I wade out just to get away from him. Across the water, the Sacred Isle in all its flatness, and the temple of the Atrebatic gods.

'Come along, come along!' goaded the ferryman, helping our party of about twenty on to a flat-bottomed boat. 'Tide's going out. Come along, lad,' he said to me, his king, but how was he to know that if I walked with the rest?

Once on the island we had another long walk across mudflats, although here ancient causeways had been maintained. The chief priest, forewarned of my arrival, awaited me at the temple. 'Your disposal of your father's ashes,' he said, 'throwing them into a confluence of rivers. Legitimate but unusual and some think that Verica has not gone into the Otherworld but remains in this one. He was king here for a good many years.'

Tired of the druids and their constant reminder that he had raped a priestess and taken her for wife, Verica had banished them from his territory. 'He hardly merited a temple burial,' I said, but the priest was turning a blind eye on the past in order to serve the future.

'After Verica left Britain for Rome, our temple to Cocca was abandoned to neglect. It is in dire need of repair. In fact, it needs rebuilding,' he said. 'If we were to make it a shrine to Kommios, your grandfather, we could treat it also as a memorial to Verica and bring everything to rest, including his spirit.'

He needn't have wheedled. Temple-building was a priority with me, over any basilica or forum, and I agreed without argument. He gripped me by the arm. 'The Romans are ousting our gods.'

'I'm doing my best to make sure that doesn't happen.'

'But it will happen. If we rename our god here Mars-Cocca, how long before it is just known as the Temple of Mars? Even if the Romans do not force it, it will happen, perhaps in just one generation. You are the son of a druid priestess, and have Apnodens himself as your counsel and companion, so you know that a druid without his god is no druid at all. A bear without claws, a snake without fangs: our power would be gone. You may protect us; you cannot protect the gods. There are already stories of desecrations.'

I nodded. 'I've heard some of them.'

'Togidubnus, if it happens here we shall not be able to stay. We shall move west, joining the trickle that will soon become a tide. All druids will be moving west.'

I looked at him, shocked. 'You know I am not my father. Druids are not only welcome in my domains, they will be protected.'

'You believe too much in the promises the Romans make. Oh, some will remain, such as bards and perhaps healers, but the priests and the wise, they will go.'

'To the Silures?'

'No, further.'

'To the Ordovices?'

'No, further. The call is sounding: we are to withdraw to our centre, our beating heart, Mona.'

Mona. It was a place spoken of by my mother with such rapture that, as a child, I'd presumed it was in Annwn.

'Of all the sacred isles of Britain, it is the most sacred, and separated from the mainland by a treacherous strait,' the priest told me. 'We are being called there by the gods. One by one, two by two. Overnight a man will rise from his bed, pack his bag and take to a moonlit road leading west. I have not yet had the call myself, but it will come. Meanwhile, we need to get this temple rebuilt.'

At supper together, Katuaros and I discussed the temple and the funds required for its rebuilding, which I said we could raise from the sale of grain to the Romans.

'What about this census?' he asked. 'It will raise a lot more tax than our tradition of a tenth to the temple. You could start to live like a king.'

'I've agreed with the governor that our people will not be taxed.'

Katuaros's eyes bulged. 'Without speaking to me?'

I apologised. 'I presumed you would feel the same way. We are doing so much to help the Romans in calming the country down and settling it as a part of the empire, far more than they could do tramping about with swords, it seemed little to ask. If we now govern the only part of Britain at peace, it is because of this and other agreements made.'

'What other agreements?'

'That we shall maintain our customs and laws.'

He grunted his approval and drank deeply of the expensive wine that came into his house as a part of the harbour dues. 'I still think you're being over-generous regarding tax. By all means, let's not pay any to Rome, but we should still tax people, if nothing else to maintain the militia to protect them.'

I told him that Plautius had asked me to expand the militia into the size of a cohort, to be trained and maintained at Rome's expense.

'But would they be ours to command?'

'Yes.'

'Would we have to join the army?'

'No. Plautius says we can act independently and not be attached to any legion.'

'That's highly unusual.'

'It is, but not without precedent. An auxiliary cohort of local warriors.'

'With the purpose of keeping our territories safe?'

'Yes.'

Katuaros rubbed his hands together. 'And what is a cohort?'

'A unit of six centuries of eighty men and four *turmae* of cavalry, the entire cohort consisting of four hundred and eighty infantrymen and one hundred and twenty cavalry. Six hundred all together.'

'That's too much infantry.'

I laughed. 'Shall I inform the governor?'

'If we are to be independent, the make-up of the unit should be determined by the task and the terrain.'

He was right. Our warriors were horsemen, not trampers, and I said I would raise it with Plautius.

Ricoba, unable to stand any more of Debonia's chatter about babies and infants in mangled Latin, left the women's couch to join us. To her annoyance, Debonia followed.

'Husband!' Debonia said sharply, addressing Katuaros as if he were a farmer. 'Lord' did not come easily to her tight, disapproving lips. 'Husband, you should not even be discussing such things in holy month! No new actions! No planning!' Anger had reduced her to speaking in dialect.

My foster brother, my twin of the spirit who shared my kingdom, turned coy and apologetic. He looked at me, shrugged and smiled as if to say, 'What can I do?'

Divorce her, I thought. It was hard to fathom, but he seemed to enjoy being under the power of his wife.

'I'm serious, Delfos,' Debonia said. Her use of my cradle name, and she a midwife of the Cuda people, infuriated me but, like Katuaros, I felt peculiarly unable to put her in her place. 'Very serious. He's not fit enough to fight.'

'Well, it's all in the future,' I said.

'He'll never be fit enough, bless him.'

'That's a crushing prediction,' said Ricoba. 'May I examine you?' she asked Katuaros, inviting him to rise from the supper couch.

'Yes,' said Katuaros willingly.

'No!' said Debonia. Ignoring her, Ricoba began to poke, pull, probe and rotate his shoulder joints.

'There is a serious weakness,' she concluded, 'and this shoulder could dislocate again at any time.'

'Told you,' said Debonia.

'That in itself would not be fatal,' Ricoba replied. 'We can always put it back, but I wouldn't like to see him on a horse wielding a sword in the heat of battle when it happened. That would be fatal.'

Debonia reappraised Ricoba with a single glance. 'That's settled then, my lovely,' she said. 'He's not doing it.'

'Though he would be able to lead a cavalry unit well enough,' said Ricoba. 'Just not fight.'

It was so subtle, these movements between the two women, and after a moment's unity they were apart again. Debonia looked stormy but Ricoba stepped forward and removed Katuaros's spear and shield from where he kept them on display, which appeased Debonia.

'Don't break them!' said Katuaros.

'We should perform the ritual surrender,' said Ricoba.

'No! I might need them in the Otherworld.'

'Don't you worry, my darling,' said Debonia. 'I'll look after them.' She took them off Ricoba.

I could see where Katuaros's desires lay. 'If Plautius agrees,' I told them, 'Katuaros will lead the cavalry section of our cohort. It is not being designed as a fighting unit and will be involved in no battle. At no time will I allow him to engage in battle.'

Debonia sniffed. 'So, you have command of the future, do you?'

She was right, of course. I did not.

14
THE RIDERS OF THE SALMON

The first task of a cohort was to escort the surveyors commissioned to locate a good site for a fort at Gleva. I was glad that there was going to be a fort but apprehensive about going to Gleva. I'd spent the summer at Corinium engaged with the formation and training of the cohort, putting off the inevitable, which was negotiations with the Glevenses. Apnodens wanted to come with me, but not with armed men, so he set off to walk there alone. He always preferred his own feet to burdening any beast with his weight, such as it was. Although it was only a day's journey from Twelve Elms he said he would aim to arrive at full moon, which was in a week.

'It will take you that long?'

He shrugged. 'Who knows? Might be less but not longer. I intend to be there when the Salmon returns.' He meant the tidal surge that sent the river back on itself. 'The Sacred Salmon of the Sacred Lake,' he said. 'I've never seen it.'

Nor had I. I calculated that, within the week, I could hold the necessary councils, do my work with the military surveyors and send the escort back to Corinium. I told Apnodens I would wait for him.

I rode at the head of the unit with Mandred and Ricoba, Maglos loping out ahead as if leading the way. That hound seemed to belong to all and none of us. Mostly he was at the side of Apnodens but, whenever I came home from a journey, he leapt up so wildly he could knock me off my feet. He and Mandred walked and talked of an evening (well, Mandred

112

did the talking, but Maglos was a good listener). He slept with Ricoba, draping himself heavily across her shins until she complained and pushed him off. Reaching the escarpment and the Rim of the Cauldron he stood there and yowled over the vale, to be answered by all the dogs of Gleva.

The way down was a steep ribbon track on the flank of the Creig. If Ricoba felt anything at being back on her hill, she didn't show it but kept her eyes on the vale stretching out below us. At every bend in the descent was a shrine, to Cunomaglos, the Lord of Animals, to Cocca, the god of war, to Nodens the Catcher, to Sucellos, Father of All, and to the Three Mothers, to whom Ricoba always blew three kisses. I heard one of the surveyors scoff at our gods, saying that our depictions of them with triangular bodies and protuberant, almond eyes didn't look human. 'Why should they look human?' I asked, rounding on him. 'They are gods. Our gods. Please respect them.'

'Or take the consequences,' said Ricoba with a disarming smile. They behaved themselves after that, for all were in awe of my wise woman, not to mention that hound who at the shoulder was chest high to the average legionary.

Gleva was the heartland of my mother's people. I had only ever visited it as a child. In my imagination, I always looked down from the heights of Cuda's Hills upon Gleva, shrouded in blue-green mist, watered by snaking rivers, a portal to Annwn. It was governed by wise women and learned men. It had traditions that went back further than anywhere else in southern Britain. Gleva – Clevo as it was known in ancient times – was the cauldron of the stories that enchanted us all, the den of monsters and giants, the garden of speaking animals, the home of heroes, the cave of wizards. It was not an oppidum, nor was it a settlement with a centre, but strings of deep-thatches raised up on stilts along the banks of streams. We were received by the council of elders, the cohort billeted and the surveyors shown a site above the flood plain of Severn river, which the elders deemed best for a fort – as, indeed, it proved to be.

As expected, the elders did not offer me a friendly welcome, but I wasn't quite sure why. In council with them, we discussed at length the perilous situation of Gleva with the Romans to the east of them, Silures to the west and Enemnos to the south. I learned that Ferylloog was 'infested' by Silures. The wooded hills between Severn and Wye had always been debatable lands but for the past generation or so had been unquestionably Dobunnic. Now they were once again the object of contention. Because of the past, because of the stories I'd been raised on about the ferocious neighbours of my mother's kin, I had an image of the Silures bordering on the fantastical: dark little men with pointed teeth, far worse even than Catuvellauni.

The priest of Nodens took issue with me. 'I am of Ferylloog myself,' he said. 'Whatever our ancestry, we think of ourselves as Feryllooges. Yes, Ferylloog is rich in iron, but it is also a place of sanctuary. We welcome all to our many temples, Silures and Dobunni – even Atrebates – and treat everyone as they truly are.'

'And what are we truly?'

'Lost.'

I asked his meaning. 'Cut adrift,' he said. 'The Romans believe they are here to take what they want from the Mother. Anyone who associates with them cuts himself off from that which sustains him. You drift like twigs on a mighty river.'

The presence of Ricoba smoothed everything and made it easy, for she garnered more respect in Gleva than any mere king. Despite – or because of – the steady migration of druids westward, at Gleva there was no shortage of them. They walked the paths and rowed the streams of the settlement as they had always done, different and yet the same. The same as everyone else except on sacred days when they wore their fine ornaments and colourful mantles and plaited their hair and beards. They felt unthreatened by my cohort, even if it did escort surveyors from the army. Our reputation for protecting the downtrodden against exploitation was growing, and the druids approved. So when it came to making my claim to be king of the Dobunni, druids arranged a simple ceremony and pronounced me king-in-waiting. 'Then, on the return of our true queen, if she agrees, you will be king.'

I felt safe enough with them to ask, 'Why is the daughter of Esius your true queen? It seems Esius was not well regarded.'

They told me that Branwen was the daughter of Gwynedd and therefore of the true royal line. Although I myself had been born of a woman of great power, I had spent almost ten years in Rome and such reminders gave me a jolt. Ricoba, noting my discomfiture, gave me a toothy grin. 'When you marry Branwen,' she said, 'I don't think things will be quite as you presume.'

Once the site of the fort had been marked out, I had the cohort accompany the surveyors back to the legion. That I was prepared to stay in Gleva with only a freedman and the wise woman of Creig as my companions increased the respect of the Glevenses and I was encouraged to broach the signing of a treaty with the elders on behalf of Rome: in exchange for access to mineral wealth, and for the peaceful acquiescence of the Dobunni, I could secure a guarantee of safety for them. They would suffer neither from the Silures nor from Enemnos. The elders asked me to consult the people directly, addressing them from the rampart of the fortified hill called the Speaking Wall.

The moon rose full as the sun began to set. There was an enchanted air to this place that allowed the voice to carry to the crowds below. I said that, as king-in-waiting, I wanted the Dobunni formally to submit to the Romans to ensure their safety and future prosperity. 'At least until such time as the empire extends westward and Dobunnia is no longer divided by the frontier.'

'Why should we trust you?' one shouted, lacking all the courtesy that had been shown to me by the elders. 'We know who you are.'

The crowd seethed. 'Shame! Shame!'

'What is your grievance?' I cried, although I knew what the answer would be.

'You had our warriors betray Caratacus and submit to the Romans!'

'They changed sides so that they might live!' My voice boomed like a bittern.

115

'But they didn't come back, though, did they?'

I frowned, momentarily wrong-footed. Why had the Dobunni warriors not returned?

'My son!' the same man shouted. 'My own son, recruited into the Roman army! Robbed of all honour and lost to his family!'

I learned that all the Dobunni warriors were now in an auxiliary unit in Gaul. So I understood when the crowd took up the protest and made a ruckus. I thought I must drown in their rage when suddenly there was a sound weaving through the air, a sweet sound that made us all stop and listen. I knew who it was before I could see him. When I did spot him, higher up on the hill, he whistled. The sound glided like a bird and then rose on an uplift and flew away. Apnodens halted the conflict with a vocos.

Silence followed and when I spoke again, the mood had changed. 'These young men of yours have chosen a new life with secure rewards. They will get opportunities to visit home, and their families could join them in Gaul if they wish to. In twenty to twenty-five years, they will retire on a generous pension with a piece of land to farm.'

'Twenty-five years?' said someone close by. 'That's a lifetime.'

'Do you have no understanding what honour means?' one of the recalcitrant objectors called out. And I stood abashed, wondering. But the day was a victory for peace, and most accepted the terms of the treaty.

It was the Feast of the Salmon. My mother had told me of it often enough, how each month after full or new moon the sea can run up Severn river in a wave, how twice a year the swell is large, once in the early spring, once in the autumn. And occasionally, in years which seemed unpredictable, the swell was mighty as the Salmon of Wisdom returned to Llyn Llyw, the Sacred Lake of Gleva.

Along with my companions, which now included Apnodens, I partook of the feast at the fire of the elders. As the mead swam inside us, and we forgot the trivial business of this world with its invaders and resisters, we began to look forward to the morrow which, the druid augurs said, would see the coming of the Salmon. Stories – long, long yarns – were told, epic songs sung, and by sunrise I was five years old again, unable to sleep for excitement.

We followed the track down the hill. There was activity everywhere. Men were paddling along the various streams towards the river; those going overland with coracles on their backs looked like beetles walking on hind legs. Taken to a privileged vantage point on a small bluff, we had a view of a stretch of the river north of that great loop called the Torc where a hundred coracles bobbed, waiting for the swell to come round the bend. Our hosts told us who of the Salmon Riders were most skilled and who to put our bets on. Amongst the augurs was the priest from the Temple of Nodens in Ferylloog, whose long hair hung in a curtain of thin plaits from a bronze circlet round his brow. He was accompanied by two hounds who were clearly kin of Maglos. The priest stroked Maglos and, bending, whispered in his shaggy ear something that sounded like, 'Well done.' It was this man who had predicted that today would see the Return of the Salmon of Wisdom and Apnodens, impressed by his certainty, wanted to get to know him better and to learn from him.

There were all the sounds of the morning: birdsong, chatter amongst people, some of whom were singing, some shouting insults or encouragement at the Riders; but everyone fell quiet, even the birds, as a distant carnyx cried out downstream. 'Sandbanks!' someone called. A while later, another blare: 'Long island!' And so it went on, the sound of the carnyces getting louder and more shrill as the great fish approached. 'The Torc!' Suddenly it became eerily still, as before an earthquake. Silence fell upon the river for just a moment, then leaves on the trees began to rustle with increasing agitation.

Something strange happened within, as if all the waters of my body were being sucked out by a tide. Some have been known to faint at that moment when this world and Annwn touch each other. Now I understood why. A carnyx blared out beside us and, with a dull roar, the wave surged round the bend and picked up all the coracles. It was bigger than even the

Priest of Nodens had predicted and a collective gasp went up from the watching Glevenses. You could almost feel the fright of the men in the coracles caught up by this wall of water. At least half the flotilla upturned and unmanned coracles were carried forwards spinning like leaves. Bits of coracle, paddles and a few flailing men slammed into the banks and, after the wave had passed, drifted like flotsam in still water. Those who maintained control, waving their one paddle back and forth, back and forth in front of their round boat, struggled madly to ride the Salmon and stay on its back as it pounded out of sight round the last bend before the Sacred Lake.

Only two coracles finished the course upright, one of them manned by the eel-catcher who had won every race for the past twenty years, the favourite on whom no one made any profit. Four were drowned and about fifteen required bone-setting and treatment for cuts and bruises. It was declared 'a good wave' and the rest of the day was spent feasting in honour of the Salmon of the Sacred Lake, of Havren, goddess of Severn river, and of the winner of the race who wore the crab claws of victory on his head.

Now that they had me to themselves, unprotected by my cohort, the Dobunni were much more forthcoming and we were treated to what Apnodens called 'the Gleva sweetness'. Tall and fair like my mother, they look at you with bright eyes and a closed-lip smile that made their rosy cheeks bulge. It is impossible not to smile back.

'These are your people,' Apnodens reminded me. After my reception at the Speaking Wall, I'd been thinking 'my people' were either cantankerous or downright hostile, but, apart from other grievances, it was my connection to Esius they objected to, Esius who had 'united' the Dobunni by the simple expediency of killing his father, Boduocus, King of Gleva. 'The stinking boar,' they called him. That I had been betrothed to Esius's daughter, and that she had been sold into slavery, was no cause for their commiseration, although they did think it was my duty to fetch her back from Rome. No, they were not much interested in kings, heirs and successors. But my being the son of Innogen of the Creig, that gave me almost godlike status in their eyes, endorsed as I was by the support of Ricoba.

The Night of the Salmon was spent at a fire built at the edge of Llyn Llyw, the Sacred Lake. As the moon rose, women walked into the water, their skirts floating around them. When they were submerged up to the waist in the glittering light of the moon rising above us, they began to slap the water in a rhythm and sing an ethereal song to the Salmon. Apnodens took up their rhythm on a hoop drum and was joined by other bards, one on a buzzing lyre, one on pipes, and each musician followed his own line to weave the music in the air. Apnodens was dressed in soft hides with long fringes. Most men wear clothes either to establish status or as protection against the elements and prickly weeds. Apnodens loved his clothes for their own sake, and the older and more crumpled his boots, hat and birrus cape became, the better. He had sewn these skins together himself with his own bone needle, made symbolic designs either with hot metal, with beadwork or with paint. Living, for Apnodens, was an act of love.

He abandoned the drum for his long, bronze trumpet, his cheeks expanding like pig bladders as he blew across the waters, giving the instrument a voice to make spines tingle. Overtones and drones, slapping, clapping, buzzing, chanting: it was soft, this song to the Salmon of the Lake. It had no melody or lyric: this music was like trails of bubbles in water and would make any god sit up and listen. Owls swept low over us, and bats, too. Falling into a half-trance, I was staring at the bat hanging upside down in Branwen's rebellious hair. Then at Esius, her father with whom she had just been reunited, plucking it out and snapping its neck all in one action, thinking she didn't know it was there. Branwen, the girl who had been dragged screaming from the grove and her goddess, Swale, when Apnodens decided to move the bardic college from Kennet to Hot Springs. How she had howled for Swale, blaming me for what was happening. It was all my fault, all my fault. As it was. Given the choices Apnodens had as the Romans approached, I'd advised him to move the college. To both of us it had seemed common sense and we looked on helpless as Branwen flailed with grief.

'Are you all right?' Ricoba asked softly.

'Caught in memory's snare.'

'Cut yourself free. Look . . . ' She pointed to the far side of the lake, where a swan was approaching us along a silvery path of moonlight. The women stopped slapping the water, held up their arms and linked hands, their song fading into silence. The music stopped, the lyre and the pipes. Everything was breathless until the swan, a fine old cob, had come to the jetty and raised its head to look at Apnodens. Apnodens, who always carried food for animals, held out a piece of bread. The swan, who could have broken his arm had it wanted to, opened its beak to receive the morsel, cocking its head now this way, now that, as if to say, 'Greetings, brother. Llyn Llyw welcomes you.' The priest of the Temple of Nodens looked on, nodding to himself. When the women came out of the water and Apnodens returned to the company at the fire, the priest praised his courage and gave him a blessing. Thus far, the elders had not been quite sure how to treat Apnodens. The son of the archdruid, who had been expected to follow his father in office, had been sent spinning by the wave of events like an unmanned coracle. What was he now? Was he even druid? After the communion with the swan, however, they had no further doubt.

At the autumn equinox there was a formal signing of the treaty. I sat with the elders in the main house of Gleva, a very large deep-thatch that could seat two hundred people, for a celebration that would end with a sharing of the Dreaming Cup. Since I had last partaken of it, the localised pain in my ribs had become a more general, dull ache I could live with, while my nightly dreaming had become enriched with the image of riding on the chalk hills, just for the joy of it, in the company of a girl, a female, a woman, who rode to my right on her white horse. A woman who both was and was not Branwen. Who both was and was not Theana. Who both was and was not Epona the horse goddess herself. I took the cup when it came my way: honey mead, of course, but with an earthy taste on the back of the tongue.

I can't remember returning to Llyn Llyw. Perhaps it was only the dream, but at once I was watching where herons and egrets moved among bulrushes in the sun and swans swam on moonlight. Apnodens was playing mournfully on a flute, a song of the wind, and the reeds began to sway. Then the surface of the lake began to froth and foam as if a thousand fish were feeding there, or one giant salmon, but it was a horse that reared out of the lake, its mane streaming with pond weed and water bubbles. It stood patiently, waiting for me to leap on to its back. It was time to ride again the swelling hills and vales of vision.

Vision. A room in Rome. A boy asleep. A snake beneath his pillow.

15
THE SNAKE

Rome, with its stinks and noises, is only tolerable in winter. After a long summer spent at the house with its blinding view of the sea, they return to the city house of Passienus Crispus on the Palatine Hill. They say the properties of Crispus add up to a fortune of two hundred million sesterces, but the young slave who teaches his stepson has no idea what that means. She pads across the mosaic floor in bare feet, keeping her knees together. Here, gods and goddesses have human form and are most beautiful, crowned with laurels and sunbeams, suckling wolves, riding dolphins. Many of these floor gods wear a lascivious smirk and she does her best to tread on their faces.

'Do you have a problem with your feet?' Agrippina once demanded of her. 'Are you lame? Always shambling about barefoot, except when you are outside. Then you have the grace of a fawn.'

She has become fluent in the language and Agrippina has dedicated her to the service of her son as singing tutor. The boy has a fine voice and a love of performing in front of dinner guests. And Branwen has a voice to make the hair on your arms stand up.

Since she has been in Rome, she has never made a vocos, never sung any song of origin or any invocation to a god. Her gods are not here. She is in a land of foreign gods who have no care for her except salacious interest. What she sang, and what she taught Domitius, were simple songs about bears, wolves, deer and eagles. Childish songs to make him laugh and forget himself for a moment. When she was caught teaching him in the Dobunnic dialect, she was slapped.

Having seen Domitius into his bed and making him drowsy with lullabies, she makes her way to the balcony. It has been an exhausting day. 'Uncle Claudius' visited Agrippina in the afternoon and spent hours in private conversation before Domitius was summoned. Branwen took him into the reception room. It was not her first sight of the emperor, but it was his first sight of her. He had a kindly face and seemed very fond of his niece and her son. He tested Domitius on his Latin, his knowledge of the poets, his abilities in numbers. 'I can sing,' said the boy, growing bored quickly. 'She teaches me to sing, my Dobunnic princess.'

Claudius glanced then at Branwen and, with a fleeting expression of guilt, looked sharply away. Everyone noticed it, except Domitius.

'Shall I sing the Song of the Eagle?' he asked. 'It's very long and I know it all by heart.'

'Forgive me,' said Claudius. 'I have to leave soon. Rome won't govern herself, eh?'

She pulls aside the silk curtains that drift and flutter in the lightest breeze like butterflies. She has heard that some women wear this gossamer and that, just as she can see the moon and stars through the fabric, so you can see their bodies. Passienus Crispus forbids the wearing of silk in his house, not that his wife would have indulged. She is a magnificent woman who needs no aid from fashion or cosmetics. Branwen likes to do her hair, spending hours on the plaits and pins, wondering about the source of her mistress's power. It is in the sound of her voice, yes, but also in her posture and bearing. Sister of Caligula, exiled for years for fomenting a plot to kill him, in every way mauled by life, she has emerged from those years as if nothing had happened. Branwen is learning from her how to survive. Agrippina is the great-granddaughter of Augustus, and somehow you would have known it even if nobody had told you. Brought home from exile on the accession of her uncle, she never tires of expressing her gratitude to Claudius, whose own wife, Messalina, stopped flattering him after she'd had the babies. He comes often to the house of Passienus Crispus.

Out on the small balcony of Domitius's chamber, Branwen looks northwest towards Britain. Bats, tweeching in their shrill voices, are flittering across the face of the moon in its fullness. She stands on the balcony, her hands out in the forlorn hope that a bat will land and hang from her finger. Below her, the lighted windows of tenements on the lowest slopes, the sounds of families at suppertime, the clatter of pottery, the sharpening of knives, the bickering of children and nagging of women. Sometimes a man's bellow shuts everyone up and gives a moment's respite before the racket starts again.

So noisy, Rome, but it is comforting in its way, to have so many people around you; it makes you feel safe. She hears a swishing sound in the room behind her, presumes it's the disquieting curtains. At the age of seven, Domitius is showing signs of an unhealthy delight in silk. He is growing up too quickly. He no longer squeezes her budding breasts curiously; he fondles them and she can do nothing about it.

After making her silent valediction to the bats, she turns from the balcony and sees two shadowy figures moving towards the boy in his bed. Knife blades gleam. She can make no sound. It is all happening too quickly. Madly, she doesn't want to wake him. If he's going to die, it's better he's asleep. And she'll be next, as soon as they notice her, which they do . . . But then something slithers.

We are primed to react to slithering. Horses, men, dogs – no one likes a snake. She gasps. The men fall backwards over each other in their haste to escape. She stands frozen as the snake comes out from under the boy's pillow, zigzagging across his coverlet, over his belly, between his legs. She swears it looks at her, collusively, before it disappears over the side of the bed and into the deepest pool of shadow. At which point Domitius wakes up, rubs his eyes and asks her what's going on. Why is she staring at him like that?

'What happened?' Agrippina asks. 'Tell me again!' Branwen has regressed into her own tongue and they send

124

for an interpreter, who takes a long time coming. Meanwhile, Domitius does the interpreting. 'She says two men came in to kill me, but a snake slithered out from under my pillow and scared them off.'

'Men with knives? A snake?' Agrippina does not know which she fears more. She has her son by the shoulders and keeps running her hands down his arms, as if to reassure herself that he is warm to the touch. 'Are you unharmed? You are sure?'

'I was saved by a snake!'

Agrippina does not believe it. Snakes are not known for public service. 'There was no snake! Tell me the truth!'

Domitius, who has withstood the frights of the evening so far, now begins to cry. He hates it when people accuse him of lying, especially when he isn't. 'There was . . .' he sobs.

A chamber slave goes to the bed and pulls back the sheets. He finds nothing, but then he lifts the pillow. Membranous, colourless, the sloughed and empty form of a snake, complete with head and eyeholes, lies there. Agrippina sits down heavily and raises her hands to receive it.

No one bothers with Branwen. She is left to pick up the pieces of herself alone. Eventually she goes to her own bed to lie there sleepless until dawn. She has no idea what happened. Who would want to kill the boy, and for what reason? Domitius tells her himself the following day, mouthing the name and doing the stabbing thing. 'Mess-a-lina,' he snarls, bringing his curled fist down repeatedly into his own chest. 'Mess-a-lina.'

Branwen can make nothing of it, cannot understand why the wife of the emperor should want to be rid of Agrippina's son. She has her own son, after all, the one now called Britannicus. Branwen has no idea of the complex web she is part of, or that in Rome a common way to divest anything of power is to kill it. But Agrippina knows, and after oblations to the goddess Salus in the Temple of Concordia, gives the snakeskin to a goldsmith to be lodged in a hollow armlet.

AD 47

16
DISPATCHES

Over the following years I was too busy to enjoy visits to the Otherworld. Life was one long, dusty road. Or muddy road. Or flooded. Or lost in snowdrifts. I went from Noviomagus to Calleva to Verulamium to Corinium to Gleva to Noviomagus. A circuit of judges, kings and judge-kings. One evening Mandred and I arrived back at Twelve Elms and found Ricoba swathed in the pungent smoke of incense burners and scrying in her bronze mirror. It was heavy and she held it aloft with both hands. Apnodens sat close by, breathing into a bone flute and gently shaking a rattle. He stopped as we came into the deep-thatch to warm ourselves at the fire. Ricoba remained in her trance. I did not speak until she had returned to us.

'What did you see, Mother?' I asked, squatting beside her.

'I saw him. Caratacus. He has leaves for hair and branches for limbs and skin the colour of alder. He has become one with the wooded hills of the west, and, like a boar, is brooding, biding his time.'

My breath shortened. Whether Caratacus lived or not was the subject of rumour, speculation and conjecture. The reports of scouts were confident but, as the years passed and no one in the army had seen him, it became easier to believe that only his reputation lived. It would suit the Silures to have us think our enemy was just waiting for his moment: it put everyone engaged in frontier skirmishes on edge. But now Ricoba had seen him in her mirror. 'You are sure it's him?'

'I am sure.'

'And when will he move out into the light?'

'Not yet. Not yet. That's all he ever says to his men when they ask him that question. Not yet. And he hefts his javelin in his hands, feeling the weight of it, knowing the range of it, understanding what it requires of him, and only when he is ready will he draw back his arm and hurl it.' She blinked and turned her gaze to me. 'Be ready. Be vigilant. Be careful. He hates anything Roman, but you he loathes.'

Although we were called a cohort, Plautius wanted nothing Roman from us and had agreed to us training as a cavalry unit. We knew the terrain, spoke in all dialects and wore chainmail rather than armour. We rode small horses bareback. We were light, flexible and, visually, British. He told us our mission was to penetrate Siluria and gather intelligence. 'We must find out where Caratacus is.'

Plautius bestowed me with the rank of auxiliary prefect (I, a king!) and had me train my men to comport themselves like Romans whenever on the parade ground, to look out for their comrades and to obey orders, but I did not have them trained to fight like Romans. Our talent, our excellence, was hunting, and our skill in catching boar we now turned on humans. We were light and fleet-of-foot. We knew how to track and flush out prey. Slowly there began to emerge from warriors driven by passion an elite troop of *exploratores*, controlled like fine horses by the lightest touch on the rein. Finding Caratacus became our passion. I encouraged all our men to speak their minds and ask questions of me but one went too far when he described the rebels in Siluria as 'the Britons'. 'They are not the Britons,' I snapped. 'We are.'

Katuaros raised his eyebrows questioningly.

'They are rebels,' I muttered.

'But British ones.'

I rubbed my face wearily.

'It's a good question,' said Mouse Ears, scratching the soft fuzz of his chin. 'Are we Britons? What are we now?'

'We are not Romans, that much is certain,' I said. 'And yet we are not what we once were. We have to find out what – or who – we are. We are something new. We are the child of a strange coupling. As my grandmother used to say of her stew, "take the best and spit out the rest". She wasn't much of a cook.'

The tension dissolved in laughter.

After a long day of practising with arms at Yellowhammer Fort, I left our men to their suppers in the mess, to the taverns, to shoe-mending, belt-polishing and language lessons, and joined Vespasian. We both enjoyed sitting together, warmed by braziers, drinking the finest available wines as we studied and discussed the latest dispatches.

'It seems I am destined to be stuck forever in the southwest,' Vespasian said. 'Just as I demolish a fortified hill of the Durotriges, the Dumnonii erupt. Now we've had to establish a small garrison at the Hot Springs to contain your Enemnos.'

It was a terrible juxtaposition, a wolfish warlord at such a sacred place, a sanctuary of healing.

'He's hardly mine. I haven't even met him.'

'Yet he is Dobunni, with a claim on the kingship.'

'He has no such claim. He's just a self-serving chieftain driven by lust for power. No claim at all.'

'He claims to be fighting for freedom.'

I blew through my lips. 'Freedom to rob his neighbours.'

'Perhaps, but there is talk of him making an alliance with the Silures. Who knows, he could be working with Caratacus.'

'It's been so long since we've heard anything of Caratacus that it's hard to believe he's not dead.'

'Oh, he's alive all right. One of my scouting parties crept up on a band of Silurian warriors, feasting and drinking round their night fire, and plainly heard talk of him, though they called him Caradoc.'

I nodded. 'That's his name in Siluria.'

'So, we need to nip in the bud any plans for those two to work together. It is not easy. Occupying all the strongholds on the hills around the Hot Springs, Enemnos spits on us from on high and it's taking more men and time than I can afford.' He seemed to think it was my problem and that I was the one who should deal with it.

One bundle of messages, which had been held up at Calleva by snow that lay in drifts for weeks, was particularly large and came in on a cart. Vespasian dutifully read through piles of tablets about grain supplies, troop placements and matters of the fleet before turning to the scrolls from the Imperium.

'Anything about Branwen?' I asked.

These days he did not even bother to reply to this question. He was looking for things that related to his own affairs, for in the coming spring his term of office was due to end. I tried not to think about it for I dreaded who would take his place. All these years I'd found shelter in the shadow of the Second. Who could take his place? Among the Romans he was my only friend. Plautius was also due to return to Rome. Who would the new governor be? For everything depended on that. Plautius, for all his arrogance, had ruled well.

'Any interregnum is tricky.' Vespasian pulled on his chin as he continued to read through the correspondence.

'Any news of Lucius Seneca?' I asked.

'No. Presumably he's still sunning himself in exile on Corsica and complaining about his lot.' He opened a tablet from his mistress, Caenis. His snuffles and grunts of pleasure at her amorous words made me think I should leave but he stayed me with a raised hand. 'Messalina!' he said. 'Scurrilous!'

'What is?'

'You know Messalina, don't you?'

'Well, I . . .' Just the sound of her name and once again I am in her bed between crumpled sheets, fingering her hair that fans across the pillows.

'I mean, you must have met her when you lived in the house of Claudius, before he was emperor? Was there anything in the behaviour of Messalina that made you suspect her virtue?'

'Why do you ask?' I rasped, as if I had a fishbone stuck in my throat.

'I only know her as a sweet young woman, mother of two, but Caenis tells me she is being accused of being a whore and turning the imperial palace into a brothel. Caenis says it is a pack of lies. What are they up to?'

'Who?'

'Who? Well, Agrippina for one, of course.'

'Agrippina? The wife of Passienus Crispus? What does she stand to gain?'

Vespasian looked at me as if I were a simpleton. 'I suppose the only letters you get are moral essays from your philosophical friends. If you want knowledge, get the gossip. What does Agrippina stand to gain? Claudius, that's what.'

'Claudius?' I had lived ten years in Rome but I was still capable of being shocked. 'But he's her uncle! She's married to Crispus! Claudius is married to Messalina!'

'So, step one, get rid of the wife. Messalina is in danger. And so is Passienus Crispus.'

Having pulled at his chin as much as it would bear, he rose up to pace the room, back and forth, back and forth.

'What are you thinking?' I asked.

'Is this the hour Caratacus has been waiting for? If Plautius leaves in the spring but the new governor doesn't arrive until the autumn, he's got the summer to cause as much trouble as he likes.'

'Provided he has the troops.'

'Yes. Hmmm. Huh.' He called for his secretary and dictated a letter in which he asked for an extension on his term of duty. 'Another two years.'

'Two years?' I gasped once he'd finished. 'I thought you were longing to get home, to Caenis if not your wife.'

'I am, but I've grown fond of you hairy barbarians. I'm not going to let him roast you on spits. You need me.'

I think my eyes may have twinkled.

'What is it?' he asked.

'Tell the truth. You're staying because you're frightened of Agrippina.'

'I'm not frightened of anything,' he said stiffly.

'Liar.'

'Why should I be frightened of a woman?'

'Because this particular woman is the great-granddaughter of Augustus and you signed the warrant for her exile.'

His face collapsed, only momentarily, but enough to reveal the real man.

He went on to the next tablet. 'Ah. Oh! One for you, sent on from Calleva.' He pushed it across the table.

The small papyrus scroll bore the imperial seal and a label: 'TOGIDUBNO REX ATREBATUM CALLEVAM'.

'Is it from Claudius?' Vespasian asked. 'What does he say?'

But just because it bore the imperial seal, did not mean it had come from the Imperium. 'Branvena, filia regis Esii Dobunnorum, Togidubno suo salutem.' My fingers slipped on the tie. I didn't know what to expect. No one ever wrote anything personal in a letter, so what was it? A list of things she wanted sent to her? What could they be?

'Open it, man. It's not poisoned,' said Vespasian. 'Or is it?'

'To her Togidubnus,' she wrote, in simple but correct Latin:

I have recently discovered that you are alive, for I thought you dead. Surely only death would explain your silence? Or have you just forgotten me? You have married another, perhaps. In case you are troubled by any commitment to me, I am setting you free from all obligations. But perhaps you've forgotten you had them, as you have forgotten about me.

There was a fluttering in my stomach, a quivering in my body, the prickling of tears. Struggling not to cry in front of the legate of the Second Legion Augusta, I stared at the letter for so long that Vespasian reached out and took it from me.

'I have to go to Rome,' I said hoarsely. 'No more obedience to you on my part. I shall leave with Plautius.'

'And do what? Snatch her? She is right, you do have another woman, one called Britannia. Your duty is to remain here, like a good Stoic.'

I looked at him in unstoical fury.

'Of course,' he added, 'since she has learned to read, you could always write back.'

And what would I say? Sometimes it seemed there were long stretches when I did indeed forget about her, but never entirely. She was always there, like a soft lullaby buried in your memory, which you can only hear when you stop trying. When you are thinking about something else – troop placements, wounded men, grievances – up floats the music. What would I say? Be patient. I have no other woman. I have no wish to be released from my obligations. I do not see you as an obligation. You are . . . you are . . . In my mind she was still a child, with the wonder and playfulness of a wood spirit. I didn't like to think of her growing up, developing not just in body but in mind, becoming watchful, critical, sarcastic. No, not Branwen, no! Composing responses to this unknown being became my last act before sleeping, displacing Seneca's recommended exercise of reviewing each day and seeing what you did right and what you did wrong. 'Togidubnus to his Branwen . . .'

Vespasian ground me down with his arguments, saying it was my duty to my people to remain. I said it was my duty to the Dobunni to bring home their queen. He said if I persisted in arguing, he'd have me locked up.

I did not leave with Plautius. I did reply to Branwen, but it was to take me almost a year, and not only because of the distractions of administration, or because I did not know what to say. It was to take so long because Ricoba told me not to worry or interfere with the work of the gods. She invited some druid women from their hiding in the hills of Cuda to come and live in our grove. Previously students of Apnodens at the Sanctuary of Kennet, they were delighted to come under his tutelage again, and thus began the Song to Bring Branwen Home – a never-ending chant, often monotone and wordless, sometimes an incantation, or an invocation, or spontaneous verse, but usually a continuous drone.

The large deep-thatch we had built as a retreat for women on their moon days hummed like a beehive. No man was allowed to enter. The women, night and day, hummed, moaned, sang and, at full moon, keened a vocos to the sky. Meanwhile, in Rome Branwen could never sleep at full moon for the pull on her body, like the waters of the tide, towards home.

17

THE CALL OF NODENS

It was Imbolc and a moon before the departure of Plautius; at Twelve Elms the trees were hazy with the colour of returning life. In her dyeing house, Ricoba was stirring one of her cauldrons, trying to simulate the silvery-green colour of lichen. The floor of the house, a crazy mosaic of colour drips and spills, yearned for its spring whitening. Apnodens sat outside, talking to her through the open doorway as she whispered over the cauldron the names of the various plant roots being boiled. I was banished for suggesting she might use lichen to get the colour of lichen. 'Do you know nothing?' she had growled. 'Use lichen? Are you stupid? Everyone knows lichen gives you purple. Stupid boy!'

I crossed to the house of Apnodens where he sat outside whittling a god out of a small piece of oak. The smoke of hearth fires, the smell of hot wool, the perfume of green shoots that push out of the brown earth in that season: just breathing it all in was as close as I could get to being no one in particular. Just a man with his friend. I was hoping to speak to him about the letter I had received from Branwen, but he seemed unapproachable. Apnodens was changing. His love of the world was becoming soured like milk in a thunderstorm.

'I see the fort at Corinium is—' I was about to say 'almost finished' when he interrupted.

'Forts! All the same! All cast from the same mould. East gate, north gate, west gate, south gate, shops, taverns, barracks, bathhouses. Everything ranked in order, the same as the men. All the same.' He arose to prowl among the trees, giving them a good whack with his staff as he passed, telling them to wake up, a rite of Imbolc usually reserved for children. Children and druids.

'How do you know?' I asked when he returned. 'You've never been inside a fort.'

He snorted. 'I wouldn't last the day. For the crime of being druid, the punishment is death.'

'That', I said, 'is a typically druid exaggeration. I've never heard of anyone being killed for his beliefs.'

'So why are all my fellows fleeing west?'

'You tell me! The exodus of so many of our chieftains and kings with their clans – and wealth – I can understand, but the druids?'

'I would go with them if I were not a prisoner here, living as I do under your protection.'

'I'm sorry if you see it that way.'

'The Romans are dividing the land between local chiefs and the State.'

'It is their land,' I said, but without conviction. I had been caught up in countless wrangles about boundaries and demarcations. How many people had been uprooted for the mere crime of being where the Romans wanted to be? If a family had been on a plot for generations, renewing their thatches every ten years with help from the neighbours, building beehives and pig pens as required, ploughing and manuring fields until the soil was fertile and friable, what could it be but utter tragedy when the Romans levelled the land for building?

'Is it theirs?' Apnodens demanded. 'Whose air is it? Whose water? Land is earth, and earth is an element that no man can claim to be his own. Look how much more men have to work these days, so that they can produce yields that will feed an army as well as keep their families. Look how little they get for it. They are no better than slaves, paid slaves with no stake in the future.'

'That may be true in some territories but not in mine,' I said. 'I've worked hard with Plautius to ensure everyone gets a fair deal.'

'He's leaving soon, I hear.'

'How do you know that, isolated here in the grove?'

'The bronzesmiths.'

Yes, of course, those loitering, eavesdropping gossips.

'What happens next?' Apnodens asked.

I shifted my position as if I were sitting on ants. Would anything I'd achieved survive the change in governors? While I was worrying about it, Apnodens turned to lamenting the decimation of the forests.

'All that timber! Timber for palisades and forts. Timber for temporary buildings while they wait for enough stone to be ripped from quarries. Good, living trees reduced to planks, whole groves smouldering to make fuel for the incessant smelting of ores. And those baths, those unholy baths you are so fond of. Stagnant water! Do you want to die young? Do you want others to die young for your pleasure? Next time you go to the baths to luxuriate in hot water, think of what is underneath.'

'Underneath?'

'Down there, below the hot pool, the furnaces fed with good, living trees and stoked by slave children just to make your muscles relax.'

This happened not to be true: there were no furnaces and no child labour or any insufferable heat. Just one fire and an astonishing feat of engineering.

He continued, 'And I tell you, if you weren't party to all these crimes against the Mother in the first place, your muscles wouldn't be screaming. It is guilt that is causing your pain.'

I glanced at Ricoba, who had come out to hang up her coloured wools. She said nothing but her expression told me: 'He is ranting.'

The part about muscle pain, however, unsettled me. It had been four years since I had cracked my ribs and I could no longer blame the unhorsing for the constant ache in my chest.

Celatus the smith approached her. 'Here you are, Mother, some rusty iron. You said you wanted some.'

'That was last autumn. But thank you, dear.' Ricoba took the bundle of old nails gratefully. 'I'm not saddening at the moment but the nails can have a good long soak.' The bronzesmith seemed to understand this dyers' talk, which wove the air with mystery, but then the smiths do the same with their processes, using words to deepen the magic of the forge. Apnodens, however, continued to seethe and, once the smith had gone and I was asking Ricoba what she needed rusty iron for (it dulls the colour, apparently), he started on a new list of complaints. The school that we had established at Corinium to teach local children to read and write was, he said, a nursery for evil. Other such schools had sprung up in all the main oppida, and he had heard stories from some of them about children being beaten if they spoke their own dialect, and parents of newborns being ostracised if they gave their babies anything but a good Roman name.

'You are asking them to speak differently, dress differently, and follow that wretched calendar,' Apnodens snapped. 'They are having their native culture wrung out of them like mud from a rag.'

'We don't do those things,' I protested. 'Not in our schools.'

'Not overtly, perhaps, but with everything your teachers say, you are feeding the little ones with the idea of the superiority of Rome!'

And then the place names being Latinised, as in Kyronion becoming Corinium. I myself was guilty of referring to the Hot Springs as teo Sulis, which Apnodens thought was a wound on the British soul.

'I have to be seen to be complicit,' I said. 'Besides, we need to bring the two cultures together.'

'Statues!' Apnodens continued, as if I had not spoken. 'Bringing in Gauls to carve statues in stone! The woodcarvers of Corinium say you think they lack skill.'

'I never said that!'

'You imply it.'

'What do woodcarvers know about working in stone?' I protested.

He waved his whittled god with its wood knot for a head in my face. 'We know that the gods do not look human!'

His certainly didn't. It looked like a peeled twig.

'I have to decorate my temples with something the Romans recognise as divine,' I retorted. 'And, yes, that would be Roman gods. In stone. If our local men refuse to sculpt gods in living likeness, then I must import those who will and can. I do intend', I said, my voice rising to match his, 'that they should learn from the Roman sculptors, not be replaced by them. I also intend them to carve images of our own gods. The Romans would expect it and accept it.'

'Do you understand *nothing*?' My mild friend was now storming. 'There is no living likeness of a god! They are seen, if seen at all, out of the corner of your eye, in a dream, as a sound, a fleeting image at most. You know that! Our images, our wooden images, that gently decay and return to the soil, *provoke* such dreams and visions. They stand between the worlds. Your Roman ones are a parade of beautiful people on a marble stage here in this world. Which is *preposterous*!'

Maglos, who had been sitting with us, now stretched out on the ground, his paws over his ears.

I reminded Apnodens, mustering all the authority I had, that he was speaking to his king, a king who was doing his level best to please the new overlords and avoid bloodshed.

'Perhaps bloodshed would be better,' Apnodens thundered. 'It would be more honourable.'

Ricoba stooped to stroke Maglos. 'I wonder what it would take', she said to the hound, 'to sadden these two? Their tempers are too bright.' The hound moaned.

'Mother?' I said.

'Don't ask me to take sides,' she said. 'Adding two colours together gives you a third. Remember that.'

Two days later, two blisteringly silent days, came the call of the hounds.

It came in the hour before dawn, an otherworldly howling that, as I woke up out of deep sleep, I took to be a carnyx. Maglos joined in. Presuming it was an attack, I rushed out to find Apnodens standing at his door, holding the straining hound by the collar. All across the land dogs were howling. The sound seemed to emanate from the west. Maglos threw his head back and crooned into the sky. It really was like a carnyx.

'His brothers are calling,' the druid said. 'The Hounds of Nodens.'

'What are they saying?'

'They are calling me to the temple. Dog to dog across the land, they are calling me.'

At dawn a messenger arrived, having followed the white track by moonlight. The priest of the Temple of Nodens had gone into the Far West, he told us, and had nominated Apnodens to succeed him.

I objected. 'If one man flees, he should not ask another to take his place.'

'Don't argue,' Apnodens said, laying his hand on my arm. 'This is a call from Nodens himself.'

'But you are a bard, not a priest, and you are forbidden to hold office since abandoning your course of study.'

'Nodens,' he repeated, 'my father god. Ap Nodens, son of Nodens. Can't you hear him in the voice of every dog?'

It was ethereal to stand on the hillside at the Grove of Twelve Elms and hear the relay of barking coming from the west. Maglos continued to howl. A call from Nodens himself, it seemed, and it was natural that Apnodens should accept it. Since his liberation from the strictures of the order, the healer had come to the fore. Sound, of which he was a master, was a way of healing, and this call he understood to be the divine seal of his own god upon the path that had opened up before him and which he now chose to walk.

The Temple of Nodens in Ferylloog.

'You know how dangerous that land is,' I said. 'The battleground between Dobunni and Silures.'

'You think I have something to fear from the Silures?' he said coldly. 'Why would that be?'

Was all this set up by him as a way of leaving the grove, and leaving me? Sensing my hurt and sorrow, Apnodens softened and laid his hands on my shoulders. 'There will always be a place for you in my heart, brother,' he said, 'and in my temple if you should need it. It is you who are in a dangerous place, not me. You were mistaken to put your trust in these overlords.'

Before he left, he gave me a gift in gratitude for the shelter and protection I had afforded him. A soft and beautiful plaid, made of the undyed wool of dark sheep from Cuda flocks, it was brown except that it had faint lines of colour in it –

woad blue, madder red, weld yellow – threads running in a numerical sequence of three, five and eight that only a druid would recognise and understand. 'It will help you move unchallenged among Britons.'

Maglos, whining, sat at Ricoba's feet and gazed up at her. 'Go,' she told him. 'Follow the god, not me.'

He dipped his head, licked her foot and rose. When Apnodens set off, jumping down the sloping path like a goat, Maglos went with him. I stood watching them go, feeling grief in the pit of my stomach that he was free and I was bound. Bound to my duty, which now was to make my way over the country to Camulodunum for the great farewell to Plautius. I swung round to Ricoba.

'It's not too late,' I said. 'You could catch him up.'

'What for?'

'I am constantly on the move. My life is dull with so many councils and negotiations. As the weather warms, I must leave the grove and go out into the world to bid farewell to Aulus Plautius. Mother, I want you to go with Apnodens.'

'Do you,' she said, and it wasn't even a question. 'You'll find me at my loom when you need me, as you will. Apnodens doesn't need anyone.'

'Why will I need you?'

'He's coming, Delfos. He's ready now.' I knew whom she was looking at within. And what it meant: Caratacus. Alive and on the move.

'If that's the case, I refuse to leave you here at your loom.'

'Excellent!' she said, coming to her feet as if ready to leave at that moment.

'But you are not coming with me!' I insisted. I wondered where she would be most safe. 'Noviomagus. I'll send you south.'

'Katuaros will be joining you?'

'Yes.'

'So I'll be alone with *her*?'

'Yes,' I said, but not so insistent now.

'Forget it!'

In the end we agreed that she would move into the hills in the company of the bardic women, 'for the song must continue'.

'Just you and me, then,' I said to Mandred as we left for Camulodunum. 'And an armed escort.'

I smiled. A gleam of sun through the rain of sadness.

On the morning of the Tubilustrium at Camulodunum, after the purification of the war trumpets, Plautius ceremonially relinquished the governorship. I was sorry to see him go, and more than glad that Vespasian had been given leave to remain. I had tried a hundred times to write a reply to Branwen that I could send with Plautius's party, but no words came. No sincere words. All I could produce were formal words. Stiff words. Proper words. Empty words. Mandred was beginning to tire of rewriting letters with one word changed. 'There's only so much papyrus in the world, and you are exhausting all supplies.' As the unit mounted to depart, with no letter from me to carry, I looked on Plautius's smooth, chiselled face, presuming it was for the last time. He might be hated by the Britons, but they did not know how much he had done to lessen the burden on them. Things could have been much worse, and were about to become so.

18
INTERREGNUM

Before he left Britain, Plautius had told me to concentrate my troops on the frontier at Gleva. 'It's a weak spot,' he said. 'Caratacus has about three good crossing places, but Gleva is the best, and it's your own territory. Of course, the new governor may have different ideas, but for this summer at least, base yourself at Gleva.'

Plautius had barely set sail when reports began to arrive of attacks across Wye river, more planned and powerful than the usual incursions of the Silures. Caratacus was attempting to establish a base on the frontier, not at Gleva but further north, on the border of Cornovia, where you can cross the Severn without getting your knees wet. Had he made a pact with the Cornovii? It seemed that, far from spending four years licking his wounds, he had been regrouping, training his fighters and preparing to return. Now, at the time between governors, was his moment.

And ours. The Cohors Atrebatum was out in all weathers, ranging the hills, encircling some wood where the enemy camped while our swift infantry ran in with spears. Ran in, ran out. We never stopped long enough to bury anyone. We tried to persuade those we captured to reveal the whereabouts of Caratacus but I was not happy with the process and, having decided that they were never going to speak, sent them off to the nearest slave market.

When I got back to Corinium I found Ricoba waiting for me. She looked tired. 'Would you like to spend some time at Gleva?' I asked.

'Of course I would!'

'So, keep your bag packed, Mother. The cohort has been charged with patrolling the Silurian border. I won't be around much – I'll be sleeping rough with the men – but we'll house you with your kin.'

'Take me there, now. Take me away from Corinium. These people! Supposed to be good Dobunni but their brains have melted like tallow. All they want to talk about is rank, wealth and possessions, as if those things count for anything. When I offer to heal the sick, they say they'd prefer to consult a Roman physician. As if that's going to do them any good! Sawbones, that's all they are. They know nothing about healing with the help of the spirits.'

'Come on,' I said, 'stop your grumbling.'

'I need to prepare for the journey. When are we leaving?'

'Not for a week at least. We'll rest first at Twelve Elms.' Ricoba was not alone in her weariness. The land was growing ever more lush and fragrant and I wanted to enjoy the spring in my grove, not out on campaign.

When at last I could turn to the messages, I found the one on top was from Vespasian. His tone was matter-of-fact, offering no personal opinion on the matter he had to report: the new governor was to be Publius Ostorius Scapula.

Katuaros joined us on the eve of Beltane with news of the growing power of the southern Dobunni, wanting to know why I was going to Gleva and not hurtling south along the Albios Way to deal with Enemnos.

'Because Caratacus is on the move east, heading for Cornovia.'

Katuaros's eyes widened. 'Do we have a battle ahead?'

'No, we do not, especially not you. Our job is to corner the beast and leave the kill to the army.'

We arrived at the Rim of the Cauldron at the start of the annual Wheel Rolling down the precipitous slope of a hill on the escarpment a few miles from the Creig. It was a great chase where the prey was never caught. Launched at the top of the hill, the wheels of fire came down at twice the speed of the men and boys who chased them, as mad and as fast as hares. Not all the flaming wheels reached the bottom. Some snagged on brambles and scrub fires ensued. I directed my men to the valley where, together with the locals, we formed up, three deep, to catch the chasers. No one got down the hill on his legs but instead turned into a human wheel. I joined the cohort, putting myself in the way of the people who tumbled, rolled and turned head over heels towards us like an avalanche of bouncing boulders. One man who broke his fall on me was a sweaty farmer so red in the face I feared he was close to a seizure. He thanked me brusquely, said he'd been perfectly capable of stopping himself, and went off, hooting breathlessly with the rest as if they had won something. Perhaps just staying alive was the prize. Many bones were broken that day and Ricoba moved about the field of the fallen, helping to splint limbs, telling them they only had their stupid selves to blame.

I had arranged with Plautius that we could keep our fire festivals. In the spirit of the famous Roman tolerance for foreign cults, he had agreed but stipulated that there should be no more gatherings of the peoples since 'assemblies are seedbeds for rebellion'. But Plautius had gone and Scapula had not yet come. That year's Beltane at Gleva was wild. Fire-dancing, fire-jumping, running cattle through the flames to rid them of winter, everyone drunk and dancing naked. With all reason abandoned, they gave themselves up to the spirit of the season.

'They make the Bacchanalia look tame,' Mandred observed.

Why is it that such ecstatic celebrations of life cause reflections on death? It was as if they knew what was coming and were not so much defying fate as inviting it to do its worst.

Mandred stayed sober and went about gathering intelligence. The Silures, he reported, were pouring into Ferylloog and did not fight clean. They were subversive, setting fire to hay barns, stealing livestock, burning deep-thatches. That was one version. The other was that Ferylloog was Silurian by rights and it was the Dobunni who were causing trouble. And then there was the opinion that the people of Ferylloog belonged to Ferylloog and nowhere else.

I decided we needed to go in and find out for ourselves what was happening there. I asked Katuaros to stay back with a detachment to protect Gleva should the enemy break through. He moaned but accepted it and Mandred took his place as second-in-command.

How do you describe Ferylloog? It's trees, trees and more trees, gnarled roots, hollowed, twisted trunks, fallen branches, hanging ropes of old man's beard. Owls. Squirrels. Goshawks. Crags and ravines, mossy boulders, rickety bridges over rushing streams. Iron being mined in caves where it hangs in nodules like stalactites, being worked in forges by brown men in brown leather, all soot and ash and red-hot metal. My men, now fully trained in arms, were more frightened of Ferylloog than of the Silures. The Silures they could hack down, but what do you do with a forest that closes in on you with menace? A forest that eats men? Swallows them up and spits out their bones. A good warrior needs more than muscle and discipline: he needs a strong mind.

We explored the tracks and trails, and sometimes, just when the trees seemed to be at their thickest and darkest, we suddenly broke out blinking into sunlight glancing off the slow brown river which is Severn. At each bend, it seemed, there was a temple. I would have liked to have visited the temple now in the care of Apnodens, but it was too far south for a quick visit, my troops too volatile to be left for any length of time. As it was, we had only spent two nights in the forest before I had a near mutiny on my hands. These men had been children once, had been told stories by grandparents and bards who liked to send the young ones to bed in terror. It wasn't a good story if it didn't make your audience gasp and tremble. Now here, grown men in Ferylloog, they could not sleep but stayed awake all night and began to report strange things after their daytime patrols. Silures living in trees, ready to drop on an unwary traveller. Bear pits, when there were no bears. Or perhaps there were. Were there bears? Boar, of course, snuffling, snorting boar with tusks the size of a stag's antlers. Wolf howls. Or was it dog? Was it that grey, shaggy hound that many had glimpsed running between the trees? Whatever it was, and probably all of it was the Shee, they'd had enough. On top of which, there was the Woman who lived alone in a temple in a very high place, who could blind a man with her beauty at forty paces, they said.

I didn't know how to deal with them or what to say. I thought perhaps I should lead by example and go off into the woods on my own in a display of bravado, but their fears were getting to me. I made quick work of interviewing locals and found that all stories of their allegiances were correct. Some were Dobunni, some were Silures, most were Feryllooges. None of them welcomed our presence. As soon as we could, we made our way back upstream to Gleva and the fort, but when we came to the ford across the Severn, we found our way blocked by a small force of Silures. About two hundred of them, most dressed in sheepskins, only their captains in chainmail, their faces painted for war. Animal skins, horned headdresses, pointed spears – the stuff of childhood nightmares.

At last, faced with a real enemy, my men showed their metal and went for them with an energetic enthusiasm. The Silures were quickly overcome and taken prisoner.

'What shall we do with them?' Mandred asked.

Vespasian would have dispatched them. Plautius would have enslaved them. Both responses would have been done with maximum cruelty as 'a deterrent'.

'Well?' Mandred prompted me.

'Let's go and talk to them,' I said. They were penned like animals, bound with ropes and chains. Far from being the swarthy brutes with dark curly hair the geographers write about, they looked like the Dobunni.

'Do you understand my language?' I asked in the Dobunnic dialect.

They did.

'Where are you from?'

'Llanmelin in the south, close to the estuary.'

'West bank? Siluria?'

'Yes.'

'What are you doing up here?'

'We heard there was no opposition, that the Romans had left for the summer.'

'Only one of them,' I said, and explained about the change of governors.

'Did Aulus Plautius die?'

'No. He'd done his duty and was recalled to Rome.'

These men were shepherds before they were warriors and, living the slow life, were not too quick on the uptake. They could not understand the concept of a general who only serves a few years.

'Who sent you?' I asked.

They shook their heads and said no one had sent them.

'Who is in charge of the Silures?'

'You call us Silures. We call ourselves men of Llanmelin.'

'You have no king?'

'A chief and our elders.'

'But does Siluria have a king?'

Despite their miserable circumstances, they found this amusing.

'Not Caratacus?' I pushed them.

They denied it. Mandred spoke into my ear. 'They are just raiders.'

'So you are a looting party?' I asked them. 'We have punishments for that crime, and whether it is death, slavery or maiming is at my discretion. Which would you prefer?'

'Kill us!' they shouted.

'I wouldn't make it quick. Probably three to five days,' I said, and described the details of the long death. 'Surely slavery is preferable?'

'Kill us!' they said, but not quite so emphatically this time.

'If you opt for slavery, you will be sent to the lead mines. You might last the year.'

'Kill us!'

I glanced round the pen of beaten warriors and saw, as I hoped, that some were beginning to have doubts. 'Maiming,' I said. 'I could have your right hands cut off. If it doesn't go green and rot, you would recover but never wield the sword again. Or stroke your woman's thigh. Or get on your horse easily. All of these things can be done, but not easily.'

There was no response.

'Or it could be hamstrings. A quick cut behind the knee – all over in a second. Lame, you could become artisans without any loss of honour. Artisans these days are getting rich. So, which is it to be?'

'We'd rather die,' claimed one in front of me, bearing a catskin helmet in honour of Ocelos, the Silurian god of war. Cat paws rested on his shoulders, the tail hung down his back. He looked alarming but, when I gave an order for him to be given his wish, there was a quick rush of urine staining his breeches.

Suddenly I remembered Seneca telling me once what makes the difference between a king and a tyrant. He quoted Virgil: 'This will be your genius – to impose the way of peace, to spare the conquered . . .'

'There is a fourth option,' I told him. 'I could offer you clemency.'

'Are you insane?' Mandred said out of the corner of his mouth. I ignored him.

'By that, I don't mean I'm going to set you free to make more trouble on my borders. Are you prepared to sit down with me and make a treaty? If it comes out right, you will be free to return home, on one condition; that you give me any information you have about Caratacus.'

Now the silence erupted in grumbling, which grew into protest and much shouting. I left them under guard in the pen without food or water. When I returned the following morning, they had settled and elected a council. They said they were unable to comply with my demand. Caratacus was on the western border of the Cornovii. That was all they knew.

With that I had to be content, and let them go.

Mandred threw up his hands in despair. 'We went through all that to let them go? Stoics!'

19
SCAPULA

Immediately after his arrival in the late summer, Publius Ostorius Scapula held a Provincial Council at Calleva and made it clear that, as kings, we meant nothing to him other than what we had to offer. We'd barely been introduced by Vespasian before he was snapping at me, 'Are you any closer to catching that coward Caratacus?'

'Coward?' I asked.

Scapula was not a patrician like Aulus Plautius before him; he was born and bred military. Trained to be tough, the son of the first commander of the Praetorian Guard, did not have the desire to be loved that weakens most of us.

'Yes, coward. Always on the run, is he not? Leaving a trail of destruction behind him. Never standing to face us and fight. A loping wolf who leaps in, takes a lamb and runs off. Yes, coward.'

It was a sore point. The summer had passed in fruitless pursuit; far from leaping in and running off, Caratacus had been sublimely evasive. We only knew where he had been once he was somewhere else.

'He has the land working with him,' I said, 'and knows every hiding place it has to offer. But we are familiar with the area he's in now, north of Siluria, on the border of Cornovia.'

'Where's that? All these names . . .'

Mandred stepped forward to draw a map in the sand box. While Scapula bent over it, the kings exchanged troubled glances. One thing was for sure: we were missing Aulus Plautius. As if our thoughts had been spoken out loud, Scapula, still staring at the sketch map, said, 'Plautius was a fool. There will always be trouble while we have the frontiers where they are, providing refuges for rebels in native lands beyond. What an idiotic policy. I hear that Dobunnia is even split down the middle?'

I nodded. 'By the first frontier, the Albios Way, yes, but Plautius moved the frontier west to Severn river to make the split more natural between the Dobunni and the Feryllooges. It's helped keep the peace.'

'I am not here to keep the peace,' Scapula said. 'I am here to get rid of the opposition and quell the rebellion. There is no point in having half a country within the empire and half without. I trust I have your support,' he said to all of us.

I swayed, trying to keep my balance as if standing on a boat on a swell. While the other kings – and queen – were assuring him that he did, I dared say nothing for fear of throwing up. *I am not here to keep the peace*. All that I had striven for over the past four years fell in a heap at those words. *I am not here to keep the peace*. I noticed Mandred watching me closely. My hard-bitten Durotrigian ex-slave had a compassionate eye for any animal or child in trouble. Now it was turned on me. I could do nothing about Scapula, but I could remind myself of my purpose. *I am here to keep the peace*. I smiled and Mandred raised his chin, relieved.

Strength returned, enough for me to dare to broach the subject of the calendar.

'Governor,' I said, 'the Month of the Bear begins at the equinox.' I went on to explain our intercalary months and to stress their importance. 'Plautius said that the Britons could keep their calendar alongside the Roman one for a generation.'

'That's a druidic calendar, is it? Same as the Gauls?'

'Yes, the same.'

'No need to change that agreement,' he said. Prasutagus of the Iceni, standing behind Scapula, raised his arms in gratitude to the gods.

On learning the extent of my territory, Scapula straightened up and asked about the treaty the Atrebates had made with the Dobunni. 'Is it holding?' he asked.

'Very well,' I replied. 'We have peace in both territories and prosperous trading. The Atrebates are more or less responsible for keeping the army supplied, receiving cargo at our harbours without any danger. You will find us loyal to the emperor.'

'And the Dobunni?'

I told him about the hostility of the southerners, led by Enemnos. 'An ancient rift has reopened. Dobunnia is splitting in half.'

He had the details from me and turned to Vespasian. 'Where is the Second?'

'On the south coast, where the Albios Way runs into the sea. But we have a small garrison at Aquae Sulis to contain Enemnos and frustrate his ambitions.'

'I want him on a spit, not contained. Send more men if necessary.'

'Can I have Togidubnus and the Cohors Atrebatum?' Vespasian asked.

Scapula looked me up and down, taking in the length of my hair and my tattoos. 'You need to convince me of your loyalty,' he said. 'I've been told that you made a pact with the Silures of Llanmelin? Offered them clemency?' He came close. I noticed then a kind of tremor in his eyes.

'Yes, in return for—'

'Never – do – that – again,' he said through clenched teeth. 'Not on behalf of the Roman army.'

If I dipped my head it was only to give me pause to check my mounting rage.

'By Mars, what officer of the Roman army offers peace to the enemy?' Scapula continued. 'Never again, Tiberius Claudius Togidubnus, *never* again. Citizenship can be withdrawn, you know, and then where would you be?'

Once I had accepted the rebuke and apologised, Scapula granted Vespasian his wish. 'Yes, you can have them. When can the campaign start? I want Enemnos wiped off like shit on a shoe.'

'It's too late to begin anything now,' I said.

'Why? We have a clear month before the season ends.'

'Because of the Month of the Bear. I shall be at Corinium with my people.'

The more he stared, the wider his eyes, the more mobile the pupils.

'The Month of the Bear,' I repeated. 'A time of peace, when there is no fighting. Enemnos will be celebrating it as much as I.'

'Good time, then, to pounce on him. Vespasian, can you spare four units?'

'No. The Durotriges keep all the Second occupied.'

'By the gods . . .' muttered the governor. 'No wonder this is taking years. As the land so the men – treacherous and boggy.'

'I knew him in Egypt,' said Vespasian when we were alone, 'the son of the prefect. Huh.' He pulled on his chin. 'Huh.'

'What is it?'

'Hmm? Oh, I'm just remembering him. Son of the prefect, and didn't we all know it, especially me, the son of a moneylender,' he said. 'He fed off his father's reputation; at the same time, he fought to build his own.' He looked me in the eye. 'Prepare yourself, my friend. This will be a jolting, like riding one of your creaky chariots over rutted tracks. Have you ever wondered why Caratacus has been so quiet? Licking his wounds, yes. Establishing his authority in Siluria, yes. But I suspect that his support is dwindling. This is the enemy he needs. Either Scapula will turn Britain against Rome and generate support for Caratacus, or he will squash Caratacus like a beetle. Either way, prepare for unrest.'

After all members of the council, including the governor, had departed, I remained in Calleva to oversee work on my house and the adjacent baths. Although the building of the basilica and forum had barely begun and the oppidum remained more or less as it was, with each passing day Calleva was becoming ever more Roman. My house by the ditch was proving to be as I'd hoped and expected – out of the way. Sometimes I sat outside of an evening and gazed up the rise in the land to the temple I was having built for Kommios and his line, Kommios, my famous grandfather who, while living in Gaul, had sometimes supported Rome and sometimes hadn't. After a failed attempt by the Romans to murder him, he became an out-and-out rebel at war with Caesar. They achieved a pact in the end; Caesar gave Kommios some lands in Britain and, coming here with his people, he founded Calleva. This is a very succinct version of my family history, gleaned from what my kin could remember, as well as what Caesar himself wrote in his book on the Gauls. I'd asked friends in Rome to search libraries for any other material, for I wanted the royal bard of the Atrebates to make a new song of origins. They found little.

I went to Corinium to keep the Month of the Bear. The journey from Calleva took me past farm after farm where they were ploughing the wheat fields for the next sowing. It had been a good harvest and the sun shone down on a land that was peaceful. It was a deceptive view. When I led the cohort in through the gates of Corinium, we were met by an agitated, querulous mob. As unit after unit of the cohort entered, the Corinians stood back, faces full of thunder. Celatus, the bronzesmith from Twelve Elms, pushed his way through the crowd and shouted up at me to retreat at once to the royal house on the hill overlooking the river.

'What is it?' I asked him. 'What's happened?'

'The Month of the Bear has been cancelled! A messenger came from the governor this morning!' Scapula had overturned Plautius's decision.

'Did he give a reason?'

Celatus shrugged. 'Does he have to?'

No, he did not. It was obvious: why waste good fighting time on a sacred custom of the conquered? Aulus Plautius had said it would take a generation at least to make the transition from one calendar to another. We'd been given days. As strong as he was in military matters, Scapula was weak in political acumen. Clearly he did not realise that what for him was a simple decision to establish his authority was for the people a sudden, inexplicable cancellation of a month of reflection, fasting and thanksgiving, marked by rites culminating in a great feast. Now it was gone. Cancelled with the stroke of a Roman stylus. This was the mark of a man who meant to establish his rule through might not right. *I am not here to keep the peace.*

Someone amongst the crowd was agitating the horses, sending dogs running through their legs. The cavalry struggled

153

to keep control, and the Corinians took advantage, pressing towards me,

'Go!' Celatus shouted. 'They see you as Roman! Do not linger!' I ordered the cohort to leave the oppidum and led them upriver to the steep road to the royal house on the flinty plateau. The earthworks might be decayed but were strong enough for us to defend ourselves. It was only when I was safe within the house that the final realisation dawned: Scapula could have warned me and had chosen not to. Indeed, he had laid a trap for me. In his wavering eyes, I was just a barbarian with patterned skin and too much hair. A barbarian amongst the Romans, a Roman amongst the barbarians. I sat in this house of Dobunnic kings with my head in my hands, awaiting my fate.

No mob stormed us. The only thing that came up the hill was an account of the Corinians being berated by an old woman who stood on the rostrum in the marketplace and in a clear and carrying voice told them that the only Romans here were themselves. 'How easily you moved your houses into the valley! And now you are edging them closer and closer to the new fort. Where is your hair? Where are your plaids? Nova-togas, the lot of you! I, Ricoba of the Creig, spit upon you and, worse, will curse you if you set one finger on your true king, Togidubnus!'

'King of the Atrebates! What does he have to do with us?'

'You know full well. He is your king-in-waiting. One finger, one finger, set one finger on Togidubnus and I'll turn you all into frogs!'

When she arrived, striding up the hill aided only by her beloved staff – a whittled gift from Apnodens – I came sheepishly out of the royal house to receive my champion.

'You good-for-nothing runt,' she said. 'What are you doing hiding?'

We moved from the royal house to my retreat at Twelve Elms. Ricoba's first act, before the ritual house-painting, was

to summon the aunts of Corinium to council. It did not take her long to convince them of my innocence regarding the cancellation. Once persuaded, they set about the uncles. Within three days, Corinium was calm again. Sulky, but calm. I held various councils but could not reach any decision as to what we should do. The people did not respond well to anything I said about taking blows without reacting.

Ricoba insisted on looking after my toga, saying she would carry it to the river for washing. She insisted on it.

'We have slaves to do the washing,' I said.

'I am not washing a toga. I am serving my king, and I want everyone to see me do it.'

'I'm not happy . . .'

'Give it. Give it to me, Togidubnus!'

I handed over my toga of fine wool.

'Bleached white – how can you bear it? Would you not like me to give it the dappled colour of the woods in spring?'

'Get going if you're going, Mother.'

'How do they get it so white?'

'Urine.'

Mandred chuckled at her expression. 'True,' he told her. 'Great tanks of urine, with slaves to tread the cloth like grapes.'

Now Ricoba had no cause to find this remarkable. She kept her own piss pot outside her hut, inviting contributions from passers-by, using it to fix her dyes, but she washed in water and, having once heard that Romans even clean their teeth with urine, had decided that 'civilisation' was what they lacked.

'They wash togas in piss?' Ricoba said. 'Now I've heard it all. That explains everything.'

'You knew that,' I said.

'Not about the trampling. That is disgusting. Imagine sharing a bed with someone who has had his feet in stale pee all day.'

'If you would serve your king, Mother, stop your chattering and go!'

'And this stripe of purple . . . How do they get purple?'

'Boiled snails,' said Mandred.

'Snails?'

'Not any old snails, special ones.'

I suffered a vivid olfactory memory of the stench of boiling sea snails in workshops outside the city wall of Rome. Not something anyone forgets.

'I get a better colour from lichen, more subtle and soft.'

'And how do you get that?' I asked.

She mumbled her reply.

'What did you say?'

'I said, from fermented lichen.'

'Fermented in what?'

Another low mumble.

'What did you say?'

'Oh, all right! So I use pee. Old, male pee. You know that. But I don't trample cloth in vats of it. This stripe on your toga, it has no subtlety. It smacks you in the eyeballs.'

Ricoba folded the toga in such a way that it sat – and stayed – on her head. 'I'm taking it for a proper wash in running, fishy waters, as the Mother wills it.' Ricoba left to walk two miles down to the river singing a washing song, eager to tell any women she found there how Romans clean their teeth. We could hear their screams of laughter even high up in the grove.

It is one thing to ban a month, another to enforce that ban. We kept to our rites and rituals for it was impossible not to. The rhythm of our bodies and our lives demanded it. For two and a half years we had eaten and now we had to fast. We had been fully engaged with the business of the world, and now we had to turn inward. It was the time to draw in breath, to be quiet and ask for nothing. It was the time to give of ourselves, to be with our friends and family. It was a time of peace, the peace which arises naturally and is not something that has to be fought for. At the end of the month which no longer existed, we feasted and lit every lamp. Some even lit beacons, risking remonstrance from our new masters, but if anyone noticed, nothing was said. In all the temples, peg calendars were adjusted to keep the time of the seasons in line.

At the Armilustrium we stepped back into Roman time. Although I had no appetite for facing Scapula, my presence was expected at the great gathering of troops and I rode at the head of the Cohors Atrebatum. Katuaros and I watched the low sun gilding Scapula's parade dress. He was a well-exercised man and for once the muscular curves of the cuirass matched what was underneath. He stood proud at the rostrum wearing his bronze helmet and red plumes to announce to the assembled troops that the first four years of Roman administration had been a dismal failure.

'We are not here to administrate! We are here to conquer! Rebels harry our frontiers daily – howling packs of barbarians! We shall destroy those mangy wolves. Under my command, we shall push for the western coast and offer anyone who is in the way a choice: accept *humanitas* or go to the underworld. You' – he addressed the massed units representing the four legions – 'you, my army, were born to fight, not to dig dykes and build palisades. The frontier of the empire must be Ocean itself!'

His words caught like sparks in the dry tinder of disaffected soldiery. The peaceful years of Plautius were not what they had enlisted for. Yes! Ocean! Yes! My horse grew restless beneath me, side-stepping and snorting, a reflection of my own feelings. I exchanged a glance with Katuaros. Was everything we had planned to be overturned? His expression reflected my concern.

Scapula brought his oratory to a climax with the announcement that, though we were celebrating Armilustrium, the army would not be retiring for the winter.

'Our enemies play dirty. They have no rules of war. They are quick to mobilise, much quicker than us, and only have to wake up early on a fine day to launch an attack on the frontier. All troops will remain stationed where they are.'

There was a lot of grumbling at this. Scapula berated them. 'What are you? Soldiers or road-builders? Show us your mettle!'

I sent the cohort to Aquae Sulis under the charge of the deceptively sweet-looking Mouse Ears to deal with Enemnos. 'If you have to act, act,' I told him. 'Don't wait on any orders from me.'

It was at Samhain that Enemnos made his move, crossing the river to take possession of the Hot Springs, but the Cohors Atrebatum drove him and his wild forces back over the river to a camp on a broad-browed hill.

It was with some pride that I reported this to the governor in person.

'So, you have a treaty?'

'No, just the defeat of an enemy.'

Scapula frowned. 'I'll believe he's conquered when I see his head on a spear.'

20
THE COUNCIL OF DRUIDS

At the winter solstice I garrisoned the cohort at Gleva. It was unseasonably mild but the men needed a rest. While the fort was distracted by the week-long feast of Saturnalia, I went alone with Mandred and a small escort into wild Ferylloog to attend a council of druids at the Temple of Cuda, one of the many temples that lined the west bank of Severn river, each on its own high place. The day was short. Any trepidation we might have felt in the dark woods crackling with mast and snapped twigs was exacerbated when we found ourselves at dusk accompanied by loping, slavering beasts. 'Hounds!' I told the men. 'Not wolves!'

They muttered behind me. Hounds? On their own? Were they feral?

'They are leading us safely to the Temple of Cuda,' I said. 'They are our eyes!' More muttering, about Feryloog being haunted, but soon we came to the path leading up to the temple and found Maglos waiting for us.

'Greetings!' I said, and he wagged his tail. 'Is your master here?' Maglos gave a short, gruff bark and turned to escort us up the bluff to the temple. At the end of the steep path we paused to get our breath back before entering the outer sanctum where about twenty druids sat cross-legged around a fire. Apnodens rose to welcome me, his eyes full of affection and friendship. I knew several of those present and was accepted not as King Togidubnus, or the prefect of the Cohors Atrebatum, but simply as Delfos, the son of Innogen. He wore the regalia of Nodens and sat in the priest's chair. 'We hear there was a battle at the Hot Springs?'

'Enemnos tried to take the place by force. We expelled him.'

'You need to heal this rift in Dobunnia.'

'How?'

'Sulis will help. She is angry at what is happening at her springs. You need to placate the goddess and what she wants most is to see Branwen safely home, for Branwen is the priestess of the Swale spring, Swale being just another name for Sulis. Branwen's love for the goddess is heartfelt and genuine. Get her home.'

I slumped under the feeling of helplessness. And guilt. *It's your fault*, I heard Branwen say. *You took me from Swale. It is all your fault*.

Apnodens explained that the council was engaged in deep work. The great bronze calendar that had always been kept at Venonis, the place of the great gatherings, had been ritually buried to save it from the smelting forges of the Romans. Now three of the druid priests, including Apnodens, were making wooden versions; part of the purpose of this council was to compare their work one with another and check their computations.

'Can you predict eclipses?' I asked.

'Yes, and many other forms of celestial phenomena, but the druids of Brigantia look after that. Here we predict the coming of the Salmon.'

'What is the Salmon?'

'A great big fish,' he said, staring at me with mocking eyes.

'I mean, what causes that surge in the water?'

He shrugged. 'I've examined it as often as I can, standing in the water and letting it wash over me – with my back to it, of course, despite all temptation to look it in the eye. It's powerful here, but not as much as it is by the time it reaches Gleva. Then it's a wave. Here a swell; there a wave. That's all I can say. A gift – or a warning – from Oceanus. It relates to the tides, of course, but has a nine-year cycle, which makes it possible to predict the days of its coming.'

'The day and the hour?'

'No, not so precise. We know that it will come each month when the tide changes direction, but the great swell happens only twice a year. We can compute whether it will come in the spring or the autumn, morning or evening, and can even find the day, but the hour remains a mystery until it's upon us.'

Reports were made to the council, coming from all over the country, about druid sufferings at the hand of Rome, about the exodus west, about fears for the future. I expected them to be supporters of Caratacus but they saw him as a breaker of traditions and recognised him as a cause of our troubles. 'But', they said, 'we are old. It is the younger ones amongst us who flock to Caratacus, prepared to fight.'

The druids have never fought in any battle throughout our long history of tribal conflict. An audible shiver ran round the room. 'We break with our laws at our peril,' said Apnodens.

'Do you know where he is?' I asked.

'Caratacus? He is here.'

'In Ferylloog?'

'Sometimes. He travels a lot, like you. From the coast of the Durotriges to the borders of Brigantia.'

'What?' I was staggered. 'As far as Brigantia?'

'Like you, he is establishing his kingdom and negotiating, always negotiating with the neighbours.'

'But the Brigantes are loyal to Rome.'

'Tenuously,' said one.

'Cartimandua would never desert Rome,' I replied.

'Not while she stands to gain wealth, no. But what about her husband, Venutius? His values seem purer than hers.'

'He is her consort; he does her bidding,' I said.

They all looked at me quizzically.

'By law,' said Apnodens. 'But in practice?'

I'd met Venutius several times at the Provincial Councils. He'd never said anything to make me suspect him of disloyalty, either to his wife or to Rome. 'He might look like a Carvetian chieftain, but he plays the part of consort well,' I said.

It seemed that Caratacus was forming a chain of allies across the country, from the land of the Ordovices to Icenia. 'Making a rope of them to choke Roman expansion,' they said.

'Icenia?'

'Prasutagus is finding it difficult to be the obedient servant.'

I remembered the high priest with the forked beard who had offered to be my father. He had so much of Verica about him that I had not given the offer any thought.

'And then there are the Trinovantes, to the south of the Iceni, always at their border, weeping and wailing and calling for help.'

'What's happened to them is unjustified,' I said. 'Rome is exploiting their weakness and making an example of them.'

'While Prasutagus declares himself a king friendly to Rome, he takes in refugees.'

'So Caratacus is talking to all these tribes?'

'It was hard for him to raise a resistance army during the time of Plautius. Now Scapula is doing it for him.'

Mandred and I exchanged a worried glance. 'Does Caratacus intend to engage with the enemy along the whole frontier, from Lindinis to Lindum?'

'Face to face. Right across the country. Gaining Brigantia as an ally is imperative. Previous battles have been impassioned and ill-thought-through. Now he's planning everything. And the core of the plan is this: once the battle begins, disaffected Britons within the province will rise up behind the Romans.'

The scale of this disaffection shocked me. 'Why are you telling me this?'

'We fear that the Dobunni will be destroyed.'

'Destroyed by whom?'

'Caratacus and Scapula both, for Dobunnia will be their battleground.'

'When?'

'Soon. Before Imbolc.'

'So, a winter battle?' Scapula's prediction was coming true.

'The Britons are not bound by the same conventions as the Romans. Winter gives us advantage over men who need to wear socks.'

The company laughed, but I was not in the mood.

'Where is Caratacus going to strike first?'

'Gleva.'

I jumped to my feet, agitated.

'It is the first safe crossing point on Severn river,' they said. 'You have a month to warn Scapula and get the place properly defended.'

'You want me to warn Scapula?'

'We do not want war. It would be carnage. Caratacus thinks he can win through sheer weight of numbers, but those numbers would rapidly dwindle under the onslaught of Roman weapons and missiles.'

'Will you warn Scapula?' Apnodens asked.

'I have no influence over the governor,' I said. 'He doesn't trust me and will want to know where I got this information.'

Apnodens leant forwards and looked me straight in the eye. 'Everything depends on you. You are the linchpin. Your good relations with Aulus Plautius have kept Britain steady these last four years. It is imperative you forge a similar relationship with Scapula.'

'They are very different men,' I said morosely. 'It's Vespasian I shall warn, and he will pass it on.'

When the moon was high in the sky and owls were hooting over the land, I was offered a mattress by the fire where I lay awake, tormented. Had I been born to oversee the destruction of my mother's people? Had I been born, even, to cause it? I tossed and turned feverishly. This hour was memory time for the druids and I was mercifully distracted by their soft chantings of all the metres of our poetry, the names of the months and the mnemonics for remembering intercalary years and the cycles of the heavens. As the calendar of the Britons became threatened, the druids were taking it into themselves, into their ancestral memory, to be stored there like a hoard of gold in the ground until better times. At last I fell asleep and the names and knowledge dropped into my own well of memory.

When I had time alone with Apnodens, I spoke to him about our troubled friendship. 'I regret my anger, back in the spring.'

'As do I,' he replied. 'But it saddens me that you must ride with them, fight with them, be one of them.'

'I don't do any of those things. The Cohors Atrebatum is independent, but yes, I do keep good relations with the Romans. It is the only way I can achieve peace and feed the people.'

'Achieve peace? Is it something that may be achieved? Do you even know what it is?'

His words put me on the back foot. I had never questioned the word peace. It's something everyone knows. 'Keep peace?' I ventured.

'That's better. Not right, but better. How is your health?'

'I am fit in body, but not in soul.' I told him about the letter I'd got from Branwen. 'She's released me from all obligations.'

'When did you receive this?'

'Almost a year ago.'

'And you didn't tell me?'

'I was going to, but if you would care to remember the mood you were in . . .'

'Ah, yes.' He smiled. 'I was in the wrong place and was working my way out like a thorn.'

I could not think of Twelve Elms being the wrong place.

'The wrong place for me,' he explained. 'It was too comfortable. I was shirking my duty so the god sent his hounds. Have you replied to her?'

'A thousand times in my mind, but I've written nothing. I can't find what to say.'

'Do you have the letter with you?'

'Always,' said Mandred, who fetched it from our bags and handed it to him. Apnodens opened it, held his palm just above the words for a while, then lifted it to his ear as if to listen to it. 'Harsh words,' he said, 'coming from hurt. Behind them, the sound of her crying. Oh . . .' He felt the impact of her sorrow.

'I don't know what to say,' I muttered.

'Would you like me to write it for you?'

'You can't write.'

'Well, I can, but I prefer not to. I could always dictate.'

And so it happened, this strange letter written from the two men who loved Branwen, acting as one.

Branwen, this is the voice of Apnodens in the hand of Delfos. We both miss you as we would miss air if deprived of it. He remains faithful to the promises he made to you and your father, but, should you wish to be released from your vows, he would honour that. For he loves you. Branwen, I do my best and pray to the spirits and gods for your return, but understand that this is not the place you left. I can say no more. Delfos is exhausted by his efforts to keep the peace and uphold justice. Do not be angry with him. Do not be angry. He is a man of duty who trusts the gods. Your Apnodens, in the hand of the king, in Ferylloog.

'The hand of the king . . .' Apnodens mused. 'How are you king?'

'Well, my father died,' I said lamely.

'It's just assumed, then? Who by?'

'The Atrebates, the Romans, the other kings of Britain.'

'By you? Is it just assumed by you?'

'What do you mean?'

He tapped me on the chest. 'Has that assumption changed anything in here? No. Assumption of position – it gives you nothing.'

'What do I need?'

'Authority. The authority of the gods and good spirits.'

'How is that obtained?'

'Through the ceremony of investiture.'

'I was told it must wait until either Branwen was home or the heavens smiled upon it.'

'Leave it to me. I'll help you.'

And from that day on we were planning, trying to find an auspicious time and place, but each time we did, Rome got in the way.

Apnodens intended to stay at the temple. 'If I need to move, then my dogs and I will go deep into the trees and the Romans will never find us. You do understand, don't you, my friend?' He reached out and squeezed my arm. 'We've called you because we need your protection. Not necessarily overt. We're not asking you to stand up for us against Scapula. Just continue the work you are good at, work of a subtle kind of influence.'

'I think you overestimate my powers.'

'I think we do not. In the years since the invasion, the Sanctuary of the Wheel has remained invisible to the Romans. You and the Shee have done that. Work that magic on our forest. Put around rumours of wolves.'

'Rumours? The wolves are real.'

'I mean the wolves with eyes that glow like red embers in the night, who can sniff out the scent of sleeping soldiers and have their guts before they've woken up.'

'Oh, those wolves,' I said, laughing. 'Yes, I'll warn them.'

'And then there is the Salmon.' He moved the day peg in the wooden calendar. 'The Salmon is coming.'

AD 48

21
SURRENDER OF WEAPONS

After the strange mildness, a brutal winter set in. We rejoined the cohort in barracks at Gleva. Around Imbolc I grew restless, wanting to be back at Twelve Elms to help with any foaling that had started early, for the newborns would not survive these temperatures and must be housed. Mandred made me stay put, saying that we would die on the road, that the centaurs had coped before I had come and would be coping now. About half a moon after Imbolc, when the days were stretching out and the woods alive with birdsong, there was a rapid thaw and storms, one a week it seemed, thrashed the trees and flooded the rivers, already in spate with meltwater. The troops at Gleva were shamed one evening by the arrival of Vespasian and a unit of the Second, marching through torrential rain as if nothing were happening at all.

'There are rumours of a planned incursion here at Gleva,' Vespasian told me as he dismounted, water dripping off the peak of his helmet. 'Apparently Caratacus has not punished the Dobunni enough for their betrayal of him. He's killed their king, taken the king's daughter, and still wants more.'

'I doubt even Caratacus will come out in such weather as this. The fire of rebellion in his men will be, well, dampened.'

'That's a Briton for you,' he said. 'Always dashing into smoky huts whenever it rains.'

I bristled but said nothing and ushered him indoors.

'Heard the latest from Rome?' he asked.

'I doubt it.'

'If you must live like a recluse . . .'

'Recluse? I rarely stop travelling. Do you know how much effort it takes to keep the people quiet? Recluse? Ha! I've spent years establishing schools and temples throughout my territories, explaining the changes in tax and administration to any man of reason I can find, subduing the passions of men of no reason. The trickle of druids west is becoming a torrent. So that's something else I have to reassure everyone about. You change the calendar, you make us keep records in writing, you tax us to pay for your occupation. What are the Britons left with?'

'Rome,' said Vespasian, and smiled.

'Rome!'

'Last year we celebrated eight hundred years since her foundation,' he said proudly. 'Imagine that. How many grandfathers between us and Romulus?'

'Imagine . . .' I wondered at his delusion of being a pure Roman, he whose own ancestors were Spanish peasants.

'Delfos, you seem distracted. Do you want to hear what's been happening or not?'

I sighed, expecting him to read out dispatches about great parades or political machinations.

'Passienus Crispus ,' he said.

'What about him?' I asked, suddenly alert.

'He was murdered. Midwinter. Yes, the great senator, twice consul and the richest man in the empire.'

Crispus, the husband of Agrippina. Crispus, the master of the house where Branwen was.

'Murdered? Who by? How?'

'Poison. Usually means a woman. My money is on his wife,' Vespasian said. 'It's always the wife, especially when a fortune is involved. And what a fortune! Agrippina is now the richest woman alive.'

'How? Does she inherit?'

'No, but her son does, and he is still a boy. Of course, they will blame the death of Crispus on someone else, whoever it was Agrippina hired to do the deed. Next on the hit list will be Messalina, mark my words, and then Claudius and Agrippina, uncle and niece, will be widower and widow.'

'So?' I must have looked very stupid.

'So they marry.'

'Uncle and niece? It's against the law!'

'Laws can be changed.'

'If that happened, wouldn't it be obvious to everyone that they had planned it?'

'Yes, it would. The just and the virtuous will declaim against evil in the Senate and probably lose their lives for their impudence. Everyone else will keep quiet. That's Rome for you.'

I was gripped by foreboding.

'How are things here, amongst the northern Dobunni?' he asked, changing the subject. 'Delfos? Are you still with me?' He had come up from the south on the Albios Way via Aquae Sulis. 'After his defeat by your cohort, Enemnos agreed to retreat to the Mendips, but he's still on that hill overlooking the Hot Springs. We have closed off all access routes but it's turning into a long siege. I can't spare the men, and he knows it.'

'I should have got that treaty,' I groaned.

'A treaty won't help. We need to get rid of him.' Vespasian whacked me on the back. 'Up, soldier!' Was it spite that made me choose that moment to tell him of Caratacus's plan to face the Romans along the entire frontier? Vespasian blanched but he did not crumple.

'How do you know this?' he demanded.

'Intelligence coming out of Ferylloog. Those Silures I captured and released? They repaid me with information.'

Vespasian snorted. 'Well, don't tell Scapula that, at least not in that tone of voice. "The clemency of Togidubnus" has become a euphemism for weakness amongst the officers of the governor.'

'Perhaps they'll think again now,' I said, but Vespasian was listening only to his own thoughts.

'We need to strengthen the defences here,' he said at last. 'We have talked ourselves into a false belief that the conquest was quick and victorious, that the battle is won, that all we have to do is to settle the locals and make Britain pay for it. It's not true, is it?'

'It was never true.'

The week before spring equinox, I went to Noviomagus. It was now surrounded by dykes as well as ditches. The flimsy wooden palisades of the fort had been replaced by a foundation course of hard flint with a wall of timber on top. I found Katuaros at the Equinox Fair being held in the bustling marketplace, where people were shaking off their winter cobwebs and greeting the equality of day and night with an irrepressible desire to buy something. A new plaid, a piece of the fine red pottery which shone like wax, baskets, salted meats, cheese, fresh wild greenery. Having bought myself some sweet dried grapes, I turned and there he was, walking amongst his people, a head above the crowd with a small boy with hair the colour of alder sitting on his broad shoulders. Father and son.

And now my envy of my foster brother became rank but, like a pile of rotting seaweed, it disappeared with the next backwash of a wave.

'Take him, will you?' Katuaros lifted up the four-year-old Rufus and put him on the shoulders of 'Uncle Delfos'. And so we walked the market as a family and my mood turned to honey.

I wanted to buy a brooch for Ricoba, and asked Rufus to choose one. I felt his breath on my cheek as he leaned forwards intently to see what was on offer. I was expecting him to choose a very expensive swan in silver, but he pointed to an enamelled raven. As I was making the purchase, there was a ruckus at the gate. The market fell quiet and the shoppers drew back to allow entry for a unit of Romans. 'Where is your chief?' they demanded. The very parting of the crowd led them to us.

'Tiberius Claudius Catuarus?'

Katuaros nodded and, lifting Rufus from my shoulders, set him on the ground and then straightened to introduce me. 'This is Tiberius Claudius Togidubnus.'

'Oh?' said the tribune. 'Well, that saves us a journey. I have come to tell you that, by order of the governor, Publius Ostorius Scapula, all Britons are to surrender their weapons. We expect you to make sure that it's peaceful.'

Katuaros remained standing but his knees buckled.

'Not here!' I told the tribune. 'Not in our territories. We have a treaty!'

171

'The governor is showing no favouritism.'

'Favouritism?'

'All new laws apply to all people. There are as many rebels within as without. Some of the recent attacks have involved no borders. Some of them from your own Dobunni in the south,' he said pointedly to me. 'Therefore we draw teeth. Bears without teeth bite no one.'

'Still have claws, though,' muttered Katuaros in dialect.

'I made a formal arrangement with Aulus Plautius . . .' I repeated, beginning to sound lame.

'What? That nothing applies to you?' said the tribune. 'That's also cancelled.'

How tempting to respond in kind and say: In that case, you are no longer welcome in the land of the Atrebates. But of course, the result of that would have been a lashing.

I went up the rostrum in the middle of the market and addressed the crowd, repeating the order in their own tongue, and was met with cries of fury.

'Listen!' thundered the tribune, standing beside me. 'If after a week we find any man armed, he will be immediately executed, along with his family.'

This I translated, although in a softer tone. Catching a glance from Katuaros I realised for the first time that he had doubts about my choice of allegiance. Over these past years, his loyalty had been to me, not to Rome. Would it hold?

'Do as they say,' I told the people of Noviomagus, 'and continue to live in peace.'

'At what price?' someone shouted.

'Where's the honour?'

'How are we to defend ourselves?'

'A Briton without a sword is a eunuch!'

I was glad I was there to take the brunt of their anger, sparing Katuaros, but that evening, Debonia made me less than welcome. 'What have you brought down on us?'

'Me? It is Caratacus who's caused all this.'

'Caratacus . . .' muttered my foster brother. 'With every passing day under Scapula, the name Caratacus becomes more attractive.'

'You can't be serious. He killed your father!'

'Well, that's the peculiar magic of the man. I hated him when he was head of the Catuvellauni but now he's head of Britain . . .'

I snorted.

'Of British resistance, I mean.'

'I thought you were loyal to Rome!'

'I was. I am. But Scapula is wearing my loyalty threadbare.'

He took his beautiful sword from her sheath and ran his thumb down her blade. 'Firebreath,' he said low. 'I watched you born in the crucible and the mould. You have served me well all these years. But now it is time for you to return.'

He turned to me. 'Firebreath must be sacrificed,' he said

I looked at him askance. It was his most treasured possession.

'I have let her down. She was made to fight, not be kept in an armoury. I mean to return her to where she came from, to sink down, down, down, into Annwn An offering to the gods.'

During the night, we went out of the house with his sword wrapped in linen. He had watched her born of molten metal, had seen her patterning of pewter-coloured flames emerge as if from Annwn. The deep magic of the forge. As our ancestors had done, we went to water, feeling the grief of loss, the deep pain of sacrifice. We took her to the jetty and, with a prayer to Manannan, the god of waters, Katuaros unwrapped his beloved sword and held her aloft. The ritual required the sword be swung three times round his head but with his weak shoulder he could not do that. I took her from him to perform the rite and hurl Firebreath out into the deep channel leading to the sea. Katuaros might have been sacrificing his own child, such was his cry, echoing across the water, for it was not just a sword that we threw to the deeps, but the past, and all the hopes and expectations that had proved vain. 'Kings without arms . . .' Katuaros said.

'Become prefects with a standard-issue gladius.'

He breathed deeply then nodded. 'A gladius. Ugly and utilitarian.'

I laughed. 'You think enemies should be slain with beauty?'

'It honours their spirit,' he replied. He was right and I felt chastised. We turned back towards the house, its lime-washed daub making it glow in the moonlight. A Roman-style house, in which were sleeping his wife, his son and an infant a few months old. To my consternation, Katuaros's eyes filled with tears.

'Don't look back,' I urged him. 'Or forward. You are alive, you are loved. It's enough.'

'It's not what I wanted.'

I was surprised. He'd always been very clear about what he wanted: a parcel of land, a big house, a family.

'What did you truly want?'

'To kill Caratacus with Firebreath. It was why I had her made. That was my purpose in life, and it's gone. Even if I still had her, I don't have the strength. I've lost to him. Again.'

This had been true ever since Caratacus had thrown him into the basin of the Seven Springs in the year of the invasion, but only now did he allow himself to believe it. My brave foster brother, he of the long stride, the bellowing laugh, the fearlessness; he who caught the boar; who had taken on Caratacus one-to-one in his effort to save Calleva; he, that Katuaros, had just been drowned with his sword. And here was the reality, a nova-toga, a magistrate, joint-king, but not a warrior. And still I envied him. Why? Because he was a father.

When the Romans returned a week later to collect the weapons, we made sure that enough were there to make a convincing pile. I promised an iron bar to every man who gave up his sword, on the tacit understanding that, in due course, if necessary, he could use the bar to make a new one. The most beautiful and ceremonial blades went to the gods; even then, we kept a few for the Romans, so as not to arouse suspicion. I surrendered my father Verica's own sword to make a great demonstration of our willingness to co-operate.

'Wise of you,' said the tribune. He told me about a stead in Cantia. 'Thinking themselves clever, they hid their swords and daggers by thrusting them into their thatched roofs. When we came and found no weapons, we set fire to the stead and all its stinking pigsties. The weapons fell with a clatter, one after another.'

'What happened to the people?'

'The order of the governor was upheld.'

'Which was?'

He would not say. I only discovered later that, on a charge of sedition, every male in the stead, young, old, infant, had had his right hand cut off.

The Atrebates were furious that the demand to give up the weapons applied to them. Had I not signed a treaty exempting them from such things? My fury was matched by that of Prasutagus of the Iceni and other kings loyal to Rome whose trust had been similarly abused. We were all striving to keep our peoples quiet. And failing. If I close my eyes now, I still see pictures of wretched families watching their homes burn; still smell the acrid stench of damp thatch on fire; still hear the explosive resistance of those who would not give up anything, except their lives. I smart at the memories. If Scapula had been trying to avoid a rebellion, he had gone the wrong way about it. There is no such thing as an unarmed Briton, not while there is iron in the ground, trees in the wood and stones in the river.

Over in the Far West, on those distant hills, beacons began to burn. I could read the signals. I knew what was coming.

22

COHORS ATREBATUM

Returning to the fort at Gleva, I found the post from Rome in a pile on my table. It was at least a month out of date, having come via the forts at Yellowhammer Hill and Corinium. I sifted through the tablets and letters quickly, looking for one in particular, which I found dated January.

Branvena, filia regis Esii Dobunnorum, Togidubno Atrebatum suo salutem. On this date a.d. III Kal Januarius I make a prayer for you to the goddess Sulis, praying that this finds you in good health.

Every day I read your letter from Apnodens. It gives me hope. Hope, like a single drop of water in a parched land. Hope that there will be more hope to come. To live, I must hope.

A man has died because of me. Am I lost? Is my soul condemned now to eternity in Hades? Please ask Apnodens for me. My only friend here is the son of my mistress. Five years my junior, yet he protects me. He says the man deserved to die.

Are you well, Delfos? Has everything settled under your good government? Are the people happy? Could they do without you now for a while?

You would not recognise me. I am fifteen. My mistress says she will marry me off to a fellow slave. I have only to give the word. I will never give the word. I wait on the goddess and her goodness. I pray that we shall meet again. Why do you never come to Rome? What delays you? Your betrothed, Branwen.

A letter three months old. 'A man has died because of me.' What was she referring to so circumspectly? The death of Passienus Crispus, murdered by his wife at the hands of another? I'd only just arrived at Gleva but I needed to go to Corinium to see if there was anything to be learned. I went to Ricoba's house to say hello and goodbye all at once.

She was ill. It was obvious at a glance, but she struggled against herself, more stoical than the Stoics, determined not to falter.

'You've come and now you're going?' she asked.

I explained why and her expression changed. 'Do you think Branwen killed her master?' I asked.

'Of course not. That doesn't mean she hasn't been accused of it.'

'What does your mirror say?' I handed her the beautiful disc of polished bronze etched with designs no Roman could ever understand. It was too heavy for her: she adjusted my hands so that I was holding it for her at the correct angle. She peered into the mirror, as one might peer into water or smoke. I could see its light reflected in her eyes which, I noticed for the first time, were growing milky.

'What do you see, Mother?'

'Be at rest. Be at peace. Stay still. There is no need for you to hare across the land looking for news; it will come to you in good time. There is nothing for you to worry about, and yet you worry. Go at once if you must but you'll be back soon enough. So, goodbye!'

I stared at her, she at me. The desire to gallop over the hills bit me like ants, but she – or the spirits – were calling on me to trust the mirror.

'Of course,' Ricoba said, 'a wise man would send a messenger.'

The camp prefect of Corinium was able to tell me something of what was happening in Rome. I asked him about Passienus Crispus and he told me it was now known that he had been poisoned by a slave, who had recently been put to death.

It was like drowning. It was as if he were speaking to me underwater, his words long and drawn-out. 'Was she given a trial?' I asked, and my words boomed in my own ears.

'She? It was a man.'

I surfaced. 'A man?'

'Passienus Crispus was murdered by a slave who had a grievance, we don't know what, because we don't really believe it. According to rumour, the slave was offered manumission if he poisoned the master.'

'Who by?'

The camp prefect smiled. The wife. It's always the wife.

We were dining together when a breathless messenger arrived saying Gleva was under attack. I jumped to my feet.

'Go at once if you must,' said the camp prefect, 'and blunder through the dark, or wait until morning when I can organise a unit of infantry to support you.'

Leaving the unit to follow on in the morning, I rode through the dark without blundering, my way lit by the stars and the guidance of Mandred. When we reached the Rim of the Cauldron, the view from the escarpment over the vale was a shimmering wonder which even I, in that state of supreme agitation, could not ignore. We rested the horses while we stared at the universe in its immensity. I remembered one night in Rome when Seneca had his best students stay awake by the power of their own will. One by one the lamps of the city had guttered and died until all that remained was the glow of fires from the potteries. It, too, had been a night of dark moon, and we stayed awake easily in wonder at the star fields.

'Those stars,' our teacher had said, 'seem to us to be tiny dots.'

'They do,' I had said. 'Pinpricks in the night sky.'

'Now, imagine you are on one of them looking at our world. It, too, would appear to be a dot. And if you and I are but dots on the surface of the world, how do we appear to the star people?'

'Smaller than dots.'

'Invisible?'

'Yes, invisible.'

'So your worries, concerns, discomforts, fears – what of them in the scale of the universe?'

'Nothing.'

'Nothing at all.'

Ricoba had been right. This racing back and forth had been a mistake.

I drew a deep breath. In the far distance, Ferylloog, illuminated by many fires. 'He is here,' I whispered.

'Caratacus?' Mandred whistled.

'In the forest.'

The Gleva fort heaved with those crowding in for protection. From the western watchtower at dawn, we could see a large throng of Silures hollering war cries on the far bank of Severn river. In spate from meltwater at its source in the Silurian hills, the ford was impassable and would be for days to come. I told the people sheltering in the fort to go back to their homes, that we would sound the trumpets should there be any danger. Meanwhile, I rode out to the river, expecting to see Caratacus on the far bank, but the war band was led by one of his captains.

He bellowed to me across the water. 'Just thought we'd stop by to say hello. Been travelling a lot, have we? This is just a warning, Togidubnus!' he shouted. 'Never be off your guard!' With that he wheeled away, his troops following.

I was too tired to do anything but take the advice. I resolved never to be off my guard again, no matter how pressing other business might be. As for going to Rome, it was unthinkable.

The enemy withdrew with the floodwaters. By the time we were able to cross the river, they had disappeared and the danger had passed. What worried me more was the mood of the Britons. Since the arrival of Scapula and his aggressive policies, things had become harder to control. I could see signs of disaffection everywhere, but sometimes its expression was so benign I failed to recognise it for what it was. Take, for example, our native love of confusing foreigners.

I heard about some Roman legionaries in Calleva asking directions to a particular tavern. An old Briton told them the way with great detail, turn left, second right, left again, and then left again. They asked him to repeat it. 'Turn left, first right, right again, and then left again. But,' he said, after several repetitions, each slightly different so as to addle their brains, 'by the time you get there, you'll find it closed for lunch.' This amusement, which had the Callevans laughing each time they went to that tavern – *closed for lunch!* – came at a cost. The Britons might be succeeding in making the Romans look fools, but only by appearing to be fools themselves. Overuse of queer logic was resulting in a reputation for inbreeding. But perhaps that itself was a layer of protection, for even Romans don't execute men for being stupid. Had any soldier realised he was the butt of a British joke, the outcome would have been dire. It was far safer to play at word games than hiding milestones or moving boundary markers: such things were tacit acts of rebellion. No, the Britons of the new *civitates* were not rebels; they were just cooked in the brains by their smoky homes. 'They have all the intelligence of kippers,' the legionaries said.

It wasn't just the tame Callevans having fun at the expense of the Romans. The rebel army was playing the same game. Caratacus, we heard, was in the land of the Cornovii, the land of hills, high hills, long hills, hills that are blue in the distance. But which hill was his? To baffle the Romans, the Cornovii started to call many of their hills 'the Camp of Caratacus' and misdirected our scouts at every opportunity. Caratacus had, we heard, sixty thousand men, but our scouts, always investigating the wrong hill, never saw them. How could a rebel army of that number just disappear? The locals explained by hissing that word that explains all mysteries: *Sheeee*. Caratacus, we were told, died at the Battle of Verlamion in the year of the conquest and was then reborn, fully grown, a man of nearly thirty years, in Siluria. He had powers beyond the human, could come and go at will, was beyond capture and feasted on heads. Caratacus of the hills, Caradoc of the mountains, Caradoc of the clouds, Caratacus of the cataracts. The songs about him were everywhere. I sometimes wondered if any of my men secretly admired him, but you can drive yourself mad with such thoughts. I decided to presume the best in them, and they repaid me with their best.

Ricoba was staying in the house of a nephew in Gleva. On one unannounced visit I caught her lying on a pallet under several woollen blankets the colours of dawn. I say 'caught' because that's what she called it, leaping up as I entered. 'Don't tell anyone you caught me. I'm fine, but my body needed a rest.' I did not want to trouble or upset her, but she knew right away that something was wrong. 'Well?' she asked.

'Branwen didn't kill Passienus Crispus.'

'Perhaps she didn't kill anyone, is innocent of murder but has caused a death . . .' Ricoba paused, musing.

'What is it?'

'Evil eye, sour thoughts, actual curses – we women have a whole arsenal that doesn't require poison or knives. Someone troubled her – how old did you say she is now? Fifteen? Well, yes, someone troubled her all right, and she cursed him. That will be it.'

'And he died?'

'A curse from a bardic princess? Of course. But it would look like an accident. I doubt anyone suspected her. She's just alone with her conscience and no one to guide her, poor wee thing. I wonder . . . What if she was troubled badly? What if she was interfered with? How would you react to that?'

'Well, if he wasn't already dead I'd have to kill him.'

She laughed shortly. 'Seriously, Delfos. Could you marry someone who has been deflowered?'

'That would depend on her virtue.'

'Which in itself depends on her virginity.'

'That makes no sense. It implies that a married woman has no virtue. If my betrothed had been deflowered against her will, but remained faithful, then of course I would marry her. Though I might think twice about anyone who can curse so powerfully.'

Ricoba snorted. 'So tell me, wise man, what is fidelity?'

'It is devotion to one man. A faithful woman is a one-man woman.'

'Right answer,' she said, closing her eyes. 'And from what I hear of Rome, not true of many.'

'I don't know. You hear rumours of scandalous infidelities, but then I look at the wife of Seneca, or the wife of Vespasian, and wonder if fidelity isn't the norm. Vespasian told me a story about Agrippina. After her first husband died, she married another rich and powerful man. In front of a large group of married women, her mother-in-law denounced her morals and slapped her round the face. Everyone takes that as a story against Agrippina, but in fact it is a story that tells us much about Roman wives. Agrippina is the oddity, not the norm.'

Ricoba nodded. 'Yes, I see.'

I went on. 'Seneca says that men have to work hard to gain virtue, practising the virtues – courage, patience, generosity – whereas women have to work hard to keep the virtue they are naturally endowed with.'

'I like your Seneca.'

'He would love you. Now, Mother, would you allow me to have you taken by chariot to Twelve Elms?'

'No.'

'It will be safer there, and more comfortable.'

'No.'

'Mother, obedience to your king is a virtue you do not seem to be naturally endowed with.'

Her eyes twinkled. 'Oh, all right. If it will make you happy.'

Mandred rushed in, breathless. 'Scapula!'

'What?'

'He's here. Just arrived. Unexpected.'

'The wretch gives me no notice,' I grumbled. 'I must go to him.'

'Good,' Ricoba said, 'I can have a bit of peace.'

'Now, Mother, I only want to help.'

'I know you do,' she said. Glancing at me, there was suddenly a vulnerable look in her eyes. 'But you go and may good fortune go with you. My powers are weak,' she said, 'but not so weak that I can't see the monster in that man. Take every care, Delfos, every care.'

'It's Caratacus we need to be worried about. That attack on the ford – that worried me. You were my first thought. I want you away from Gleva.'

'Get out of here,' she wheezed. 'You do me no good at all. I'll go to Twelve Elms when I'm better.'

'You will go now!'

She chuckled to herself. 'Shall I go? Can he make me? Should I resist?'

I left the house, but not before I'd had a word with the aunts, telling them she needed to be given something to make her drowsy and then to be carried on a chariot to the Grove of Twelve Elms.

The unrest on the frontier erupted every now and again in insurgencies. Scapula praised his own foresight in having had the weapons called in. It seemed not to occur to him that, had he not called them in, there would not be this level of disturbance. He looked tired, his cheeks sunken. He considered it was time to push the western frontier right up to the threshold of Siluria, which meant crossing both Severn and Wye and subduing Ferylloog, which lay in between. He wanted to hear from me details of the place and any obstacles he might encounter. He wanted to know how many troops we had and whether we needed more cohorts to be drafted in, probably from the Twentieth.

'Numbers won't help,' I said. 'Ferylloog is thickly forested.'

'So, our first move should be to cut down the trees?'

'It wouldn't help,' I said. 'It would only expose precipitous rocks and crags. It's not marching land, by any stretch of the imagination.'

'I hear you've been doing good work with your cohort, fighting in native fashion. Rushing in, rushing out, circling round and rushing back in again. No honour in that, of course, but it's effective, I can see that. So would your cohort be able to clear Ferylloog for us?'

I did not know what to say, for in truth I did not want Ferylloog cleared. It was its own self. It had to be protected. 'I doubt it,' I said.

'So what do you suggest? At least if we fire the trees, the rebels will have nowhere to hide.'

'There is a whole population there who are not rebels.'

'Are they loyal to Rome?'

'No, but not hostile either. They just want to be left alone.'

He scoffed at this and told me to write a report 'with some practical suggestions'.

We dined together that evening. I was wearing my hair in a topknot, a fashion popular amongst the Cohors Atrebatum, enabling us to be both long-haired and short-haired at once. I shared Scapula's couch, dressed in a toga with my hair done up like a barbarian. Some of my tattoos showed. He took me in with a glance. He had a winning way of treating legates such as Vespasian as his equal, but kings he made very conscious of their inferiority. He kept pausing in his conversation to give me synonyms for Roman words he thought might be too difficult for me. I wanted to push my signet ring of citizenship in his face, to impress his handsome nose with TOG.REX. Had I done so, I would have been bound to a post and flogged to the bone the next day. I inhaled and reined in my horse of passion.

'Tell me about your cohort,' he said. 'I understand it is not a standard auxiliary unit.'

'We have one century of infantry but the rest are cavalry familiar with the terrain, drawn only from my territories and thus friends of Rome.'

'Are you?'

'Am I what?'

'A friend of Rome?'

'Is it in doubt?'

'I've heard you're the grandson of Commius. Who knows what traits you have inherited from him?'

I wanted to jump to my grandfather's defence and say that if his allegiance changed, the Romans had only their own treacherous selves to blame. I resisted the impulse.

'Get your hair cut,' Scapula said. 'Your British troops can wear what they like, but their commanders must be seen to be Roman.'

23
LAKE FOR SALE

Ferylloog was quiet. The rebels had withdrawn into Siluria. Scapula, however, wanted us to make sure of it and, before he left to return north, ordered us to continue flushing out any resistance. We disappeared into the trees and spent the summer in council with local leaders, negotiating treaties when it was feasible. In times of rest, I indulged myself looking for the Woman, a druid priestess they said could blind a man with her beauty who lived alone in an abandoned temple, high up amongst the rocks of Wye gorge. Who else could it be? My dreams during those nights were filled with Theana. Before I could find the place, however, news came of more trouble at Gleva and we left Ferylloog at a gallop, heading for Llyn Llyw, the Sacred Lake and home of the Salmon of Wisdom. A nova-toga had been murdered when he tried to collect taxes.

'Set upon,' said the locals. 'Set upon and beaten up. Not murdered.'

'But is he dead?'

'Oh, yes, he's dead all right.'

There was a subtle network across the land now, like cobwebs in long grass, a layer of administration between the army and the people. *Publicani* were travelling the territories, raising taxes on the strength of the census held three years earlier, turning the tithes on our lands and livestock into coin for the imperial treasury. Tax on fields and produce we expected, but a lake? Did they not know it was sacred?

By the time we got there, the mob had calmed a little. Having no weapons other than axes and slings, in their fury they had destroyed the escort of the *publicanus*, creating a heap

185

of torsos and dismembered limbs. Who needs weapons when you have rage? Heads were instant trophies, but what to do with the rest? Some called for a pyre, some wanted to feed the fish, others to build a sky platform and give the bodies to the birds. They fell back as I arrived and greeted me as king rather than prefect of a cohort. What should they do? With the druids moving into Siluria, there was no one to consult on the right action. I came down in favour of a pyre. As they built it, they set up a chant, calling on the gods to bring death to all Romans. I was relieved to discover that they did not include me in this.

A unit from Gleva fort approached, fully armed. Not a single individual was distinguishable in this many-legged wall of metal that marched towards the people, now becoming raucous in their invocations to the gods of war. Jeering on one side; a steady tramping on the other. More helpless slaughter. I could not bear it. Before they engaged, I put on my torc and stepped out to stand between the Britons and the Romans in druid fashion, raising my arms and calling on the benign gods of the place. The junior tribune in charge approached and turned to address the crowd.

'Go back to your homes. We shall be lenient. We understand that this murder of a land agent and his aides about official business was by brute savages who do not understand *humanitas*.'

'We understand all right! This lake is sacred. It belongs to its spirits. You want to sell it!'

'Is this true?' I snapped at the tribune.

He shrugged. 'It's to go up for auction in Rome. We're having it evaluated.'

'To what end?'

'To pay for improvements at Gleva.'

Why would anyone so far away be interested in a body of water in western Britain? Where was the profit? 'So what was the agent doing?' I asked.

'Establishing the cost and practicality of drainage.'

Drainage?

Of course . . . The bronze of our grandfathers lay in that lake, and the silver. Shields, torcs, beautiful swords: given to the goddess Havren and to the Salmon of Wisdom, with which some wealthy Roman was going to make himself even wealthier. Could I tell the tribune about the Salmon of Wisdom? About swans who swim on moonlight? Of course not.

'This lake is mine,' I growled.

'What?'

'It is in Dobunnic land and, as such, belongs to the king.' He looked stunned, as did the Glevenses. Of course it was not my property, nor theirs, it belonged to the gods, but quickly the people understood what I was doing and backed me up. 'My property,' I repeated, 'and I have given no permission for its sale, let alone its drainage. This is theft! Theft by the Roman State! How dare you sell my property to some speculator in Rome?'

The tribune fell back under the force of my wrath. 'It must have been a mistake . . .' he spluttered. 'An error in the census.'

'Stand down!' I thundered. 'Have your men stand down at once! This lake will not be drained!'

He glared at me momentarily but, taking in the strength of my cohort and the mood of the crowd, quickly subsided. 'It's not for me to say. We need to consult the governor.'

'He's busy in Cornovia,' I said quickly. 'I'm sure he won't want to be bothered by such a minor consideration.'

I was worried Scapula might know that, by our laws, the lake was not mine. It belonged to itself and its presiding spirit. We calculated that, if he came at all, he would arrive in a week and a day. A week and a day . . . it allowed me enough time to get back into Ferylloog and seek counsel. I needed the wisdom of Apnodens.

I left the cohort under the command of Mouse Ears to protect the lake from further violation, and rode off alone with Mandred, wearing my druid plaid that Apnodens had given me for protection when travelling alone. A druid on a native horse without any bags or armed escort: any bandits in the vicinity would not bother to intercept me.

There are two main paths south through Ferylloog. The shortest way is through the woods but the safest follows the winding river with a temple on every bluff, at every bend. The Temple of Nodens was a long way downstream from the Temple of Cuda where the council had been held. To save time, I opted for the dangerous path through the woods.

A hilly country, Ferylloog, betwixt Severn and Wye, where the trees grow amongst the ferny rubble of moss-covered boulders, their gnarled roots splaying out like the feet of dragons, reaching for trickling brooks and springs. Even in high summer it is cold and damp in the tree-dense woods, dark under the thick canopy overhead. A sunless, dripping place. You get jumpy. A charcoal-burning camp seems threatening, as does an iron mine. Mandred and I went as fast as we could under the drooping branches bearded with silver lichens, only slowing when crossing a stream on a slippery wooden bridge. Squirrels crashed overhead, jumping from tree to tree, chased by martens. Starlings squabbled amongst the brambles. Close to where the river bends in the great loop called 'the Torc', we slowed and were starting to relax, beguiled by this otherworldly beauty, when some of the trees seemed to move.

They came out on the path in front of us – and behind – men with green mantles, leaf crowns, lichen beards, charcoaled faces. I was quiet; they were quiet. Then they parted as their chief came forward to speak to me.

'Delfos!' he cried, as if greeting a long-lost friend.

Caratacus . . . The last time I had been this close to him, my harpist lay dead at his feet. If my knees gave way, I hid it well. Caught between rage and fear, hating this man beyond reason, there in the enchanted woods I had to face him with what courage I could muster.

'Where are you off to?' he asked. 'All on your own?'

'To the Temple of Nodens. I need counsel.'

He laughed loud. 'Yes, you do!'

Ignoring the comment, I told him what had happened at the Sacred Lake.

'Now do you see? Now do you see?' he shouted. 'The nature of these overlords who spit on our gods? And on us!' He calmed, sniffed, reappraised me. 'You do well to seek help.'

'Advice, not help.'

He shrugged. 'Druid advice? There is no need to go all the way to the temple. It comes to you.' He whistled and from labyrinthine passages between the gnarled and twisted trees came Apnodens with Maglos at his heel. I stared at him in shock.

'We know about the lake,' Apnodens said, running his hand over my plaid as if greeting an old friend.

'Delfos, Delfos,' said Caratacus. 'You are like a man struggling to wake up. Join us. What are you doing fighting with and for them, against *me*? Me, your brother in spirit. Join us!'

'You don't understand. I am not on their side, and I am certainly not on yours. I pass between you, working always towards peace.'

'Peace!' He spat on the ground. 'There won't be peace until the Romans are gone. Where's Scapula?'

'On his way. He'll arrive at Gleva in a few days to arbitrate on the lake.'

Caratacus came close. I could see wrinkles on his weathered face. He was as part of the woods as the lichens. 'You are joking?' he said quietly. 'You really think he would find in our favour?'

'I shall tell him that the lake, as part of Dobunnic lands, is mine and if he requisitions it, I'll report it to the treasury and accuse him of theft. It's not mine, of course, it's sacred land, but he needn't know that.'

Caratacus stood back. 'You think that will solve it? Haven't you heard what he's doing to the Cornovii? Battering them into submission. It will be the Dobunni next spring, being rendered toothless, bloodied and servile. Where then your peace? Delfos, Delfos . . .' He came close again. 'Join me. Regain your pride, your manhood, your dignity.'

I kept my face hard against his blandishments. 'I wasn't aware I'd lost them. I also retain my wits, whereas you . . . Do you really think you can win?'

'We may not have the resources of the Romans, but we have the strength and ardour of Britons and the gods and the Shee to help us.'

'For what do you fight?' I asked. 'To protect your property?'

'I've lost it all.'

'For fame, then, or pride?'

'I fight for freedom!' he thundered, anger displacing the charm.

'What kind of freedom? Freedom from what?'

'Servitude, you turnip. Slavery!'

189

'You are going the wrong way about it. If you wish, I could persuade Scapula to hold council with you.'

'Council of what? Peace? Peace has to be fought for, like everything else. It's the only thing they understand.' Caratacus turned and strode to the nearest tree to relieve himself.

'If you would agree to becoming a client king, king of Siluria . . .' I said to his back. I turned to Apnodens with a hopeless shrug.

'Do you know when Scapula is likely to arrive?' he asked.

'Any day soon.'

'We must send him a message that you are here in Ferylloog, at the Torc, prisoner of Caratacus.'

'And am I? A prisoner of Caratacus?'

'Of course you are,' Caratacus said, rejoining us. 'My hostage, should I need one, but how much would Scapula pay to have you back? What's your value? Certainly not your company. Always yawping about peace, justice and right action, as if you know all about such things and I do not. Take him, Apnodens. I will set a guard on your camp.'

Apnodens took us to a shelter he had made himself in the woods. I told him how shocked and disheartened I was to discover that he had joined the rebels. He told me not to believe my eyes but would say no more.

Caratacus sent a fleet-footed rumour up to Gleva telling of an insurgence at the Torc, that he had crossed the Severn and was on the Roman side of the river. It was not long before we heard that Scapula was on his way with a detachment of the Fourteenth. As the Romans marched into the tongue of land, they found they had been misinformed. The Britons were on the curving far bank, a great war host gathering on the bluffs of the western side of the river, all around the Torc. Broad, placid Severn appears shallow at that place and is slashed by sandbanks. It seems you can hop across from island to island, as indeed you may if you know the tides. Scapula took advice from the locals, who assured him that the crossing was easy and that the best time would be in the morning at what the Romans understood to be the fifth hour. Tides. Peoples of the Mediterranean are not familiar with them. With regard to knowledge of tides, Britons have the advantage.

Having camped for the night, the troops rose early. When the sun was high enough to glance off the sluggish brown water in a thousand lights a roar went up from the Britons in every man's dialect, a cacophony of languages all expressing the same rage. Limed hair, white and spiky, eyes bulging, temples throbbing, teeth bared, muscles flexed, these painted men were beyond reason. Carnyces yowled; drums thundered. There would be no negotiation here. They would fight for freedom or die in the attempt. They brandished their swords and spears and stuck their tongues out of mouths gaping with rage and disdain. With their feet thundering on the turf, and swords banging against shields, they stomped their message of resistance to these foreigners who had taken their lands, their sacred places, their sacred calendar, their women, their animals, their freedom. The uproar was deafening, but another sounding horn quietened them and caused them to fall backwards. Caratacus rode forward in his chariot and came to rest on the bank facing the Romans across the river. Scapula likewise rode out across the shallows to the first sandbank. It was his first view of his enemy and he was not disappointed. Eyes wide, he stared at Caratacus, a glowing lion of a man in the prime of his years, half-naked, fully painted, standing beside his seated charioteer.

Scapula bellowed across the water, ordering the Britons to lay down their arms. He spoke in Latin. 'What?' Caratacus shouted back, also in Latin. 'Surrender to a man who wants to desecrate our Sacred Lake? Never! For your sacrilege, Manannan the god of waters will swallow you, every man of you. Suck you down into his watery depths.' If I was surprised that Caratacus not only understood Latin but spoke it perfectly well, it was muffled by the circumstances. It was only later that I wondered about it.

'I am under the protection of Jupiter and Mars,' Scapula boomed. 'Your ugly gods do not frighten me.'

'So come and get us, you oily bastards!'

Scapula ordered his infantry forward. They started to wade out, shields ready to protect themselves from spears which, so far, had yet to be thrown. Then the attention of every man shifted as the Woman of the Temple rode out of the woods on a white mare. Theana, naked but for a cloak of iridescent feathers. Kingfishers and mallards and winter ducks by the hundred had died to make her look immortal. She fluttered in the breeze coming off the river. With smiling eyes full of admiration, Caratacus watched his sister taunt the enemy.

'You!' she shouted at the troops in the water. 'Put one more step in this holy river and your seed will rot.' They were aroused and doused all in one: I knew the feeling. Halfway across and approaching the second sandbank, they hesitated but, forced to choose between a curse and their commander's wrath, pressed on. Impelled by fear and lured by lust.

Scapula, apparently impervious to naked women, was turning the colour of beef in his rage. 'Don't listen to the witch!' he ordered his men.

'As for you,' Theana cried, 'Publius Ostorius Scapula. As for you, you will never see home again! Never again! You will die in this land that hates you, and your spirit will be homeless. A yawning scream without a voice. An eternity of horror!'

The curse seemed to skim across the water. I saw him stagger backwards as if hit by a stone, but then he rallied and urged his men forward. Half the unit was wading when a sudden silence came upon the river. To a man they all stopped and looked at the water rising up to their knees. And then it came, the sea rushing round the bend upstream towards them followed by a great frothing bulge in the water. The sea was coming for them! Furious Oceanus curving and scrolling, bent on revenge for their sacrilege. The wall of water, higher than the tallest of them, uprooting trees, hurling up the slimy ooze slamming into banks and recoiling. Eels leapt skywards.

'*Retreat!*' Scapula screamed at his troops.

A carnyx sounded downstream. 'The Salmon is coming?' I asked Apnodens.

'It is!'

'You knew? You've planned this? How? Impossible!'

'Remember I keep the calendar of tides,' he said.

'But how did you get us all here at this time?'

'I didn't. That would be the Shee.'

And some misinformation from the locals.

As the Torc was the first major bend in the river there was only one blast of a carnyx before the frightening sea swell appeared.

'Look!' Theana cried to the Romans, pointing downstream. 'Look what's coming! Death!' The marooned men who had reached the sandbank turned to see the great wave approaching. Even I knew you must never look at the Salmon but always keep your back to him. Within moments it had swallowed the sandbank and all was water. 'Death to the Romans!' she screamed. 'Death to the governor! Death to the emperor! Death to you all, and an eternity in your own grim underworld!'

They stood, helpless and terrified. The Salmon surged, caught the Romans facing it and tossed them like dead twigs. On the Salmon's back rode the coracles, the men inside wielding whips to make sure any legionary who got to his feet went down again. The Romans floundered, fell, struggled up, floundered again, all to the roaring laughter of the Britons. Slingshot rained down on them; many were injured, blood stained the river, but no one died. The Britons taunted them, watching them think they were going to die, seeing their unmanly fear, laughing when hardened infantrymen called out for their mothers. Legionaries, it seems, are like cats: proud, arrogant and terrified of water. Their loss of dignity was catastrophic but only for their reputation.

I took advantage of the uproar of triumph amongst the spear-shaking, ululating rebels to slip away. 'I'm going back to Gleva,' I told Apnodens.

'Are you insane? Stay, you idiot, stay.'

'What, as a prisoner of Caratacus? No thanks. It may be preferable to being Scapula's monkey, but what would become of my family, of Katuaros, of Ricoba? What of my peoples? The Glevenses. The Corinians. What of Twelve Elms? You may be able to walk away, Apnodens. I cannot. I have a sense of responsibility.'

'Caratacus does not intend to hold you either as prisoner or hostage. He wants you as his ally. But on his terms.'

'You want me to change sides?'

'Your grandfather did it often enough.'

'I am not my grandfather! I am myself. If my allegiance is to Rome, it's because I believe they can bring peace to these fractious islands. But you, I cannot believe you are siding with Caratacus.'

'I've sided with no one. But listen to this, he and he alone is concerned about the safety of the druids.'

'So am I! He is not alone!'

'You think you can protect us by being allied as you are to the Roman army?'

'I have the ear of governors and legates. I can move things from within, gently, without force. If I can summon Reason to speak for me, she will change minds.'

'I think you have made a terrible mistake,' he said, and turned away to melt into the jeering crowd.

Thus, with our friendship bruised if not torn again, I rode off fast towards Gleva on the track which follows the river, the torpid river with its elephant skin the colour of mud. Romans on that side; Britons on this. How often have I asked myself which side should I be on? The answer is always the same: Be as the river.

24
THE TEMPLE OF DOGS

'I heard you were a prisoner of Caratacus,' said Scapula.

'I escaped.'

'Escaped? Or were never prisoner in the first place?'

'Escaped. It was easy. The Britons were drunk on victory and mead.'

'Not my idea of a victory, playing a trick on your enemy. So, I came to Gleva at your behest. Something about a lake. Were you luring me into that trap?'

'Not at all! While I was waiting for you, I went into Ferylloog to seek counsel from a temple priest. I had no knowledge of what they were planning.'

'Did you get his advice?'

'There wasn't time. Events unfolded too quickly. Events, I have to say, inspired by what has happened at Llyn Llyw, the great lake to the north of here. It has been requisitioned without my permission and is to be sold at auction in Rome. The people rose up and killed the land agent and his escort.'

To my surprise, Scapula nodded. 'Something was entered wrongly in the census. The lake was recorded as free land.'

'Free' meaning what, up for grabs? I tried to keep my temper. There was nothing inaccurate in the census record: these men had just come to drain the lake, flooding Gleva in the process, to dredge out its treasures and then confess to it being 'a mistake'. I said nothing. Scapula was still angry after his humiliation at the Torc. His eyes – they moved back and forth, back and forth. It was slight, little more than a tremor, but I could see it, the restlessness of his gaze.

'I'll ensure nothing happens to the lake,' he said. 'Those

responsible will be brought to justice. I have no desire for the fame of my glorious city to be tarnished by corruption.'

I was astonished. How could anyone believe that Roman glory was not already tarnished beyond repair?

'At least you have one thing out of all this,' I said. 'You know where Caratacus is.'

'I want those woods fired, reduced to blackened stumps.'

'Understood, but listen, the iron there is worth twice anything found elsewhere. Iron needs mining. Mining needs miners. Miners need homes and communities. Leave the clearing of Ferylloog to me and my cohort. We'll comb it, over and over, until nothing remains that is not loyal to Rome.'

'I will leave it to you,' he said, 'but show no mercy. Flush out that devil, and if I hear any word of Caratacus being harboured there, the whole territory will be torched.'

I turned to leave.

'By the way, if I see you again wearing your hair in that stupid topknot, I shall take it off myself with a sharp blade and your head with it.'

Hearing on good authority that Caratacus had withdrawn west of Wye river, I went alone into Ferylloog, leaving Mandred to look after Ricoba at Twelve Elms. The Temple of Nodens was a few miles south of the Torc, high on a bluff looking east over the river, facing the dawn. A steep path of loose red sandstone was guarded by two wolfhounds and I had to wait there until Maglos trotted down from the top to meet me and accompany me up to the gate that opened on to the temple and its precincts. Inside the surrounding wall, nothing could be seen of the world but the blue sky above, the passing clouds and swooping birds. Doors to all outhouses and accommodations were closed but you could tell by light flickering through cracks that all were in use, either for study, prayer or healing.

A friendly acolyte approached to offer a foot-wash, asking what had brought me here, what ailments did I have? 'We only have five patients at the moment – plenty of room for another.' When I explained the purpose of my visit he took me to the chamber of the chief priest. It was bare and simple with few possessions other than his musical instruments and the feathers, pine cones, and pieces of mossy bark he picked up on his walks. Apnodens offered me a cup of warmed mead from a small cauldron at the fire.

'What ails you, friend?' he asked.

'A rupture.'

'Of the soul? I'm suffering from the same condition.' He smiled as I took the mead.

'I was so disturbed to see you'd gone over to him,' I said.

'Gone over? That implies I'd previously been on the side of the Romans. Not something I'm aware of.'

I remembered the image of neutrality I'd had at the river, watching it flow between opposing banks. Don't take sides: it was the way of Apnodens.

'You're right,' I said. 'I only know you as your own man. I suppose I was thinking of the last great gathering, when your father was advocating peace with the Romans.'

'For which he was murdered.'

'So why join the murderers?'

'I haven't. Don't you see? There is no possibility for any druid to be a friend of Rome, therefore we run with the rebels by default. Or seem to. What happened when you got back to Gleva?'

'Scapula said a mistake had been made in the census and that he would make sure justice was done.'

'Truly?'

'He says he does not want the reputation of Rome to be besmirched by corruption.'

We looked at each other and then burst out laughing. 'There was no mistake, of course,' I said. 'We just caught someone out in his murky transactions. But Scapula is dealing with it and, yes, Llyn Llyw is safe.'

Apnodens laughed again.

'What is it?'

'Their faces when they thought they were going to die! Robbed of all dignity, they were.'

Our laughter restored our friendship. I crossed to the peg calendar hanging near the door. 'I suspect you can predict with a greater precision than you've claimed.'

'You think we planned to knock Scapula's troops off their feet? I promise you, we can't be that precise. If the Romans and the Salmon were in the same place at the same time, look to the Otherworld for the agency. There again, look to yourself. You appear to be the one initiating everything.'

'Me?'

'The Shee then, with you as their hapless agent. Caratacus lured you and the Romans with you, with the intention of a lethal ambush. He was fully stoked for war. But when I told him the Sacred Salmon was coming, and that the gods desired peace, he changed it into a game.'

The guard dogs at the base of the mound started barking and two priests went down to see who had arrived. Apnodens and I went with them out of curiosity, for it had not been a furious barking, more a howl for help. We found Mandred beside a chariot which bore what appeared to be a bundle of blankets on the floor. 'She insisted,' he said. 'Come out, Mother!'

'I also insisted!' I said. 'I told her she was not to travel but stay where she was!'

'You did, so you did, but you weren't there. Come out, Mother!'

The blankets stirred. One of the guard hounds whined and pawed at the bundle. 'Geddoff!' Ricoba emerged with a piece of linen tied round her jaw and knotted on the top of her head. She had the toothache. Looking meaner than usual, and tetchier, she glared at the dog. 'Geddown!' she said.

'Oh, Mother, what ails you?' Apnodens reached out to her face.

She recoiled. 'Don't thouch meh!'

'Do you want healing or not?'

Ricoba made a sound, part-moan, part-sigh, part-scream. She swore by elderwort for such infections but apparently had been lax in her collecting. Apnodens had her carried up to the temple and into a healing room where he made up a concoction of thyme, yarrow and mint for her to drink and gave her a salve of elderwort to deaden the pain.

'Rub it on the gum,' he told her, 'and apply it yourself. I don't want my hand bitten off.'

'I thought I could thleep here and the god would cure me with a dweam.'

'When did you last sleep with that pain?'

'I don't wemember.'

Apnodens sent for the temple's doctor, who poked about in a tray of metal instruments and picked up a pair of pincers.

Ricoba's noises intensified and got muddled with a curse against all doctors.

'You are swallowing poison,' Apnodens said. 'You'll be dead by the end of the week. What's it to be?'

'Go on then,' she said sourly and, unknotting the linen bandage, opened her mouth wide. Swivelling her terrified eyes to me, she held up a hand. I took hold of it and squeezed. Squeezed hard as the pincers went in. The tooth came out in a gush of pus. Ricoba yowled. The dogs outside took up her cry.

The doctor gave her a purgative and encouraged her to vomit up as much as she could. When she was limp with exhaustion, Apnodens had her taken into the inner *cella* of the temple. The door opened to a shuffling, slavering sound which I couldn't interpret; then the door closed again, trapping beloved Mother with whatever was within. She was there all night. In the morning she reappeared as her old self and would say nothing of what had taken place other than to make an expression of extreme disgust. She seemed strangely dishevelled.

'Did the god appear?' I asked.

'Ha! Did the god appear? Ha!' And she went off to the room she had been allocated to settle in and sleep all day.

Mandred and I left the temple to exercise our horses, followed by a pack of hounds eager to run with us. The woodland rides were exhilarating. Concentrating hard on avoiding all obstructions, jumping exposed roots and fallen trees, we were taken by surprise. Before I knew what was happening, I was felled by slingshot hitting me squarely in the chest and reawakening as if by fire all the pains of cracked ribs I had suffered last time I was unhorsed. I writhed crying amongst the bracken while the dogs chased off the robbers, sending them scampering into the hills, yelling that they were being chased by the hounds of Nodens. After which I remember nothing.

Mandred took me back to the temple draped like a sack of fleeces over the back of my horse. Ricoba, blaming everyone for not looking after me properly, drove off all druids and doctors and druid-doctors, and brought me round with her own therapies, mostly lullabies and little bags of dried meadowsweet waved under my nose. Once I was conscious, Apnodens re-established his authority and drove off Ricoba.

'Who were they?' I asked. 'Bandits?'

He gave a slight shake of his head.

'Silures? Feryllooges?'

'Southern Dobunni. Enemnos wants you dead, apparently without a battle.' He reached out and pressed his thumb against the place between my eyebrows and kept it there. 'You are cold.'

It was true, I was, though I had not noticed, but now the heat began to flow through me again.

'You are ill, Delfos.'

'No, I am not. I was stunned by a stone. It stung like a bee but nothing is broken. I am fine.'

'Sick in the soul. You have not healed as I had hoped. You will spend the night in the inner sanctum.'

'He will not!' Ricoba shouted from the other side of the door hangings where she had been listening. 'Don't do it, Delfos! It's terrible!'

'Sick in the soul,' Apnodens repeated, ignoring her. 'I once thought it was the loss of Branwen that was gnawing away at you, but the root is something else.'

'What?'

'I don't know. But it will be revealed to you in your dreams by the hounds of Nodens.'

He had me change into a simple linen tunic and guided me into the *cella*, opening the door to a room where five wolfhounds leapt to their feet as if to attention. He introduced me to them as Togidubnus, King of the Atrebates and Dobunni, chanted a hymn to Nodens and asked the dogs to begin the work of healing. He left softly, closing the door behind him. I stood there frozen while the dogs moved round me, sniffing at my feet. One stood up on its hind legs and put its paws on my shoulders, compelling me to sit. With a powerful nudge of its nose, I went from sitting to lying. I lay on the hard ground with my eyes tightly closed as the dogs moved around me, sniffing and nudging, then – O, horror! – licking. Long, rough, tongues drooling over my bare face and arms; warm, smelly breath. They licked me until I thought I must vomit. Then the lead dog nudged me to turn over, and I lay on my face while my back was kneaded by their huge paws. I know that the saliva of dogs has healing properties, but I always thought its use was on cuts and abrasions. Now, licked all over, I only grew increasingly tense and disgusted. Then a hound, perhaps the largest of them, sat on my rump and lay along my spine with its forepaws over my shoulders so that I could not move. Other dogs joined it until I was covered by a hot blanket of living dogs. And thus we spent that dreadful night.

But in my dreams . . . I was with Innogen, my mother, sitting on her lap and listening to lullabies. Then I was in the bed of Messalina, gazing at her beauty as she slept. Messalina, Messalina, the girl who had inducted me into the ways of love when I was sixteen. She opened her eyes, stared at me and smiled, as if to say 'all is well'. And her face became that of Theana. Then I was in a Roman bathhouse being massaged with oil and scraped clean. Then I was stretched out, my head against a pile of hides, my feet towards the communal fire, listening to a tale of giants and heroes sung by a bard. Then a young girl possessed of a pet bat skipped into my dreams, plumped down on the grass and began to sing with a voice so many years older than she was. Then I was lying on the Hill of the Albios Horse, on the chalky bed of the horse's foreleg. Next I was flying low over a green and hilly land whose beauty made my heart ache.

A dog licked away the salt tears seeping out of my eyes.

In the morning, I emerged covered in long grey hairs and drool, looking, I was told, remarkably happy. Apnodens took me into his room and had me recount my dreams. I told him what I could remember, but found I choked on the recollections of Messalina.

'Who was this woman?'

'We were lovers, when I lived in the house of her husband, Claudius.'

'The emperor?' Apnodens whistled softly. 'Do you miss her?'

I hid my face in my hands, wondering. I missed her body, that was for sure. But I didn't miss the sense of danger in being close to her. 'I didn't love her. Perhaps I should have. Perhaps that's what she needed and deserved. I just took her mind off her farting husband. She has a son.' I was almost whispering.

'So?'

Then I confessed what I had never spoken out loud. 'There's a possibility he is mine.'

Apnodens sat cross-legged, rocking back and forth while he communed with his god. 'The loss, that which you grieve for . . .'

'Branwen.'

'No.'

'Who then? Messalina?'

'There is guilt there, but not loss. Tell me more.'

The strongest recollection was of flying over green fields, woods, bare hills. 'It was warm. It was foaling time. Rivers and streams that veined the land sparkled in the sun. Flocks of waterfowl took off from a marsh, flew round me, flew on. Accepting me. It was so peaceful, so beautiful . . .'

He mused on this, then said. 'The name of your loss is Britain. That is your constant pain, your agony, to which you awaken every morning. All your efforts these past years to find a middle way, to make the absorption of Britain into the empire a peaceful one, to sow harmony rather than discord, have resulted in a shell of a man. In your heart, you swap sides daily. Flip-flop. Now on this side, now on that, as if the sheer speed of your turning will create the illusion of stillness. Do you understand what I am saying?'

'I think so.'

'Remind me what the Oracle at Delphi told you.'

I closed my eyes and returned to the trickling springs of Kastalia, with Pythia in the blue-black shadows sniffing the waters, smelling violets, and then speaking with the voice of Apollo: *Go home, O orphan, go home and marry your mother to your father*.

'Marry your mother to your father,' Apnodens repeated.

'By the time I got here, Innogen was already dead. Verica followed not long after. But I thought I understood. The Oracle did not mean my parents, but what they represented: father

202

culture and mother culture. Rome and Britain. I was – I am – to marry them.'

'Have you done it?'

'I have not.' I sat with my head in my hands. 'How is it to be done?'

'Do you know what marriage is?'

'Of course.'

'Do you? Let us be guided by the gods.' He rose up to prepare the Dreaming Cup. 'You need to go to Rome.'

'Not that way! I've just spent an entire night in Annwn.'

Ignoring me, he made his pungent brew on the fire. 'Not while the governor keeps refusing you permission.' He poured the steaming liquid into a shallow bronze dish and let it cool. At last he handed me a small portion of bread to eat, then passed the cup.

I settled down for a long journey south which would take only moments. 'You do realise, don't you,' he asked, 'that it is not the Dreaming Cup that gives you these visions? For most people, it gives a period of intense reality followed by vivid dreams. For you . . . Your visions are your own.'

25
LET THE MADNESS BEGIN

Shrieking horns, strident flutes, clattering castanets: devotees rollick along in the wild procession of the Maenads. It is the Festival of Bacchus and the narrow streets and tall buildings amplify the noise. Everywhere garlands and swags of vines. Drunken youths jumping into vats of grapes and stamping out the juice. The fountains running with wine. Branwen is standing at the front of the crowd with Domitius. Now in his eleventh year, he gives the appearance of a calm, obedient young man, the richest in the empire since the death of his foster father, Passienus Crispus. But when the procession passes by, led by the lady Messalina playing the role of Ariadne abandoned by Theseus, Domitius shows himself for what he is: pubescent. He is all but panting as she passes close by, no matter that he considers her – and her son – the enemy. She is sobbing and rending her clothes in feigned grief and Domitius's freckly face goes red to the hairline. Still in her twenties, mother of two. Still beautiful. Still the wife of Claudius. Rumours of her infidelity infest the city like rats. It seems she has decided to go out and meet her fate halfway. (If they are going to accuse her of things, she may as well be guilty.)

It is all being enacted on the Field of Mars. Suddenly Domitius screams, so loudly that Branwen throws her mantle over his head as if he were a spooked horse. It does the job and she draws off the mantle as Bacchus arrives in his flamboyant chariot at the head of his own procession. He is played by a handsome young senator, the best-looking man in Rome. Fighting off wild beasts, Bacchus takes Ariadne into his chariot where he lies down with her to offer her the sky.

The union of Bacchus and Ariadne – you would have taken it for real. Under an arch of grapes, the writhing and moaning of the divine pair is a triumph of simulation, except of course, it isn't simulated.

Domitius grunts rhythmically, his eyes out on stalks.

Branwen looks to the sky and prays, for this cannot be right, the wife of the emperor copulating in public with a senator. This cannot be right. By all the gods . . .

Clouds seem to come over Rome, plunging the city into ominous darkness as before a storm. She drags the boy back to the grand house on the Palatine which is now his property, although, like all his property, it is held on his behalf by his mother.

What is she doing? What is Messalina doing? By the laws of Rome, with this act of adultery she has just divorced her husband and married another. Claudius, who has been in the port of Ostia, is borne up the river on a surge of rage. Messalina hurries to the house of her mother and locks herself in.

All Branwen knows is that on one and the same day all Rome is drunk with merriment and then sobered by anticipation of what must surely come. Domitius seems to know what's happening better than Branwen does. He taps his nose and nods like an old senator. 'It's the end of her,' he says, 'the end of her. And good riddance!'

'Shall we sing the song about the sun and the moon?'

He looks at Branwen witheringly. He is outgrowing her whimsy. He goes off to do what he loves doing above all things: listening at doors and windows.

His mother, the lady Agrippina, has good cause to hate Messalina, who sent her and her sister into exile in the first place, and who takes every opportunity to flaunt her son Britannicus as next in line to the laurel wreath. Britannicus, Claudius's only surviving son from three marriages. Messalina's son. Messalina who has lately adopted the ridiculous fashion for crimped hair, full of tight curls, that sits on her head like a hat. Agrippina is getting crosser by the moment, apparently building herself into a thunderclap. But what follows is a radiant smile for which there is no explanation. 'It will all be over soon,' she tells her son, who nods as if he knows what she is talking about.

205

During the night, the imperial boat slides into its mooring at the bridge. Everyone in Rome is quiet, listening, wondering what is happening in the imperial palace high above the forum. The lamps burn all night long. News comes from the Praetorian camp that the man who played Bacchus has been dispatched as a traitor. Claudius sends a message to Messalina, advising her to kill herself. He'll give her an hour.

All Rome hangs in suspense. In her chamber, again and again Messalina takes up the knife, only to drop it, sobbing now for real. She cannot execute herself for something she has not done. She had not married another. Just got carried away ... At last a captain of the guard comes into her room and asks her, does she need help? He wraps his firm hand around hers as she clutches the knife.

'Like this,' he says and guides the knife to her heart; when she still resists, he gives it a deft push. As she folds into death, before her eyes close, she stares straight at me. Imploring.

Bats rise up in a flutter as the keening starts. Is it for the loss of Messalina? Or for the abuse of justice and the loss of virtue in a prince? It all becomes clearer at dawn the next day. Branwen stands astonished to learn that the recently widowed Agrippina is preparing herself for remarriage to her uncle, the very recently widowed Claudius. Obvious, isn't it? She has a son of the direct line of Augustus who has inherited the fortune of Passienus Crispus. This has all been planned for years, since she returned from exile. And somehow, Domitius knows all about it, and knows that, on this day, he is about to step out from the shadow of Claudius's son, Britannicus.

'Would you like to sing the Song of the Foxes?' she asks, and he laughs. The cruelty that has been latent in him is coming to the fore and his British princess knows for a certainty that, whatever happens next, everything is about to change.

Usually at this point I wake up to ordinary reality but not this time. I am lost on my return to this world. I am in a burning wood, trees on fire all around me, the way obscured by choking smoke. Falling branches pass through me as I pass through the fire. I wake up coughing.

'What did you learn?' Apnodens asked as I came out of the trance.

206

'Messalina is dead.' I don't know how I looked but I felt ashen.

'Did you learn anything of marriage?'

'Only that it is a transient affair governed by politics and a lust for wealth.'

'So you still don't understand.'

'Understand what? The Romans? I think I do. Apnodens, you need to leave.'

'Leave?'

'Leave the temple. Leave Ferylloog. Take all your people with you. Ferylloog is going to be put to the torch.'

He stared at me, speechless.

'It's true. He told me he'd torch the trees if Caratacus was hiding here.'

'But he isn't, he's gone.'

'Leaving Scapula humiliated. He will torch the place. Smoke you all out, for he sees the druids as allies of the rebels.'

Apnodens nodded, accepting this. 'I'm going to put the silent spell on you,' he said and, wetting his fingers in a phial of sacred spring water, he sealed my lips.

'We were planning to go, anyway. We shall follow in the footsteps of our masters and go to Mona,' he said.

Mona, the most sacred of all our sacred isles, north of the land of the Ordovices.

'Meet me there,' he said and, leaning forwards, touched my brow with his.

Scapula's troops moved into Ferylloog a month later, by which time all the temples stood empty. Many fires were started which crackled through the groves but the gods gave us a wet Samhain season that put paid to any desire that Scapula might have had for a conflagration.

AD 49

26

THE SURRENDER OF HAIR

'So, the she-wolf has got her prey,' said Vespasian, reading the latest dispatch from Rome. 'Claudius and Agrippina married on New Year's Day. I'll give them five years, by which time her son will have come of age. And then, Uncle, beware.'

'Is it not against Roman law for a niece to marry an uncle?'

'It is, but he changed the law, at least for himself. Emperors are divine, remember, and not subject to mortal law.' Vespasian's face worked with sour emotions. It must have been hard to maintain loyalty to someone so morally vacuous. While most of Rome merely acted as if the doings of the emperor gave them licence for self-indulgence, a few adhered to ancient ideas of virtue, including some of the senators born of republican fathers, and at least one legate, the son of a moneylender and tax collector. 'Oh,' he said, 'here's something that will interest you.'

I quickened. 'Branwen?'

'Seneca. He's been recalled from exile. Agrippina wants him as tutor for her son.'

'I think – I thought—' I stuttered.

'What?'

'I thought Branwen was his tutor.'

'What wild rumour is that?'

I could not tell him how I knew, that I'd seen it in a vision brought on by sacred mushrooms.

'Seneca . . .' I breathed. 'Back in Rome . . .'

Vespasian opened another letter. 'Oh, by Jupiter. I'm to go back. I asked for another extension, but it's been denied. My tour of duty ends next spring.' Sweat stood out on his brow. He feared what awaited him in a city where Agrippina was the dominant power. 'I've taken a precaution,' he said. 'I arranged for my son, Titus, to share lessons with Britannicus. To my relief, they've become close and genuine friends. Say what you like about Claudius, he loves his only son. So, even if they kill me, Titus will survive. One more campaigning season and then I'll be . . .' He opened a tablet, one of a pile that had come from the governor. 'Oh, by all the gods on Olympus!'

'What now?' I gasped, wondering what could be worse than death at the hand of Agrippina.

'Scapula! He is on his way here to review the legion!' Vespasian stared at the tablet and then snapped it shut.

There was something I needed to do before I met the governor again and I set off alone on a cold but bright day, wrapped in a birrus cloak against the weather. I kept to higher ground to avoid the winter floods that lay between the fort at Yellowhammer Hill and the Sanctuary of the Wheel a few miles to the south. Delicate white and yellow flowers on the woodland floor – the first colour of spring. Spring: it used to be a season of hope, the herald of a return to the fields; now it ushered in yet more campaigns of battle and conquest.

The Sanctuary is a promontory of land; coming in from the north, the way is level. Beyond the great circle of stones, the path ends and the ground falls away on three sides; down to Thames on the right, Charwelle on the left and, ahead, to Ford at Two Rivers. I went down the spur of the promontory to the timber walkways of the ford over shallow waters and on to the confluence where I stood watching the turbulence of Thames meeting Charwelle. My eyes began to play tricks and the moving waters took the form of my father. At first he was floating just below the surface and then he rose up to meet me. Verica was not himself: this Verica, this father, cared for me, was proud of the fighting skills of my cohort and their victories against the rebels of Caratacus. He sat on a fallen tree, water cascading from his hair, king of the river, the very picture of Oceanus, of Neptune. I squatted on my heels to talk to him as

I had never spoken to him in life, confidentially, admitting to my fears and weaknesses.

'I am related to some of these men I have to fight!' I said.

'Do you think they care? If they were holding the sword to your throat, do you think a sense of kinship would save you?'

'What should I do?'

'Fight them!'

'To what end?'

'Conquest! The Romans are your people now. Are you not a citizen?'

'I am also king of the Atrebates.'

He blew through his lips. 'Fat lot of good that will do you. Grab some land, son, get those taxes diverted your way, increase your herds. Oh, and get a wife.'

'I am already betrothed.'

He snorted. 'To that pale twig of a slave? She has been deflowered. Get yourself a good virgin and have sons. Good sons. Not like you were, you flinching sniveller, but a proper son, as you have become.'

I took up a stone and hurled it at him but of course it passed right through and I was left with his laughter.

My horse nudged me from behind. When I turned I found it was not my horse but Amabel, Verica's purple and silver darling, who came for me whenever I was here at the Sanctuary, the spirit of a horse. Not the one I rode in my flying dreams. This one, the horse of my soul.

I jumped up on her back, felt her warmth, saw her breath coiling in the cold air. She broke into that lovely run of a British horse and carried me up the spur, back to the Sanctuary, turning in through the west entrance, across the ditches and into the ring of fallen stones; across the wide circle to that stone where my father had raped my mother; the stone of my conception. There she stopped to crop grass. I slid off her, went down on my knees, put my forehead on the ground and called on the gods of the place.

'You again?' It was the old druid I had met here on that occasion when, just before the invasion, Mandred and I had been temporally lost for a couple of days in the Sanctuary. A couple of days which, in this world, turned out to be three weeks.

'Yes, I'm back,' I said to the Shee-druid.

'What's it been? Six years? You said you were going to restore the Sanctuary.'

'All in good time. For now it is enough that I am preventing the Romans from coming here.'

'You are?'

'Well, I've put about rumours of hauntings that seemed to have worked. What more can I do?' I asked.

'Set the stones up again.'

'I'm not sure that will ever be possible. The Romans are here to stay. Land is being parcelled out.'

'What?' The Shee-druid was uncomprehending. 'What are they doing to the land?'

'Giving it to men deserving of reward.'

'What? The land? It's not theirs to give!'

'Tell them that. They dig a ditch, put up a palisade, call it theirs. We do much the same.'

'But you don't call it yours.'

'No, we don't. But they have documents.'

'What are documents?'

I sat with knees drawn up and my head in my hands, wondering if in fact madness was taking hold of me. When I looked up, he had gone.

I lay on the ground, curled on my side. 'Mother?'

A whisper came out of the land itself: 'It is the time. Sacrifice what has been demanded of you.'

Before I went to Rome as a boy, we had a ceremony at Noviomagus in which Verica surrendered me, his son, to the will of the gods and to Rome. We sacrificed a young bull and I was smeared with its blood. Then, after a ritual washing, I was made to kneel before the chief of the elders – the king's most senior counsellor – who took a sharpened, sacrificial knife, lifted my head by the hair and with one whistling strike cut off a lock of it. He put it in my hands. 'Feel the weight.' It had none. It was weightless. 'Yet on your head it hangs heavy. Be free of attachments, Togidubnus. Do not take sides. You are being given to Rome as surety of your father's loyalty to

212

the emperor, but remember it is a temporary sojourn; you are merely passing through. However, you need to leave your hair behind.'

And so I had been shorn, a very close cut to the scalp, to make me less exotic in the eyes of my new masters, less the barbarian. They put my hair on the fire where it sizzled and melted. When I stood up, it was as a Roman boy, although of course it takes more than a haircut. Katuaros, who had watched this through his fingers as if it were a castration, turned away from the burning. It was more than he could bear. He turned away, tossed his own heavy hair off his shoulders, ran his fingers through it, over his scalp from forehead to nape of neck, and was momentarily convulsed by a violent shudder.

At Rome I was presented to the emperor, Tiberius, as a gift. The journey had taken six weeks and my hair by this time had begun to grow. Even so, Tiberius thought it too short. He had a greenish pallor, like a drowned slug, and seemed never to go out in daylight. 'Let it grow,' he said, 'so that we can appreciate its colour more. The colour of ripe apricots. Let it curl around your ears.' As he touched my face, everything in me clenched. I had heard about such men. They were common in Rome, especially in the company of Tiberius. Pederasts. Lovers in the Greek tradition, they claimed, though they shared none of the codes of honour of the Greeks. Men who had lost any ability they might once have had to attract a woman now turned to boys whom they could command or bribe more easily to do their will. Fat, sweaty, stinking of fish sauce, garlic and wine. Son of a barbarian king, I became the prize they all fought for.

I did my best to make myself unappealing and found a tutor of the art in Claudius, nephew of Tiberius, a man many years my senior who had developed all manner of kinks and stinks to keep himself free from unwanted attention. He had some genuinely involuntary twitches but he exaggerated them; dragging his leg, stuttering, saying foolish things, he created his own solitude, and once he had noticed my distress, he invited me to keep him company. 'Curls the colour of apricots!'

'Only in lamplight.'

'Perhaps, but your fairness makes you a honey trap to wasps.' He took me to the barber for a head-shave to repel the attentions of Tiberius, then to the library where he began to teach me to read.

As I grew older, and Tiberius was succeeded by Caligula – a man so debauched we missed Tiberius – I took up wrestling to defend myself better. Wrestling and study. I divided my time between the gymnasium, the library and the classes Seneca held in the forum. I have much to thank those unctuous pederasts for – they forced me into good company and made me who I am.

When I returned to Britain, I forgot about barbers. As simple as that – just forgot about them as if they had never been. All around me, men of my age wore their hair long, plaited, braided, hanging loose. Many of them were as hairy of face as of head and had fine beards that took a single, double or triple plait well. These beards and moustaches of the men of the south were trimmed and groomed; it was Caratacus who revived the fashion for long beards, flowing beards, scraggy beards, foxtail moustaches, eyebrows like hedges. Truly barbarian, it was Caratacus who led the rebels, their chariots careering over the ground in an oceanic wave of hair to disconcert the enemy. It was the main trick of the Britons, to put the opponent off his guard with war paint, monstrous moustaches and lion manes.

It was not deliberate on my part, that my face be Roman and my hair British: I just preferred a shave to an itchy beard; but it was taken up by young men of my generation as a statement of our friendship with Rome. It marked us, revealed our allegiances. We were Britons willing to live under the rule of Rome, as opposed to Caratacus and his nit-infested troops, who would rather die. We were the pragmatic ones. The face of reason is clean-shaven. Katuaros, spurred on by his wife, had gone the whole hog and cut off his beautiful mane. I was surprised how easily he had given up his glory until one day, under the light of the sun, I noticed his pink scalp was beginning to show. That gave me a pang of grief on his behalf but he never said anything about it.

Being clean-shaven had served us well throughout the years of Plautius. It was an easy way for the governor to know who was who: the rebels, the friends, and those oily opportunists, the nova-togas, who wore everything, including their hair, in the Roman style. Now, under Scapula, there were to be only two kinds of Briton. The hairy and the clean.

I could hear the voice of Seneca within me, encouraging me. 'It's only hair. It is not who you are. You are not your hair! The wise man conducts himself so that no one notices him. Merge with the background, Delfos. Do as you have been instructed.'

I sat up and undid my hair from its knot. An ageing hand reached out and gently took my knife from me. You'd have thought it was Ricoba. Was it another of the Shee, taking the form I trusted most? No, it *was* Ricoba, whom I had left at Twelve Elms.

'Allow me . . .' She took hold of my hair and, gently, gently, cut through it with a pair of shears where I would have hacked. When she had done, she stood back and laughed. 'You look like you've had a bad fright!' She trimmed and shaped what hair I had left until I regained a little dignity. So real, so physical – those shears creaked at the hinge and sighed at the blade – it had to be a Shee illusion.

'There you are. No longer British, but not quite Roman.'

'Why are you so good to me?' I asked. 'Why do the Shee help me?'

'Because you have Shee eyes.'

'I do?'

'And in honour of your mother. Is there anything you wish for that I can grant?'

'Yes. For my betrothed to return home.'

'Only when you learn to love her will she be able to return, not before.'

She collected up and handed me the pile of hair, the weight of down in my hands, and told me to bury half of it at the conception stone. 'Give the past back to the Mother,' she said, 'and prepare yourself for the future.'

'And the other half?'

'Leave it aside for the nesting birds.'

I did as I was bidden, dedicating the offering to the Mother and to the local god, Cuma, burying half my hair and leaving a tumble of waves by the stone.

'Ricoba?'

'Yes?'

'Are you in my future?'

'I am not.' She reached out and touched my face.

'Whatever brought you into my life,' I said, 'I am grateful.'

'It was Innogen. I was with her when she died. She asked me to look after you until your woman arrived.'

'Who is my woman?'

'You know the answer to that. I wanted so much to meet her but all I have been able to do is carry you to her threshold. Find her, Delfos, learn to love, fetch her home. Caratacus will help you.'

'*What?*'

'Go with Caratacus.'

'Where?'

'Over sea, over land, over sea and up the great river.'

'To Rome? Caratacus? What are you saying, Mother?'

A great flapping of black wings brushed past me: a raven landed, filled its beak with as much hair as it could and took off. When I turned back, Ricoba had gone.

As Apnodens had said, my visions were my own. I did not need the Dreaming Cup, especially in thin places such as the Sanctuary of the Wheel. I was supposed to return to Yellowhammer Fort but on leaving the Sanctuary I just kept riding west until I came to the grove at Twelve Elms. Almost knowing what I was to find, I went into Ricoba's deep-thatch. She lay in a coma, attended by the women of the settlement, who could do nothing for her except keep her nourished and clean. They fed her as they would an orphan lamb, gently blowing tepid broth into her mouth through a hollow stalk of straw. The aunts in charge came to meet me, hands splayed out in a gesture of relief. 'You've come at last! We've been calling to the gods to send you. What happened to your hair?'

I ran my fingers roughly over my scalp. 'Sacrificed,' I said. 'What ails Ricoba?'

'Age. Age is getting the better of her. The chariot that is her body has become decrepit and can run no more, but its driver, her spirit, carries on as ever. Or it did. She lay here, telling us what to do to put the world right, how to look after you so that you become the man you truly are, what to cook, what to brew, what to pound up as a medicine for her. She lasted a week that way, and then one morning she did not wake. But she lives still.'

'Will she – can she – recover?'

'The uncles are saying not to waste time and food on her, but to let her slip unhindered into the Otherworld. But we can't. We're women. So we've waited for you and thank the gods you have come.'

'I had a vision of her. She cut my hair. With those very shears,' I said, pointing to them where they lay with the rest of her meagre possessions: her mirror, her comb and some loom weights. She had no jewellery or precious ornament, other than the enamelled brooch I had bought for her in the market at Noviomagus.

Aunts. Aunts and grandmothers. They who raise children on stories of the miraculous and downright strange, who teach us about the spirits we share the land with, about Annwn, about charms and curses. They have a remarkable tendency to look at you as if you are mad when, as a grown man, you tell them something they really ought to believe in.

'*Those* shears?' the aunt gasped.

I picked them up, chopped the air with them. The squeak of the hinge and the sigh of the blades – the same. 'Yes, these.'

The aunt put her hand on my brow to see if I was feverish. I shrugged her off rudely and went to kneel by Ricoba. I laid my head against her chest, heard the heartbeat which, though feeble, continued. She was like an old person plodding at the end of a line of migrants, the distance between her and the rest ever lengthening. After a while, I lifted my head and spoke to her expressionless face that seemed to be nothing more now than a part of her breathing, the air quietly sucked in and exhaled through the hole that was her mouth.

'Ricoba,' I whispered. 'What do *you* want? To live or to die? To stay or to move on? They are calling on me to decide, but I need you to direct me. Give me a sign. I know you can do it.'

I heard her voice in my mind. *There is no death. Only the body dies.*

There was a rustle at the door hangings, as if a creature had got caught there.

'Out! Out!' cried one of the aunts, going at it with a broom. 'Damn crow! Are you blind? Why fly into my hangings?'

I crossed quickly and snatched the broom from her, made her and the rest stand back and then held the hangings aside so that the bird – too large for a crow, far too large: a raven – hopped in. Head now to one side, now to the other. Round jet bead of an eye blacker than the blackness of its feathers. Great fat axe of a beak. A psychopomp, for sure. It hopped to the woman on the bed, jumped on to her chest – gasp of horror from the aunts – cawed thrice and then, with a mighty beating of its wings, flew across the house and out of the door, taking her soul with it.

'She's gone,' I said.

We wrapped her in her coloured linens and made a sky platform for her beyond the grove. It was what she had wanted: to feed the birds. I knew she had gone home; I knew it. What was on the platform was just a dead body: her living spirit was in Annwn, but grief came nonetheless. 'Learn to love,' she had told me, and it seemed I had.

27
GRIEVANCES

The harbour at Noviomagus thronged with merchants and sailors being ferried to and from boats in anchorage. Jetties creaked, cranes groaned, masons tapped at samples of stone piling up. Almost everyone there was Italian or Gaulish, brought in to teach us how to cut stone, lift it, transport it, to understand and value materials that we had never bothered with previously.

Mandred and I looked for anyone who might have news from Rome other than the death of Messalina or the marriage of Claudius to Agrippina. Someone who might know the effects of these events on Agrippina's household. As I meandered about, going from group to group, I was approached by victims of minor theft, cheating or bullying, or by those claiming to be falsely accused of such things. So much grumbling . . . I referred them all to the court. When, however, a party of Trinovantes from Camulodunum arrived, seeking to consult me, I arranged for them to be accommodated at the 'villa' – Debonia's grand name for the house which, though it had doubled in size, was still only a house. Its wattle and daub walls glowed with plaster painted red and white. The floor was of clay. To the Atrebates, it was a thing of wonder. To a Roman, it was laughably rustic. The Trinovantes, the Stony River tribe, led by their wizened old chief, took no notice of it.

'The Twentieth Legion is to withdraw from Camulodunum,' the chief told me. 'They are dismantling the great fort.'

'Scapula is moving everything west,' I said. 'That should be good news for you easterners.'

219

He said that Scapula was having the site of the fort converted into accommodations for veteran soldiers. 'They tell us it is for our protection, that the veterans will be called upon to deal with any local uprisings, but what do old soldiers do when there aren't any uprisings? They get drunk and beat us up. Bullying, drunkenness and whoring,' said the chief. 'We can't go out after dark and should never go out alone. They defecate and vomit in the street gutters and leave it for us to clear up. If they want anything we have, they take it, including our farmland, our livestock and our women. They even eat our chickens, our sacred chickens! If anyone dares to stand up to them, we find their bodies in the morning. We have to suffer being called backward and primitive while they blaspheme and soil the nest, eat our chickens and throw away the bones as rubbish.'

It was part of our tradition that chickens be given the same burial rites as humans.

'The women . . . We keep our girls at home, all day and all night, and they are turning as white as grubs. We are treated worse than slaves, trampled underfoot, battered by the jeering scorn of the veterans. Can you help us? Can you ask the governor to control them?'

'I will certainly talk to him next time I see him, but I warn you, my words hold little weight with Publius Ostorius Scapula.'

'There is more,' the chief continued. 'They are laying out a temple to Mars.'

'There is nothing we can do if they wish to flaunt their power and wealth.'

'Their power perhaps, but our wealth.'

'What do you mean?'

'They are making us pay for it. They say they are building it for us, therefore we must pay.'

'You couldn't pay for a flock of goats!'

The chief bridled but had to agree. 'The Catuvellauni stole everything from us. Rome overcame them and we rejoiced, but now it's difficult to see the difference between them. Everyone wants what little we have. What can we do?'

I'd heard the argument before, many times, that the Britons would profit from new roads and the conversion of their sprawling enclosures into organised settlements, and therefore should be taxed to cover the costs. There was a logic to that. But temples? To Roman gods? To an emperor who considered himself divine? I gagged on the thought. How could the Trinovantes pay? 'If you are considering violent protest,' I told them, 'don't. Do nothing to provoke the Romans.'

'How could we mount such a protest without arms?' the chief asked.

I stared at him through narrowed eyes. A smile ghosted on his lips. Of course they were armed, if only with ash spears.

'If we stay peaceful, how can we pay?' he asked.

'I'll get all the stone you need to arrive through my harbours and sell it on to you without profit. As for our own local tufa, you can have it for nothing. My offering to the god Mars.' It was all I could do, and I made sure they were well fed and rested.

Katuaros was late back from the harbour and looking thunderous. He said there was news of an attack on the Isle of Vectis, a place that frequently changed hands between the Durotriges and the Atrebates. Vespasian had won it back for us the year after the conquest but now the Durotriges were trying to recapture it. I sent an order for the Cohors Atrebatum to leave Gleva and come to the aid of Vectis, after which I set about organising a fleet of boats to ferry them across from our coast. Mandred was anxious. We did not know how many there were of the enemy or how suitable our cohort was for the terrain, which was mostly open and flat. I sent to Vespasian for back-up.

It worried me that bringing the cohort south was leaving Gleva unprotected. There was an advance unit of the Twentieth there under the command of Manlius Valens who, I was assured, could be relied upon. I would just have to trust him. Frustrated, I grew tetchy and short-tempered in court. Case after trivial case came before me of litigious men accusing their neighbours of various misdeeds; the judgements I handed out became increasingly punitive. Mandred worked hard to mitigate the effects, reminding me repeatedly that these were my people. I spent the days waiting for the cohort to arrive, listening to tedious complaints of stolen cattle, burned haycocks or appropriated fields, neighbour against neighbour in bitter litigation.

But then came the case apart.

They stood in the courtyard of the temple, a father and two grown sons. The father's face was belligerent, that of his sons, defiant. They were accused of murdering their daughter and sister in a fit of domestic savagery.

'Not so,' the father declared, raising his chin. 'It was our sacred duty!'

Many households were divided between those ready to adopt Roman ways and those not. There were a growing number of cases where strict fathers forbade their children to speak in their own language, insisting they learn Latin, and those where the elders demanded that the hearth-tongue be safeguarded and Latin never spoken. This man's daughter had been caught in the arms of a legionary. Her brothers dragged her home, raped her, maimed her, killed her, while her father looked on approvingly.

'What is this new-found moral rectitude among you?' I thundered. 'For the sake of an idea, you will murder one you have nurtured? What an obscene perversion of nature!'

'According to the laws of our ancestors,' said their advocate, 'men have the power of life and death over their wives and their children! For the honour of the family!'

'Do not speak to me of family honour. You have dishonoured us all. If you have a grievance, fight it out in the court! Let wiser men than you be the impartial judge!'

Wishing I had druids to consult, I ordered the confiscation of all their property, castration of the brothers and banishment for all three.

'Banished? From Noviomagus?' the father cried.

'From anywhere in my territories, the lands of the Atrebates and Dobunni.'

'Where should we go?'

'I don't care, but you are advised never to be caught in my lands. You are no longer members of the Atrebates nation.'

They wailed as if I'd sentenced them to death.

When the cohort arrived, they were ordered by a tribune of the Second not to cross to Vectis, where units of the legion were sweeping the Durotriges into the sea. 'Surplus to requirements,' he said. It was all I could do not to shout in his face. On the same day, we had news that there was a violent incursion by the Silures into Gleva, led by Caratacus. Had the invasion of Vectis just been a lure? I presumed so. Hoping that Gleva would be safe under Manlius Valens, I gave the men two days' rest before leading them northwest myself, relieved to be out of the stifling banality of Noviomagus, riding over downs and through forests, feeling alive again.

We arrived at Gleva to find it picking up the pieces. Caratacus had long gone, leaving only damage behind and many dead. I demanded to know what happened and Manlius Valens shrugged in feigned hopelessness. 'We were out on patrol. You know what these barbarians are like. Nothing honourable about them. They crept up on Gleva in the dark, took it by surprise, set fire to anything flammable, speared anything that moved. That bastard! He was gone by morning!'

I said nothing but stared at him, trying to read the truth behind his words. He flinched.

On the face of it, the Glevenses were angry, but I could tell this was hiding a deep sorrow. Inside they were crying. They were tired, living in a land quartered by the Romans and Enemnos. They wanted only to tend their crops and animals.

Mandred was among them, listening to their grievances, and heard something he reported straight back to me. 'I was told that Valens took his unit out on patrol as soon as he heard that Caratacus was coming.'

'Presumably in the opposite direction. I suspected as much.'

Pragmatism or cowardice? Assuming the former, I left the cohort at Gleva and returned exhausted to Twelve Elms. It was the time of first fruits, of lying under the shade of trees, listening to stories and gossip. That's how it should have been. Instead, as soon as I lay down in the grass, tears for Ricoba ran out unbidden and unstaunchable. I seemed to be fated to lose my women. My mother, my lovers, my betrothed, now my wise woman. Mandred prescribed some dancing girls from Corinium and a good drunken supper but I declined, preferring grief. I told myself repeatedly that fear of death is unmanly; that death is inevitable; that everything dies, so why mourn? But I could hardly bear the loneliness and did not know what I had done to deserve it. Most men my age either had families or companions, were ever in a crowd, looking out for one another. Apart from Mandred and an escort, I travelled alone.

At Lughnasa the people were celebrating with dance and chatter, mead and ale, children running about with rosy cheeks making figures out of large stooks of wheat. I took myself off to the paddocks where the gentle mares stood head to tail, flicking the flies off each other in the summer stillness. Only their foals had the energy to run about. It was a good year: the Roman line was beginning to show in the height and sleekness of the foals. The sun setting behind me sent long shadows out over fields of golden barley where the scythers were at work. Then the deep peace was shattered by a carnyx sounding in the distance, hounds barking, trained men calling one to another across the hills. Everyone stopped to look, listen and wonder. After the sun set beacons lit up across the land towards us from the east. Calls and beacons. It didn't take a druid priest to read those signals. From my own limited knowledge I could tell something was afoot, and it wasn't Caratacus.

I met Mandred at the grove. 'Have you heard it?'

'Yes, I've heard, but I couldn't see anything from here. Are there beacons?'

'Like chains of golden beads across the land. It's not Caratacus,' I said. 'Something is happening in the east.'

'From what I heard in the callings, the uprising we expected – it's begun.'

'The Trinovantes?'

'And the Iceni. The Romans could hardly expect the local people to pay for their own subjugation without kickback!' Mandred said. 'If this is Scapula's idea of Pax Romana, then he is creating serious trouble. Anyone would think he is wanting unrest.'

Anyone would.

I discovered it was happening all over occupied Britain, ancient communities being made to fund their own unwanted transformation, but the temple at Camulodunum was an extreme instance. No wonder, then, that the Trinovantes made an alliance with the neighbouring Iceni. It was the temple, the building of that temple, and all it represented – not least the insensitivity of the men building it – that caused the surreptitious reforging of swords.

In the middle of the night, calls came out of the west, whistling through the dark (they said it took an hour for a message carried on the wind, picked up and passed on hill to hill, to travel across the country). Caratacus was calling up Britain to join the rebels. Scapula responded by sending the Fourteenth east. Although they moved quickly, by the time they reached Camulodunum the uprising had been squashed by the veterans of the colony. Many of the leading warriors were brutally and publicly executed 'to set an example'. There was no sign of Caratacus going to their aid.

Scapula's next move was to redeploy the Twentieth on the western stretch of the frontier and the Fourteenth on the northern stretch. He sent an order for the Cohors Atrebatum to report to the Fourteenth.

I protested that my troops were required to protect northern Dobunnia from southern Dobunnia. The next message from Scapula answered none of my concerns. It was, he said, time for the great assault on Siluria and the flushing out of Caratacus. He was intending, within a year, to be standing on the furthermost headlands of an expanded empire, looking out over the western ocean. Cohors Atrebatum, he said, was to report to the legate of the Fourteenth. From being an elite and independent cohort of *exploratores*, we would be reduced to being under the command of some legionary tribune with his own ideas.

28
ENEMNOS

We paused the horses at the place where the Albios Way suddenly shelves down to the river and the sacred springs of Sulis in the basin of seven hills. To our left, the largest hill lowered over the valley. Somewhere in the woods on its summit stood the camp of Enemnos. Below, the Romans moved to and from the ford where they had built a fortlet of timber and turf. Siege engines stood listlessly at the foot of the hill too broad and high for the missiles to do any damage. In the marshes by the river, coils of steam rose as ever from three knolls but the small temple that had housed the shrine to Sulis had disappeared. What was once the goal of sacred pilgrimage was now a war base and the atmosphere of this sacred land had changed from 'otherworld' to 'this world'.

'What have we lost?' muttered Mandred.

We rode slowly down and found Vespasian in his quarters. He was thinner than when we'd last met, and tired. He had taken a spear in the thigh during one of the assaults on Enemnos's stronghold and, despite the efforts of the legionary physician, it was not healing. We rode out together along the ancient causeway to the springs, dismounting close to where the hot water gushed forth from slimy red rocks.

'You think this bog will heal my thigh?' he asked.

'Is your wound infected?

'Deep down, yes.'

'Sulis is a goddess of healing.'

'Much like our Minerva, I hear.'

'Yes, the same attributes.'

'Will she heal me, a Roman?'

'If you win her favour, yes.'

'How do I do that?'

'Through performance of rites.'

Mandred led Vespasian to a pool where the water had cooled sufficiently not to boil the bather. He helped him down some shallow stone steps and had him sit on the gravel at the bottom with the water up to his waist. Then he began to intone a prayer to Sulis.

'Ow!' Vespasian bent into the water to rub his leg. I thought the water was affecting his wound but he claimed that something had bitten him.

'A fish – or one of our primitive spirits,' said Mandred.

'By the gods, it's not only spirits who are primitive in Britain. I mean, look at this place – an untamed triad of springs in a wild marsh. Is that how you lot honour the gods?'

'It's how our gods wish it to be.'

'I don't feel welcome here,' said Vespasian.

Mandred agreed. 'You are not. Sulis is angry. Her holy sanctuary has become a battleground.'

Vespasian nodded. 'This business of the Dobunni has gone on long enough. It's just a local power struggle and shouldn't involve the army. Not when Dobunnia has a strong king.' He peered at me sceptically.

'I was sent home by Claudius to broker peace, not make war.'

'Enemnos is fighting back hard, following the example of Caratacus. We cannot afford to be detained here by a prolonged siege. We need to try your way. If anyone can talk us out of this, it's you.'

I did not share his confidence. So far I had only made treaties with those who fell over with the slightest push. I had not made one with Caratacus and saw little hope of making one with Enemnos. Vespasian moved in the water and the light of the setting sun splintered into a pool of saffron glints. I could hear the spirits whispering. I gave voice to Sulis.

'What are you prepared to give up?' I asked him.

'Give up? Nothing! We've earned every gain.'

'The new road you are laying across the springs. How necessary is it?'

'It will carry traffic from the Albios Way to a new bridge.'

'Traffic? Military? Mercantile? Across the sacred springs?'

'It will cut the journey time by an hour.'

'An hour?'

Vespasian slapped his hand down hard on the water. 'Nothing has gone right for us here. The marsh is treacherous and we've had countless cases of bad sprains, broken bones, even death on two occasions. The horses get spooked for no reason. An entire wall of the fort collapsed during building; the water cisterns leak; some of the camp whores are breaking out in suppurating rashes. And now I get a spear thrust in me and the wound will not heal. The problems here have been delaying us for months when we should be further south, subduing the Durotriges once and for all. If I were superstitious, I'd say this place is cursed. What will we give up? I'll tell you. Being patient, that's what.'

'What happened to the skulls?'

'What skulls, you son of brutes?'

'The ancestral kings. They were kept in the Temple of Sulis, the head of Esius himself among them.'

He shrugged. 'I know nothing about any skulls, or any other disgusting relic of your ancestors.'

'What happened to the shrine?'

'That crude temple that was here? It fell down, all by itself, with no help from us.'

I could only just see him through the steam, worrying at his thigh.

'Sulis needs the agency of her priests, but they've all fled. If you wish, I could send for a renowned healer in the Far West who was once the priest of Sulis.'

'What, one of your druids? To poison me in one of a hundred subtle ways?' Vespasian growled. Having climbed out of the pool, he examined his leg and found nothing there, no blood, no toothmarks. 'Must have just been a twinge,' he said. A slave dried him with towels. He winced with pain when his leg was touched. Clearly nothing either we or Sulis had done had helped.

'You need a druid healer,' I muttered.

'And you need to deal with Enemnos,' he said. 'We can't carry on wasting our resources on one rapacious warlord.

It's an internal matter for the Dobunni. You need to reunify your territory.'

'What weapons does he have?'

'Slings and spears. If there are swords, we haven't got close enough to see them.'

'You want me to tackle him alone?'

'You're the one with the gift of diplomacy.' He gazed out over the misty marshes. 'To build the road, we'll be draining this swamp.'

Small wonder that Sulis was not co-operating in his recovery. The slow, careful approach on slippery causeways through the marshes to the three steaming knolls was a large part of the healing ritual.

'For a negotiation to succeed, both sides must enjoy a benefit,' I said. 'Enemnos must surely be hungry. Offer him restored supply lines.'

'There are countless farms on that hill, plus livestock, even game. He's not hungry.'

'What, then, does he want?'

Vespasian shrugged. 'Northern Dobunnia?'

'Let's hope he's more reasonable than that,' I said.

We sent to Enemnos calling for a council. While we waited for a reply, I explored the hills surrounding the Hot Springs. I knew there were druids hiding here and discreetly let it be known that I, Delfos, son of Innogen, would talk to them. At last a young boy approached, took me by the hand and led me to a ferny hollow, high up and with no view of the valley below. There was a natural spring issuing out of the steep land; around it, in niches carved in the rock, were the venerated skulls including that of Esius. Here I met those druids who remained, mostly elderly, too old to emigrate.

'Why are the druids on the run?' I asked.

'Just moving,' the elders told me, 'as a herd finding better pasture.'

'I hope you will stay. I need you.' I explained to them my difficulties with the law. 'I'm trying to maintain ancient customs but in the absence of druids and with nothing written down, they are becoming forgotten.' I told them about the father who had watched his sons murder his daughter.

'What punishment did you give them?' they asked.

'Confiscation of property, castration and banishment.'

'We would have advised as much, and that's all we can do, advise. It is for the king to decide. Your judgement was sound. Be at peace.'

We'd invited Enemnos to meet us at the ford but he said that, as we were the ones calling for a ceasefire, we should go to him. 'I am a true Briton,' he said via his messenger. 'You have my word no harm will come to you.' Nevertheless, Vespasian had a large force accompany us. There were three terraces to the stockade on the hill, and three walls with three gates. We were asked to abandon the troops at the second and go on with just a small escort.

Enemnos was waiting for us at the top. From a distance, he cut a fine figure, tall and muscular despite his sixty years of age, but as I approached I realised why he was rarely seen. His face looked like it had melted down one side and he squinted, perhaps to distract from the droopiness of his right eye, but nothing could hide the puckering of old burn scars down his cheek. No beard had ever grown in that place and he shaved the rest of his face to match. His hair, too, had been affected by the scarring and only grew in tufts above his chewed right ear.

'Why have you brought the Romans?' he asked me, staring disparagingly at Vespasian. The right side of his mouth remained fixed while the rest moved, distorting his speech. 'You don't trust me to keep my word?'

We were standing at a viewing place, looking out over the great circle of hills. He raised his arms and called on the goddess to help us in our negotiations. Dressed in chainmail and leather, he looked like some exotic auxiliary of the Roman army. Apart from the disfigurement, he was a handsome man who held your gaze to prevent it flickering over his tufts and puckerings.

Ushered into the chieftain's house, we were offered wine. While Vespasian called for a slave to take the tasting, I quaffed mine. Enemnos nodded his approval. 'So, we meet at last,' he said, 'O son of Verica. King of the Atrebates.'

'By what right are you challenging my kingship of the Dobunni? You have split the Dobunnic nation north from south.'

'Some might say I am reunifying it, but under my leadership.'

'Are the southern Dobunni distinct from the northern?'

'There was a merging of tribes in the time of our grandfathers, when Caesar came. Then a split. Then Esius reunified us. But we are not the same people, no. My people have always been here and we intend to stay, the people of the snake hills and the snaking river. But our grandfathers were right: we are stronger united as one territory, especially now with the coming of another Caesar.'

'Naturally I agree with you. Except that I have more right to rule the territory than you.'

Enemnos snorted.

'There is something we need to make clear. I have not come here as an equal to sue for peace. I have come to end hostilities, one way or another. The Romans have been lenient with you, contenting themselves with a siege out of respect for the sanctity of this site. Vespasian is known to be able to take a hill in a day. Ask the Durotriges. This one is large and might take two, but still, once the ballistae are unleashed . . . I am here to tell you that, if you persist with your illegitimate claim on my territory, you will be wiped out and not a man left standing.'

Vespasian turned to stare at me. This was not the kind of negotiation he had had in mind, nor was it altogether true. Enemnos, however, did not so much as blink. 'You are the illegitimate one. Esius did not have the right to make you, Togidubnus of the Atrebates, his successor. It was in the fever of the moment. The Romans were landing and no one knew what to expect. Sensing his own death was imminent, he panicked.'

'I am betrothed to his daughter, Branwen. I believe there is precedence, at least in druidic law, for me to inherit the land.'

'Only if Branwen dies. If I am claiming kingship of the whole people, both north and south,' said Enemnos, 'it is on her behalf. If she were here, she would be queen, rightfully so in everybody's eyes. She would unite us just by her presence. With your election by the Romans, my people grew angry.'

'I was chosen by Archdruid Regalis.'

'And the Romans. He was in their pay.'

'That is not true.'

'If Branwen were here,' he said, ignoring me, 'she and I would rule north and south together. How old is she now?'

'About sixteen.'

Enemnos feigned indifference but those squinting eyes told another story. 'You, you upstart imposter,' he said loudly, 'you claim kingship of the whole. *The whole!* It takes more than the Roman army to support such a claim; it takes the will of the people, and you do not have that.'

'I do in the north,' I said, confident that the changes wrought in Gleva, Corinium and everywhere between were proving popular. 'The northern Dobunni know me for who I am, son of Verica and Innogen. Innogen of the Creig,' I repeated. The revelation that I had royal Dobunnic blood threw him and he could not cover it.

'And your lineage?' I asked. 'I see you have no bard.'

He took up a small doeskin purse and emptied it into a wooden platter, making a scatter of gold coins which he stirred with a forefinger, flipping some of them over to arrange them in a line of forefathers including Coriomandu, whose conflict with his brother Boduocos had split the territory north from south. It had been reunified by Esius, who ruled from the north, but the old hostilities rumbled on. Enemnos looked at me, his eyes glittering, as if daring me to pick one up. 'Go on,' he said, 'take one. You are my honoured guest.' Have words ever sounded so divorced from their meaning? I left the coins on the platter. Where there were duplicates, he turned them to show the symbol of the triple-tailed horse running sunwise over the wheel of the year. All tribes of Gaulish origin had a version of this. It was the Sacred Mare. We are horse people, we are all horse people. He picked up one showing his own profile and name and turned it over. I gasped. This horse was not a mare, but a stallion. I felt the full force of the symbol, the reeking power of it. Such arrogance, such hubris, to turn the Mother of the Land into a rutting male, to be equated with himself.

232

'These are my ancestors,' he said. 'This is the sacred emblem of the Dobunni.'

'These are the past,' I said, 'and only of value if you melt them down.'

He looked at me with an expression of disbelief that distorted his face. I needed to douse the fire. 'My friend,' I said, 'we must learn to adapt to change and not cling to what has gone.'

'And why not? The past was a better place. We had our druid colleges, we had doctors and lawyers and judges, we had teachers, we had ways of living that served the Mother. The Romans are rapists!'

Vespasian bristled. 'Take care, Enemnos,' he said.

But Enemnos was not in the habit of taking care. Or orders. 'This is a new world you have brought to us,' he told him. 'You call it civilisation. You pave our fields, metal our tracks and strip our rocks of their minerals. Yes, many benefit, but only at the expense of others. You overwhelm us with your monstrous army. You take booty. You live off spoils. You are parasites.'

A vein in Vespasian's temple was throbbing. 'And that from a land-grabber who feeds off his own people,' he said.

I turned to the legate. 'Leave me with him,' I said. 'It is not right that you stand there, a man of virtue, listening to such insults. Leave us.'

I had never spoken to Vespasian like a king before. He understood it as play-acting and, with a stiff bow, withdrew, taking his officers with him. Enemnos was clearly impressed, even subdued, by my authority over a legate. I faced him on my own. I'd heard so many stories about him: a common man with ambition; a petty chieftain who had pushed his grandmother into the hearth fire; someone who had murdered his wife. 'What is it you want?' I asked.

'What do you mean?'

'It may be in my power to grant you whatever you want: wealth, property, reputation.'

'How? How are these things in your power?'

'In exchange for a cessation of hostilities, I'd arrange for you to receive citizenship.'

He nearly choked on this. 'You think I want that? Look at me. I am a warrior. I live a warrior's life. Me? Wear a toga?'

Several of his captains laughed. He turned to grin at them.

'Forget the toga,' I said. 'Think of rich farming land, herds of cows and horses, fine wine, finer than this muck, red pottery, silverware, glass. You are not so young that your body is not beginning to suffer from the way you live.'

He spat at my feet. 'I live a warrior's life and I will die in battle, king of a united territory, famous in songs. You, on the other hand, will rot with age and die whimpering on a bed of soft pillows.'

'I warn you, my friend,' I said, 'the Romans are tired of you. Submit to a treaty or take the consequences.'

'Such threats are empty given that I have successfully resisted Vespasian for so long.'

'All I have to do is to speak to the governor and the Fourteenth will join the Second to grind you and yours into low-grade, gritty flour.'

'All I have to do is to call the Silures to my aid.'

This caused me to stall momentarily.

'You didn't know of my affiliation with Caratacus?'

'We'd heard rumours. So where is he?' I growled. 'Do you know?'

'If I do, I'll not be telling you.'

'Vespasian will be returning to Rome early next year. The new legate of the Second is unlikely to be so lenient. If you continue to resist, the Romans will expend their full force on all the peoples of the southwest. Opposing the Romans guarantees brutal reprisals, and not only against fighting men. Have you got a family? For their sake, stop, just stop.'

'You asked me what I wanted. What is it that you want?'

'Peace and prosperity for all. I don't want a united Dobunnia under my command. I want a united Britannia, living under Roman rule but making the most of it.'

'What would Caratacus say to that?'

And now, like a snake in dappled light, I chose to deceive him with candour. 'He would call me a collaborator, weak and self-serving, without a wisp of understanding about honour. Believe me, Enemnos, I have no idea where right lies in this. No idea at all. I feel my way in the dark, adhering to ancient laws that seem to have been written into my soul. As the son of Verica, all is clear – my loyalty is to Rome. As the son of Innogen, nothing is clear. What would you do in my position?'

'I wouldn't be here for a start,' he said. 'I'd be in Rome, rescuing Branwen. That's what's missing here. That's what is causing all the fractures: your failure to do the right thing. Branwen is my queen, the queen of the Dobunni. Because of your clumsy interventions, she is now a slave. Bring her back! What are you doing here? You should be in Rome, finding her, bringing her home. This country is doomed without her. If you will not act, I shall. I'll meet you one-to-one in battle, I'll slash my sword across your neck, I'll take your head as a trophy. "Look," I'll say to my children. "The mighty Togidubnus, who had the backbone of a jellyfish. Your mother was betrothed to him, but I freed her from that, and I freed her from Rome."' He stood back and regarded me through narrowed eyes.

I was rocked by the realisation that he intended to take Branwen as wife.

'All of Dobunnia will be mine,' he said, 'you upstart usurper.'

Even as the blood rushed to my head, I was talking myself down. Enemnos, trained in the discipline of a warrior, had learned how to whip himself into such a fury that he became fearless in the face of death. The warrior's fever. I had been trained not to react. How could he ever understand me, or I him?

'Let us talk,' I said. 'We can make a deal.'

'How? How can we do that?'

'Because Branwen is my betrothed and, although it may not be evident, I am working hard for her release.'

'Not hard enough, you boneless worm. That's the task of a real hero, a man, a true Briton.'

'Perhaps so,' I said, 'but it is I who am betrothed to Branwen, not you, and it violates our laws to take another man's betrothed.'

'Not if he's dead.'

I stood in silence for a while, to let my passions subside. 'If you will not accept citizenship,' I said at last, 'will you accept unopposed rule of southern Dobunnia? Neither of us will get what he wants, but perhaps this would be better. You rule the south, I the north, and the unity of the territory would be gained in our collaboration.'

'And in return?'

'You will agree to live under Roman law, honour Branwen as my betrothed, and make peace with Vespasian. His troops would withdraw.'

Now it was his turn to fall quiet and pensive. With an enigmatic squint, he held out his arm for the wrist-to-elbow grip that sealed agreements.

'You are not human; you are some Shee changeling sent to confound us,' he said. 'But let us take an oath together.'

An oath! What was he? Inhuman? Because even as he made it, he never meant to keep it.

I left at dusk, riding back down to the ford with half a treaty. Mandred had been out and about, picking up information from the southern warriors.

'That scar,' he told me. 'When he was only two years old, Enemnos's grandmother threw him in the fire to stop his bawling.'

'So the story is skewed?'

'Aren't they all?'

'What happened to the grandmother?'

'Nothing. She was head of the clan.'

'And did he kill his wife?'

'No, but he wanted to. She blamed him for every mishap. She died of a fever, not poison. Burned up, they say, by her anger.'

'He was intending to marry Branwen.'

Mandred choked.

'He has sworn now to honour her as my betrothed.'

'And you believe him?'

'I have to.'

He glanced at me doubtfully.

AD 50

29

THE ATTACK ON DECEANGLIA

Freed from the distraction of the southern Dobunni, I returned to Corinium while my cohort went north into the middle lands to spend the winter patrolling the extended frontier with the Fourteenth.

We heard that Scapula was planning an attack on Deceanglia in the spring.

'What have the Deceangli done to deserve Rome's attention?' Mandred wondered.

I had no idea. They were a simple, pastoral folk who never bothered anyone. Over the winter, which we spent mostly at Twelve Elms, I made enquiries and learnt as much as I could about the Deceangli and their territory. The weather warmed early and it was not long after Imbolc that I led my escort in through the creaking gates of the small fort that garrisoned the Fourteenth. Built north of the Bare Hills, it was almost one hundred miles west of the Albios Way and the original frontier.

I hadn't seen Scapula for a year and decided, wisely, to visit the barber before presenting myself. He and his officers were laid out on supper couches as if they were in Rome itself and not here in draughty Britain with the rain drumming on wooden tiles. He was entertaining the company with tales of Egypt, where his father had been prefect. He was already governor of Britain – did he need to elevate himself even higher in the eyes of his officers? His status was beyond question – until I walked in. Was that why he hated me so much, because I was a king? For kings then still ranked high in the eyes of the world. He appraised my hair with a glance – then winked. I could have punched him for that wink. Coolly, I made my report of the agreement I had made with Enemnos. 'The southern Dobunni are now quiet,' I concluded, 'and will remain so if we accept Enemnos as their leader and offer no opposition. He and I will collaborate to rule all Dobunnia together.'

'You are joking?'

'To prove our good faith, the Second must withdraw.'

'And how long do you expect this agreement to last?'

'It has survived the winter.'

He scoffed at that. 'Remove the Second and he will move north to Corinium and Gleva. What is to stop him?'

'To gain trust you must offer trust.'

Scapula snorted. 'Have you had any information about Caratacus?' he asked.

'No, none. What's your latest?'

'That he's in the territory of the Ordovices, forming a coalition of all disaffected tribes.'

Scapula had chosen the ideal place for the fort, where the territories of the Ordovices meet those of the Cornovii and Deceangli. He intended to make Deceanglia at least impassible if not uninhabitable. The Deceangli were Old Folk who had been here long before we Gauls arrived, shepherds mostly who kept to their hilltops. What had been their crime? 'They have no centre, no king, no organisation,' I told him. 'They wouldn't put up any resistance if you moved through their territory. Can't you just let them be?'

'Deceanglia is Caratacus's only route east.'

'East?'

'He won't want to be in the west when we push forward. We need to block the rat's hole that is Deceanglia.'

It was why he had summoned me. 'I want your cohort to lead the attack, with you in charge. Flatten the place. Create terror – then I'll send the legion in to finish the job.'

The cohort, relieved to have a mission that didn't involve riding through enchanted woods, banged their spears on the floor when I told them this. Their enthusiasm evaporated, however, when they learned what that mission was to be. The prospect of killing people who posed no threat sickened them.

'It's against the laws of our ancestors!' Mouse Ears protested when I dined with my captains.

'Help us,' said Ten Horns, usually all but mute but now vocal. 'We've done everything you've asked of us, but this . . .'

'Be dispassionate,' I advised him. 'The duty of every soldier is to follow orders.'

'Even if the orders are coming from a madman?' asked Cow Crippler. 'Scapula hates Britons. We are Britons. I fear our men will become mutinous. Are you able yourself to be dispassionate?'

'Passion comes upon us unbidden. Reason has to be summoned. I do my best.'

'You should hear him when he stubs his toe,' Mandred told them. 'He blames the rock.'

I let them laugh at my expense and then continued. 'A Stoic would question whether this order we've been given is within our control. The answer is clearly no. The only thing within our control is how we meet it. Passion is urging you to protest, even refuse. So, what if you give your feelings free rein, let the rage burn, mutiny? How does it end? You will all be killed, your dependants will be cast into poverty and you will have done nothing to avert the fate of the Deceangli.'

'But what if you protested to the governor?'

'That's what he wants me to do, that or grovel. I will not satisfy him by doing either.'

'So the fate of the Deceangli is determined by your pride?'

I reddened. Mandred grinned at me like the mask of Comedy. It was not only Scapula I had to beat, but my own faithful companion, who kept me and my practice of Stoicism under close and critical scrutiny.

'Trust me,' I said to them. 'I will be sending out messengers to all the strongholds, advising them to submit without a struggle to minimise the damage. Deceanglia will be destroyed – by us – but it will recover. Quickly.'

'How?'

'Wait and see.'

As the days passed, I received replies from the Deceangli chieftains, most of whom said they would agree to surrender if I would ignore the streams of people moving west to the mountains of the Ordovices. I went further and promised them safe passage. Scapula got wind of it and sent his own angry message to me saying that there is no honour in submission for either victor or vanquished. 'Do the job properly.' It came on a wax tablet. I had Mandred melt the wax.

The Deceangli were a federation of small clans and had never had to deal with anything more testing than a raid on livestock. Gathering together to defend their territory was beyond them. And so, after the mass of them had departed, unopposed we tore down walls, set fire to thatches, corralled into slave pens any who remained after the exodus. I rode amongst my men tirelessly, encouraging them to show discipline. Following orders . . . It is an essential part of the training, for all manner of good reasons. However, when orders come not from the good but from power, they can be arbitrary, anomalous, even absurd. Across history there have been brave souls who disobeyed orders for the greater good, only to be rewarded by being flayed alive. I was not one of them and I did what I was told, most of the time, while schooling my men in three things:

Do not kill from love of killing.

Do no harm.

Do not steal.

The men of the cohort were barbarians for whom the slashing sword was the tool of their trade. They thought my rules were impractical; but they had also been raised by druid priests and teachers and knew that what I told them was a deeper truth than the warrior's way.

'Dispassion', I told them, 'must be as practised as your skills with weapons.'

'A warrior without passion?' said Mandred. 'You might as well castrate them. Make soft-natured geldings out of your fine stallions.'

'If only you had read Plato, you would understand. The soul is a chariot pulled by two horses. The driver is Reason; the dark horse is Passion; the light horse is Thumos, or what we might call spiritedness,'

'I've never heard of *thumos*.'

'It's a Greek term for which we have no one-word equivalent.

When you do your daredevil riding, that is your *thumos*. For the sake of glory, you transcend base emotions such as fear. By "dispassion" I don't mean the absence of passion, but a control of it. What Reason does is control and steer two wild horses. Passion is always the stronger force. Dispassion allows *thumos* to be of equal strength to passion, not governed by it. If you want an example: Caratacus is Passion; Scapula is Thumos.'

'And the driver of the chariot would be . . .?'

I have read the records of these events. They say that the hostile resistance put up by the Deceangli provoked a massacre. I was there. There was no resistance and no provocation. Neither was there a massacre. We did harm, we could not help but do harm, and there was much sorrow and impoverishment, but few died.

Only when Deceanglia had been reduced to smoking ruins did the legion arrive, bringing with them a message from Scapula informing me that Venutius was harrying the northern border of Brigantia. I was stunned by this news.

'Why are you so surprised?' Mandred asked. 'I told you, no man is happy being a consort, and he least of all. I've seen this coming for years.'

Perhaps so, but it was the surrender of weapons being applied to the Brigantes, and Cartimandua allowing it, that had soured his loyalty, that and the fate of Deceanglia. When Cartimandua advocated taking no action, he returned home to Breghed in a sulk, taking his Carvetii warriors with him. The Carvetii, the people of the deer, dwelt in the lands beyond Brigantia, a mountainous territory with broad valleys and lakes called Breghed. It was much further north than anywhere I'd been, and yet beyond it were the rough lands of untamed tribes and, beyond them, the deep, black forests of Caledonia. The north: the very thought of it was oppressive. The Romans were absolutely dependent on Cartimandua to keep Brigantia as a buffer zone between north and south.

'Imagine', said Mandred, 'if Venutius allied with Caratacus.'

I blanched. Mandred studied my expression and then smiled crookedly. 'You may think you are neutral – no one else does. You are seen as an ambassador of the emperor. If such an alliance were forged, it would be the next boat to Rome for you, if you could get to the coast fast enough.'

There soon came reports of attacks on Brigantia's northern border and insurgencies by the Carvetii. Scapula ordered me to visit Cartimandua and see if she required any help. I led the cohort through Deceanglia to her base at Rigodunum, passing heaps of rotting animal carcasses and field upon field destroyed by fire, the grain reduced to black stalks, the air heavy with the smell of smoke. There would be no harvest this year. Famine was certain.

The queen greeted me cordially with an exchange of gifts in the ancient tradition. For my part I apologised that Scapula had not come himself but she said she was glad of it. 'I'd rather bite on granite than spend time with that man,' she said low into my ear. The scent of her wafted over me.

We were having supper in the Roman style, with imported wine and the best olives. Braziers filled the hall with light, warmth and the perfume of fragrant oils. Dancing girls, flutes, singers – at first I took these as shallow entertainments but soon realised that she was using them to limit what could be heard of our conversation.

'I hear', I said, 'that your husband has left and returned to Breghed.'

'The call to surrender our weapons – he felt unmanned by it. And then he was angered at the oppression of the Trinovantes, but it was what happened in Deceanglia that tipped the scales. He won't be away long – he can never leave me for long.'

'I was shocked to hear that Brigantia had been included in the surrender of weapons. North of the frontier, you are free people. You have – wisely, in my view – pledged loyalty to the emperor yet retain full independence. So they had no right to demand your weapons.'

'We could have fought it but I decided it would be best not to. That may have been a mistake. It's not just my husband and the Carvetii who are upset but many tribes of the Brigantes nation.

To placate them perhaps I should have you disembowelled for your part in the massacre of the Deceangli.'

'I arranged for evacuation of the territory,' I said quickly, in case she wasn't joking. 'Only nineteen died in battle, if you can call it battle.'

'Is that true?'

'It was a wretched affair but we saved thousands. What happens now I cannot say.'

'Anyone would think Scapula wants unrest.'

I agreed. 'He's sent me to find out if you are facing trouble from your husband but I wanted to see you on my own account. If there is a massacre of the Deceangli it will be by starvation. I am trying to organise aid. Would you be willing to supply them with food?'

'What, and upset Scapula? No, I would not.'

Any thought I might have had of allowing her to seduce me – clearly her real intention – ended there and then.

I awoke at dawn to blaring carnyces sounding the alarm. Cartimandua was at the ramparts, shouting down at the warriors at the gates.

'They are rebels from northern Brigantia,' she told me, 'led by the chiefs of the Lopocares, the Gabrantovices and the Setantii.'

'What do they want?' I asked, looking down on a massed throng gathered under a mingling of tribal emblems, enraged men with painted skin, hair limed into spikes.

'You,' she said.

'Eh?'

'They want me to surrender and hand over "Togidubnus the Killer".'

'I hope you do not intend to comply.'

She was not in the mood for levity. 'My grandfather built this nation,' she told me, 'pulled it all together, all the tribes, clans and families, pulled them into one, and swore allegiance to Rome. Now the people are turning on me.'

'Not on you, on Rome.'

'It's the same thing. So, are we to do battle?'

244

'Against your own people? No.'

'No?'

'Let them exhaust themselves in a siege.'

Our warriors spent the day raining down slingshot, driving the enemy into the perimeter ditch so deep no one could climb out of it. Screams came up from those who fell in and were impaled on the stakes that bristled in the ditch. Only when the sun began to set did we give the signal for the main gates to open. Out flew Cartimandua's troops and my cohort to whoop and holler around the ditch of the dying. Cartimandua led her warriors to the left, I led mine to the right. We caught many in our pincer action, netted them and hauled them into Rigodunum.

I stood with Cartimandua as she harangued the captives, her soft voice now grating and shrill.

'You know what the Romans do to rebels!' she cried. 'It will be a mass execution at dawn! We'll have you dig your own grave pit and then we shall fill it with your miserable corpses!'

She was met with spitting disparagement and such a swelling of chests you'd think no chain would be strong enough to hold these men. She trembled, not so much from fright as the fear of anarchy. Even so, I considered her threat too harsh. 'We're not Romans,' I told her. 'What would execution achieve other than more hatred and resentment? Show leniency, my lady. Hang the ringleaders, no more. Pardon the rest and let them go. If you want to maintain the federation of the Brigantian tribes, let the rest go.'

She stared at me. 'What would Scapula do if he were here?'

'He would have them all slaughtered. And then the whole of Brigantia would rise up in a body, you would be deposed, the Romans would come and everyone, in time, would be subject to the empire.'

That event has gone down in history, though in the Roman record it was Scapula's idea to be lenient. Naturally.

We waited. Would there be a full-scale rebellion? Would Brigantia split? We waited. Three days later, a large body of riders was seen approaching from the north. Our eyes ached with the effort of reading the pennants and know who was coming. Cartimandua was the first to recognise them: the Carvetii, led by a strong man wearing a horned headdress. 'Venutius . . .' she breathed. We waited. Was this it? The end of her rule? But then, as they approached, we saw pennants of peace on their spears. They came in through the gates, the Carvetii warriors, as grey with dust as the rocky roads they had travelled on. Venutius alone dismounted and bowed before his wife.

'My queen!' he said affectionately, taking her hand to his lips. 'We heard about the trouble and came to help but rode straight into an uprising among the Lopocares which was threatening to spread like a moorland fire. We've put it down. On the way here, however, we met many rebels returning home saying you had pardoned them and let them go. True?'

'Togidubnus advised it,' said Cartimandua.

Venutius glowered at me. It was hard not to feel intimidated by this man with his bare-chested bravado. I stood firm. 'It seemed the wise thing to do,' I said, though suddenly doubtful.

He spat on the ground. 'Wife!' he said to the queen of the Brigantes, 'you have no business taking advice from any man other than me.'

'You were not here!' she countered, and thus began a violent row which ended only when Cartimandua flounced off, calling for her chariot. And her shield-bearer.

I stayed one more night at Rigodunum, during which Venutius softened towards me. He had washed off his war paint and was back in his toga. Cartimandua, thrilled by her husband's coming to protect her, celebrated a little too heartily and was laid out in a stupor between us on the supper couch. We talked together over her, Venutius absently stroking his wife's hip and leg as if she were his dog.

'The Deceangli are facing famine,' I told him.

'Whose fault is that?'

'Scapula's,' I said. 'I did my very best to obey orders without creating harm, and now I want to make sure the sufferings of the people are not prolonged. We need food but the queen has refused to offer aid.'

Venutius lent down and kissed her on the cheek. 'You bitch,' he whispered. He straightened up. 'What can I do to help?' he asked.

'What indeed? Cartimandua must never find out.'

'It is of no consequence if she finds out. I can easily reach Deceanglia by sea from Breghed to avoid crossing Brigantia. Tell me what is required and I'll have the ships in Breghed's ports loaded and ready.'

'Grain, dried meat, livestock, whatever you can spare.'

'Leave it with me,' he said.

Cartimandua was no lightweight but he lifted her easily from the couch. 'Come, my darling. It's time for you to receive me as a wife should.' He grinned at me. 'It's so much easier when she's unconscious.'

In the morning he had me join him on the walkway above the main gate. There was still a hostile throng below, though much depleted.

Venutius shouted down to them. 'Go home. Go home, now. There will be no rebellion in Brigantia. This man, Togidubnus of the Atrebates, is innocent. There was no massacre in Deceanglia, but there will be famine. We call upon Brigantia to help with relief. Go back to your farms! Bring in the harvest! Let us share it with our neighbours!'

Cartimandua, hungover and dishevelled, joined us to look down on the rebels. 'Yes!' she cried. 'Let us feed those who are starving!' Her husband looked at her not so much with pride as with self-congratulation.

30
A PLAN TO CATCH CARATACUS

When it came to the time of departure for Vespasian, the Second Legion expected to accompany him to Camulodunum and give him the farewell he deserved, full of admiration and praise, but Scapula insisted they stay at their posts in the southwest, that the Fourteenth would stand in for them. The Second were having none of it.

Camulodunum seethed with soldiery, all buffed up to a high sheen, nodding red plumes, proud standards of the boar, the cavalry in parade helmets. If the Trinovantes had had any further thoughts of rebellion, this alone persuaded them to be quiet. Although the temple foundations were still being laid out, we could see its extent: it would be overwhelming.

And I, a Briton, stood amongst the dignitaries watching one of the few Romans I was pleased to call friend going through the rituals of an honourable departure. Life in Britain without Vespasian. Life in Britain with Scapula. I was full of foreboding.

During the feast, I found a few moments alone with him.

'What do you advise me?' I asked.

'Carry on as you are and keep out of Scapula's way,' said Vespasian. 'He truly hates you.'

'Why?'

'Why?' Vespasian laughed. 'To have you in the same room reminds him of a virtue he does not possess. That and the humiliation you delivered at the Severn.'

'That was Caratacus, not me.'

'You just stood by and did nothing, eh?'

I cleared my throat. 'More or less.'

'He will never be persuaded that you are not in league with the rebels. If I were you – and this is my parting advice – make sure it's you who captures Caratacus.'

Now I scoffed. 'And that would win Scapula's approval? He'd hate me even more.'

'But he would never be able to express it. It would fester inside him. Get that bastard Caratacus. Once he is dead, Britain is ours.'

'Rome's.'

'Yes, Rome's.'

'Wouldn't Rome rather have him alive?'

'I suspect that would be impossible. But if it could be done . . . Claudius would shower you with gold and whatever else you desire.'

'A certain young slave would suffice. When you get home—' I began.

'First thing I'll do is embrace my wife and children. But the second thing, no, third thing, after I've bedded my mistress for a week, is to find out what I can about Branwen. And then you shall have a dispatch worth reading.'

'It's a dangerous place for you, home,' I said, 'with Agrippina become so powerful.'

'Claudius knows how much he owes to me. Who was it, after all, who really conquered Britain? I'll be fine.'

I looked at his broad face, etched with various emotions, eyes twinkling above the strong nose, the chin. The chin. Was it quivering? 'The gods be praised,' he said. 'Back to civilisation! My wife's arms! My lover's thighs! The laughter of my dear son, Titus, whom I will not recognise after all these years.' Had he convinced himself? It did not look like it. He was going to miss Britain, the campaigns, the camaraderie, the victories.

'As soon as I can, I will join you,' I said.

'A man of your stature is wasted in these bogs and puddles on the outer edge of the world, but this is where you belong and where your duty lies.'

'I sense that Scapula would like to see me gone.'

'All the more reason to stay. Delfos, my friend, listen. We have been here seven years and things are no easier than on the first day. The whole frontier is one treacherous, unstable, whiplashing line. All the legions are deployed along the Albios Way and making incursions ever deeper into the west, which only increases the instability. Britain has never needed you more, keeping the rear with your countless acts of diplomacy. You must stay. The fate of southern Britain depends on it.'

The next Provincial Council was held at Calleva. Cartimandua arrived in her glorious chariot, driven by her equally glorious shield-bearer. Her husband, Venutius, had returned home to Breghed again, this time for good. The days were long. I sat alone with the queen after supper in a triclinium watching fireflies dancing in the warm, still air.

'It will soon be midsummer . . .' she mused. 'Do you remember the great gathering of tribes we used to have at Venonis?'

'Of course. Your Brigantes occupied half the hill and got all the best deals at the livestock markets.'

'I miss those gatherings, but we had to sacrifice them for a better life. Do you remember Caratacus?'

'At the gatherings? I remember him, the second son of King Cunobelinus and a worse bully than his brother, Togodumnus. I remember him beating me up when I was four and he was eight. After Katuaros came into my life, he left me alone.' I stared into space baffled. 'Did he leave me alone, or . . .?'

'Or was he not there?' said Cartimandua. 'He seemed to disappear.'

I nodded. 'Yes, that's right. I remember the sense of relief. We didn't know where he had gone. I hoped he'd died.'

'When he came back amongst us – well, it was obvious enough where he'd been. The brute now had style. And so manly . . . although naturally I hated him for being Catuvellauni. Always strutting and taunting us. He had aspirations to have a territory to match ours.'

'He still does,' I said, wondering what it was that was so obvious.

'When, oh when, is he going to come out into the open? Everyone is tired of this restless frontier and the constant skirmishes.'

'It is my deepest wish to see the whole land united, even if that means united under Rome.' I brought my head close to hers so that I would not be heard by servants or slaves. 'Could we talk in private?'

'Come to my bed tonight.' She ran her finger down my cheek.

'I was thinking of an audience in my house down by the south gate.'

'Were you? Down by the palisades? You want me to come to you, down by the palisades? If you want to talk, you know where to find me.'

The scent of her when angry. Musky. Did she bathe in ass's milk like Cleopatra? Was it spiced? Dwelling on such idiotic questions, I followed her meekly. It was, after all, a harsh life of deprivation in the army.

After the preliminaries to our audience were over and to her satisfaction – apparently I debunked the reputation of the Atrebates for being better on horses than on women – I broached the plan that was germinating within me. 'Caratacus, we believe, is somewhere in the hills that lie between the Cornovii and the Ordovices. We are getting closer every day.'

'By destroying every hill fortification you come across, I hear.'

'Yes, well . . . Even so . . . We are coming close. It is my ambition to take him alive. Vespasian thinks that would be impossible, that Caratacus would kill himself rather than be taken.'

'I doubt it.' Cartimandua reminded me that suicide was a habit of cowardly Romans, not Britons. 'Imagine the rewards if we did take him alive,' she said, replacing the golden torc around her throat and pinning her hair into shape.

'You could have anything you wanted.'

'I could . . .'

'So, what is it you want?' I asked her softly.

'Security. And some of those lovely perfumes from India.' Her cheeks dimpled.

'You could have enough gold to pay for a wall around the entire boundary of Brigantia, and enough sandalwood and patchouli to sink a galley.'

She all but purred. 'I suppose the governor wants the rewards himself,' she said.

'The only reward Scapula is interested in is a triumph. Gold would be welcome, of course, but he'll not risk a triumph for it, so Caratacus dead or alive will get him what he desires most, and dead is less risky. We need to corner Caratacus somehow,' I said.

'Obviously.'

'And then let him escape.'

'Escape? To where?'

'To you.'

'Why would he do that?'

'Tell me the truth. I ask you what you want and you talk about perfumes and defences. You have not mentioned getting your husband back. How do things stand between you and Venutius?'

'We are finished. I do not want him back. This separation is final. When I discovered that, against my will, he had been funnelling aid to the Deceangli, undermining my authority and my relationship with Rome, I banished him from Brigantia. I'm going to divorce him and take another. Have you seen my shield-bearer, Velocatus? Somewhat my junior, I know, but so athletic. Like you, he doesn't have to wait until I'm asleep or unconscious.'

'We need to convince Caratacus that Venutius has left you, that you are still in love with him and will do anything to get him back. If Venutius is in touch with Caratacus, we can be certain that that is the version he's told him anyway, that he left you, not that you banished him. We need to make it clear to Caratacus that, lovelorn, you are desperate to regain your husband's affection and would even offer Caratacus refuge in Brigantia if it would win Venutius back.'

'Why would Caratacus want to go there? If he escapes, surely he will go further west? If he gets to Mona, it's a hop and a skip over the waters to Ireland.'

'That's what he wants Scapula to think, but his aim, like mine, is to unify Britain, only under his command, and for that he needs the eastern and northern tribes with him.'

She blinked twice, smiled. 'Oh, I see. He wants Brigantia on his side.'

'It would make him invincible. The Romans would be driven home. Britain would be free.'

'Free to murder each other.'

'Quite. Think of the wealth, my lady, if it were you who captured him. Rome's gratitude will arrive in carts groaning with gold.'

'Which we must share?'

'I'm not interested. It's all yours.'

She looked at me incredulously. 'You'd be content with the glory?'

'I'm not interested in glory, either.'

'What then? What is it that you desire, Togidubnus?'

'It seems such a small thing, but all I want is to wrong-foot Scapula and irritate him like a swarm of bees.'

'Nothing small about vengeance,' she said. 'If all this comes to pass and Caratacus flies into our trap, don't you risk coming into Brigantia unless you have the Fourteenth with you. The mood of my people will be incendiary. No. Let us meet at Venonis.'

The Fourteenth were concentrating on the Bare Hills where they destroyed every defensive camp they came across until the hills were bare indeed. But if Caratacus had ever been there, as rumoured, he was no longer.

Scapula moved the legion to the great grey hill that lies on the land like a sleeping hog. The Wrikon was the capital of Cornovia and he needed to take that territory to block an obvious route of escape for Caratacus. While he was making a beacon of the Wrikon to light the sky, my cohort took Blackstone Hill. Took it without a fight. I made a treaty with the chief and counselled him to put up no resistance should Scapula come.

'Why should he come?' the chief asked, his brow furrowing.

'He should not, of course, since a treaty has been made, but there is no accounting for the governor's moods. Be assured, he won't last forever. At the end of his term he will be gone. All this will come to pass within three years and then the governor, this governor, will be gone.'

But it was to happen sooner than that, thanks to Pulchritude.

31

PULCHRITUDE

In the fort at Viroconium on the edge of the blue hills they'd given one of the captives a room to herself. They said that any man who lay with her knew happiness for the first time but it was like a drug: it wore off, and the next time he needed twice as much. The night had the first chill of autumn and I'd wrapped myself in my fine mantle made by Apnodens with the coded threads that no Roman could read. With the colours arranged in the sequence of number which is growth, any druid I met would recognise me as a brother. Her keeper looked me up and down. 'Can you afford even a moment with her?' he asked, doubtfully.

I opened my mantle to show the embossed cuirass. 'I don't have to.'

'Excuse me, Commander!' he said hastily. 'Of course you don't.'

I peered in through a grille in the door. The room, though locked, was well furnished with hangings and a fine bed on which she was sitting, hugging her knees. Seeing me, she gave a little cry and then hid her face.

They had captured her during the sack of the Wrikon, where she had retreated during the scourging of Ferylloog. They didn't know who she was. The only name she would give was 'Pulchritude'.

I returned to my room and tried not to tremble when Theana was shown in. The passing years and the deprivations she had suffered had merely ripened her beauty.

'What is it you want of me?' she asked.

'Just to talk.'

254

'Truly?'

'Truly.'

'They are using me as a whore again. It is not the way to treat a priestess.'

'At least they feed you, and pay you, I believe. Challenge them and they will just take what they want without any recompense.'

'They can use my body, but if they want pleasure beyond the bounds of anything imagined, that's only mine to give. As you know.'

'Why did you leave?' I asked, my voice like the drag of the sea on shingle.

She shrugged. 'I was bored. You were out for Samhain. I was left behind like some housewife or concubine. It is not my way. And I knew that, soon enough, you would be touring your territories and would not want me with you.'

'I was keeping you safe! You could have been so easily recognised and betrayed.'

She leant forwards. 'Delfos . . .?' Her voice was like silk, this Circe. 'Shall we pick up where we left off?'

I cleared my throat. 'There is only one pleasure you can give me, and that's knowledge of the whereabouts of your brother. We know he's in the blue hills but which hill? There are dozens of them.'

She smiled. 'You would rather know where Caratacos is than lie with me? What are you? Not a man, for sure,' she said, her face brushing against mine. 'That is why I adore you, because you resist me. Everyone else, from governors to centurions, would sell their mother to lie with me. But you, you stoical piece of self-composure . . .' She leant forwards again, kissed me chastely on the cheek and then sat back.

'I don't remember resisting you,' I said.

'Oh, but you do resist me, in your heart. That's reserved for another. You want my body, but do you love me? As you love Branwen?'

I was taken aback. 'Branwen is my betrothed, my duty, the one I must protect. I'm not sure that adds up to love.'

'You worry about her all the time, get agitated at the thought of her. Do you ever worry about me?'

'Worry, no. You will never be anyone's victim. Theana, I do love you, but I must fulfil my duty towards Branwen or else risk breaking my vows.'

'Desire, that is what you feel for me, just like every other man. What makes you different is my feelings for you. I love you: there is the truth of it. But you are right, I will never be anyone's victim and shall not shed one tear over you.' She sat back with a sigh. 'All you want of me is knowledge of my brother. As ever, I do not know where Caratacos is. Why should I? We share the same father, that is all. There is no love lost between us.'

'I always thought of him as loyal to his family.'

'Try asking the family, uprooted, pulled hither and thither by their lord's passions. Dryadia will do anything for him – she's besotted – and the same with the children. Some of his brothers and cousins are loyal, but not all. And then there is me.'

'You looked loyal enough during that confrontation with Scapula across Severn river. Riding with him, playing your part in the great trick.'

'I was living in Ferylloog, alone in an abandoned temple. When Caratacos arrived from Siluria, he sent for me, saying he needed my unearthly powers of distraction. Well, it made a change from hiding. When he left, I returned to my lonely abode. It seems I am condemned to hide – or be captive.'

'At least until I turn up,' I said. 'Where did Caratacus go?'

'When Scapula took Ferylloog, he moved north from Siluria into the territory of the Ordovices. He's united all the tribes of the Far West. Calls himself the king of the druids and they follow him like puppies. I had decided to go to Mona but Scapula's attack on the Deceangli blocked the road and I stopped with a cousin's family on the Wrikon. I do my best to keep away from Romans, but here I am again, and no doubt another interrogation is planned.'

'Why? I'm the only one here who knows who you are.'

No one would recognise this priestess in a simple gown as the befeathered, face-painted Morrigan hurling curses across Severn river.

'Prostitution is not my chosen life. Once again I need your help to escape, and your permission.'

'Permission for what?'

'Ostorius Scapula needs to be dealt with.'

I laughed. 'You're asking my permission to murder the governor of the province?'

'Is he not a tyrant, caught in a passion for destruction? What has happened in Deceanglia . . . All those lives ruined just to block my brother? Scapula, having started, cannot stop, therefore he must be stopped. It is permitted within our laws, as well you know. But where is the man of courage who will stand against him? Somewhere in the mountains of the Ordovices, biding his time. When men cannot act, then women must. I am not violent. I never take the course of crude intervention. All I intend is to invoke the gods for aid, but I need the permission of a king.'

'To lay a curse like the one you laid on him at Severn river?' I asked.

'That was done in haste and fury. Only his pride was wounded. That was all. As for the one I laid on Vespasian – he was saved by his own gods.'

'You cursed Vespasian? Why?'

'For the sacrilege of the Hot Springs.'

'Will he die?'

'No, but he'll limp for the rest of his life.'

I blinked. No man of right mind wants to believe in curses so it's uncomfortable when he finds evidence of their efficacy. Of course, she could have heard via gossip about the legate's wound to the thigh.

'It's Ostorius Scapula who must die but I need the power of a king behind me,' she said. 'I need your permission.'

I did not give it. 'Tell me precisely where Caratacus is.'

She hesitated.

'You know he cannot win,' I said. 'It's impossible. Scapula has him more or less surrounded.'

'Only you don't know where?'

'As soon as we do, it's over.'

'And you want me to tell you, to hasten that moment?'

'Where is he, Theana?'

'Caer Caradoc. The hill of Caratacos.'

'Which is where?'

'This hill, that hill, always on the move, could be anywhere.'

'But where is his base? Where is the family?'

'He is his own base, and the family is with him. Are we Britons not famed for our loyalty? If my freedom depends on betraying my brother, then you must kill me.'

'Me? Kill Pulchritude? I'd be dead myself within the hour, legitimately executed. As my friend Seneca is wont to say, there is always a route of escape: we always have a vein we can open.' I took her hand, which was trembling slightly, and turned it over to show her where the vein pulsed in her wrist. 'There – that one.'

'I know which one,' she snapped, and tried to tug her hand out of my grasp but I kept hold of it. 'Theana,' I breathed.

'We Britons do not believe in self-sacrifice, not of that kind.'

'No, we don't, although I've been hearing examples of it.'

'And why is that, if not because your Romans drive us beyond what we can endure? Delfos, let me go. Let me walk out of here.'

'I cannot do it without your telling me what I need to know. Are you going to die or are you going to walk free? Your choice.'

'I DON'T KNOW!' she shouted. 'You must ask the gods. Either they will show you where he is, or they will not. It depends on the purity of your heart.' She turned away, drew a tiny pouch on a thong from her cleavage, took something out and put it in her mouth.

'What are you doing?' I asked, alarmed.

She came close. Seneca used to test my powers of self-denial, making me fast for a day, for two days, while having onions and bacon fried in his kitchen. As ordeals go, that was nothing compared to what I was going through now.

She stroked my face. With the lightest of touches, she pushed on my shoulder and I fell backwards. I squeezed my eyes shut and tried to concentrate on anything but her. Floggings, maimings, crucifixions, anything to douse my passion. And surely, with Theana, I shouldn't have to: she would be waiting with the bucket of icy water when the moment came. She straddled me. She brought her mouth down on mine, opening my lips with hers. And just as I surrendered, she spat into my throat, some fibrous, masticated leaf.

I struggled under her, trying not to swallow but too late. 'Theana! What was that? Poison?'

She sat back, smiling. 'Why should I want to kill you? Just trust it: something far superior to those mushrooms Apnodens is so keen on. It will show you everything you need to know. Or it will show you nothing.'

'How long?' I asked.

'You will be back around tomorrow noon. And I shall be far away.' She touched the fine druid mantle Apnodens had given to me. 'What's the truth of you?' she asked softly as I fell backwards into a bottomless well.

Time collapses. There is no chronology, only a present moment where everything that has happened is happening now. Scenes are whipped up by a draught of time like the leaves of the Cumaean Sibyl, and I cannot put them together to read the book of all knowledge.

Everything has changed. Branwen is walking head down, carrying bed linen through the grand halls of the imperial palace on mosaics of gods ravishing women. The walls are of porphyry, stone the colour of dried blood. She stands aside, gaze dipped, as her mistress sweeps past, answering a summons from her husband, the emperor.

'She's a witch!' The high, warbling voice of Claudius echoes through the halls. 'Get rid of her!' he demands.

Agrippina pleads on Branwen's behalf. 'She is a Briton of royal blood!'

'I know who she is. Whom she belongs to.' Claudius seems to glance my way, and then stare moodily at his son, Britannicus, who is standing by his father's chair, biting a fingernail. 'Get rid of her!' Claudius storms. 'I am surrounded by astrologers, witches and Jews. Send them all to the flames!'

'Why?'

Claudius cannot tell her that he is being haunted by Messalina, who seems to be watching him from behind every column, wishing his downfall. A downfall being predicted in the forum by prophets, diviners and fortune-tellers. He has to clear the streets of their inflammatory sooth-saying.

'She has taught Domitius so much!' Agrippina protests.

'Such as? How to dress as a barbarian and sing like a painted actor? You wheedling woman. Why do you want to keep that witch who poisoned your husband?'

Not true, not true, Branwen mutters under her breath. I didn't poison my master, and you know that well enough, since it was you who had him killed.

Domitius is leaning against a marble pillar with a half-smile on his face. He has heard everything and gives her a slow wink. 'You'll be all right. I'll see to it,' he says quietly as she passes.

'Branvena!' Agrippina calls, and Branwen goes trembling to her mistress's chamber. Agrippina is crying. 'I have done everything I can, my darling. You who saves lives, not takes them. I want you here, in the palace, not sold off to a street entertainer as my husband is threatening. Fire? Burn you alive? No, he wouldn't do that. You have too much value. But he'll only agree to my keeping you if . . .'

Now she is emptying the chamber pot of Agrippina's handmaid, making her bed, washing her clothes. A slave to a slave. It was the only way, Agrippina said. The only way to stay in the palace and not be sold off. Deep within, Branwen prostrates herself before her goddess, Swale, and sings to her. She likes the smallness of her new accommodation in the dark, cramped cellars. It helps her dream. At night she sits with Apnodens by a flowing brook and they sing together to the moon and the stars, the foxes and owls.

During the day, although she keeps her head down, she is aware of much of what is going on.

Now she is in the kitchen, feeding acorns to the dormice in the fattening jars. 'Free him,' whispers the boy standing next to her. Since the marriage of his father to the woman who, when all is said and done, is his cousin, Britannicus loiters in the kitchen to get away from his tormentor, Domitius. 'Free the mouse!' he says to her.

'I cannot. I will be whipped.'

'Poor little mouse.'

She wants to hug Britannicus who, himself, is the poor little mouse. Since his mother Messalina died, he has hardly seen daylight. He himself is in a fattening pot, being fed acorns. Claudius has adopted Domitius, who has a better bloodline than his own son, and renamed him. Poor little mouse. Britannicus doesn't stand a chance.

'Hail, Britannicus!' says the one who is now his stepbrother as they pass within a colonnade.

'Hail, Domitius!' Britannicus replies, as if nothing has changed.

'My name is Nero!' shouts Domitius, banging into Britannicus. 'Nero Claudius Caesar Drusus Germanicus. Remember it!'

And here comes that stooped, barrel-chested old man who has been recalled from exile on Corsica to tutor the one now called Nero. 'Come, dear boy,' says Seneca. 'You are late for your lesson.'

As Nero goes with Seneca, he turns to poke his tongue out at Britannicus.

Now she is in the *hortus* where the gardeners have their sheds. She likes to watch them sowing seeds of exotic plants like cucumbers and lettuce. The gardeners are all out, picking figs, taking down spent vines, digging over beds in the various gardens around the imperial palace. She prefers small things and, in the shed, she bends over neat rows of cuttings of bay and box trees. A shadow fills the doorway. 'Branvena?'

She looks up, wincing in the sun that is making a corona behind the crumpled face of Seneca. He comes in to join her, asking questions about plants she is able to answer, calming her, overcoming her shyness.

'I became quite an expert in growing grapes during my eight years on Corsica,' he said. 'But this is not your duty, is it? Does helping the gardeners bring peace to your mind? Yes? It did for me, too. Each time I felt anxious or frustrated or bored, I went and got my hands dirty.'

She smiles quietly and nods. She is not going to tell him how she feels.

'Do you know who I am?'

'Yes. Lucius Seneca. Tutor.'

'Are you aware that one of my students before I was exiled was a certain Togidubnus?'

'Yes,' she says, and he can barely hear her.

'You are his betrothed.'

'Perhaps,' she says.

'Perhaps?'

'I don't think he wants me. All these years and he has never come for me.'

'I doubt that's his fault. Legate Vespasian is back in Rome and tells of growing unrest in Britain. Poor Delfos, he was thrown into a bear pit. "Go ahead of the army and promise the kings peace and prosperity if they will only submit." That's what Claudius told him, and young as he was, and over-confident as he was, he set off to do just that.'

Branwen's eyes are welling.

'And I myself have come home to learn that he is king of three territories now: the lands of the Atrebates, the Belgae and the Dobunni. He was even offered Catuvellaunia but declined it. High King, according to some. Branvena, I instilled in him a sense of duty not practised by many, and I'm certain that's what is holding him together, but of course, it prevents him from coming for you.'

'He has no duty to me?'

'Yes, of course he does. He asked Vespasian to seek you out, but it took him some time. You had become invisible.'

'I was Nero's first tutor.'

'Well, one of them. You taught him singing, I understand.'

'Now I am the slave of a slave, one who treats me cruelly. Only when I come here to look after the little trees do I feel safe.' And now Branwen is crying. Seneca takes a corner of his toga and swabs her face, saying, 'There, there,' lost for words as he always is when confronted by a woman in tears.

She pushes him away and runs down paths lined by clipped hedges, to a pool at the place where all paths cross. Frogs live there. She leans far over the rim of the marble pool, looking for them but seeing only herself reflected. Her tears hit the water like raindrops. She peers into slimy green depths, willing gods to appear. And then comes the *vocos*, a wild lament of loss and longing, the same chant being sung for her continuously at Twelve Elms. A sparrow on a lily pad washes its wings in a shower of light and a frog hops out from under a stone. Seneca catches up with her, drawn like the animals by her Orphic song. 'Calm, calm, Branvena,' he says softly. 'I shall speak to Agrippina, see what I can do to help you, but for now, be calm and stop making the spirits weep.'

From water to fire. I am drawn through flames. Such dreams. Fire everywhere – Londinium, Camulodunum, Rome, Judaea. The world is on fire. It is the end of the world. Red skies in the east. These images are brief, flashes of light as I keep falling, down, down, down, beyond Annwn to the Underworld. That place of limitless dark where there is no existence. *Or it will show you nothing.* And then, suddenly, back to air.

I woke up gasping with the taste of vomit in my mouth. Scapula, summoned by my alarmed Mandred, stood over me. 'Where's your armour, your mantle, your shield? Lying there in woman's clothes!'

I glanced down in horror. I was not dressed in her gown, but it was draped over me.

'What's the matter with you?

'Nothing! Something I've eaten.'

'Or drunk, you barbarian. Did you forget to water the wine?'

I heaved again at the thought of it. 'Leave me.'

'Where is Pulchritude?' Scapula demanded.

'I don't know. She was here.'

'Did she drop something in your drink?'

'No.' I pointed to my mouth. 'She dropped it in here. Soma.'

'Soma?'

'A leaf. I've never felt like this before.'

'Did you eat fish for supper?' He turned to Mandred. 'Did he?'

'Yes.'

Scapula glared down at me. 'Soma and fish do not mix. You deserve to be sick, you ignorant Gaul. If we've lost her, if we've lost Pulchritude . . .'

Realising that even Scapula has been using Theana, I rolled over and threw up on his feet. He jumped back in disgust.

A servant ran in to say that my tunic and armour had been found in a pile as neat as the spoils of war in a triumphal display, not far from the palisade ditch.

'Tunic and armour only?' Mandred snapped.

The servant shrugged, his hands spread out palm upwards. Theana must have ridden out in the misty dawn, dressed as me. And now she rides for the hills wrapped only in my druid mantle. As I was savouring this vision, in a flash I saw a forbidding cliff of grey rock rising from a floodplain. I knew what the gods had given me: the image of a hill, an image of the hill.

Meanwhile, Scapula was intent on another hill entirely, to the west, and I knew there was no point in telling him it was the wrong one. Scapula would want to know the source of my information and preferred what was wrenched from captives to anything coming from 'the gods'.

I went to the bathhouse to soak and scrape Theana off me, wearing a Scapula-like scowl to discourage any jeering from my fellow officers about how I had been found. A cleansing usually works on my mind as well as on my body, but this time it merely uncovered something I find it difficult to admit even to myself: *I want this nightmare to end; I want to stop haring around the hills killing my own people.*

Scapula's hill proving as fruitless as all the rest, he ordered the Cohors Atrebatum to scout another in the vicinity, a simple cone with a 360-degree view. Near the summit we found an undefended druid grove, recently abandoned. At the very summit, bald of trees, was the view of all directions. There was no one there. I ordered the cohort to return to the plain but held back as they disappeared through the tall bracken – Mouse Ears paused, looked back and nodded – and for a short while I had the place to myself. Then, moved by some spirit of the place, I performed the rite of the eight directions and blessed the land with the blessings of a king. Everything seemed to open, as if the heart of me were the centre of a flower, an unfolding, opening beauty that was limitless. I made a *vocos*, not as enchanting as that of Branwen, but as sincere, a cry to the gods for help. *I seem to have spent years chasing a part of myself I do not want to meet, and now I am getting close.*

A few moments later, I turned to follow the tracks of my men back down to the war.

AD 51-2

32
THE HILL OF CARADOC

Cornovia is a land of ridges, scarps, valleys and hills: steep, rounded hills; rugged, mostly bare-topped hills with wooded slopes; gentle hills, hostile hills, wild hills – all of them with their ramparts and defences, many of them blue in the distance, all of them islands in times of flood.

I was sick of hills; we all were. The hard slog up rough tracks to ramparts defended by a clutch of warriors pretending to be the army of Caratacus. After a long winter of such fruitless toil, I'd forgotten what the hill I'd seen in the vision looked like, for I'd seen too many contenders. One rock rising high out of the ground looked much like any other. And yet he was here somewhere, he and his thousands. You could feel it.

The Fourteenth was camped close to Brei Dun, a high and extensive hill embraced by Severn river close to its confluence with Vyrnwy. Camped where the ground was flat and dry, we watched the hill for any sign of movement. Scapula was loath to have his legion cross the river for nothing; he waited until he had sound information from his scouts. They told of Brei Dun as a hill rising in natural terraces, many of which had stone or timber ramparts, none of them new. They learned that within the uppermost tier of defences was rolling, wood-fringed pastureland. It was very quiet, but they could hear the snicker of horses. There was no other sign of the enemy, although some reported the feeling of being watched, but then scouts often do. Scapula waited for further intelligence before deciding whether to attack or not.

'I have my doubts about this one,' he told me. 'According to a man we captured last night, there is no one called Caratacus nearby, but if we mean the one they call Caradoc, then he is on Caer Ogyrfan, an ancient fort with tortuous ditches and ramparts about half a day north. It could be another goose chase, but you might as well be checking that out while we sit on our rumps, not knowing what to do. Just observe. Do not engage. Hear me?'

The land in those parts is low-lying and sodden with puddles and ponds. The Cohors Atrebatum, guided by Mandred's eye for ancient ways, picked their way north and came to a crossing place on the Vyrnwy. On the far bank there was an escarpment of a hill that had seemed small in the distance but, the closer we approached, the more it rose up to loom over us. My skin prickled. This was not Caer Ogyrfan, our destination, just a hill no one had mentioned. Soaring grey rock capped by a single rampart, the main defence being the terrain itself, a sheer cliff face that no army could scale.

I sent scouts ahead. They splashed across the river which, here, was foaming wavelets on a broad, shallow bed. An easy enough crossing for a few but not for an army.

'The main approach must be elsewhere,' said Mandred.

I watched our scouts gain the far bank and follow a worn track to the wall of stone rising out of the marsh which looked as if it had been built by giants. In my innermost being I knew that this was it, the place the gods had shown me. I wished, as I so often wished, that Katuaros could be here, sharing this moment, his nose lifted to the scent of prey. He rarely rode with us these days and never when there was any threat of trouble. He seemed to have adopted his new life with equanimity, content to be making deals with foreign merchants, amassing a fortune, but never enough to pay for what he wanted to build. It was I who did the missing, sorrowing at his transformation from warrior to nova-toga, wishing we were boys again.

When the scouts returned, they reported that the main approach was on the far-side where the hill rose less dramatically and was defended with traditional tiers of ramparts and in-turned gates.

'It's quiet,' they told me, 'the gates are undefended but you get a strong sense of being watched, as if by an animal gone to ground.' A new rampart at the base had been recently and hastily constructed. 'According to some local shepherds it's called Copper Hill, being an ancient mine long out of use.'

'A mine, you say? With tunnels?' I asked. The scouts didn't know. The local Cornovian dialect had been difficult to understand.

'Oh, it will have tunnels all right,' said Mandred, 'worming through the hill, chasing the green ore.'

'Could they hide an army?'

Mandred was blanching. 'Not an army, no. The tunnels will be tiny, some as small as the children who dug them. You worm in, and in, and in, and there is no turning place. When you need to return, you have to wriggle backwards from the stifling dark, dragging the green rock after you.'

He swayed on his feet, as if he were going to faint.

'How do you know this?' I asked.

It had been one of his grandmother's favourite stories, about the little boy who had been so naughty that he ran from his people, out of the gates, over the dykes and ditches, into the woods where he lived wild. But then he'd been captured by hunters, sold as a slave and condemned to a short life in a mine in the Far West. 'Oh, the rock is cold and drippy,' he said, in his grandmother's voice. 'Cold, so cold and dark, the tunnels so twisting that you can only wriggle along them and never stand up. You are alone with only the voice of your whip-master urging you on. And you hammer at the rock until your fingers bleed, until your lamp gutters, until the air runs out, then you scrabble backwards and backwards, trying not to panic.' He took a deep, shuddering breath.

'Not a place to hide an army then,' I said, to break the spell of terror he was weaving.

But Mandred was ensnared by memories. 'And what happened to me? I became that naughty boy. I bodged the sacrifice which was my initiation. I ran out of the gates and over the dykes and ditches to live wild in the wood. Can you imagine, when I was captured? I was all but suffocated by fear of the mines.'

'Mines that haven't been used for a thousand years!'

'But they are in the stories . . .'

'And yet here you are, my whole and hearty freedman. Now, where would an army hide?'

'There will be caves on the hill, and caverns and galleries within them, but they wouldn't hide in the tunnels, no, no, no.'

'So if we take the gates, there is no escape, no tunnels exiting the hill at any point?'

He shrugged. 'There are bound to be some, made by springs.'

We stood together at the river, looking across at the hill which guarded a road to the Far West. Traditionally sworn enemies, the Silures and Ordovices, had become united under the warlord known here as Caradoc, but there were no signs of him, not on this side of the hill which faced Cornovia, so steep and sheer that its only man-made defence was a stone rampart at the top.

Mandred gazed at me. 'You've got that strange, milky look in your eye. What are you seeing?'

'We have him,' I said. 'They're here. They are all here. Hundreds of them. Can't you hear them holding their breath? Warriors, warriors' families, the family of Caratacus, Caratacus himself.' I could feel him on my skin, like the irritating sap of wild parsnips.

'Whatever you are thinking of doing, think again. You were told not to engage with the enemy.'

'So what do I do? Send a message back to Scapula that I have an intuition which is giving me goosebumps? I have no intention of engaging, but I do need to be sure. We need to scout the hill thoroughly, get them to reveal themselves.'

The following day we followed the scouts across the shallow but treacherous river. On the far bank I split the cohort into two parties, one led by Mouse Ears to go around the hill eastwards, the other, led by me, westwards. We passed through dense woods, mostly ash choked by ivy, so married to the rock that the only defence here was a ditch. We could only suppose stronger defences above the woods. Mandred rode ahead, following the tracks of horses which, he said, were fresh.

'Riders?' I asked.

'No.' He studied the trees and found no sign of broken branches. 'A herd.' Although I would obey the command not to engage, nothing stopped me crippling the enemy if I could.

I chose a few men to come with me while sending the others on round the flanks of the hill to meet the rest at the north gate.

The further up the hill we went, the denser and darker the trees. The winding track was a series of long steps formed by gnarled roots. Caratacus had herds of horse, or had done once. Now he was reduced to his core stock and would hold them most precious. Where were they? On the top, inside the ramparts? Or secreted somewhere close? It seemed there was nothing in the world but trees and brambles. After a while of hacking our way through, I called a halt. When it was quiet, I whistled. My mare's ears twisted backwards. I didn't know if Caratacus's horses spoke the same language as mine but immediately came a whinny. I turned back, studied the undergrowth more closely and suddenly found myself looking down into an old disused quarry where about two hundred horses were being guarded by young boys. If this was what was left of Caratacus's magnificent herd, it was a sorry sight. They were battle-scarred, weary and apprehensive. They could smell conflict in the air. There were chariots there, too, upended, their poles reaching for the sky like the necks of swans launching into flight. But they, too, were in a bad state of repair and had been stripped of their gorgeous trappings.

I asked for volunteers to attempt a precipitous descent into the quarry. Cow Crippler thought this was a mad idea. 'The best thing would be to lob fiery brands in to stampede the herd. They'll find their way out right enough.'

As we had no time to make fire, I had them to make a ruckus around the lip of the quarry, telling them to keep hidden, instructing the slingers to aim small stones at the horse-boys, enough to sting but not to injure. When everyone was in place, I set off the first call and thrilled to hear my own yowlings echoing around the quarry. Screams, booms and ululations followed, while the horse-boys were thrown into agitation by the stings. Screeching banshee calls and slingshot were all it took for the lead mare to crash out of the compound, taking everyone with her, including the boys. They careered down the hill on a path we had not noticed.

When we got down to the valley again, we could see their dust in the distance. I sent four men to chase them and keep them running while we met the other arm of our cohort gathered close to the main gateway on the north side. Here the hill rose in three terraces with ramparts, most of them ancient and in disrepair. Spears bristled above the palisades. The defenders did not engage or provoke in any way, just watched and waited.

'Is it him?' I asked Mouse Ears.

He nodded, met my eye, grinned.

As I sent off a couple of my fastest riders to inform Scapula, the gate opened and a messenger came out to invite me to enter and meet Caratacus.

'Scapula said . . .' Mandred began.

'Do not engage. So I shan't. I just want to talk to him.'

'And what? Make a treaty? You're insane.' Mandred turned to Caratacus's men at the gate. 'This is our commander and our king. What can you offer us as surety for his wellbeing?'

To my astonishment, they offered Dryadia, the wife of Caratacus, as a hostage. Out of the gate came a chariot bearing a pregnant woman, a daughter of about twelve years and two younger children. Despite the passage of years, Dryadia was still beautiful, her fair hair curling like a cloud of pea tendrils. We nodded to each other as we passed. I ordered that she and her children be taken to an abandoned stockade we had found a mile or so to the south.

Caratacus was waiting for me at the mouth of a large cave. He looked sombre and grim. Our hunt was over and I closed my eyes in a momentary prayer of thanksgiving.

'So, you have found me,' he said, arms folded over his broad chest. 'I take some solace that it is you and not that bitter-faced rat called Scapula. Yes, the gods are with us.'

'You should be grateful to him.'

'For what? His brutalities?'

'For swelling your numbers.'

He grunted. 'True enough. I've never been so popular. They come to me in droves. I have the Silures and, now, the Ordovices, but daily we get contingents from all directions: Corieltauvi, Durotriges, Brigantes, the Iceni. Oddly, none of the Atrebates. Such loyalty to their king!'

He set off up through the last of the gates. 'Copper mine,' he said, flipping his hand towards the cave as we left it. 'Grim.'

We came out on open ground that was all dips and rises from centuries of surface mining. Caratacus told me to walk behind him, 'Or risk a rapid descent into the Underworld without time to wonder what is happening.' On the highest ground were clusters of deep-thatches surrounded by ramshackle tents. Men and their wives and children went about their daily chores as in any settlement but hey all stared at me with hostility as we passed, the women in particular hard-faced and determined. Of mixed tribes, they were united by one desire: to keep our lands and traditions. They were willing to die fighting for the Mother. And for the druids.

The largest deep-thatch stood on the highest knoll. Inside the gloomy house, Caratacus had us stand in what light the doorway offered. It was three years since we had last met, on the banks of the Severn in Ferylloog, and he had spent those years in tireless negotiations with Silurian chieftains, moving from camp to camp, territory to territory, often living rough. He looked exhausted and his hair was beginning to grey but he stood as tall and proud as ever.

'So, this is it,' he said. 'This is the time. Either I live or I die. If I live, all Britain will rise up in my support and Rome will withdraw. If I die . . . If I die, I will go to the Otherworld and take my place among heroes.'

'Caratacus, there is a third choice. Submit.'

He still had a laugh like a thunderclap. '*Submit?* Oh, you never give up, do you? Here I stand, having to choose between world renown and immortal honour and you offer me *servitude?*'

'If you reject the third choice, you are left with just two: life or death.'

'You are wrong, so wrong, Romey! The choice is between life and eternal life! Honour and greater honour! Your pinched little stoical views of what life is all about. Happiness? Duty? No! It's about honour! I am prepared to die for it. What are you prepared to die for?'

I struggled to find an answer.

'I'll tell you what you are prepared to die for: *nothing*. You self-serving, comfort-seeking, pathetic excuse for a man. You *Romey!*'

And now my blood was roaring through me like a river in spate, and carried helplessly in the flood was any memory of Seneca's lessons on anger. I don't know what held me together in that moment, what stayed my hand from my sword. It was not fear. Anger knows no fear. Here he was, my enemy, the snatcher of Branwen and the murderer of her father, here he was, and here was I, bearing a sword and stopped from using it by some inner force, some part of me that commands the rest: Reason.

Caratacus smiled suddenly, mistaking my inaction for cowardice. 'Delfos, Delfos,' he said, 'what is it about you that brings out the worst in me? I never meant to provoke you. I can't help it. You're like a boy who is just asking to be pushed over.'

'Except I never fall,' I said.

'True enough. Resilience – I admire it. Come, let's stop the antler-clashing. I invited you here for a purpose.' Drawing me into the shadows of the house, he reached out and pressed his thumb above my nose, between the eyebrows. 'You will not speak of this. You will not speak of this. You will not speak of this.' The opening formula to an oath of silence that binds anyone who agrees to it.

'I will not,' I said, even as I wondered if I could keep such an oath.

'I have no intention of dying,' he said. 'I'll be gone by tomorrow eve.'

'Gone where?'

'You will not speak of this!' He pressed again with his thumb.

'I will not!'

'Mona. All my activities on the mainland have been to protect the sacred isle; now is the time to cross the strait. No Roman will ever land on Mona's shores, not while I am there.'

'You will never make it, not with your mangy forces. You are trapped,' I said. 'This hill will be your last stand. Scapula and the Fourteenth are already on their way.'

He stood there, breathing hard. I tried not to flinch: I knew his temper, his dramatic swings from charmer to killer. His eyes suddenly narrowed. 'Scapula is at Brei Dun? Two days march?'

'He could do it in one.'

'Once he's got the message Hmmm, yes, I'll be gone by tomorrow evening.'

'Not with your ragtaggle forces. He'll catch you up easily.'

While he mulled this over, I relaxed, let my shoulders drop, became less confrontational. 'Of course,' I said, 'there is another option. I've seen Theana.'

He softened. 'Where is she?'

'She was a prisoner at the fort near the Wrikon but she escaped.'

'Do you know where she went?'

'I think northward.'

'*North?*'

'I can only presume she hopes to find refuge in Brigantia.'

'That's impossible! Cartimandua is wedded to Rome!'

'She's wedded to Venutius and is heartbroken at their estrangement.'

'He's left her?'

Ah, the power of assumptions! I felt the thrill of a plan taking root.

'Yes, he stormed off, appalled at what happened at Deceanglia, wanting nothing more to do with Rome. Cartimandua has tried to persuade him to return but he is stubborn and remains in Breghed. I'm surprised he hasn't made contact, for he rides with you now.'

'Probably couldn't find me.'

I laughed sharply. 'No, he probably couldn't. But the fact remains that Cartimandua is distraught and will do anything to get him back, even switch her loyalty to you.'

He stared at me, slack-jawed.

'It's true,' I said, relaxing my hands which had clenched. Nothing would sever Cartimandua from Rome but, such was his vanity, Caratacus now believed the opposite. How easy that had been! Was there going to be retribution for lying under an oath of silence? It's not the same as a truth-speaking. But if the gods were going to frown on me, I did not have the time to worry about it. The lives of thousands, of tens of thousands, depended on my lying and I would have to take the consequences. 'Cartimandua has turned and Theana knows it. She's gone to Brigantia.'

Second lie. I had no idea where Theana was and presumed she was somewhere in Ordovicia, as west as west could be.

'Cartimandua would join forces with me? That fragrant bitch? That dimple-faced Romey?' His eyes were bulging. 'I find that so hard to believe. But it is even harder to believe that you, O man of virtue, would lie. Oh, by my god, Brigantia! Imagine! My forces are large, drawn from almost all tribes, including the Southern Dobunni, but this would double, even triple, our numbers.' His eyes glistened.

'Enemnos is your ally?'

'Of course. With the Brigantes we would number, what, three hundred thousand? We would bear down on their paltry four legions and they would run for it. North, you say. Could I go north?'

'Make your way across Deceanglia to the border with Brigantia and throw yourself on the mercy of Cartimandua. Believe me, she has turned and will do nothing to harm you, not if it means the return of Venutius to her bed.'

'Are you speaking the truth?' he asked again.

'I am.' Tendons in my shoulders twisted like braid.

'Why? What do you get out of this?'

'The absolute joy of frustrating Scapula. My people will not be joining your rebellion – I'll get you one day, you barbed arrow in my soul, I promise you, but for now – I want you to escape.'

He smiled then, a wan smile which seemed to hold a glimmer of affection.

'You do owe me two,' he said.

'Two what?'

'Escapes. That Beltane on the Hill of the Albios Horse. You think it was Theana who helped you? It was me, by turning a blind eye to what was going on. And then in Ferylloog. I had you prisoner but you walked off while we were celebrating the humiliation of the Romans. Did you not even wonder why it was so easy?'

'Why would you want to help me?'

And then the smile of the charmer was back. 'I've always hoped you'd be the man to tame my wild sister. This is no time to be a druid priestess! She must know that. She needs

276

someone to look after her. Is it possible that I could welcome you into my family? My large and loyal family? I want you supporting my cause.'

'Never.'

'There speaks your head, as usual. What about your heart? Do you not love my sister? Do you not love our land? Think on these things,' he said. He pressed his thumb again into my brow and this time kept it there. 'How often must we meet, you and I?'

And something inside me, something beyond the rage, turns to him. Time collapses on me like loose soil. Under the spell of the oath of silence, I am confused. I am not sure who he is, who I am, or where we are. Then I recognise a Gaulish sky over a place called Alesia. He is at the walls of a besieged camp, where the Romans have trapped him by building their own wall around his. Carnyces are calling on all tribes to come to his aid in this, his last stand. Though I think he is a fool for putting himself – and the people – in this peril, yet I heed the call. I cannot help myself. I, Kommios, rush to the aid of Vercingetorix. I, who have made a pact with the Romans, risk my life and everything I possess to save my fellow Gaul. The story of my grandfather was finding its echo in my own life, and it was not difficult to see Caratacus as an incarnation of the great hero, Vercingetorix. Vercingetorix who was captured by the Romans, taken to Rome, kept in a rank pit of a dungeon and, eventually, throttled in public to the jeering of the crowd.

Why had Kommios changed sides to support him? Was the same being asked of me? In the depths of me I believed what Caratacus had said. His was the way of glory and eternal fame; mine the way of a long life that will end like a lamp that has run out of oil: in darkness and a smell of burning.

Whom would I die for? I will not know until the moment comes.

He releases his thumb. The vision frays and I am left with Caratacus, smelling unwashed and greasy. 'Whatever happens, wherever I go, to the Otherworld or to sanctuary in this world, I cannot take the family,' he said. 'Dryadia is heavy with child and my youngest ones are too small for a perilous attempt to escape. Please, Delfos, I have given them to you as hostage, but I want you to keep them. Protect them.'

'If I take them, they'll have to be enslaved,' I said coldly. 'There is no other way.'

'Then let them be enslaved,' he said.

'You? You who would rather be dead than a slave yourself, you click your fingers and sell your family off?'

'No! That is *not* what I am doing. I want you, you pernicious weed, to take them. Enslave them but do not send them to the mines. Keep them for yourself. You are the best slave master I know. You bought your Mandred deformed and maimed. Look at him now – healthy, virile, shackled to you by love and loyalty only. That's what I want for my family. If my child is to be born into slavery—' Here his voice caught in his throat. '—let it be you who is its master. Delfos, Delfos . . . For the sake of the gods,' he pleaded, 'for the sake of our ancestors, for the sake of our religion, our people, our children, for the sake of honour, will you help me?'

'For the sake of those, but not for the sake of you, I will.'

'Say nothing of this meeting. Look the other way when I retreat.'

'Retreat? Your horses have gone. Will you run away on foot?'

'You found my horses? So all this talk of escaping north . . . You duplicitous wretch. They were the last of my herd. The last. My fine, fine herd. Finer than yours.' He grunted in pain, head in hands.

'I'll get them rounded up and returned,' I said.

I didn't realise then that, when it comes to bending the truth to achieve a desired outcome, he was my equal. 'Don't bother,' he said. 'I am exhausted, spent and shall die here in battle. Do what you must, but please, look after Dryadia and the children. They are in your keeping now. I am finished. You have won, Delfos. I am done.'

Something niggled within my soul that I could hardly understand let alone give voice to. It whispered to me that, if Caratacus died, I would regret it forever. I wanted Caratacus to live. Do not ask me why.

'If only you would submit,' I said, 'you could look after your family yourself.'

'In servitude?' He spat at my feet with disdain. 'You never give up, do you? No. Neither do I.'

33
DEFEAT OF CARATACUS

Scapula arrived two days later, riding with a light escort in advance of the cumbersome legion. After a show of warriors on the ramparts of Brei Dun, the Romans had launched an attack but it had been just another trick. Lured by a small decoy unit, they had assembled the engines and fired their missiles on an empty place. Scapula left the bulk of the legion behind to dismantle everything and follow on. 'So,' he said grimly to me, 'he's here?'

'He is.'

'Are you certain?'

'I know it.'

'How do you know it?'

'I've spoken to him.'

'*What?* I told you not to engage with the enemy! Are you two collaborating? Is that it? I've always suspected it. Where are they? On the summit?'

I told him about the defensive walls on the far side, where the hill was not so steep, the gates, the tricky path, the layout of the camp and the dangers of the terrain. 'It's an ancient, disused mine and the ground is perilous.'

He wasn't listening. 'What did you talk about?'

'He wants my help to escape.'

Scapula looked as if a fishbone had caught in his throat.

'He thinks he's getting it,' I said.

'What are you up to, you weasel?'

'For a start, I've taken his horses. We found the herd and chased them off.'

'Where did they go?'

'Far across the valley. They won't be wandering back.' In truth, my men had already found them and herded them back to the hidden quarry.

His anger subsided. 'Good work.'

'I tried to persuade him that his position is hopeless and that the only option is to submit.'

'But you failed, presumably.'

'He'd rather die. Take this hill, Legate, and you have Caratacus.'

Scapula looked moon-faced at the prospect. He rubbed his hands as if by a fire on a cold night. 'Good work,' he said once more. 'Well done. You have given us all the intelligence we need.' Despite his praise, it was clear he still did not trust me. I cannot imagine why not.

'His wife and family: he has put them into my safekeeping.'

The pupils of Scapula's eyes moved rapidly. 'We'll be taking them as prisoners of Rome.'

I folded my arms across my chest. 'I claim them as my booty. I'm giving you Caratacus. He'll be easier to take if he believes his family is safe.'

'Hand them over!' Scapula demanded. 'Or I'll know you as a collaborator!'

'What will you do with them?'

'I'll tell you what I'll do. I'll capture Caratacus alive and send him and his family together to Rome as my gift to the divine Claudius.'

'And what will happen to them then?' I asked.

'They will be executed together in public.'

'She is pregnant and there are three children.'

'The plebeians will love that.'

'Call me what you will,' I said, 'but Britons do not break a vow.'

'You should not have made it!'

'Yet I did. Dryadia is my hostage. However distantly, she is kin, and I'll not send her to her death for the pleasure of Rome.'

'We'll see how much choice you have when it comes to it. Where is she?'

I pretended I hadn't heard.

'Togidubnus?'

'I thought she would be safer away from here.'

'Where?' He caught me by my kerchief, twisted it in his fist and brought my face close to his. The pupils in his eyes wavered like jellyfish. 'Where?'

'I took an oath,' I said. 'I will not break it.'

Scapula was clearly fighting the desire to throw me to the floggers. With a snort, he got the better of himself. 'You would not be much use to me flayed to the bone, but believe me, I want to do it.'

I regretted not having given Theana my permission to lay her curse upon him.

Once the legion had arrived and set up camp, the Cohors Atrebatum was ordered to start up the slopes. Under a constant hail of missiles from the ramparts above, we edged forward in the testudo, using Roman shields held over our heads and locked into a carapace. The sound of heavy rocks hitting shields went on until nightfall but the worst injuries we had to deal with were grazes, concussions, dislocations and jarred muscles. Unable to get even to the lower terrace, we were forced to rest for the night at the base of the rock below the first ramparts. I sat with the captains round a fire. They were troubled. When I asked why, they wouldn't say, but eventually Cow Crippler told me that they were not happy attacking Caratacus.

'Claudius promised peace to those who freely submitted,' I told them, 'and has by and large kept to it. What is to be gained by joining the rebels?'

'Freedom from tyranny,' said Mouse Ears.

'It's not just that,' said Ten Horns. 'If we lose our land, we also lose who we are. This land, ploughed by our fathers, sown by our mothers, is where our spirits dwell. We are born of this land. Now the Romans claim it in conquest and call their occupation peace, but their idea of peace is not ours. Roman peace means Roman everything. They claim the land is theirs and all that it yields. They feed the soil with the blood of our kin. They beat our children for speaking their mother tongue and say they are civilising them. They take our temples and use them to worship their own gods. Temples intended for healing are now places where priests get rich.'

'All this is true,' I said. Ten Horns's words had been delivered in a soft tone, but that he was speaking at all when he usually preferred silence made them more powerful than a diatribe.

'And yet you advocate submission,' Mouse Ears said. 'Do you really believe it's the better way? Look at what has happened to the Trinovantes. They submitted, and a more downtrodden, miserable people it would be hard to find.'

I sat, hugging my knees and rocking. How to make two into one? How to marry my mother to my father? Britain to Rome? How to find the middle way? I felt pressure on the nape of my neck and shivered at the touch of a foreign goddess. *Show me, Athena, show me the way,* I said inwardly.

'I am Sulis,' she replied with some annoyance, 'goddess of the healing waters. You think I am the same as Athena and Minerva? Listen to Ten Horns. He understands.' And then she began to whisper in my mind the words I addressed to the men. 'Ten Horns is right. It is vital that we do not lose who we are, yet resistance is destined to fail, for no matter what the size of the rebel force, they do not have the weapons or the discipline of the Romans. But then, submission is not the answer, either. We've all seen the slaughter of men who have surrendered. Yet we must preserve our culture. This land: it is more than rolling hills, craggy mountains, wide rivers. It is the very seat of wisdom. The druids follow a teaching that is beyond ancient, a truth once known to all but then forgotten. They have brought it back into the light. Learned men, seekers of truth, came here, the misty edge of Ocean, to study in our colleges. They come no longer and the druids are withdrawing, taking their knowledge to the heart of this sacred land which is Mona. We must enable them to live unmolested, enshrining wisdom in poetry, while we . . .' Everyone hung on my words but Sulis was no longer inspiring my speech.

'We?' Mandred prompted me.

'We are here, now, part of the Roman army,' I said, 'and we obey orders.'

They looked at me disbelieving.

'I never submitted to the Romans,' I said. 'I didn't have to. I came home to help them in their conquest. I am, they say, a friendly king. But I am eight years older now, and sufficiently buffeted to think more deeply on these things. What my smiths would call being made malleable by fire and shaped by hammers. We Britons are called on to submit – not surrender when exhausted by battle – submit before the event. To survive, even prosper, it is for everyone to obey the overlords. But no one said anything about submission of the spirit, for that is impossible to enforce. Live, my Britons, live, and know that freedom is within you.'

This won some of them over, but not all. I continued. 'If you think that under the rule of Caratacus we would return to the old life, you deceive yourselves. Use your senses. He says that what we had before the Romans came was better. Perhaps it was, but it is lost now, and not his to regain. Look at his life. He lives among ruin and wreckage in fear of death. He is turning our fair land into a pile of rubble which he uses as a barricade. Is that the life you want? Believe me, the old one is gone. When you fight in the morning, it is not for the emperor or for Rome, it is for yourselves and your grandchildren. What we want is all Britain at peace; to achieve that, we must rid ourselves of this ruthless warlord.'

'And the ruthless governor?' Mandred asked.

'He will be replaced once his term has ended.'

Though some still gazed at me doubtfully, I could sense their loyalty regaining its strength. My men. I was so proud of them; out of years of training and discipline, a bunch of raging warriors had become an efficient fighting force, loyal, obedient and brave. Then one asked, 'What do we do if we find ourselves in battle with one of our own kin? It could happen.'

'Your duty,' I said.

'You mean, kill him?'

'Act as a warrior and do what is necessary to defeat the enemy.'

They looked stricken. I told them to relax. 'I made an agreement with Caratacus: Britons will not engage with each other.'

'So whom do we fight?'

'Await orders but make sure they are my orders and not the barking commands of a centurion. You are not the Roman army, you are the Cohors Atrebatum. Follow the orders of your king.'

I spent the night sleepless, and not just at the prospect of the morrow. I was caught in a net of my own making. Had I made the plan with Cartimandua just to annoy Scapula? Why? I drifted in and out of sleep, lost in the waterweeds of dream. And in one of those dreams, I was the one escaping Copper Hill and taking off for Brigantia. I woke up suddenly as an inner voice commanded me, 'Let him escape!'

At dawn we began to excavate, prising out the massive boulders that formed the lowest course of the first rampart. Each dislodgement caused stress to the wall above. Suddenly Cow Crippler shouted to retreat. The men sped down the hill left and right, out of the path of the falling wall, its boulders rumbling past down into the surrounding ditch. Trumpets sounded and the legionaries arrived to enter through the breach.

Progress then was swift. The soldiers marched up the hill, rampart to rampart, under a hail of slingstones. My cavalry formed a wing; the cohort infantry, at my insistence, kept the rear. Each time we reached the enemy they scattered, withdrew, backed up higher and higher until they came to the summit. We paused when we got there, went into formation, my cavalry protecting the flanks of the army. To our surprise, Caratacus stood at the head of his men who were arranged in lines like Romans. I realised that he had covered the mine hollows with willow lattice and scrub and was going to draw the army into them. I ordered our infantry to hold back and not enter the fray. Carnyces and war horns blared and the two sides engaged. At once the Romans were floundering, falling like bears into the pits, screaming with pain and rage. Scapula rode up to me on a short rein, his horse snorting and agitated. 'It was a trap, damn you! And you knew it! Why are your men not fighting?'

'I knew only what my eyes told me when I looked. I warned you about the terrain!'

'There is not a man or a mosquito in this world who irritates me more than you do! After this, after all this is over, I'm going to send two prisoners to Rome: you and him. And my only regret is that I won't be there to see you put to death!'

I wondered how I could reach Theana, given that no one knew where she was, but in truth souls do not need physical communication. She knew, as if I had told her to her face, that she had my permission to lay her curse.

The role of cavalry is to harry, not to fight. The riders of the Cohors Atrebatum, keeping to safe ground, caused mayhem without drawing swords. The rebel warriors had entered battle dressed in helmets and chainmail, ranked like Romans, but soon enough they were engaging in the native manner. A Briton under duress fights naked, unencumbered and dramatically intimidating. I encouraged our men to do the same. Most did not need the encouragement. They were already casting off their own mail shirts and helmets. Long hair flew wild and armour was tossed away; when the warriors of Caratacus met the Cohors Atrebatum it became difficult to know who was who.

It is impossible to look on battle and see what is happening. All is a blur as if your eyes are filled with blood, your ears with screaming. But I began to detect a swelling of my numbers. The more they fought and fell, the more there were of them. A mystery to which Scapula, lost to battle-rage, was oblivious.

The fierce certainty of the women was hard to face. Maids, wives, mothers, armed with swords or spears, stood ready to sacrifice their lives to save Caratacus and all he stood for. I avoided engaging with any of them, but I saw many hacked down by legionaries acting as if they were in a granary full of rats. I heard babies crying. I wanted to throw up my arms and shout STOP! Just stop . . .

Passion. The passion to destroy and the passion to resist. All was passion. There was nothing of reason on either side. If I could get Britons and Romans to sit in council, what would I say? Would I tell Caratacus to give himself up for the sake of others? That was all it would take to stop this. Would I tell

Scapula to stand down, to banish Caratacus to the Far West and strengthen the frontier? Why should he? This was his moment, the moment when immortal fame was guaranteed. Publius Ostorius Scapula – the man who caught Caratacus.

By the time the sun was beginning to set, there were many more of us than at the beginning of the day even though a vast number of both Romans and Britons lay dead or dying. Did his flittering eyes make it difficult for Scapula to see? While riding about in a sweat, urging his troops to take Caratacus alive, he was blind to the rebels among my cohort.

'Find him!' shouted Scapula. 'I want him alive! Alive!'

Where was Caratacus? I looked about. Had he already escaped?

Roman trumpets sounded for withdrawal back into formation. Keeping to the shadows, the Britons who had concealed themselves within my ranks began to run away, like children playing a game of Find Me. A short run, a pause in hiding behind some rocky outcrop, another short run, all heading across the plateau. As you can drain an amphora with strips of rag, Caratacus's people wicked themselves off the hill, going down any path made by goats or springs following the lead of Caratacus himself.

Scapula had left a unit on the plain to pick off anyone trying to escape. These men, on foot, would be easy prey. But the escapees did not go far down the hill; they concealed themselves in the woods.

'Where is Caratacus?' Scapula thundered. 'Is he among the dead?'

I had seen him go with the rest but said nothing. The setting sun caught the gully where the large cave was. My horse snickered.

'What's in there?' Scapula demanded. 'Has anyone searched it?'

No one had, put off by local stories about giants who lived underground. Just as soldiers approached the cave, high-pitched whistles came from the woods. As if Zeus or Taranis had been trapped inside the hill and was now free, a great thundering came from the depths, amplified into something monstrous. Hardened fighters jumped back in terror and ran off. In a storm they broke loose, the finest horses of Caratacus. A stampede thundering, as it were, out of the ground, a pounding froth of British horses exploding out of the cave.

He had tricked me! The horses I had found and chased off were a decoy of nags!

Scapula roared to get himself heard over the thunder of hooves. Roman infantry fell aside, charged by riderless horses who, guided by the whistling, seemed to know what to do and where to go. Rearing, kicking out, they surged across to the west, down into the woods to meet their waiting riders. Coming out of the cave behind them was one man alone: a faithful kinsman of Caratacus, who surrendered to the Romans.

'Where is Caratacus?' Scapula shouted at him.

'Gone,' he said simply, and got a back-handed slap across the face for it. Scapula, merciless when it came to dealing with those who surrendered, ordered him to be taken away and scourged. It was all in a day's work. Women who came out to search for survivors fell to Roman swords. One orphaned child, a small boy naked from the waist down, bawled helplessly for his mother in the field of carnage. That nearly undid me, and any man who saw it, but then Mandred, with tears flowing, stepped forward. He took the child, hugged him until he stilled; then, with a prayer to Camulos, he slit his throat and drained his blood into the ground. To be a sacrifice today or a slave tomorrow: no one would have chosen differently for himself or for another.

Scapula, so confounded by events, maintained his authority with savagery. An enemy who had melted away, to be collected by horses? Escaped? How? Where to? He had the expression of one who has at last caught a butterfly only to open his hand and find it gone. He was somewhat mollified when, two days later, a scouting party brought Dryadia and her children before him.

'We found them hiding in an old stockade, Legate.'

He forced her to kneel, even though she needed the help of her daughter to do so. And then the interrogation began. Where was her husband? Which direction had he gone? Who had offered him sanctuary?

I tried to intervene, thundering at the governor that the family was my booty, that I intended to sell them and he had no right to damage my property.

'Is that what you arranged with Caratacus? Why should I take any notice of what two barbarians agreed?' He unsheathed his knife.

There was one thing that could stop Dryadia's suffering, but the oath of silence intoned by Caratacus had been a strong one and kept me gagged.

You will not speak of this.

Scapula took hold of a handful of Dryadia's extraordinary hair and hacked it off at the root. She cried out in pain. The smaller children were howling.

'Well?' Scapula demanded of her. 'Where is he?' He took another handful and some of her scalp with it.

You will not speak of this.

An oath of silence is a sacred thing; one never breaks such an oath, but Dryadia was crying out in pain and her eldest daughter was staring at me with eyes wide and pleading.

I snapped. 'Stop this!' I shouted. 'I know where he has gone! Ask me!'

Scapula turned. 'You know?' he asked, coming towards me.

'Brigantia.'

'*What?*'

'Cartimandua has offered him refuge.'

'How can that possibly be?' he demanded, his face crimson. Almost purple. 'Cartimandua has turned? How can that be? We shall move on Brigantia, flatten the place, destroy it utterly!'

'It's a plan', I told him out of earshot of the family, 'laid by me and the queen to catch Caratacus. We've made him believe she's switched her loyalty, to win Venutius back. The moment he crosses the border, the Brigantes will take him.'

He stared at me, so agitated I thought he was going to burst a vein. Such was his state that I realised Theana had laid her curse. 'Who has made him believe that?' he demanded.

'Me. It's not Caratacus I've been collaborating with but Cartimandua. I want him dead as much as you do. You only have to wait and, if the trap is sprung, he will be delivered to you.' What did I expect? Praise? Gratitude? Scapula steamed like a deep-thatch after rain.

'You want the Roman army to *wait*? Soldiers are not trained to wait!' He stood breathing hard, knowing he had no other option. 'Togidubnus, it's not only Caratacus I want dead!' He turned on his heel and went off, calling his tribunes to him to arrange a deputation to Brigantia's queen.

'Imagine you are the general of a legion,' Mandred said later when we had returned to camp. 'Governor of Britain even, with a single purpose, which is to catch and kill the enemy, and then some jumped-up petty king who has been negotiating behind your back tells you to sit and wait for the enemy to be delivered. Where's the glory?' He whistled softly. 'The glory is all yours. He's as mad as a spider in a broken web.'

'Jumped-up petty king?' I asked.

'In his fractious eyes. No one else's, of course.'

Although I had access to all official reports, I also had my own men, running 'errands' as we called them, men who could merge unnoticed with the tribes and find out what I needed to know. One of them coming from Brigantia slipped into camp and sought me out. I listened, striving not to let my sense of triumph show. So far as anyone knew, he was just a groom consulting me on horse feed. After I'd dismissed him with a coin, I went to an ancient altar I had noticed in the woods, there to kneel, lay my forehead on the ground and commune with the spirits of the place.

'She's got him,' I told Mandred later.

'The plan worked? Oh! You fox. You foxy fox.'

'He's alive.'

'Have him killed! Before he kills you!'

'The spirits tell me that if I want Branwen back, I must take him alive.'

Mandred rolled his eyes. 'That's not what they are telling me.'

A day later, a message arrived for Scapula telling him that Caratacus had been captured and was in chains at Rigodunum.

He ordered the Fourteenth to make ready to go north but told me to remain behind with the cohort. 'No need for you to come,' he said. Had he asked, I'd have told him the that I'd arranged with Cartimandua to meet at Venonis. But as he did not ask. I did not tell him; I just watched with some satisfaction as he set off. Once the troops had left, I ordered the cohort to make ready to go east on the Via Claudia to Venonis.

Mandred looked at me questioningly.

'As arranged with the queen,' I said.

'Now what are you up to?'

'Me? Nothing. I just happen to know the handover will take place at Venonis, and Scapula happens not to know.'

'There's more to it than that.'

'The queen wants to hand Caratacus to me. She trusts Scapula even less than I do. Once he has Caratacus, he'll ignore any promises I made to her. She wants her reward.'

'Uh, you play a dangerous game, my King. I've been meaning to ask if I could take some leave of absence to visit my family.'

I cuffed the back of his head. 'What family?'

The following morning, the Cohors Atrebatum set off into the rising sun.

34
CARATACUS CAGED

On summer roads, it took us only two nights and three days
to reach Venonis, the centre of Britain. It has always been
called thus – the centre of Britain – but are we talking of all
the Britannic isles or just the main one? Either way, how do
you discover where the centre is? Druids of old were great
mathematicians. Legend has it that they taught Pythagoras of
Samos. With their sky maps and stone circles and knowledge
of the sun, the moon and the zodiac, somehow they established
that, if you stood on the summit of Venonis, the limits of the
north, south, east and west were equally distant. But how
could that be? Britain is a long island, not a round one; when
I used to ask that sort of question of my own druidic teachers,
they said that if I couldn't work it out for myself then I must
have faith and just believe what I was told. Truth is, they didn't
know themselves. It was lost knowledge. Our ancient elders
claimed that the art of writing spelled doom for the memory –
Plato said the same thing. But whereas the Greeks *wrote* about
the perils of writing, the druids forbade it. None of our young
had been, before the occupation, taught how to write. To sing,
yes, to memorise vast epics and genealogies, but not to write
them down or to read them. And the result? Druidic feats of
memory remained phenomenal but we were forgetting things
that had not been ritualistically committed to memory, such as
how to find the centre of an irregular shape.

As the great bald hill of Venonis came into view, there was an
uprush of memories. When I was a boy, every midsummer we
made the long journey here to meet family, kin and strangers
from all eight directions. Seeing the hill, I was a child again,

coming up the road from the south, frisky with anticipation. Here the peoples of Britain gathered to talk, barter, forge alliances, draw up treaties, settle legal disputes, arrange marriages and, when the sun went down, to feast under the never-quite-night sky, to drink, to tell stories and sing. And, of course, to dance. The great circle dances. The weavings and stampings that got the blood of men racing and small children over-excited. Time after time I was plucked from under the feet of the dancers, pulled out of harm's way, to be put on my mother's lap or on my father's shoulders. They were happy then, Verica and Innogen. All year long they lived separately and snarled at each other but, come midsummer, they were the cosmic couple, the sun and the moon, the king and the queen, and I their son, a lonely child given the gap in age between me and my brothers, who had a different mother. And then came Katuaros, fostered from the chief of the Belgae, to end my loneliness. At midsummer, he was expected to spend the feast time with his own family, and me with mine, but we were too busy, roaring over the vast hill, looking for enemies, finding friends, killing off imaginary giants and monsters. The sons of Cunobelinus sat apart, restrained, dutiful, respectful of their father, the king of the Catuvellauni.

I must have grunted, for Mandred asked me what the matter was.

'I came here every year as a child,' I said.

'Who didn't? I wonder if we played together?'

'Atrebates with Durotriges? Never! But listen, do you remember the sons of Cunobelinus, holding solemn court around their father?'

'Of course,' he said. 'They seemed to think they were the lords of all.'

'But do you remember Caratacus among them?'

'As a child, yes. Complete thug.'

'Do you remember him when he was older?'

He squinted. 'I didn't go again after I was banished from the Durotriges.'

'I went every year until I left for Rome. Caratacus seemed to disappear. I wonder where he was?'

Mandred shrugged. 'Fostered out somewhere?'

'But at the great gathering, all fosterlings are reunited with their families,' I said. 'I wouldn't have thought of it, but it was something Cartimandua said, about him being missing for a few years.'

My ruminations were interrupted by Mouse Ears suggesting we camp for the night before ascending the hill. 'We don't know what we're going to find there,' he said, which was true enough.

Venonis had always been a great crossing of ways, the centre, we were taught, of the eight-spoked wheel, the wheel remembered in the tattoo on my forearm. The wheel of the chariot and the wheel of the dance, the wheel of directions, the wheel of the year, the wheel of the stars across heaven.

The wheel of eight spokes. Two crosses superimposed. There is the cross of directions – north, east, south and west – and the cross of time, X, the chiasmus that gives us the cross-quarter days. Those who understand the wheel know that space and time are one and the same. So I am told. Things on earth never quite reflect the perfection – the ideal form – of heaven. At Venonis, the dominant roads were diagonal. Alignments were not perfect because of all the bumps and troughs in the landscape, but once this had been an ancient pilgrimage track, the Albios Way, that ran from the southeast to the northwest, passing through Venonis, the place of great gatherings of the tribes. The chiasmus and the cross. A phenomenon of the heavens. The symbol of a forgotten god. All lost now to the tramp of hobnailed shoes and the rattle of carts on the new road which, running from southeast to northwest, from Dubris via Londinium to Viroconium, had been renamed the Via Claudia.

Even in the gathering dusk it was obvious that the hill of Venonis, once our most sacred omphalos, the centre or navel of the land, was dead, like a whitened, barkless tree that still stands yet bears no leaf. The spirits had gone. In the wind I could no longer hear the shouts of children, the boomings of prophets, the wild music of bards, the enticements of the market-sellers. In the wind I could only hear the mewling of a lonely buzzard. This place was the heart of all Britain, and it had stopped beating.

I couldn't sleep for the waves of memories that washed over me, of my parents happy and together, of the great gatherings of all the nations of Britain, the Gauls and Belgae of the south, the Caledonians of the Far North, the Ordovices, Iceni, Brigantes, all weaving together in a great web of connectedness, forged by so many alliances and marriages that in the end one thought of oneself as 'Briton'. The merchants peddled stories from afar, of the lands of spices, of great civilisations, of the Romans who had 'pacified' both Gaul and Germany but who had yet to pacify us. While we craved exotic goods, we were not prepared to become part of anyone's empire. And that is how we grew: independent, proud, complacent.

Caratacus was certainly present at the last great gathering, held just at the time of the invasion of Claudius, for it was then that he was crowned druid king by the young militants who had broken with the age-old custom of non-violence. To see a druid take up arms . . . It was shocking, a breach of natural law. But it happened, and Caratacus had been behind it. He it was who put about the idea that the druids were in danger, when they were not. He it was who stirred up the younger ones, telling them in his great booming voice that the way of peace led to slavery.

Why? Son of a great king who had been an ally of Rome – what had caused Caratacus to become anti-Roman and the instigator of resistance? Cunobelinus had not been dead a year when his dutiful sons had rampaged across the southern territories, establishing their own kingdoms.

At first light, we dismantled the camp and began the long and gentle ascent to where the north–south and east–west roads crossed each other on this vast hill. Some trees grew here and there, copses and groves on the hillside, but there was no skirt of woodland. The summit was encircled by a ditch, an earthen rampart and a wooden palisade, all in a state of decay. The gates stood permanently open. At the highest part, where we had views of all four quarters, and the clouds and the light changed every time you turned to one of the eight directions, was the main place for the investiture of kings.

We had only been there a day when a lookout on the summit alerted us to the approach of Cartimandua, driving her dazzling chariot at the head of a very long procession of armed Brigantes. The priests among them wore antler headdresses and, beating on skin drums, brought an ancestral solemnity to the day that sent a shiver down my spine. I rode down the hill to greet her. There were a host of captives shuffling along in her train, one caged on a cart. I recognised Caratacus even though he sat with his head down, hugging his knees. He only came out of his stupor when several men lifted the cage off the cart and set it on the ground. He stared at me and if, indeed, looks could kill . . .

'Gotcha!' I said to him.

'For some reason he thought I would give him refuge!' said Cartimandua.

Caratacus jumped up and threw himself against the cage, roaring like a bear. And we goading him.

'Venutius?' I asked the queen.

'Still in Breghed. If he was angry with me before, he is incandescent with rage now, saying I have betrayed all Britons. Our divorce is being finalised.' Cartimandua glanced at her handsome armour-bearer and smiled but Velocatus discreetly kept his eyes averted.

'Traitors!' Caratacus rasped, his voice hoarse as if he had a mouth full of sand.

I called for him to be given a horn of beer. 'What was that?' I demanded, once he had quaffed noisily and got his voice back.

'I said TRAITOR!' he shouted. 'You lied! Your damned clever lies! I gave you my family for safekeeping, that was the deal, and you passed them over to Scapula! Why did I ever trust *you*?' He hawked. I dodged the beery ball of phlegm he spat at me. 'Everyone knows why you haven't brought Branwen home,' he continued. 'You don't want to share anything with her. You and your greedy acquisition of more and more territory. All by negotiation? No! All by lies and deception!'

Then I came back on him. We met face to face through the bars, both of us snarling. '*You?* Dare to call *me* a liar?'

'Cartimandua was ready to turn, that's what you said. You said Theana had joined her. Yes, I dare to call you liar.' This was rich, given his duplicity regarding the horses. All that play-acting: *Oh! My herd! My precious herd lost!*

I'd had enough of him. I had the chain securing the cage unlocked. Mandred and Mouse Ears tried to stop me, but I shook them off and, as thunderous as Taranis, went in to meet my enemy nostril to flared nostril. We hissed like a pair of bristling cats. Head to head, we glared.

'I am Caratacos. I rule this land. There is only one, and it is me. This land, all this land, is mine. As foretold by the druids, one shall come to be king of all, and that is me. Through me, and only through me, will Britain be united.'

I said nothing but bent my arms ready, looking for the first grasp. I was dimly aware that someone had locked the cage door to prevent Caratacus escaping.

'You told me the bitch was lovesick for Venutius!' His spittle sprayed on my face.

Cartimandua, watching all this with delight, laughed and clapped her hands. 'So lovesick I threw the braggart out of Brigantia!' she crowed. 'Whatever made you think otherwise?'

'Togidubnos! I believed him!' yelled Caratacus. He drew back his head and smacked it into my nose. An explosion of blood and pain. Momentarily in charge, he threw me against the cage. I rallied, shouldered into him, grabbed him round the waist and flipped him on his back. He rolled over and caught me by the knees, bringing me down. The cage creaked and rocked. I was surprised that he wrestled in the Roman style. Our British style was less mannered, more chaotic, pushing, shoving, grabbing, winding – a fight with only one aim: to win. But in this fight, we stuck to Roman rules, at least to begin with. By the end it had become wholly British. I heard someone issuing an order. Or was it a cry? At the same moment, we both fell from exhaustion. Entangled in the small cage, we lay together groaning, broken, bruised, bloody, apparently dead but for the gasping and the sweat. Again that cry, more urgent, but I was deafened by the drumming in my ears. 'Where's Dryadia?' Caratacus asked through blood-caked lips.

'She's at the fort at Viroconium,' I panted.

'You spineless runt,' he gasped. 'What possessed me to trust you?'

'Think what you like but in truth I saved your wife from being tortured.'

'How so?'

'I claimed the family as my capture and therefore my booty.'

He tenderly felt the swelling around his eyes and winced.

'It was to keep them safe,' I continued. 'I have no argument with them, only with you. And another thing,' I said. 'When you are taken off to Rome, the family will go with you. If they had stayed in hiding, you would never have seen them again.'

'But they would have been alive,' he said.

I tried to sit up but the world tipped and I fell backwards. Mandred crying: '*Get him out of there!*'

Scapula and the legion arrived the following day. He had not been very far from Viroconium when he had learned that Caratacus was being transported to Venonis. He peered at me, his face so contorted with pent-up rage that his eyes were reduced to slits. He could barely speak, overcome with the triumph of the capture on one hand, with hatred of me on the other. He looked from one to the other, both of us bruised and swollen. 'Who won?' he asked gruffly.

'I did,' said Cartimandua. 'Caratacus is my prisoner, whom I surrender to you.'

'You bilious sow!' Caratacus snarled.

Scapula's fury suddenly subsided; now he looked like a boy on his birthday. 'On behalf of the divine Claudius, I accept the gift of the queen of the Brigantes,' he replied, standing before her, his feet firmly planted, his gleaming helmet tucked under his arm. 'Great rewards will come your way, my lady.'

'Togidubnus played a part in this,' she said graciously. 'He would share the honour.'

'Would he now?'

Caratacus growled like a bear with a blocked nose.

'There will be an Ovation in Rome in which you will be personified,' Scapula told Cartimandua, 'unless, of course, you would like to be there in person?'

'In the Ovation?'

'Well, no . . .' Scapula had trouble keeping his face straight. A woman glorified by Rome? That could never happen. 'One of the onlookers,' he said.

'Looking on my personification?' Cartimandua sniffed in disdain.

Scapula did not answer but ordered two of his men to arrest me and tie my hands behind me with rope. 'As I promised you,' he said, 'I am sending you to Rome as prisoner for conspiring against the empire and collaborating with the rebels. You and Caratacus can travel together, chained to the same anchor. Sweet.'

Everyone protested at this, even Caratacus, who shouted in fluent Latin that he was no collaborator of mine, that I was a two-faced, oily dog who was a lying deceiver. 'Man of virtue? As slippery as a buttered eel!'

'As a lying deceiver, I've met my match in you!' I protested.

Scapula stood, pinching his lower lip thoughtfully and then addressing the gathered throng, captors and captives alike. 'What shall I do with the king of the Atrebates?' he asked them.

'Free him!' they all yelled.

Scapula looked disappointed. 'Togidubnus, all I've ever wanted since arriving on these blasted isles is to see the back of you. Free you may be, but you will go to Rome. I'm putting you in charge of the prisoner's escort. With luck, you will kill each other on the way. If not, and if you make any attempt to liberate the enemy, you – and he – will be hacked down on the spot, no trial.'

My head was spinning and I was beginning to feel sick. As they released my arms, all I could think was, At last. Rome!

We took the captives to the nearest fort and incarcerated them for two weeks while transport was arranged. Caratacus was joined there by Dryadia and the family. I ushered them into his prison. There was a tearful reunion in which Dryadia promised him she had not been harmed or troubled in any way. 'Togidubnus made sure of it.' Caratacus glowered at me. I said nothing.

Once all arrangements had been made, Scapula and two centuries of the Fourteenth, along with my own cohort, escorted us down the Via Claudia to Dubris, our treasure of such value that we were on constant alert against attacks. None happened. I intended to put the cohort under the authority of Katuaros but Scapula ordered them to join the Twentieth under Manlius Valens, the legate who would leave a fort and everyone in it if an attack seemed imminent. At the port, before embarking, I addressed the cohort, thanked them for their loyal service in recent trials and promised them I'd be back as soon as I could to join them.

'With Branwen?' Mouse Ears asked, combing his soft beard with his fingernails.

'With Branwen,' I promised, and the ageing, battle-scarred members of my old fianna went dewy at the thought of the return of the one they had known and loved as 'Little Sister'.

Scapula came out to the anchorage to see me on board. It had been a long journey from Venonis and he looked tired, although he worked hard to cover it. He gave me letters for the emperor which, I had no doubt, made it clear that these captives were his gift, not Cartimandua's or mine. As we said our farewell, I took him by the upper arm. And immediately let go. He was cold to the touch, in a subtle, not physical way. I had come across this before. It is a well-known symptom of a powerful curse.

'Consider this a banishment,' he said. 'Do not return while I rule here.'

'I promise you, Governor,' I said. 'I shall not.' I looked into the eyes of a man who, it seemed, would never know rest again under any circumstances. Such was his weariness that his eyelids were fluttering like a pair of trapped moths.

'Farewell, Governor,' I said.

'May we never meet again.'

'Careful what you wish for,' I said.

35
CHIASMUS

When I went on board, I was met by the cold gaze of the prisoner chained to the mainmast. The oarsmen set to work, grunting and splashing to shouted commands until we moved out into the sea and headed for Gaul. Once we had set sail, he was moved from the mast and chained by the ankle to the anchor.

Although he was a master of coracles and claimed he could ride the Salmon, he was not happy on the sea. He stood in green-tinged silence, watching Britain dwindling in the distance, his land, his life, his freedom, shrinking on the horizon like melting snow. I joined him and stood in equally reflective silence. As the western wind caught us, the commander had the sails fully unfurled but what was good for our progress was bad for the hero's stomach. Caratacus seemed to hold himself together by will-power and each time his gorge rose he overcame it, lord and master of himself.

'Just let it out,' I said. 'Food for the fish.'

'Leave me . . .' he said, swallowing and swallowing.

I was carrying a small phial of garum sauce for this purpose and, taking out the stopper, waved it under his nose. At once he was retching in a stupendous arc into the wake of the ship. Seagulls swooped in ecstasy.

'Or food for the birds,' I said. 'Most of us use buckets.'

'You are a bastard,' he growled, wiping his arm across his mouth.

I ordered watered wine for him and left him to it. The longer he had to reflect on things, the better.

The crossing was uneventful and, once we had anchored, the tribune in charge said officers could go ashore to rest for the night. I opted to remain on board, however, and share my supper with Caratacus.

'I don't want to eat with you!'

'Then don't eat.'

He was half-starved and had no choice. At first he chewed in silence but then he said, 'You told me Cartimandua would do anything to win the love of Venutius. Stupid of me, to believe you, to expect things such as honour and loyalty from a Romey. Man of virtue? Ha!'

He tore meat off the bone with his teeth and went back to his chewing. I'd not noticed it before, how long he chewed before he swallowed. It seemed to give him time to think. 'Cartimandua presents me as a gift to Rome and will be given a fortune in return, including anything I once possessed. Whereas, presumably, you got nothing for handing over my family?'

'Why would I? It wasn't a gift. I tried to hide them but they were found.'

'You betrayed me. You broke the sacred oath of silence!'

'I said nothing of your family's whereabouts. They were found by scouts. As for where you were: Scapula was torturing Dryadia in front of me. What would you have done?'

Caratacus turned and looked out to sea.

'I saved your wife, your family, your unborn child. Would you have acted differently?'

He snorted with disdain. 'Dryadia will give birth on this journey, and it will likely kill her.'

I was quiet, wondering if that wasn't the best option, to die on the road. Caratacus turned to face me. 'What are you thinking? That she's bound to die, anyway? Will they kill her? With me? In public?'

'I doubt it. They will kill you, yes, for the sheer theatre of it, but they will more likely enslave her. They will put her in a good position, in the imperial palace itself in all probability. Dryadia as handmaid to Agrippina. Just like Branwen.'

'Branwen? Is that what happened to her?'

'What do you care? You got the gold from her sale.'

He ignored this. 'She's a slave in the imperial palace? So, you will meet her again soon. Ah . . . at last you can rescue her, after how long?'

'If it hadn't been for you, I'd have rescued her eight years ago. Each time I hoped to make the journey, trouble flared on the border. My border. Your incursions.'

'You must hate me.'

'Must I? I was not woven on the same loom as you. Anger, yes, sometimes rage, but hatred? There are some emotions I just turn away from. It is the stoical way.'

'How long is this journey? How long do I have to suffer your pompous philosophising? I'd rather be in Rome, meeting my fate.' With a rattle of chains, he kicked out one foot, then the other, to release cramp.

The following morning we began the run down the serrated coast of Celtica, sails being furled and unfurled, oars lifted and lowered, the music of the galley commands to the oarsmen. Between sail and oar we maintained a steady speed. There were no storms on the Sea of the Basques but the waves crashed violently against the rocky shore. The next time we stopped for an overnight rest on land, I again stayed on board.

'Will they put me in the Tullianum?' Caratacus asked.

'So, you've heard of it?'

His eye twitched. 'It's where they kept Vercingetorix.'

'All the prisons are much the same, deep underground with a stone ceiling so low neither Briton nor Gaul is able to stand up straight but must endure weeks with his head bent while sewage laps at his feet,' I said.

'Yet Vercingetorix lost none of his glory.'

'True enough,' I agreed.

'What happened to your Kommios?' he asked.

'He died in bed at a grand old age.'

Caratacus hawked and spat, adding to the slime of the deck. 'Is all your family averse to honour?'

I shrugged. 'I think we just prefer to live, even into old age. The Tullianum it could well be.' I shuddered at the thought of it, the old underground cistern with a hole in the floor through

302

which they throw important prisoners awaiting trial. 'Your reputation runs before you,' I told him. 'The great Caratacus! King of the Britons! I wonder what will satiate the Roman lust for your humiliation? Garrotting is perhaps too quick, even after weeks in the foetid cellar. The most common lingering death for a non-citizen is crucifixion.' I stopped suddenly, realising I was enjoying this. He would know for himself the gory and graphic detail about the three-day death. I'd tortured him enough. 'Let's pray it will be quick. And then you can have the immortal honour you long for. However, given your reputation, we could argue for a healthier incarceration, out in the open air where people could see you. The great Caratacus!'

'And when I come before the divine emperor? What then? If I maintain my pride and dignity . . .?'

'Your death will be prolonged. If you want a quick death, submit.'

'Submit! Here we go again! Never! I am Caratacos! I do not submit to any man, least of all some jug-eared, drooling lurcher. Me? Submit to Claudius? Ha!'

It was the old Caratacus, his voice booming across the ship. Sailors and troops paused in what they were doing to stand and listen. Close by, a school of dolphins leapt out of the water in a spray of sunlight.

'Look at that,' he said, in awe.

'Claudius is vain and vulnerable,' I said. 'If you played on it, if you were to ask for clemency . . .'

'*Clemency?* I would rather bawl him out for his theft of my lands and property! Then I would die having done something worth doing!'

'Caratacos, if the opportunity is offered to you, take it! Use it! Stand up before the Romans and tell them what you want them to hear, but not so as to anger them. Your main weapon – now as ever – is your voice, your wonderful voice that can make mountains tremble and dolphins leap. Let Claudius hear your voice.'

'Saying what?'

'That's up to you. You could plead for mercy or say something to hasten your death. It's up to you. You must decide for yourself which is for the greater good, whether to die or to live.'

'To live? Would they set me free, let me go home?'

'Impossible.'

'So the choice is easy: an honourable death, preferably quick.'

'Whichever you decide,' I said, 'let your voice win it for you. Am I right in thinking your Latin is passable?'

'Better than that. Like you I spent my youth in Rome, but only three years of it.'

I was taken aback by this – he was so thoroughly the barbarian rebel – although it made sense of his missing years. 'Obvious,' Cartimandua had called it.

'You lived in the glorious city? And you are not a Romey?'

'Only three years. It was during the rule of Sejanus. Rome was rancid with evil. When the purge came, they executed Sejanus and anyone thought to have supported him. All those executions: they included my host and all his family. There were more bodies than rats in the streets. I couldn't get away quick enough. Before I went there I had, like my father, been a friend of Rome, but after all I saw, all I witnessed and experienced, on my return I became a friend of Britain.'

'Friend of Britain! You land-grabber. You stole Calleva!'

I tried to regain my composure. Was it true that I did not hate him? Was it only rage that made me want to take him by the throat and throttle him? I remembered Seneca telling me that hidden hatred is so much worse than open hatred. A hatch was lifting on a dungeon within me that I had not suspected existed. I took a very deep breath and reminded myself of the job to be done. For the dignity of Britain herself, Caratacus had to die a noble death. Any humiliation he suffered would be shared by our people, the downtrodden, the vanquished.

'However good your Latin was, it's probably rusty now. We have a few weeks to tune it up like a string on a harp. Mandred will help. If, when it comes to it, you make mistakes, it would not matter. You are an educated barbarian after all, and not a pretend Roman. No, I just want you to be able to say what you have to say in the best way possible, and from the heart so that Claudius will listen to you. A quick death has to be earned. In what is left of this journey, Mandred will drill you in vocabulary and sentence structure, and teach you how to use language to engender emotion.'

'You think I don't know that already?'

'In our own tongue, yes, undoubtedly. But in Latin? The last thing we want is you standing before the emperor and speaking like a schoolboy.'

He stared at me hard and wonderingly. 'Is all this really to earn me a quick garrotting? It sounds as if you want me to live.'

'I can't imagine life without you. It would be like day without night. Summer without winter. Heat without cold.' And suddenly I realised that I needed him, my enemy, to keep myself in balance.

I had no further conversation with him before we reached the port of Burdigala and the beginning of the Via Aquitania which crosses Gaul to the Mediterranean. The honey-coloured road of packed gravel stretched out in one long, straight line into hilly country. It was busy with merchant traffic and patrols, the way bordered by shrines, each mile marked by a stone, and every eight miles with an overnight camp for troops.

I had secured a covered cart for Dryadia. Caratacus shuffled along in leg irons with Mandred walking beside him, keeping him distracted with principles of rhetoric. Watching Caratacus shuffle I remembered how Mandred himself used to walk, long after his own leg irons were removed, lurching pitifully until we had him cured at the Hot Springs of Sulis. It was as if we had the same thought simultaneously, for Mandred suddenly looked over his shoulder at me and smiled.

I rode along the line to the tribune in charge. It did not take long to persuade him that the great hero must look his best when presented to the emperor. I gave him my word that Caratacus would not escape.

'How can you be so sure?'

'You have two guards with him always. The leg irons are only for humiliation.'

At the next stop, Caratacus was unshackled. I walked with him to rest my horse. 'Mandred tells me your Latin is superb,' I said. 'There's not much he needs to teach you.'

Caratacus rubbed his ankles. 'Just another of your false presumptions about me. A scruffy barbarian, a rapacious warlord, an illiterate bandit. That's what I am to you. Just because I took Calleva, which was bequeathed to me by my uncle. It was your father, Verica, who was the usurper.'

I had never heard that before, but rallied. 'Not to mention the killing of King Esius,' I said, 'and the sale of his daughter into slavery. Yes, these things do have a bearing on my opinion of you.'

'I am none of the things you take me for. I am the druid king, elected to save the druids from annihilation by the Romans. I have given my life to serve my holy elders. That is what I am prepared to die for: our law, our religion, our culture. Our wisdom.'

'Would it come as a surprise to learn that Scapula has no ambition to wipe out the druids? He has only ever been interested in wiping out you.'

It was Caratacus's turn to be wrong-footed.

'You have created all this,' I went on. 'Was it your idea to form a militant wing? That's when the troubles of the druids began.'

'They began with rumours spread by Rome that we are superstitious magicians who practise human sacrifice!'

'And what was the murder of the archdruid, if not a human sacrifice? A good man, a wise man, having his throat cut even as he began to address the throng at Venonis.'

'It was necessary. He was so like you. *Submit, submit, it is our only hope!* We couldn't allow any more of that. What worked in the past between warring tribes when, with a *vocos*, the archdruid stepped between them to restore peace, no longer works. Our magic has no power over the Romans, so we must fight them on their own terms, with weapons.'

I shuddered. 'That is an aberration of the druid way.'

'It is necessary for our survival.'

'Claudius is fascinated by our religion. Julius Caesar's best friend was a druid. Why on earth would Rome want to be rid of us? If there is such a plan, it is to be rid of anyone fomenting rebellion.'

'Rebellion! Why am I a rebel, to fight for what is mine? What am I rebelling against, if not an aggressive occupying force who wants all we have? Rebel? You're the rebel. It is you and

Cartimandua, and Prasutagus, and any one of you Romeys, who are the rebels. Rebels against our Mother, Britannia. You have never understood, have you?' Caratacus said. 'What, you think I've suffered all this, the years of rootlessness, of indecisive battles, for my ambitions? You think when I call for freedom, I only want wealth? Is that it? You were never crowned with the mistletoe, were you? It is I, not you, who am the druid king, elected by our wise men to be the one to protect them. To *protect* them. Do you understand? Do you really believe the Romans have no wish to wipe us out? While I was in the glorious city I learned of the plan to exterminate the druids in Gaul; I realised by extension they would do the same in Britain. I came home. I warned the druids of what would happen if there was an invasion, and I began to build my army.'

It felt like an earth tremor, when the ground beneath you unexpectedly shifts. Had I got it wrong?

'We did it all by rumour and whistles. Remember how we disappeared off Copper Hill? The druid way. And that is where they are, in the high mountains, or over the strait and on sacred Mona. I was crowned druid king and given the duty to protect them. The fighting druid. It was my duty to be always between them and the Romans. That is over. I am removed. Do you think I *care* what happens to me now? Just let it be quick. Clemency? I despise you, Togidubnus. I utterly despise you.'

I spent the next two days riding alone, flea-bitten by my thoughts, my fears, my guilt. I was taking Caratacus to his death, and every step was growing heavier. Now, with the truth revealed to me, I knew it was not only Caratacus I was killing, it was the druids. I wanted to fold up in my mother's lap and sob. Mandred grew concerned, thinking I was developing a fever. There was only one cure for this, a long ride over the chalk downs, but that was not available.

'Dreaming Cup?' he suggested, but I shook my head. I would never take that stuff without the presence of Apnodens.

'Soma?'

'Mandred! The solution, if there is one, lies in wisdom, not in some smoking cauldron. Be quiet now and let me think.'

'So think, but stop picking at the scab of what happened.'

I consoled myself with the thought that soon I would meet Seneca again. I could ask him. He would know what to do, and if there was nothing that could be done, he would know how to endure it. I needed Seneca!

I rode apart from the columns, letting the rhythm of my horse and the clopping of its hipposandals on the long road fill my being. A sandal lost: clop-clop-clop-pad. I dismounted and went back to pick it up where it lay by a marble shrine gleaming in the sun. I stopped in its shade to rethread the laces while the long train of soldiers and captives passed by as if in a trance. I'm not one of those who seems obliged to read every epigraph, every dedication, every milestone he passes as if it is his duty to read any word that comes before him, but an altar in the shrine caught my eye. It had been donated by some travelling merchant, a Greek: 'TO THE GODDESS MINERVA, DELPHIDIUS OF ATHENS WILLINGLY AND DESERVEDLY FULFILLED HIS VOW'. In his mind and heart, presumably he had meant Athena. But here, Minerva. Athena – Minerva – Sulis. I sat on the marble seat of the shrine, fiddling with the hipposandal, wondering about this unknown man who had my soul name and worshipped the same deity; and what it was the goddess had done for him that he had repaid with this altar and its finely engraved letters. The tramping of the passing unit; the clinking chains of the captives; the heat of the day. Suddenly all was dark and I was plunging. Into Annwn? A black lake? A crevice in the Temple of Apollo at Delphi? The Dreaming Cup? It was all and none of these, just bottomless space.

Delfos, Delfos, Delfos . . . She was calling my name. *I am with you now as I have been with you since the beginning. I was there at Delphi, there at Hot Springs. I am Athena; I am Sulis; I am Minerva. It was I who carried you to Rome in your visions, as today I carry you in person to fulfil your vow. Your vow to your betrothed. Do you think I do this for someone despicable? Weak? Unheroic? Do not believe what he says about you, for he does not believe these things himself. He is scared of you.*

Why scared?

Because he cannot control you. He is scared of your moral strength; of your true devotion to me; of your devotion to truth itself. You have what he lacks.

And he has what I lack.

It is so. Live to die or die to live.

Mandred, having missed me, came back and found me slumped on the ground, my head resting against the altar.

'It's the heat,' he said, giving me spring water from his flask. 'Don't let Caratacus know you fainted – he'll hee-haw like a donkey all the way to Rome.'

At the Mediterranean coast a large, square-sailed corbita awaited us, accompanied by two galleys carrying an escort of Praetorian Guards, all gleaming bronze armour and bobbing red plumes.

'What's this?' Caratacus said. 'A merchant ship? Is that what we are now, just cargo? More goods being delivered to Rome, which already has more than enough?'

'Look at the escort,' I breathed. 'Praetorians! That is something reserved for consuls or the emperor himself. I told you: your reputation runs before you, and you will be treated with honour, great honour.'

'And my family? My men? How will they be treated?'

'That's up to you. It's not just your life in your hands, though you seem oblivious to that. Everything depends on how you meet Claudius, what you say, and how you say it. By all means hasten your own death, driven by that monstrous pride of yours, but think of Dryadia and the children before you do, think of your loyal warriors. Their fate depends on you.'

On this third leg of the journey, Caratacus became so immersed in his studies with Mandred that he had no need for seasickness medicine, even when it got a little choppy between the islands of Corsica and Sardinia. I stared up at the rocky heights of Corsica as we passed. It did look barren, yes, if you kept a blind eye to the vineyards on its southern slopes, the opulent villas perched like gannets' nests, the busy little fishing harbours. I realised that Seneca had used poetic licence to describe it as a barren rock. It was well populated, thriving, dramatically beautiful. But it was not Rome. That was his grievance. He had been shut out of Rome. But he was shut out no longer. I wondered with a flutter of impatience what our reunion would be like.

At Ostia, we disembarked and boarded a river boat to carry us up the Tiber. My mood was as choppy as the waters, churned as they were by so many oars on so many craft. The captives were to spend the following days in a prison on the Field of Mars. Caratacus was making a fuss, saying he wanted to be in the Tullianum. I told him to calm down, that I would do what I could to get him transferred to the place where Vercingetorix had awaited his own trial once he had been sentenced. We never discussed it, our identification with our heroes. Mine, Kommios, was my ancestor, my grandfather, but his? He was not related to Vercingetorix yet he had a sense of kinship with the heroic Gaul that went beyond being a blood relative. I made to leave, intending to enter the city at once. Caratacus took me by the shoulders. 'Look on me, Delfos. We shall not meet again. You have got me wrong. And now I wonder if I haven't got you wrong, too. You are not like the others, lusting for wealth. You are your own man, and it's been a struggle for me to understand you. But I've been watching you these last few weeks, watching and listening. While we were at sea, you spoke of my voice. I've been thinking about that. Yes, I have a loud and carrying voice. I use it to stir men up. You also have a voice, calm, measured, quiet. You soothe; I thunder. I slice off heads in war; you negotiate treaties. You say you have walked away from hatred. You haven't. You don't even know what it is. Let me tell you. Hatred cannot exist except where first there was love. Hatred is love gone bad. You are not going to believe what I am about to say, but I shall say it anyway. I am grateful for what you have done for me, and I bitterly regret what I did to Branwen's father, and to Branwen.'

'So you don't despise me, then?'

310

'Of course I do!' He laughed – like the Caratacus I once knew, whose belly laughs echoed in the hills – but then sobered. 'Understand these things were done neither for my cruel pleasure nor for vengeance. I needed to break your power. We could not have you married to Branwen. That would have made you too strong. But now, you have won, and you will see her again, very soon.'

It was my turn to feel seasick, even though we were on land.

'You have been loyal to her,' he said. 'It's a quality I value above almost all others, loyalty.'

'How do you know I've been loyal to Branwen?' I asked.

'Everyone knows that, even my sister,' he said, and winked.

I stared at him, hard, as if to see into his soul. He stared right back. 'You are the one', he said, 'whose name will be garlanded with glory. The man of reason who felt his way across the marsh in the dark, trusting instinct, trusting the gods, intent only on reaching dry ground. If only I could swap souls! Would you swap with me?'

'What, and be a hero? Adored by all who love freedom and hate servitude? Even here, on the doorstep of death? Of course I would! But Reason tells me that would be the choice of a child.'

'O son of the son of Kommios,' he said, 'do you not know yet where your heart lies? Not with Father, but with Mother.'

O man cast in the mould of Vercingetorix, I am the product of both.

36
OUTSIDE THE CITY WALL

We disembarked into a crowd straining to catch a glimpse of the famous rebel. Pushing them back, Praetorians created a passage for the captives to the Field of Mars, the land between the city and Tiber river. Once a swamp in a loop in the river, it had been reclaimed and was now filled with monuments, gardens and theatres, a place for nobles at leisure to meet, converse and parade. The Portico of the Argonauts had been turned into a temporary prison. Caratacus and his family stumbled along, each ringed at the neck with heavy iron joined to a long chain. Within the portico they were released from their chain but had their feet shackled and were put in a small room at ground level.

'What am I doing here?' Caratacus thundered. 'Take me to the Tullianum!'

Everyone stared at him as if he were mad.

'They want you here,' I explained to him, 'in honour of your status.'

He hawked and spat.

'Every great man of Rome – the imperial family, the senators, the military commanders –all will want to come and speak to Caratacus. They would not be happy to enter the stinking pit which is the Tullianum.'

'I want to die in the manner of Vercingetorix!'

'Don't worry,' I said, becoming irritated by his histrionics. 'You will still be garrotted in public. Think of your wife for once, and your unborn child.' Dryadia had folded up, sitting on the floor in a corner weeping. 'Do you want her to give birth in the Tullianum?'

'She can stay here.'

Dryadia's weeping became louder. I needed fresh air and left them to it.

Outside the spacious square in front of the portico was filling up with those wanting to meet Caratacus, mostly senators and nobles with their grandsons wishing to touch history in the flesh. I saw Vespasian in the toga of the consul, accompanied by his son Titus and his friend, Britannicus, son of Claudius. Titus was a handsome lad but you could already see signs of the crumpled face that marked the Flavian family. As he grew into manhood he would become the image of his father. Britannicus, on the other hand, had no mark of Claudius in him at all. Nor any mark of me. Clearly Messalina had been faithful to neither of us. He flinched under my gaze and looked away.

'What are you doing here?' I asked Vespasian. 'Surely you have not come to idolise the rebel.'

He smiled. 'I want to see him, that's all, see my enemy face to face. I'll spit on him if no one's looking.'

I turned to those milling behind him. 'Form a queue!' I demanded, taking it upon myself to patrol it, acting like the gatekeeper to Caratacus. They did as bidden, even Vespasian, and I allowed a few in at a time. I noticed that he still limped as he walked, that the wound received in battle in Britain had not healed. At the end of the day what was left of the queue dissolved only to form again at sunrise. And so it continued, day after day. An invitation came from the imperial palace to visit the emperor but I explained why I could not.

'Go,' said Mandred. 'What's the matter with you?'

'I'm too busy.'

'Procrastination, that's what it is. Go to the palace! Reunite with Branwen! It's why we are here!'

Any leisure I did have I spent at the gymnasium wrestling with men and pretending that women had no power over me; in truth, I was scared of the wrath of my betrothed. Those stiff letters we had exchanged. She had released me from any bond I had made with her father, but I had refused to be released. How would I face her? What would she look like? In my mind's eye she was a tousle-haired ten-year-old, fearfully independent except when in the company of her beloved teacher, Apnodens. I remembered them singing together, he chanting a line, she repeating it. I remembered her playfulness, her teasing, her bubbling laughter. She had been a slave for eight years. Surely the laughter had died? I was in no hurry to find out and thus I avoided the imperial palace.

The queue, as I say, was formed mostly of fathers and sons, but I came across a small group of Jewish women whose interest in the prisoner I could not fathom.

'What is your business with Caratacus?' I asked them.

'We have come to clean him, feed him, help allay his fear,' they told me.

'Fear? Caratacus?'

'Everyone fears their own end. Add public humiliation to that . . .'

Suddenly there came the swelling moans of a woman in travail coming from within the prison room. The women looked at me, their eyes large. 'It's his wife,' I said. 'Go. Do what you can to help.'

They hurried to the front of the queue.

'Let them in!' I shouted and the guards acquiesced. It was these Jewish women, who referred to themselves as 'Followers of the Way', who helped bring forth the daughter that was born to Caratacus in Rome.

I'd expected the trial of Caratacus to be over and done with by Saturnalia. I would overwinter somehow with Branwen in Rome and we would return to Britain in the spring. I would take her to her people and oversee her investiture as queen of the Dobunni. Having formally relinquished the title of king-in-waiting, I would marry her and become king of the Dobunni. Why does the mind persist in viewing the future as a straight line of cause and effect? One has only to look back to realise that there are no straight lines in life, only divergencies, deflections, accidents creating a series of twists and turns that brought you here, to the present, and thus it must be in the future. We may indeed reach our goals and fulfil our intentions, but it will not be by a straight path that cuts through all obstacles; no, it will be on a splintering path that finds its direction by bouncing off events to bring you where you need to be, leaving you to wonder who is driving this chariot with its pair of wayward horses. In truth, the future is unimaginable. All we can safely expect is surprises, such as the trial of Caratacus being delayed until January, when it would be the culmination of the annual celebration of the Conquest of Britain and Triumph of Claudius. A piece of theatre, in other words.

'Are you really going to spend all winter here in these cramped quarters, overseeing a queue?' Mandred asked. He himself was out and about, gathering intelligence not just in the forum but in poorer quarters where, he said, you were more likely to learn useful information. And I was grateful for it, cooped up as I was.

'I seem to be doing the work of a secretary,' I said pointedly as he threw his cape round his shoulders.

'You're very good at it,' he said.

That morning I had a visit from the secretary of someone too important to follow the protocol of the morning queue to see Caratacus. 'You are requested to bring the prisoner, under cover of darkness, to my master's house on the Quirinal.'

'And your master is?'

'The praetor of Rome, Lucius Seneca. He asks that you bring the prisoner yourself.'

Seneca – the name on every man's lips. I'd heard that the queue to see Caratacus was nothing to the one that greeted Seneca every morning, stretching from the atrium of his house halfway down the Quirinal Hill to the city wall. Seneca, my humble master had returned from exile to become the most exalted person in the empire, apart from the emperor himself. Seneca. Seneca. Seneca. Was it any wonder I was avoiding meeting him? I did not wish to besmirch my cherished memories with the powerful new form that had hatched from his dormancy on Corsica.

'On the orders of the emperor,' I said haughtily to the secretary, 'Caratacus is not to be moved.' That much I had intended to say: the rest came of itself, unbidden. 'But I,

315

Togidubnus, King of the Atrebates and Dobunni, shall come gladly.' And so I went with the secretary and his retinue into the city and up the hill of the Quirinal, where senators and consuls live in luxury behind high, private walls shaded by laurels. Seneca received me himself in the atrium.

'Delfos!' he said, stepping forward, arms wide.

Eight years had passed. Everything was different and nothing had changed. 'Lucius!' I said and returned his warm embrace.

37
REUNION

The last time I'd seen Seneca was in prison, struck down by one of the wheezing attacks that seemed must kill him. He had been in his late forties then, so troubled by his lungs that he had begun to look on every breath as if his last. Now here he was, closer to sixty and looking fit and healthy. Though still barrel-chested and thin of leg, he had the ruddy complexion of a peasant. He stood before me, holding me at arm's length, studying my own transition from youth into manhood.

'It suited you,' I said, 'Corsica.'

'Rest is a wonderful thing,' he said, leading me through the atrium of his house where marble busts filled the niches in the walls and exotic fish swam in a long water channel. There were chambers right and left, quiet places with closed doors and, at the end of the atrium, his study flanked by a dining room and his own main bedroom. All doors were closed, yet I had the prickling feeling that we were being watched. I was glad that Seneca, drawn by the din of sparrows and the dancing play of light, passed on to the walled garden with its colonnades, its flowering plants in urns, its privacy.

'I enjoyed it at first, the solitude and the leisure to study nature,' he said. 'But after a while, one would readily swap a sky full of stars for the company of friends, as you yourself foretold when we were last together. The mind must be exercised like the body, and mine grew flaccid.'

We walked through the dappled shade. 'Once lassitude gains entry into your soul, it is hard to dislodge. It takes the very energy you no longer have to be rid of it. I lost interest in my studies. Lifting a stylus to make a note seemed too heavy

317

a task. I began to enjoy sitting in the shade with a glass of wine, doing nothing and calling it "thinking", happy to put off until tomorrow the work of the day. You can have too much solitude.'

'Solitude? On our way to Rome our ship passed Corsica. It seemed to my eyes to be a popular summer resort for wealthy Romans.'

'Wealthy Romans of the most tedious kind,' he said. 'And then, of course, there is the winter.'

'But "barren rock"?'

'In the winter, yes. Though any man of letters worth his salt would know I was quoting Ovid. It is the common fate of poets, to be banished. We know too much and are not afraid to speak out. Eloquently. Very well, so I wasn't exiled to some remote barren rock like Ovid, but I was relegated to a villa on the mountain from where I could see the sun glancing off Rome on the far horizon. I may not have been abandoned to starve amidst desolation, but I did feel like a dog shut out.'

'And whining to be let back in.' I intended it as a joke, but he cast me a dark glance. Picking a stalk of lavender from an urn as we passed, he crushed it between his palms to breathe in its loveliness.

'At my lowest ebb, I heard the voice of Reason. "Resume your practices," she said, "with no thought of success or failure." And so I did. Rising early, eating frugally, spending the hour before bed reviewing the day. Suddenly my interest in what was around me sprang back to life. I could spend hours watching hawkmoths ravishing the flowers, listening to cicadas, marvelling at eagles. They were hours well spent. Soon I was returning to my books and reading again. And then it happened. Words began to flow. Words to be written down, many of them to be crossed out or thrown away, of course, but not all. I began to write things I was pleased with: plays, essays, letters. I was happy, Delfos, happy in the act of writing, of rising each day with a sense of purpose, even a sense of not having enough hours in the day. And then fate intervened.'

A message had come from the imperial palace. His sentence of relegation had been commuted and he was invited to return. 'It would be an honour for my new wife and me,' Claudius had said, 'if you would accept the tutorship of my newly adopted son, Domitius Ahenobarbus, henceforth to be known as Nero Claudius Caesar Augustus.'

I glanced around his garden, the beds of herbs lined with clipped box, its fountains and statuary. 'I don't understand. You had achieved happiness and you gave it up. For wealth and position? You?'

The sun was setting on a warm autumnal evening. He sat down on a marble bench next to a brazier and patted the place beside him. 'Close your eyes. Put yourself in my position. I had a choice between two things: I could either enjoy personal happiness and freedom from duty, or accept a duty that put me in charge of the education of the next emperor.'

I opened my eyes. 'Next emperor? That will be Britannicus, surely?'

'Britannicus is the son of Claudius, but Nero's claim is greater. He has the blood of Augustus flowing in his veins. Up to now he has been taught literature and history by two decrepit freedmen and has developed an unseemly taste for theatre under the influence of a certain barbarian princess. Really! Branvena is a lovely girl, but really!'

I went to speak, croaked, coughed to clear my throat. My eyes stung and I moved downwind of the brazier.

'She had to be removed from her post. She was leading Nero into the land of whimsy when what he needs, so desperately, is philosophy.'

I grunted.

'What did you grow up on yourself, if not philosophy?' he asked.

'Well, I started with whimsy.'

'But from the moment you entered my little school, you began to become who you are.'

'And what is that?' I asked, dabbing at my eyes.

'A fine man with an acute sense of justice, who knows right from wrong and acts accordingly. A man who, himself, chose duty over personal happiness, who remained in Britain when his heart was here. Now do you understand why I decided to return to Rome? To do my duty for the greater good. I do believe you would have done the same.'

I gazed on the opulent garden and, rather than understand, felt confused.

He sighed. 'It wasn't the money, the new house, not even the most elevated office of praetor, that lured me back. It was the realisation – and acceptance – of duty.'

He rose up and led me to a triclinium of grey stone, open to the garden with ivy creeping in and vines swagged between pillars, heavy with pendulous grapes. A cold meal was being set out for us.

'Is it working?' I asked. 'Are you guiding Nero on to a straighter path?'

'I am. After only two years of my tutelage, he is showing fine qualities, qualities that became apparent to all when he assumed the toga virilis. Only thirteen but already beloved by the people. He can hold the stage like no other. Have you met him? No. But you must. I'll arrange it. You have much in common.'

'We do?'

'Through my influence, he is falling in love with Greek philosophy, art and culture. You two together would talk for hours. And poetry. If he wasn't who he's destined to be, he'd either be a fine poet or an actor.'

Was Seneca smitten by his pupil or by the idea of a philosopher king? Good government by the wise: an experiment that has been tried many times and has never succeeded.

'So, you see, I made the right choice,' he said.

Perhaps, but on a false basis. The rightful heir was Britannicus.

Seneca adjusted his toga and took his place on the couch. 'I am a wealthy man,' he said. 'From rags to riches in what seems to be but a day. I am the praetor, the imperial administrator. I have estates, vineyards, businesses, money to lend – anything you want, dear friend, just ask, and I won't be looking for it to be paid back – but all my time is taken up with imperial business, with visiting clients – have you seen the queues? – with lessons for my very special student.'

'You're not whining again, I hope.'

'No, no! I'm not complaining! I just wonder if I can maintain my stoical principles in the face of plenty. Poverty is conducive to a life of virtue. Plenty? It is so much harder. How should I live? Moderately, of course. All things in right measure.'

He played with his food. Confronted by plates piled with fruits, silver dishes of shelled nuts, a main course of three birds, one cooked inside another, I looked back on his frugal meals with painful nostalgia. *If you can't abstain, at least be moderate,* he had once said. And if you can't be moderate, then what? There may not have been pheasant brains, roasted dormice or marinated sow's udders on the table, but the plentiful salads and cold meats had been arranged by the master cook in the kitchen, whose speciality was delicate dressings.

'I'm sorry this is not a feast,' Seneca said, 'but I thought with you I could be myself.'

He thought this was moderate? My dear friend, my wise old tutor, the man who had taught me everything that was worth knowing, the one I had considered the wisest of men: he should be sitting cross-legged on a hard floor eating cheese and olives, not propped on an elbow nibbling food that upset his digestion. Grief, not for anything in particular but for the transience of things, even qualities of character, took a hold of me.

'Dear boy,' he said, leaning forward with concern. 'Is that a tear on your cheek?'

'I'd forgotten what pepper does to me,' I said, dabbing at my eyes again.

'I apologise, Delfos. I have been talking non-stop when what I truly want is to hear about you.' He called a slave. 'Clear the table of all this nonsense and bring us some bread, cheese and olives. And some of that roasted ham. He turned back to me. 'Now, tell me of all that has happened since we last met.'

I told him of the conquest and of the years since, and my own wearying work of establishing Roman law and administration. 'My people have come to accept changes such as the names of the months, numbers, language, the need to be able to read and write, but they resist the taxes. There is much grumbling! They pay up, once I've reminded them of the benefits: greater prosperity, easier travel, safer roads, efficiency. I'm making it sound easy, but most of my days are spent listening to cases in court of unfair distribution, even loss, of land, of being made to pay a higher tax just because a new road runs straight through your settlement – all manner of injustices stemming from heavy-handed overlordship. I try the governor's patience with my endless petitions. I thought I would grow up a warrior but most of my battles are fought in the law courts and treasury. A negotiator carefully edging towards a fairer, more peaceful co-existence.'

'As a gardener with weeds. Just when he thinks he has all the beds cleared, he looks back.'

'Exactly like that. Nettles and dandelions.' I told him of the insurgencies and skirmishes and how often memory of his wisdom had guided my actions. 'Time after time I've wanted to kill my enemy but a thought of you stayed my hand.'

He looked troubled. 'Why? What did you think I might say?'

'That killing is evil.'

'I may have thought so once. Now I see that a greater evil is to allow murderous aggression to go unchecked.'

'Meaning?'

'If your enemy has you by the throat, you must shake him off, by whatever means. Let this be your guide to action: always for the good, even if it means killing.'

It took a while to absorb this shocking new view. 'Life was so much easier under druid law. Through law, our druid elders guided us in the ways of peace. Now they are forbidden to act as lawgivers and we have to live under Roman law, which is to say, Pax Romana: peace by the annihilation of the enemy.'

'That is not true peace.'

'No. So I keep telling them. Negotiated settlement leading to a cessation of hostilities. That is the better way.'

'Perhaps, but it is still not peace.'

'What then is peace?' Seneca asked.

'Peace of mind. It's the only thing within our control, whether we are agitated or unmoved by events.'

I realised how agitated my mind had become over the years. He nibbled on olives like a squirrel, satisfied and contented.

'Why are you holding court so much?' he asked.

'Our druid colleges and law courts have closed. Some druids have dissolved into the communities but many, knowing exactly what Pax Romana means, have migrated, either to the

Far West or Ireland, or our most sacred sanctuary, the Isle of Mona off the northern coast of the land of the Ordovices and Deceangli.'

'Are they safe there?'

'I hope so.'

I felt slightly light-headed, realising why it was I'd wanted Caratacus to live. Not for himself, or any of his ludicrous ideas about freedom. It was because he'd been protecting the druids. 'Aulus Plautius was a good governor,' I said. 'Ruthless, perhaps, but not over-ambitious. He really did want a peaceful absorption of Britain into the empire. But Publius Ostorius Scapula is a driven man. He will reach those western shores if it kills him.'

'It has killed him. Scapula is dead. Without reaching his goal.'

'*What?*'

'We heard yesterday. He fell from his horse in the heat of battle with the Silures, but not from any wound. No one knows what killed him but it was probably exhaustion.'

'Probably,' I said.

'So we shall look for a new governor and need to make sure he's a good man. When will you return to Britain?'

'At first sailings in the spring.'

'I strongly recommend you postpone until we've found you a governor that you can work with.'

I nodded gratefully and rose to leave, saying I needed to return to my accommodation to look after Caratacus.

'I hear he is being looked after very well by just about everyone,' said Seneca. 'The Campus Martius is an unhealthy place. For all its fine buildings and monuments, once a swamp, always a swamp. Not healthy. You are tired, Delfos. Stay with me here on the hill above it all where the air is fresh. You would be very welcome. Who knows, after a few days you might even relax enough to ask me the question.'

'What question?'

'The question.'

I slumped back down on the couch, my head in my hands.

'Have you been to the imperial palace yet?' he asked.

'No,' I groaned.

'Surely you've been invited?'

'Several times. How many times can you refuse the emperor without being flogged?'

'Why do you risk it?'

'What can I do?' I cried. 'Arrive in the great halls with my composure intact? You know what he's like. He'd play with me. He'd attend my reunion with Branwen like a malevolent spirit who feeds off human embarrassment.'

Seneca nodded. 'It's true. They would not have given her up lightly. Agrippina, who had more or less thrown her away, would have suddenly become very possessive. They would have toyed with you mercilessly.'

'You're speaking in the past tense.'

'Past conditional tense. Did you learn nothing from me?' He smiled his winsome, satyric smile. He, too, was toying with me. 'They would have done these things, if they hadn't already sold her to me,' he said.

From being too hot I went cold. 'What are you saying?

'Branvena is here.'

Here?

'In this house. As soon as I got back from Corsica, I made enquiries. She had been for some years in the house of Passienus Crispus, serving Agrippina. On the death of Crispus – bad business, that – and the marriage of Agrippina to Claudius – *very* bad business – Branvena was transplanted into the imperial palace. She did not fare well and, from being a tutor of Agrippina's son, she was made the slave of her handmaid. When I finally caught sight of her, she was looking brittle from exhaustion. Agrippina had tired of having her around, especially given the influence Branvena continued to have over her son, corrupting him with her peculiar ways, encouraging him in plebeian activities like acting and singing. When I offered to buy her, Agrippina agreed without a struggle. Indeed, I got her cheap. She is now here at my house, being restored to good health.'

She is here . . .

'I thought it would make it easier for you,' he said.

My own senses became acute: the song of the breeze, the patter of leaves falling to the ground, distant conversations beyond the garden walls, the constant trickle of water falling into stone basins. Overhead, the high-pitched whistle of an eagle gliding over Rome.

'Be prepared for a shock,' he said. 'She has been sadly neglected.' Seneca nodded to a servant. The man returned the nod and quietly left. 'Apparently she was a wonderful singer who offered unique entertainment for the family. They dressed up for it, Nero wearing a wolf pelt, his mother a torc, Claudius in an expensive plaid with a very beautiful brooch. Nero wrote little plays about barbarians, with songs that your lady sang. She sings well, but it's not her real strength, is it? Not what she has been trained in. But she would never perform a sacred chant for mere entertainment. I've heard it, you know, a *vocos*.'

I felt something pressing on my lungs so that I could hardly breathe. That rib pain was back. Heartache, Apnodens had called it. 'I'm not sure I want to see her,' I said.

'Ha! She is positive she does not want to see you.'

My pride was stung. 'Oh?'

'What kind of lover does not rescue his beloved?'

'A busy kind with a nation to look after! You know . . . Don't you tell me . . . If it comes to the choice between a small, selfish action and a greater one related to the common good . . .'

Now Seneca's face clouded over. 'Beware of philosophical hogwash, especially that spouted by me. Follow your heart. If your heart is large enough to encompass a nation, well, that is a great good, but yours? Mine? Perhaps it is better to be selfish than a hypocrite.'

Hypocrite? Me? What was he saying?

I roared with grief and frustration at his betrayal of his principles and Seneca flapped his hands, telling me to watch the anger and take control. I wanted to wrestle him to the ground, to smash down Rome and the gods with it, and whoever the tormentor is who holds the sacred mirror up to a man's face and shows him his own image. I do believe Seneca was considering sending for nets to catch me. I looked at his expression of consternation mixed with fright, stopped shouting, calmed down and began to laugh.

He sat down heavily. 'By Jove, I hate barbarians,' he said, wheezing.

'You and I have a duty to the greater good, whether we like it or not,' I said, as if it were a slogan for someone seeking election. A truism. Something worth repeating.

He gazed at me. 'You, at least, can have both worlds. You can marry Branvena and take her home to continue your dutiful work together. Perhaps I, too, can have both worlds. If only I could find the Corsica within, the place of inviolate solitude and endless time.'

'She never liked me, you know,' I said, beginning to gibber. 'Always preferred Katuaros. All women prefer Kat—'

'Oh, stop your nonsense, boy. At the first Triumph celebrating the conquest, they put on a re-enactment of the death of Caratacus's brother. Usual thing. Strong, hairy Gaul dying under the hooves of a Roman cavalry officer. I was told that when she was assured it was not real but a re-enactment of the death of Togodumnus, she heard Togidubnus and collapsed.'

I wanted to say, 'I know, I was there,' but resisted. How old had she been then? Eleven? A slave in charge of the son of Agrippina but lost and alone in this unbelievably strange city for which no story nor florid account had prepared her.

There were the sounds of footsteps approaching. My skin prickled. I expected the shuffling steps of a nervous slave, but it was the tread of a woman who had business with me.

The door opened and Seneca's wife entered.

'Ah, Paula, where is Branvena?' Seneca asked.

'She is indisposed.'

'She was well enough when I saw her first thing.'

'Now she is indisposed,' said Paula firmly. 'She begs your forgiveness, King Togidubnus.'

'How long will she be indisposed?' I asked, believing that Seneca had been right: Branwen did not want to see me.

Paula shrugged. 'It could be weeks.'

'Weeks? Is she ill?'

'No, dear, she is bald. My husband here had her deloused and the barber was a little too enthusiastic. In the end, with her hair left in clumps, we decided to shave her head. She cannot bear for you to see her.'

So it was not hatred that kept her away? That thing in my chest again, heavy.

Seneca harrumphed. 'All those years she's waited and now she postpones the moment because of her appearance? Women!'

38

BRANWEN

I had thought of her so often. As a voluptuous young woman who rejects me; a sullen slave reduced to skin and bone; a truculent girl as fierce as a wild cat; a numbskull with that high-pitched laugh of women that sounds like a mouse screaming. Then sometimes she appeared as the child I had known; sometimes as the queen she was destined to be.

In my visions, which had been so right in the details, she had been faceless, her features scrubbed out as you see sometimes in a wall painting, or chiselled off a statue. As if someone would erase her from memory.

Waiting for her hair to grow became a torment. I kept myself busy on the Field of Mars, trying to sieve out the genuinely curious from the mob in the queue. Seneca persuaded me to stay in a guest room at his villa but I could hardly bear the knowledge that my betrothed was behind one of those many doors. I wanted to shout along echoing colonnades, 'Branwen, come out! Show yourself! It doesn't matter to me if you are bald!' Instead I went restlessly from room to room or, when seated, drummed my fingers on tables.

'All those years you delayed coming for her,' said Seneca's wife, 'and now you are impatient?'

I was invited to a dinner party at Vespasian's new house lower down the hill. During lulls in the entertainments, the dominant topic of conversation was Caratacus, who had met him and who had not. What a fine figure of a man he was, beneath all the grime and unkemptness. Noble by birth, surely, the way he holds himself, that voice. He lived wild in Siluria for years but you can see the king in him. How will he die? Not crucifixion – that's for low-born criminals. This man is a hero. A most worthy opponent, he took on the Roman Empire. Lost of course. Ha – ha – ha. Garrotting, then, in public. Like Vercingetorix. Yes, the same as Vercingetorix. I made my excuses and left early, returning to Seneca's villa.

So far I had seen no sign of Branwen but, on this night, perhaps because she did not expect my early return, she was in the garden, singing an incantation to female spirits deep and resonant. The language was British, the dialect Dobunnic. The hairs stood up on my arms. Treading silently, I made my way through the house to the garden where, in front of a wall fountain pouring water into a semi-circular basin, she stood singing to the nymphs the story of the Golden God and the Silver Maiden, a young woman, slender, boyish with a fuzz of hair over her scalp, wrapped in a blanket against the winter chill. She turned, suddenly aware of me, and swiftly lifted her blanket over her head like a *palla*. She stared at me, horror mixed with something else, and shrank back when I drew the blanket off. 'Oh,' I said, feigning disappointment. 'I thought you were Branwen.'

'I am Branwen!' For a moment the ten-year-old shone through, the one who enjoyed being teased.

'How can that be?' I asked. 'I don't remember your head being so beautiful, but then it was always lost in that uncombed thatch of knots where bats roosted.'

'Just one bat,' she muttered. If she had intended to be frosty with me, she failed. She ran her hand over her scalp. 'Beautiful?'

'Any sculptor would have you as his model.'

She stood back to appraise me and appeared to find me wanting. 'I never imagined you in a toga.' She came close again and looked up into my face, tracing my angular jawline with her hand. 'You've grown craggy,' she said. 'In my dreams . . .'

'Yes?'

'You are eight years younger.'

'As are you in mine.'

'You dream of me?'

'Often.'

She took my hand and studied it. 'Knobbly knuckles,' she said. Suddenly I could hear and see Little Sister again, full of curiosity and wonder. Palm to palm, finger to finger, our hands found each other, hers small and pale, mine large and brown. Our fingers interlaced and locked together.

'I'm so sorry,' I said lamely. 'I swear to you, I tried to come, I longed to come, but every day there was a new emergency keeping me bound to Britain.'

'I understand: Master Seneca gave me a lecture on the topic of duty,' she said. She was quiet for a while. 'I gave up hoping. I thought I'd never see you again. Then, when you arrived, I decided I didn't want to, anyway. Now you go and creep up on me.'

I led her into the warmth of the garden room where braziers burned, feeling a mellowness of being, a softening, that affected us both. Hatching from the shells we had developed to protect ourselves, we were both new and vulnerable. But, as she gazed up at me, rosy-cheeked in the lamplight, her eyes narrowed suddenly. She became angry, lifted her arms, balled her fists. I embraced her, to pinion those threatening arms.

'What is it?' I asked.

'Theana,' she said into my shoulder. 'You think I don't know about her? It got back to me, so it did. Sleeping with the enemy's sister! Making a home with her in my grove. My grove! The place where we were betrothed.'

'I sent her away!'

'She is a druid priestess, she is wise, she left of her own volition.'

'Are you in touch with her?' I asked.

'Enough to know that she is the one you desire. Not me.'

'Desires can be relinquished. One thing she never required of me was my protection. Help, yes. But not protection. And that is my duty to you. Love and protection. Branwen, Branwen, Branwen,' I whispered, holding the back of her head as if she were a baby and pressing her face into my shoulder. Great sobs began to rack her body. I held her tighter. The garden fell quiet, the only sound the whisper of the glowing charcoal in the braziers. Her muttering, hiccoughing grief was on the surface of the well of peace. True peace, which is found within and has nothing to do with negotiations or ceasefires or even peace of mind. Peace as a quality of the soul. The true condition of being: utter stillness.

Branwen quietened and suddenly relaxed as if she were melting into me. Her breathing became slow and even.

'I cried a whole year for you,' she said softly.

'Only one year?'

She punched me in mock anger. 'I ran out of tears. I forgot about you.'

'Oh, you did, did you? I believe you saw a re-enactment of the killing of Togodumnus and, thinking it was me, fainted.'

'How do you know about that?'

'It got back to me, so it did.'

She looked doubtful.

'Seneca mentioned it.'

'How would he know? He was in exile. It never happened.'

I stared at her, one eyebrow cocked.

'That old gossip,' she muttered. 'I was out in the sun. It was too hot.'

'In January?'

She sniffed irritably.

'Branwen, it grows late. We should retire to our beds,' I said.

'What? No! Don't leave me!'

'The mistress would be down on us like a falling tenement if she found us alone together.' Paula somewhat outdid her husband in shows of morality. What Seneca wrote, Paula practised. 'In the morning I will arrange your manumission,' I told Branwen.

'That's already been done. Seneca arranged it. I am a freedwoman.'

Surprised, I kissed her lightly on the head. 'What you are in truth is a queen. Remember it.'

Having risen early, I had a long wait before Seneca was up and ready for the day. The queue of clients was already forming outside the villa but the praetor would not be hurried from his bed, his barber or his breakfast. I spent the time in the library reading a copy of Plato's Seventh Letter which Seneca had pressed on me, wanting to know my thoughts about the education of a ruler. To be sitting in a room full of books, unscrolling a text of Plato, was a pleasure beyond pleasure. Suddenly I heard Branwen squeal, greeting someone in joy. I followed the sound to the garden where I saw her by the pond, a fair-haired boy turning in front of her to show off his toga.

'Look at you!' She was saying, clapping her hands. 'A man!'

He looked far from that, bouncing up and down on his toes in pride and delight. 'Where have you been? I missed you!' he cried.

'In the women's quarters for a year, before your mother sold me to your new tutor. Seneca is your future now. I am your past.'

'But, Branvena, you are bald! What happened to your hair?'

'I had to be deloused before Seneca would take me in. I caught nits in the imperial palace! That slave cellar is infested, and not only with lice.'

'I must deal with it.'

'Do you have that power?'

'I'll speak to the emperor, my stepfather. He'll deal with it. What else is it infested with?'

'Gossip and intrigue. You really shouldn't fill a small windowless space with people who have nothing to thank you for.'

'I'll deal with that when I am emperor!'

They laughed together again. Although I was hidden in the shrubbery, he was facing towards me and I could see his striking blue eyes, gingery hair and freckles. For all his Augustan ancestry, Nero had Gaul in his blood somewhere. Either that or divinity. Everyone said he had the colouring of Apollo. And the gold armlet in the form of a coiled snake he wore, containing the sloughed skin that had been found beneath his pillow, reminded others of his supernatural qualities.

'Look at you!' she said. 'Too old now for my foolishness.'

'I am not! As soon as I learned you were here, in my tutor's house, look, I brought my kithara. Please, please, please, the dance of the fawn!' He began to strum a dramatic sequence of notes. Branwen, who had disappeared into a hedge of laurels, tiptoed out, looking left and right, a fawn wondering where her mother was. In a sliver of time, I was captivated, reading the story easily from her expressions and exquisite gestures – accompanied by this rather fine music – her sense of abandonment, her fright at the sound of hunters, her delight at seeing Orpheus with the kithara, who held out his hand to her. She, the little fawn, came to him and brushed against him trustingly.

Their laughter was doused by a shout from inside the house. 'Nero Claudius Drusus Germanicus! Stop your acting! Come here at once!'

The boy she had always known as Domitius pulled a face and sloped off, making ape noises, his knuckles dangling. He straightened and looked back. 'If you are Seneca's now, we can see each other again?'

'I'm not his. I am a freedwoman.'

'Freed? Oh.' He straightened up as if the pleasure had been taken from the day.

'I'm returning to Britain with King Togidubnus.'

'King? Not for long. Britain is ours now. When we execute Caratacus', Nero said, passing into the atrium, 'the conquest will be complete and rebellious Britain will become the Province of Britannia. No place for kings there.'

Branwen stood before him shyly. 'I am marrying the king as soon as it can be arranged.'

'Oh?' He looked angry. 'Well, that's fitting. A hairy barbarian and a bald one.'

I knew then that Nero was someone to be treated with caution.

Seneca's wife arranged for us to be married in a short, private ceremony. The day before, I invited Branwen to come with me to visit Caratacus. She declined, saying it would be unseemly, not to mention unlucky, to have your bride spewing up in public the day before your wedding. 'I don't ever want to see that man again.' I nodded, understanding. 'But', she continued, 'I would like to see Dryadia.'

'Do you know her?'

'I know of her, and can imagine her sufferings.'

Leaving her with a prison guard to be shown to Dryadia's cell, I went into that of Caratacus. Tired of the constant stream of fawning Romans, Caratacus was grateful for my visit. 'I feel like a gladiator, hailed by the crowd while yet a slave.' He kicked out his legs to ease the weight of the chains. 'Or a bear, only of value while he dances. I'm glad this ends in death and not neglect. How long do I have to wait?

'Two months.'

Caratacus growled. 'They call me a hero while all I suffer is humiliation. Triumph indeed.'

I grunted in agreement. 'Apparently Britain was conquered by Claudius in a matter of days.'

'Britain has not been conquered yet, nearly ten years on.'

'They believe your capture will end the resistance.'

'The only thing that will end the resistance is their departure.'

'Have you heard that Scapula has died? Fell off his horse in the heat of battle and was dead before he hit the ground. No weapon involved.'

Caratacus stared at me disbelieving.

'Theana laid a curse on him,' I said.

Caratacus smiled. 'She's powerful, my sister.'

'I was of a mind to return before the equinox, take the last sailing before winter sets in, but Seneca wants me to remain in Rome until a new governor has been chosen.'

'Sound advice.'

'Is it? What will happen in the absence of a governor? As I remember it, you were never as active as during an interregnum.'

'True enough, but I'm not there.'

'So, you share the delusion that the conquest ended with your capture?'

'Not at all. There are others to take my place.'

'Such as?'

'Venutius of the Carvetii for one. And Enemnos of the Dobunni.'

I sniffed. 'I have signed a treaty with Enemnos. On the return of Branwen, he will relinquish all claim to Dobunnia.'

Caratacus gave one of his belly laughs. 'Perhaps you should set sail at once, winter seas notwithstanding. But I was hoping you would be present at my execution.'

'Is that your wish?'

'Yes.'

'Then I will, after which I shall return to Britain with my wife, the queen of the Dobunni.'

'So, have you met her yet?'

I nodded. 'We are to be married tomorrow.'

'A Roman rite?' He looked astonished.

'A necessary ritual to keep the moralising women of this city quiet. You wouldn't believe what sticklers they are for propriety. Branwen and I shall be married to avoid their disapproval but of course we shall not be married in the eyes of our own gods. We'll do it properly once we are home.'

He sighed. 'I wish I could attend.'

'Even if you live and are free, you would not be welcome. Not so far as Branwen is concerned.'

He leant forwards, touched my arm. 'When the time is right, tell her that I – or my spirit – seek her forgiveness. I was a brute and I am sorry for it. But brutes are required in brutish times.'

Told that Branwen was waiting for me, I left him and met her outside the prison.

'How is Dryadia?'

'Let us play a game.'

'A game?'

'You are the wife of a rebel leader, destined to die with your husband in a few weeks. It will be a public execution and you will die with the bloodthirsty howlings of Romans in your ears. You will die having seen your children garrotted one by one. Even the infant you bore so recently will be killed before your eyes. You have not recovered from that birth but are malnourished in body and sick in the soul. Your gods are powerless against those of the Romans. You were born to be the wife of a king, not a warlord. You have been faithful during all these years of hardship, travelling from place to place seeking refuge and shelter, because you love him. But as the day of death approaches, you wake up each morning loving him less, until now, when you love him not at all. Now, dear one, tell me, how is Dryadia?'

I was speechless with guilt and grief. I felt as if I'd been stripped of all pretensions and left as I truly am, a naked man possessing nothing. I was still in that mood when I woke up on the day of our marriage.

Branwen was neither nervous nor shy as we went through the brief ritual: it was just something that had to be endured, and her powers of tolerance were strong after years of enslavement. Although we slept together from then on, as Ricoba had advised me I did not claim my rights as a husband but left it to Branwen to choose the time. 'Men always want more coitus,' Ricoba had said. 'Women always want less. Know that to be true. Be patient. Let her come to you.' Given the nature of Cartimandua, I presumed there were exceptions to that rule, but I adhered to what Ricoba had taught me. On that first night, Branwen sat against the bed-board, watching me as I lay beside her.

'Get some sleep,' I said.

'No. If I close my eyes, you'll disappear. You are the cause of my every sorrow but I mustn't lose you.'

I rose up on one elbow. 'How am I the cause?'

She pushed the heel of her hand into the mattress. 'What's this stuffed with?'

'Feathers.'

'Of dead birds or living birds?'

'Dead. Presumably.' I'd never given it a thought. 'How am I the cause?'

'I was happy at the Spring of Swale, studying with Apnodens, so happy, but then you came, closed down the college, forced us to move west.'

'That was Apnodens, not me! He wanted to protect us all from the Roman army.'

'You tore me from Swale, goddess of the sacred stream. It was you.'

'I advised Apnodens to move the college to the Hot Springs, that was all. I didn't expect a ten-year-old screaming as if I were ripping her apart.'

'You were ripping me from Swale.'

'And yet you agreed to our betrothal.'

'I was being dutiful to my father, doing what was expected of me. What choice did I have? From the day you arrived in my life, I, a small child of ten, was being stripped of all possessions. There was nothing solid beneath my feet any more. The future was a heat haze over a field of drought. And then you left with Apnodens for the great gathering at Venonis and wouldn't take me with you. You left me behind with my father.'

'At his insistence, and rightly so. You were still his daughter, and too young for us to be wed. As part of our agreement, you were to continue your studies with Apnodens for five years.'

I don't think she had known of this arrangement I had made with Esius. She inhaled sharply, re-evaluating her father.

'What happened, Branwen? What happened after we'd gone?'

'I was down by the river and they came hollering out of the woods like bandits. Caratacus. He looked worse in reality than in my nightmares. He himself pulled me up on his horse by the hair. He stank of hog roast. I tried to poke out his eyes but he just laughed.' She ran one hand over her head, as if to soothe away the memory. 'They rode up the royal hill, breaking through all the defences, and set fire to the royal house. Flames leapt from the thatch. Everyone inside flew out to find themselves surrounded by the rebels. Caratacus dismounted and gave me to one of his men. When my father appeared, coughing and blinded by smoke, I cried out to him. It was a cry for help but became a scream of warning. Caratacus, having cleaved the air with his heavy sword once or twice, stepped forward, sword aloft. My father was staring at me as his head left his body.'

She began to breathe rapidly and I stroked her to quieten her down.

'People, my people, were running everywhere, trying to collect up children and livestock. "This", Caratacus bellowed at us, "is the reward you get for your treachery! You Dobunni, you changed sides! You deserted Britain and crossed to Rome!" He ordered his men to fire all our thatches. Everyone young enough to work was caught like rats and thrown into carts. The elderly, including aunts and uncles, were dispatched. Once the carnage was over, Caratacus took hold of me again, made me ride in front of him on his horse, holding me tight to prevent escape. We made our way to a port on Severn's estuary, where I was sold at a very high price.'

'Do you feel', I asked tentatively, 'a sense of relief at his capture, or justice?'

'No.'

'No? I thought you might want to be the one to throttle him. You blame me for your ills, but it was he who murdered your father and sold you into slavery.'

She leant forwards and stared at me with lizard eyes. 'I hate him so violently it makes me sick, but it is you who are to blame for my ills,' she said.

Heat burned in my face. 'How?'

'It was you who persuaded Esius to change sides. You thought you were so clever! A devious trick. Sending the levy that Caratacus had called for, and having them surrender to the Romans. You strutted about Kyronion as if you could win battles with tricks. That's why he came for my father's head. That's why I was made a slave. Because of you.'

My skin was crawling. I wondered if indeed she did have nits and I'd caught them from her. What was I thinking, allowing her on my bed? I jumped up and stood staring at her.

'I was made a slave,' she continued. 'I expected you to come for me. But you didn't come,' she whispered. 'I had nothing left. All had been taken. My life with Apnodens, my Swale, my people, my father, my country. Everything gone.'

The putative nit attack passed and I sat down on the bed, lashed by her accusations.

'I'm sorry,' I muttered, head in hands.

'You're as bad as Seneca. You don't mean what you say.'

'*What?*'

'Your actions contradict you. You say one thing, do another. You blame Caratacus for all the ills of Britain. Take a look at yourself. Son of your father. Oh for my mirror. I would hold it up to you now.'

The heavy bronze mirror I had given her at our betrothal. Presumably taken by Caratacus and now part of the heap of spoils here in Rome. I'd commissioned it from the same workshop that had made my mother's mirror, with the etched curves and cusps that had fascinated me as a child. And suddenly I remembered something, the day Innogen caught me playing with it. Her fury. Almost a curse. And here she was again, in this young woman I had this day married. The torment of Branwen's words was becoming unbearable. I cried out loud, a roar of grief from the belly. The cry of one who had also been ripped from his family and homeland and sent to Rome, not as a slave perhaps, but as a hostage. My life might have been pampered but it had always hung on a single thread – the loyalty of my father to the empire. And suddenly it struck me that that thread had held. Could it be that Verica had cared? Loved me, even? Again that light-headed swaying as if the ground of my soul were shifting.

'I do what I think is best. It's all I can do. Sometimes I get it wrong,' I said, sitting with my back to her.

She spoke in a whisper, close to my ear. 'Did you know that Seneca has five beds and uses all of them each night? You used to tell me how he slept on stone floors. Now he has five feather mattresses. It's live birds, by the way. Baby ducks. They grow the feathers back and get plucked again. He's like a nomad after dark. Wandering from bed to bed.'

'Have compassion. He's nearly sixty, has old bones and a weak bladder.'

'Poor little ducks.'

Exhaustion took me unawares. The night was troubled by images of headless kings and bald ducks. When I awoke in the morning, she was curled on her side and I was curled around her, our bodies enfolded like two leaves in a bud about to open.

39

THE TRIBUNAL

The day began before dawn as the people rose early to get a good place along the processional route to watch the Triumph and see the empire's greatest enemy, Caratacus, son of Cunobelinus of the Catuvellauni, paraded through the streets in chains. Mandred asked permission to spend the day in Transtiberim, the Jewish quarter across the river. I had looked at him askance. It was not like him to miss any spectacle, let alone a chariot race. He shrugged and said that his boyhood was behind him.

'I enjoy listening to the Followers of the Way,' he said. 'They tell of a rebel who stood up to Rome by appearing to yield. "Love your enemy," he had said, and was rewarded with a flogging. Apparently he didn't flinch.'

'I don't believe that,' I said.

Mandred shrugged. 'Many do. This man performed many miracles. But he didn't save himself from death, he yielded to it, and in yielding he brought about his own rebirth. Three days later.'

I blew through my lips. 'Great storytellers, the Jews.'

Claudius and his retinue arrived at the Field of Mars and made ready to lead the procession. Claudius was unsteady on his feet and servants helped him into the imperial chariot, but once he had the reins of the four white horses in his hands he became capable again, the triumphator in purple toga, riding in a gilded chariot, reliving an episode in his life that had never quite happened, given that the 'defeat' of the Britons had been effected by Aulus Plautius and Vespasian. Claudius had only been engaged in a staged fight outside Camulodunum. Now he and his retinue set off as the sixth hour was sounded. Next to go were the great carts carrying the spoils of war, then a troop of Praetorians in pure white togas escorting the miserable captives. Following them, various dignitaries, consuls, ex-consuls and the like, and foreign kings such as myself. I rode with Vespasian in a silver chariot. While I was wearing a toga with a narrow purple stripe – and proud enough of that – he was wearing the *toga picta* – purple and embroidered with gold – and a coronet with dangling gold ribbons. As we made our laboured progress, following about five hundred men on foot, we were of scant interest to the populace, who were climbing on top of each other to get a view of Caratacus. Cheering started at the back of the crowd and spread until all Rome was acclaiming its enemy. Vespasian glanced at me and rolled his eyes. About a hundred captive Britons in leg irons shuffled along in front of us, heads bowed, spirits crushed, but Caratacus, chained to his family with the neck irons, walked with head up, returning the stares of the crowd with laughing eyes. Caratacus walked tall. Dryadia shuffled with her head down over the infant she clasped to her breast.

The route, from the Field of Mars up the hill to the Praetorian barracks, passed through the forum. On raised platforms and stages in a cacophony of conflicting national songs and dances were jugglers from Libya, wrestlers from Egypt, acrobats from Greece and young Spartan boys waving their swords in the pyrrhic dance. The doors of the small Temple of Janus were closed – something that happened so rarely – for it signified peace. Rome was at peace with Britain. The spectators were held back by soldiery in tunics, for it is traditional in triumphs that no one bears arms, not even the Praetorian bodyguard of the emperor.

What could often be a ponderous event lasting days was over in a morning, unarmed troops marching, cavalry trotting, both riders and horses wearing silver masks, everything brisk because, unlike most triumphs, this one had a particular purpose, which was to carry the barbarian king to his trial outside the Praetorian barracks. And thus the procession, having wound through the populous heart of the city, made its way up the Quirinal, past the senatorial villas to the massive barracks at the city walls. Two tribunals had been set up a short distance from each other in front of the gates to the barracks. What was this? Two emperors? Claudius was already in his place on the curule chair. At the foot of his tribunal were piled the spoils of war: swords, shields, helmets, torcs, jewellery, mirrors – all our beautiful bronze-work embossed with semi-circles, triskeles and basketweave hatching, the script of a people in touch with Annwn. A defeated people present in the person of the chained captive now approaching.

As we left our chariot, Vespasian helped down by an aide, he asked me where I would be sitting.

'With Seneca.'

His lip curled but he said nothing and went up the steps to stand behind the emperor. I walked across the ground to join Seneca, who was sitting close to the mysterious second tribunal. All around were people watching from three levels of tiered seating, noisy in their opinions as to how this tribunal was going to play out. One more common criminal to be crucified on the Appian Way? Or the honour of a quick death? Surely Caratacus deserved no less. I squinted against the sun and saw Branwen in the women's section beside Seneca's wife. She had her eyes closed, her face upturned to the sky: she was praying.

Everyone was intrigued by the empty seat on the second tribunal. Even while I was wondering what or who it was there for, the gate of the fort opened and the newly appointed prefect of the Praetorians, Sextus Afranius Burrus, rode out, followed by two lictors bearing their bundled rods, behind them a two-wheeled cart painted scarlet, gold and purple and covered with exotic fabrics and golden tassels.

So there we were, onlookers to a scene of piled treasure, a famous barbarian king in chains, the emperor himself – and what did we all stare at? That curtained carriage.

Seneca smiled at my hesitation to sit down.

'It's not. It can't be,' I said.

'Why can't it be?'

Burrus dismounted and drew back the curtain on the carriage. The first we saw of her was her sandalled foot.

Why was I so shocked? Perhaps I caught it from the atmosphere – perhaps shock is contagious in a crowd. At home in Britain we have powerful women who play the role of king. It may not be common, but common enough to be unremarkable, so the sight of Agrippina, a military mantle draped over her shoulders, being helped by the prefect of the Praetorian Guard to her place on the second tribunal should not have made my stomach flutter. But it did. This was so new for Rome. A consort equal in status to the emperor. Beautiful Agrippina in the ripeness of maturity, her hair meticulously plaited in loops and girdled by a golden chaplet. She glanced around the crowd and achieved the ultimate victory: she stole attention from Caratacus.

What was it like for him to look up at these men, the victors, who had taken all he had? One could not tell. His expression gave nothing away, not even when his warriors, coming first to the tribunal for judgement, abased themselves by begging for their lives. I knew several of these men, had myself suffered at the hands of some of them. Even so, I hoped the emperor would listen. But he did not. Condemning them to slavery, he had them taken away to who knew what unendurable fate. The mines, the galleys, the quarries – anywhere muscle was needed.

Dryadia continued to gaze into the face of the swaddled baby that had been born on Roman soil, but her sons and daughter outstared the Roman audience with contempt in their eyes. Caratacus himself looked neither downcast nor contemptuous, nor did he beg for his life. Released from his neck chain, he stepped forward when bidden to pay homage to the emperor.

As he knelt, he dipped his head and raised his hand, requesting permission to speak. Claudius acquiesced. I listened, ears as pricked as a hare's, wondering if all the tuition of Mandred would bear fruit and that Caratacus was about to earn himself a quick and honourable death. He stood up, studied his audience in silence. His words, when they came, were in faultless Latin, so correct indeed that they seemed lifeless. You'd have thought he was a schoolboy training in oratory rather than a man on the point of execution. I shifted uncomfortably in my seat. The crowd was beginning to mutter, even to laugh.

A dog was barking. Why shouldn't a dog bark? It's what dogs do, except this was more of a croon than a woof. Other dogs joined in. I glanced over at Branwen, remembering something she had told me when a child: that bards could sing songs that only the gods can hear, gods and dogs. Everyone began to take notice of the croonings which were now all over Rome. Caratacus paused, glanced over his shoulder at his weeping wife. Then he took a deep breath and began to speak as Caratacus always spoke, in that mighty voice which could turn a tide. Whatever anyone was thinking or dreaming or musing upon was stopped by that voice that could bring an enemy to his knees. But to my astonishment, it was Caratacus who knelt, submitting himself Claudius with the words, 'I surrender to you, great Caesar, Light of Jupiter in this world.' What had I expected? Bravado. Insolence, Resistance to the end. Not this. 'You are the mightiest of the mighty; you command the greatest empire, you have lordship over the seas. Such is your power, you have even crossed Ocean and brought rude Britain into your fold. I surrender to you and lay everything down, even my life and the lives of my loved ones. Take me, Caesar. It is your right.'

Claudius frowned, wrong-footed by this surrender. Where was the defiance? Where the deliciously humiliating pleas for mercy?

Caratacus played the pause at least three beats longer than any orator would have done. 'But,' he said, just as we were wondering if he'd dried, 'what will happen once you kill me? I'll tell you. I shall be forgotten. And what will happen to you, after you die, as you surely will in time? You, too, will be forgotten.'

Claudius laughed and glanced around at all the signs of himself in temples and statues. Forgotten?

'What do we know or think of Tiberius now, or your nephew Gaius Caligula, other than their cruelty? Their statues have been defaced or pulled down by those who hated them. Their temples renamed. Augustus is the one who is remembered, but why? For his conquests? His triumphs? His wealth? No. He is revered – worshipped – for his goodness, his generosity, his justice, for the peace and prosperity he brought to Rome and her empire. He is so revered for these things that his memory will endure forever. His name, Caesar Augustus, is your title, and will be the title of every emperor henceforth.' Of course, no one present believed this glowing portrait of the father of the dynasty, but everyone wanted to.

Abject surrender? Caratacus? What was he up to? Claudius was now wide-eyed, while over on her dais Agrippina was thrilling to this barbarian king reminding everyone that having the blood of Augustus in your veins rendered you semi-divine. She even put her hand on Nero's knee, possessing her son, promoting him, in this moment of supreme validation. Nero, for once interested in official proceedings, hung on everything Caratacus had to say.

Catching the eye of Agrippina, Caratacus smiled in that great-hearted way of his, the smile that none could help but return. With just one smile he had her.

He looked back to Claudius. 'Caesar!' he continued. 'Do you think killing me will bring you glory, as if I were some kind of trophy? An elephant or a lion, killed in an arena? Do you suppose the conquest of my land and peoples will bring you glory? I tell you, it will bring you shame! You will be remembered only for killing an enemy after he had surrendered. Had I chosen the fate of King Togidubnus over there, I should be sitting where he is, as a friend. I have ancestors more illustrious than his; I have a lineage more noble than his but I stand before you scorned and derided – for what reason? I tried to resist you. I had men, horses, arms and wealth – do you wonder that I didn't give them up without a struggle?'

Oh, Historia, believe me, his version was at odds with the truth! And yet such was the power of his speech that we believed every word.

'So now you intend to punish me. Kill me then, and let us both enjoy oblivion.'

Oblivion? Claudius looked ready to have him run him through there and then.

Caratacus glanced again at Agrippina. 'However, were you to save my life, for such an act of clemency you would

345

be remembered with affection forever. Whenever the name Caratacus is spoken, Claudius and his beloved consort, Agrippina, will be remembered. My fame shall be your everlasting memorial that no one can destroy, melt down or smash. We would live forever in the minds of men.'

Clemency? I shifted on my seat, as thrown as Claudius. If Claudius made no reply, it was because he could not trust himself to speak and, besides, did not know what to say. A slave hurried to him, carrying a message from Agrippina. Claudius nodded and raised his hands palm upwards in a gesture of magnanimity. 'Let him go free,' he declared. The audience ranked on the stands stood up as one, cheering. The stiff senators and Praetorians shouted their approval. Nero jumped up, clapping as if at great theatre.

'Now that', Seneca said to me, 'is what I call a speech. Emotion, you see, you have to have emotion and reason in fine balance. Neither reason nor emotion alone will win an audience, but get the two running together, and the people are yours. What a voice!'

'I trust we have historians present.' I meant it as a joke but Seneca nodded.

'Each evening, Agrippina dictates the day to a secretary, keeping a diary with the intention of writing an autobiography. And why not? The most powerful woman since Cleopatra, she cannot trust a male historian with her story.'

Agrippina looked relaxed sitting on her curule chair, her hands clasped in her lap, wrapped in an ermine mantle against the sharp winter air. You could tell she had absented herself, had gone within to memorise what she needed to repeat later, and she wanted that barbarian's speech in praise of Augustus.

Burrus, the prefect of the Praetorians, whispered something to her. Agrippina blinked, glanced at Vespasian and laughed. Vespasian saw it and looked as if he had a bee in his mouth that he must ignore. And suddenly I saw it all, as if a veil had been drawn to one side. Yes. Like going behind the scenes. This play had been about the sharing of power and the beneficence of the powerful, but in truth the whole field was divided into two camps, that of Claudius and that of Agrippina. He had the Senate, she had the Praetorian Guard. And I realised with a sudden twitch of apprehension that, as friend and guest of Seneca, I was in Agrippina's camp. No wonder Vespasian's lip had curled.

On the dais of Claudius, Vespasian was screwing up his eyes as if to keep his thoughts in check. For years he had fought the Britons, had lost many men in the battles, and now Claudius, for the sake of his own fame, had released their leader? Beside him, Britain's first governor, Aulus Plautius, he with the face of polished marble, remained expressionless but, as anyone else present who had served in Britain, he refrained from cheering.

Veil after veil was dropping from my eyes until, behind the scenes, behind the very theatre itself, I glimpsed another reality, governed by women. Agrippina – Dryadia – Branwen. They were just as unconscious as anyone else, but, because of Branwen's silent song, the gods could work through them. And, thanks to those gods, Dryadia would not have to watch her children die. But what would happen to her, to them? It seemed inconceivable that Claudius would allow Caratacus to return to Britain. When he said 'Let them go free', he meant remove their chains. Whatever status he was awarded, Caratacus and his family were slaves and condemned to live in a city and culture they abhorred. Condemned to dress as Romans, eat as Romans, to worship emperors, to speak Latin. For the sake of his family, Caratacus had chosen a living death.

I didn't see him alone again, only at a distance, he the honoured guest of every rich man's supper party. To my dismay, he seemed to be enjoying his notoriety and not to care that some of these men had gained their wealth through mineral extraction in Britain, or the trade in slaves and hunting dogs. He stood proud of all that and declaimed his deeds and victories like an orator. He always ended on the same note: that, despite his greatness as a hero, Rome was the greater.

I began making arrangements to return to Britain at the equinox, wanting to be away as soon as possible, whether or not a new governor had been chosen from those strutting about, presenting themselves for the position. I did not want to linger in the city to see Caratacus gradually fall out of favour and, like a performing monkey, die from neglect, scabby and half bald with mange. I gazed on him from afar and wanted to ask: What price heroism? All he would be remembered for is sycophancy and hypocrisy. I was angry and bitter but deep inside, beyond any feeling of betrayal of principle, I was glad he lived.

Branwen and I were alone in the garden. I had been somewhat guarded with her since the tribunal, aware now that my wife had godly powers strong enough to change events. She herself, however, acted as if nothing special had happened. She had started singing, so high that only dogs could hear her, but did not seem to make the connection with the change it had brought about in Caratacus, giving him the strength to put aside his rehearsed speech and use his own voice. When I asked her about it, she said she'd been making a *vocos* for Dryadia to help her soul fly when the moment came. 'But the moment did not come.'

'Tell me, does Apnodens have that power or is it only available to women?'

'No, he can do it. He can go up five scales and into the sixth, when he can't even hear himself.'

I remembered the dogs howling, that time when Apnodens said he had been called to the Temple of Nodens. But who had done the calling? He or the dogs? Clearly he had called himself, leaving me in awe of the hounds.

Branwen wanted to know what would happen when we returned home.

'I plan to land at Noviomagus to discuss things with Katuaros, and then we shall go to Dobunnia.'

'I meant,' she said tartly, 'what will happen with you and me.'

'We've discussed that. We shall marry according to our own customs.'

'But then what? What are my days like?'

'Well, you will be queen, and accompany me everywhere.'

She said nothing. I began to wonder if that prospect had any appeal for her. 'How would you wish your days to be?' I asked.

She shrugged.

'What was your mother like, Branwen? How did she spend her days?'

'She was a bard. She died when I was in my seventh year. I don't remember her ever referring to herself as queen, although she wore the torc on holy days and looked like a queen. But first and foremost she was a bard.'

'Was it she who taught you to sing?'

'She said I was born singing, that most babies scream on entry into this world, but I sang like a bird. Not a bard, a bird.'

We smiled at each other.

'I mean it,' I said, 'tell me how you want to spend your days.'

'As she did.'

'Then you shall.'

'Because', she said, cutting across me, 'I am called to a sacred duty. This I know. This I have been told. Your duty is to guide our people peacefully into a new life, I understand that now. Lucius Seneca explained it to me. My duty is to protect and retain all that is good and true from the old life. I am to look after the stories that contain our history, our genealogy, our gods, our heroes, our monsters.'

Our 'whimsy'.

'I am to encourage mothers to maintain the lullabies, the bards to sing the epics, the grandmothers to tell the tales of magic which teach us to recognise danger and have courage. That's what I want to do, to keep our traditions flowing like a running brook that is hidden – you just hear it now and again and know that it is there.'

Almost imperceptibly she came closer. When I felt the touch of her next to me, I put my arm round her and felt the warmth of her. It was dusk. We rose to walk through the garden and into the house. The scent of daphne trees filled the evening air. We walked slowly and in silence, our paces matching, our tread on gravel in time with each other. The scent and the gravel. Two bodies moving. I wondered at us, how my arm could rest on her hip so easily, how her head could brush my shoulder. It seemed we had been cut from one block with a curved line, and now we were together again with no gap between us. I, the tall one, the protector, she the shorter one, the supporter; she the protected, me the supported. Two halves of one unity.

'Plato, in his dialogue *The Symposium*—' I began.

'Ssshhh. I'm listening to that mistle thrush, high in the tree. See him? Up there? He's calling me home.'

I listened with her and it was as if I had never listened before.

We shared my bed that night as usual in innocence, although, at her invitation, we did make love. The true act of love is pure. It is not a taking but a giving, a sacred act in honour of the gods who protect us. I lay beside her, my arms round her. 'I am the first?' I whispered.

'Of course. What are you saying?'

'I heard a rumour, that's all.'

'And you believed it?' She was stiffening, becoming frosty.

'And there was something else I heard,' I said, to deflect the subject. 'That you killed a man.'

'Yes, so I did, with a curse.'

'What was his crime?'

'Trying to force me against my will. Take heed.'

My powerful wife. I had the ability to see, she to act. Together we could heal Britain, I was sure of it.

They awarded Caratacus a pension, gave him a fine house on the slopes of the Viminal Hill and kept him like a dancing bear.

'Do I detect anger in you?' Seneca asked me. 'Why are you angry?'

'I try not to be. It was, after all, the will of the gods that he live.'

'And yet you simmer.'

I sighed. 'All my efforts to win him an honourable death were thrown to the winds. Now he struts about playing the hero, but is it heroic to wheedle your way to clemency, to life in a fine house and a comfortable pension?'

'As you say, the will of the gods. This story is not ended.'

'But we know how it will end. The Romans will become bored of him – quite soon – and he will be left to grow old, recounting his past deeds to anyone who will listen. Which will be fewer and fewer until he dies, forgotten, ignored.'

'Death is the end of everybody's story: the only thing in our control is our reputation.'

'Yours is assured,' I said.

'For the moment, but anything can happen between now and that event. Enough talk of death! I may be old but I have work to do, getting this once-great city back on her feet. And you, too, have work to do, making Britain's transition into a province of Rome as painless as possible. Write to me. Anything you need that I can give, just ask. When are you returning?'

'At Branwen's insistence, as soon as possible. We'll be leaving at the spring equinox.'

'We still haven't decided on the new governor. You should be here to give your verdict on all candidates.'

'Branwen will not tolerate remaining here one day longer than she has to.'

'Too many bad memories?'

'Too boring. She is expected to keep company with women like . . .' I hesitated, but then continued, '. . . Vespasian's wife. Stiff, unsmiling, disapproving and, worst of all, dull. Branwen is already refusing to go to their parties. Says she'd rather keep company with slaves.'

'You artfully avoid implicating my Paula in this, but you're right. It's Agrippina's influence. She of the incestuous marriage is busy setting high moral standards among the women. Yes, keep Branwen free of it.'

Branwen kept herself free. She spent time with Dryadia, whose company she preferred, although it took some time to win the wife of Caratacus over. Dryadia refused to leave the house they had been given and to wear anything Roman. She kept her hair loose – as loose as a cloud of curls can be – and spoke in her own dialect at all times. Little by little Branwen won her confidence and after a couple of weeks she was braiding that lovely hair, singing a braiding song that made Dryadia weep for home.

'I thought you hated Caratacus,' I said.

'I do, but I've nothing against Dryadia. Can we take her with us?'

I thought it so unlikely we'd receive imperial permission that I didn't even ask.

While we waited for weather good enough for travel, Branwen returned to tasks that had occupied her as a slave, working with Seneca's gardener to take cuttings, sort seeds and raise little plants to introduce to Britain. She had cages made for the transportation of rabbits and exotic chickens. 'Not everything about Rome is evil,' she told me. 'There is much we can learn from them.'

When I could, I worked with her as a delightful relief from the forum. Sometimes, watching her delicate fingers potting up seedlings, or glimpsing the back of her neck as she stroked a docile hen that had jumped on her lap, there was a pain in my chest, familiar, worrying. I'd had so many diagnoses over the years: cracked ribs, a bruising slow to heal, a sense of loss. How could I be suffering a sense of loss now? With every passing day, Branwen and I grew closer. But the pain only intensified.

Does love hurt? I cast my mind over the poets to see what they had to say and got no answer. I asked Seneca. His brow furrowed as he tried to remember relevant passages from Plato's *Symposium*. 'It's like being two halves of one whole,' he said.

'But does it hurt?'

He didn't know, couldn't think why it should. I went to the shrine room in his house, folded up on myself, forehead on the cold stone of a floor mosaic, sank within, down, down to that underground stream which is Inspiration and consulted Pythia, the priestess of Apollo at Delphi. 'Does love hurt?' I asked her. 'Of course,' she said. I asked the spirit of Ricoba. She said, 'Love? Hurt? No. Loss of love – that hurts. Like an arrow in the heart.'

'But I have gained my love.'

'Branwen, yes, but you have lost Britain.'

I sat back on my heels and gazed at the figures in the mosaic. The central image was a winged boy with a bow and arrow riding on a dolphin.

Branwen found me there, 'sobbing like a child' as she put it.

Those arms that cradled hens and rabbits folded round me, pressing my head into her shoulder. 'We need to go home,' she said. 'Home to Kyronion.'

I sat back. 'Corinium,' I corrected her. 'Branwen, you will not recognise it as home. They've built a large fort there and the people have moved their homes to live in its shadow.'

She shuddered. 'What can we do about that?'

'Nothing. We must learn to accept it.'

'You sound like Seneca.'

'What would you do, then? Fight?'

She looked hopeless. 'I'll do what I said I'd do. Nurture the stories so that we never forget. And . . .'

'And?'

'Remind you daily that I am not content with half of Dobunnia. The Albios Way, which runs from the Hills of Cuda down to the Hot Springs, once a sacred way that crossed my territory, has been desecrated and now splits my land in two.'

'It's the frontier of the empire!'

'So say the Romans. The gods see it differently. It is a white way, a way of peace, and I am not content that this path of spirits be tramped on by military patrols. And then there are the enemies within. Claudius believes that, with the taking of Caratacus, the conquest is complete. But others will rise up to take his place, and continue to rise up while injustice prevails.'

'Yes, I agree. I long for peace, peace of the true kind, where opposites are reconciled. But I fear the killing will continue.' I reached out to her; she grasped my hand with surprising and reassuring strength.

She could be so many things: a child, a bald recluse, a shy fawn, a willing lover. Since her song of silence at the tribunal, however, she had started to become a queen, to be firm in her convictions and speak her mind. This was not going to be an easy marriage with me making the decisions, giving orders and being obeyed. I was king to her queen; she queen to my king. We had to run together like a pair of fine chariot horses in the sacred union of Father and Mother. The future of Britain would depend on us.

HISTORICAL NOTE

The fort at Yellowhammer Hill was one of the first to be built after the Roman invasion. Later it was linked by Akeman Street to Verulamium in the east and Corinium in the southwest. So why was that site chosen? It was a place where three territories met: those of the Atrebates, the Dobunni and the Catuvellauni. But it was also, as it were, a corner where the frontier stopped facing the west and began to face the north. In the early years of the conquest, anything west or north of the frontier zone remained, in Roman terminology, barbarian. The history of the Romans in Britain consists largely of pushing these lines further west and north. Brigantia was the exception. Although very much north of the first frontier, the alliance of Queen Cartimandua with the Romans kept it free of aggression. All its troubles came from within.

Most of the story in *The Albios Way* takes place in Dobunnia, which equates to a large region stretching from the Bristol Channel as far north, perhaps, as Worcestershire, but its main area corresponds to Gloucestershire with its capital at Corinium Dobunnorum (Cirencester). I am indebted to Stephen J. Yeates for his imaginative study of Gloucestershire and have followed his suggestion that Welsh mythology has its source in the 'cauldron' which is the Vale of Gloucester. There is evidence of Dobunnia splitting north and south, perhaps several times during its history, but no evidence at all of who the king was at the time of the invasion. Esius and his daughter Branwen are my invention, as is Enemnos (although he takes the name of a historical figure of the time).

The Fosse Way, running from Lindinis (Ilchester, Somerset) to Lindum (Lincoln) is a great route for going north from the Cotswolds without touching a motorway. They say it was built by the Romans but it seems likely that they followed an ancient track. These days it is the A429 from Cirencester to Halford, Warwickshire. After that, the B4455. A stretch of it may be walked at Sharnford, Leicestershire. It crosses the A5 (Watling Street) at a place now called High Cross, then Venonis, the great gathering place of the tribes akin to Autricum (Chartres) in France.

Ferylloog, or the Forest of Dean, was marooned by geography. The Severn separated it from Dobunnia, the Wye from Siluria. Perhaps because of this the people of Dean developed a formidable sense of independence which remains today, although when I asked a cider-maker if he considered himself descended from the Dobunni or the Silures, without blinking an eyelid he said, 'Oh, the Silures, of course.' Temples have been excavated at Lydney and Littledean but many more may have followed the course of the Severn.

Gloucestershire retains many customs that may be prehistoric in origin. The almost suicidal race to catch a round of cheese rolling down Cooper's Hill, held every spring, echoes an ancient practice of chasing a flaming chariot wheel. The winner of the ladies' race in 2023 finished unconscious and only learnt of her victory later.

Crickley Country Park contains at its summit an ancient hillfort. That it was a royal seat of the Dobunni is my invention. The name Crickley derives from Creig.

As to names of characters, there are two main problems: lack of records and the question of how to spell or pronounce old British names in the Roman style. Therefore there appear to be inconsistencies, especially in the endings -os and -us, but the spelling has been determined by who is speaking. So far as we know, there are no names beginning with K but I was worried that there were too many characters beginning with C which, for the more visual readers, would cause confusion.

It has long been held that Fishbourne Palace was built by King Togidubnus and used as his residence. There is no evidence for this except circumstantial: the engraved dedication to the temple of Neptune and Minerva at Noviomagus (Chichester) which mentions Togidubnus as 'Great King'. His foster brother, Katuaros, although my invention, is based on a signet ring, found on the site of the palace, on which the name TI (BERI)

CLAUDI CATUARI is spelt in crude letters. There is no record as to who this person was except that, being in possession of the ring, he was a citizen of the Roman Empire. My invention of a dual kingship gives the building of the palace to the foster brother.

Catuarus must be seen as a Briton of wealth and social position who owed his citizenship to the favour, direct or indirect, of Claudius or Nero. The classic example is of course the client king Tiberius Claudius [To]gidubnus ('Cogidumnus'), already attested at Chichester (https://romaninscriptionsofbritain.org/inscriptions/91)

Catuarus is likely to have been his kinsman or ally, rewarded like him for collaborating with the Roman invaders. (https://romaninscriptionsofbritain.org/inscriptions/Brit.27.48)

It proved very difficult to picture the Hot Springs of Sulis before they became Roman Bath. Repeated visits helped me gain some sense of the three knolls, and a November swim in the rooftop bath of the new spa gave a good sense of how hot the springs are (the water has to be cooled for bathers, even in November). In the course of my researches, I met people involved in the building of the new Thermae Bath Spa and heard about the obstacles they met in trying to reach the deadline of the Millennium within budget. Things fell down, leaks were sprung, even one or two lives were sadly lost. A geomancer was called in and advised appeasing Sulis who was upset by the building works, so redolent of what the Romans did nearly 2,000 years earlier. A ceremony was held after which the works proceeded smoothly to completion, albeit six years late.

Sometimes fiction struggles to match fact.

For more historical notes see www.lindaproud.com

ACKNOWLEDGEMENTS

My first thoughts go to the land itself, the hillforts I have climbed, the ditches I have stood in, the fields I've stared at hoping for at least a ghostly image of the fort that was once there. The sight of Crickley Hill and the Vale of Gloucester from Barrow Wake at Birdlip. The broad, brown Severn sliding past the Forest of Dean. The view over Cornovia from Titterstone Clee. White Horse Hill, Uffington. I travelled the Fosse Way many times with my husband, David, delighting in the discovery of a hidden England (Barton in the Beans) and magical places such as Brinklow.

Memories are held in the land, and some of the people I met knew to which tribe they belong. Two women passing at Verulamium (St Albans) chatting about the Catuvellauni; the staff at Corinium Museum who introduced me to one who was definitely Dobunni (though he looked like all the rest, if a bit more shy); the cider-maker at Awre who told me all the foresters consider themselves Silures (Welsh in today's speak). It's been a glorious exploration and I was glad to share it not only with David, but also with Sally Dunn, Geoffrey Parks, Anna McClelland and Peter Sullivan, friends who so generously accompanied me when I went to look at a field, a ditch or a hill.

And now the people of the land. As ever I was surprised by the willingness of academics even to speak to me, let alone spend time answering my very demanding and slightly odd questions. Only one proved sniffy, but even he helped, if unwittingly, when he told me that Ambrosden, near Bicester, does not get its name from Ambrosius Aurielanus, as many think, but is a Brythonic name for yellowhammer.

As with *Chariot of the Soul* I am deeply indebted to the work of Revd Prof. Martin Henig, and to his readiness to discuss my work-in-progress. Martin introduced me to Dr Daphne

Nash Briggs, expert in British numismatics, who taught me so much about coins of the time, how they put names to forgotten characters and how to view them. When I agonised about facts, she encouraged me to go with the Muse. 'It's fiction, after all.' Dr John Creighton's book *Britannia: The Creation of a Roman Province* (Routledge 2005) is in my view the best of the many studies of early Roman Britain and enabled me to visualise Calleva as a place that lived and breathed. I approached him for advice nervously but, once again, was greeted with generous enthusiasm.

The archaeologists have been just as helpful and I am indebted to Eberhard Sauer (head of excavations, Alchester fort near Bicester), Graham Soffe (archaeologist, Hayling Island, chairman of ARA), Kate Adcock (editor, *Journal of the Association of Roman Archaeology*) and Dr Roger Tomlin (archaeologist specialising in inscriptions). Good guys, one and all. The well-known TV archaeologist who was outraged by my suggestion that tribes need more mention, rather than being described as Iron Age A, B or C according to their crockery, is not included in this list. Really, that kind of thinking depopulates history and reduces it to potsherds, aka 'evidence'. But then that's archaeology for you, and why we have historical novelists.

Another group of experts to be thanked are the unsung heroes of every major town in Britain: the directors and staff of local museums. They struggle with so much and can often be overwhelmed by underfunding and school visits. They are the guardians of our past. Specifically for this project: Dr Rob Symmons (Director, Fishbourne Palace near Chichester), Elizabeth Johannson-Hartley (Director, Gloucester Museum), Staff and Directors of Corinium Museum, Cirencester, and Verulamium Museum, St Albans.

Heartfelt thanks to the friends who have supported and encouraged me throughout. Whenever I lost faith in myself, I only had to look to them to have it restored: Angela Burdick, Alison Coles, Denise Cullington, Dr Jude Currivan, Sally Dunn, Towse Harrison, Dr Jenny Lewis, Steve Lunn, Jane Mason, Caitlin Matthews, Ed Murray (bronze sculptor), Rhodri Samuel, Hugh and Dorothy Venables.

Lastly, my gratitude to those who have contributed their amazing skills to this project: Richenda Todd (editor), Martin Lubikowski (cartographer), Amanda Roberts (author-typesetter), Phil Greenwood (printmaker).

There are no sacred and unsacred places; there are only sacred places and desecrated places. Wendell Berry